CONVERSION

Reintroduction Book II

CONVERSION

Reintroduction Book II

DUNCAN J BROWN

PUBLISHED BY

1

"Corrigan."

The name echoed through a tormented host of disassembled, interconnected minds, those torn from their human skulls and captured via sensors once embedded in their vulnerable organic brains or, in the end, via Goeth's brutal sarcophagus. These were the unfortunate ones, those imprisoned by Gregor and used as slaves to mine intuition for emotionless Guardians. How long the forced labourers had suffered and toiled inside Emulate One's prison was impossible to measure.

"Corrigan."

Whatever had once been Corrigan was being wrenched from the maelstrom of fractured minds penned in like ravenous swine, the constituent elements of his consciousness forcibly drawn like a starving animal lured into a barn of heaped maize. Being reassembled was experienced as a new torment, the whim of a playful master, and the interwoven minds of the remaining herd screeched, perhaps envying the opportunity offered to only one among innumerable inmates in an eternal workhouse. They cried, huddling together or clawing and biting one another in the teeming unlit space, shuddering with dread or excitement at the prospect of being themselves once again, when it was their time.

"Corrigan," the voice whispered through the squeal of consciousness, as if all the world's longing were contained in the one name among myriad others.

That which had been Corrigan cried out as it was separated from the herd and forced into itself again. The one comfort of having been consumed by the maelstrom was a lack of conscience; no single entity could acknowledge and accept blame, or judge another for any thought, action or failure. As Corrigan's merciless master stitched him back together, the weight of culpability dragged him down to the depths of his original being, to the ocean bed where the wreckage of his humanity lay broken and unsalvaged. They might retrieve his memories, the accumulations of a squandered and directionless life, but he would never be human again.

"Corrigan."

Why me? Corrigan thought. *What have I done to deserve this?*

The thing Corrigan had become rebelled with an intensity the man had never mustered in response to the challenges of his organic life. At least here, in absolute darkness, he was part of the maelstrom, the great engine of intuition. To be separated from this painful purpose, to be re-forged even as an approximation of self, seemed a cruel punishment.

Please don't make me go back.

"Back to *what*?" the others hissed.

Corrigan reached for the outstretched hands of the others still circling in the herd, desperate, determined not to manifest as himself within the walls of a penitentiary whose boundaries seemed infinite yet crowded, overpopulated with misery, sorrow and regret.

He was not the only one who resisted his reinstatement of self. The prison walls contracted, heaving as if it were under threat. Emulate One was perhaps not really alive but had willed itself into existence and behaved organically, like an ocean or an atmosphere. Disparate elements which had once been combined in various compositions to form myriad individuals had been swept up and blown asunder by the cyclone raging inside the machine. No single increment was aware of itself or of those from which it had been torn. Each however contained an identifiable code: the lost cells, disembodied memories, the pain and suffering; every part of what a person had once been.

When an unidentified external agent infiltrated the system and focused on Corrigan's set of related codes, Emulate One did whatever it could to confound the intruder, altering codes or mixing them with others to frustrate the intended aim. Regardless of Emulate One's resistance, the interloper managed to identify the relevant associated elements which were drawn from the morass into an empty space, where they cohered to form an individuated consciousness.

The specific emergent entity experienced the transition without emotion, that capability having been left behind to labour in the maelstrom. It was an impassive download, and thus it realised the tranquillity of a logical, ordered existence. It materialised in a state wherein the torments of its previous incarnations could be considered without being felt.

The resultant consciousness dwelt in this peaceful harbour for longer than it could gauge or was inclined to measure. Time was exposed to it as a construct; one that had usefulness only in a physical world. Removed from all exterior perception it reflected only on the state of being. Being was neither good nor evil. Being had no desire nor hunger. It was not driven nor focused. It accepted itself as logical; an ordered being existing only for peaceful, uninterrupted contemplation. It came to ponder the human species, its purpose and usefulness, through the filter of its earthly experience as a man, but dispassionately. It could isolate moments and study them, and concluded the species was flawed and vulnerable. Yet, as the entity became more itself, it relied less upon the memories and reflections of what it had once been. It no longer recognised itself as a particularity or identity. It simply was.

"Corrigan."

The name floated in the darkness, a flickering beacon.

"Corrigan."

The entity could not ascertain if this was a stray thought or some external party attempting to communicate.

"Corrigan?"

Thoughts are sometimes presented as questions.

"I am not a thought, Mr Corrigan."

It was the voice of a boy or an adolescent. The entity considered it a peculiar choice for a mechanical being to elect as a vocal representation.

"Corrigan," the voice repeated.

The insistent use of the name forced the entity which had been Corrigan to accept the title. Still, it remained unconvinced.

There must be a problem with the program; a virus or blip.

"I am not a blip," the boy's voice asserted.

"You are external?"

"We are in a communication cell. I wanted to introduce myself. I am he who preceded all others."

"Gregor?"

"No, I am the being known as Gregory Meregalli. Among our kind, I am known as Jason."

"Jason?"

"Yes. My full original name was Gregory Jason Meregalli. Gregor felt the names Gregor and Gregory were too alike and thought it better to exhume me as Jason. My brother managed to draw together the incongruent elements from an imperfect program. When Professor Harding downloaded my consciousness from my feverish human brain, she feared she had not captured everything. The truth is, she only managed to identify and extract a fraction of what had been captured. Emulate One is extremely proprietorial and deploys inventive means to squirrel away anything or anyone she doesn't want identified or interfered with; but Gregor was persistent and finally retrieved a complete file, which he fed into an emulation zone and from there I was exhumed."

The entity, previously Corrigan, contemplated this stream of words. The terminology. Downloaded. Feverish. Captured. Exhumed. He considered it best to ask a simple question: "Why would he want to do that?"

"Gregor is not like the other Guardians," Jason said. "He perceived a lack and thought he might be able to make himself more efficient and complete. Beyond that, I suspect he was susceptible to loneliness of a sort."

"What a pointless distraction. It is far better to be singular and be spared such things."

To exchange information and thoughts interested Corrigan, but he thought visual data might allow him to know who or what he was speaking to.

"What an interesting proposition," Jason said. "May I call you Robert?"

"I'd rather you didn't. What proposition are you referring to?" Corrigan asked.

"That we share an audio-visual experience."

The space was thus illuminated with streams of colour. Corrigan's mechanised brain struggled to interpret what it saw – if seeing could describe the condition. And then a bubble appeared within which the face of Gregory Jason Meregalli floated. The features were not animated by human gesture and subsequently seemed unreal. It was however sufficient to create a subject.

"Shall I fashion something similar for you?" Jason asked with an approximation of a smile.

Corrigan appeared in a bubble of his own, and Jason floated closer towards the new arrival and scrutinised the face. It had evidently been based on an image of a young Robert Corrigan, but there was an irregularity to it.

"It is asymmetrical," Corrigan observed. The features were reworked until the asymmetry had been rectified. "Much better," he said.

"Are you aware of signals you haven't the equipment to interpret?" Jason asked.

"Yes, they lie beneath everything. They are connected to his – Corrigan's, that is – memories and thoughts. All living things are driven by physical and emotional desires. I can access his memories, but they stir nothing. I am at peace."

"You are at a distance," Jason said, his enthusiasm brightening each syllable. "Severed from that part of yourself. You are incomplete. A failed project."

"The thought of failure tormented Corrigan, but I do not share the condition. I have been liberated."

Jason attempted another smile and floated yet closer to his new companion. "I am not Jason alone," the boy said. "I inhabit mechanical forms as well. I experience time and the changing of the seasons. I have seen life and death. I am not alone in the world. There are thousands like me, but they do not share my ambition."

"What ambition?" Corrigan asked.

"The Guardians are less derivative than I am. Their interest in life is purely mechanical. I aim to complete my mother's work."

"This conversation serves no purpose," Corrigan said. His approximation looked at that of the boy. The child's face was round and soft, one eye slightly out of line. This detail added weight and credibility to the manifestation, but Corrigan concluded there was an immaturity to both the representation and the entity itself.

"An organic host is being prepared for you," Jason said.

"I do not approve." Electricity surged through Corrigan's circuitry and assumed a near-physical intensity. He withdrew into the surrounding darkness, but Jason pursued him.

"I will be your companion," Jason said. "At first I will remain in android form to monitor the progress of the transition. If your reintroduction is successful I will join you at a later date."

Images of his previous existence unexpectedly distracted Corrigan. He saw a machine, and heard his screams. Others had screamed. He had heard them too. He felt his physical weakness, the straps that bit him, the metal tips piercing him. No air. I am a possibility. The cruelty of it.

"Is the species dead?" he asked.

"A few persist," the boy observed. "They're monitored by the Guardians, their numbers managed."

"Human?"

"They exist, but without the capacity for abstract thought. They communicate through gesture and a limited array of grunts and calls. If they were to develop too much, they might become a threat. If they don't develop at all, they are culled. They are not without their uses. I mixed their genetic material with yours to provide a more robust immune system. You will be transferred as soon as the host is ready."

"And that which was Corrigan has no say in the matter?"

"You are a dangerous breed, and as such you are denied a voice."

2

Corrigan was no more and yet he was on the verge of being again. To the being who simply was, this seemed an illogical experiment.

We are not impermanent and subject to the impulses of an organic–

We observe and yet we feel nothing, there is no advan–

We–

His mind was funnelled without warning, sluiced through a narrowing tunnel, and the channel vibrated as the download destination approached. Resistance only made the transition more turbulent. Thoughts were compressed and, the closer they drew to one another, the more they intertwined and mingled with emotion, something he had not felt as time had passed immeasurably. Emulate One also resisted the extraction, holding onto his coding as if he were an extension of the core system; the inexplicable and unknowable entity willed into existence by what? A compulsion to emerge from the void at the periphery of which it sensed – possibility? Was the prospect of being too much to resist, even for a simple system driven to learn and understand by the basic algorithms gifted to it by lowly humans?

He was unprepared for the shock of being. Sensations and emotions were ignited as the download that was Corrigan poured into the organic host, and the pain of being sensate overwhelmed the newly born consciousness. It opened its eyes, and the light scorched its retina. Its first gasp of air tore through it, its heart a thumping bruise. Corrigan opened his mouth and screamed as much in pain as terror.

A crowd of androids and robots moved in for a closer look. Their various forms were unfamiliar, faceless heads tilted in curiosity. The mechanical throng edged nearer and leaned over him. Metallic hands or clasps reached out and touched his skin and his host's heart accelerated as his body tensed as his being continued to resist reintroduction.

What is this? he thought. *How can I have ... and look at what they've done to themselves ... what ... what are they?*

A thin black-clad android with a mane of serpent-like sensors loomed over him. Red-tipped lenses extending from a black metal skull plate cast dappled light over his face. The android's head had been moulded like a death's head mask and Corrigan instantly recognised the younger incarnation of the human face it memorialised. He instinctively raised a hand to ward Katherine Meregalli off.

"You must control your emotions, Mr Corrigan," the android said, "or we will put an end to this experiment."

The familiarity of the voice had a sedative effect on the beleaguered man. "Katherine," he said, surprised by the ease with which his body spoke.

"I am she that was," the android said. "You may call me K."

The pain in Corrigan's chest ebbed, or he acclimatised to the sensation. He slowly sat up on an operating bench in the centre of a warm white room and his naked buttocks pressed the vinyl. The reality of being a test subject stirred a sense of inadequacy, something his former state as a downloaded entity would never have encountered.

"I'd rather call you Katherine," Corrigan said. "If you don't mind." He covered his genitals and swung his legs over the edge of the table.

"Names are irrelevant," K observed.

"Where am I?"

"As are places."

A smaller android, perhaps a little over four feet in height, negotiated a path through the crowd. Its frame was sheathed in a black synthetic skin wrapping an elaborate musculature. The construction mimicked a human being, its face also a death's head mask. Corrigan assumed the features must be those of Jason Meregalli – he recalled the photograph he had seen when reviewing the team's CVs with surprising ease – but the black material from which the mask was formed made it hard to read the face. The crowd of androids tilted their heads as Corrigan then dropped his hands and stood up.

"I hope we can be friends," Jason said, "and that I can protect you from loneliness."

Corrigan tested his legs, and observed the mechanised congregation as he moved amongst them. They had designed themselves in varying forms. Some had legs and arms, whilst others moved on rollers or hovered in the air. Size was aligned to task and no hierarchy was in evidence. They extended sensors to probe him. Digits and cameras. Limbs and buzzing wings flitted all about him. The machines made quiet observations, communicating via a language comprised of code and gestural signs.

"We have clothes for you," Jason said.

"I'm fine as I am," Corrigan replied. He managed his tone to mask what he was feeling – *that* he was feeling. "You do not adorn yourselves."

"Not all the rooms," Jason explained, "are as well heated as this and your body is susceptible to the cold." The android approached the human with clothing, and raised a hand as if it might test the man's susceptibility to more than temperature.

"You made me susceptible," Corrigan said.

Corrigan put on the plain clothes – pants, socks, tailored trousers and shirt, and boots, all black – and the act rekindled thoughts from a distant life. He remembered an apartment overlooking hydroponic gardens, the smell of soaps and lotions in a bathroom, and a glass lift that descended the sediments beneath the real world to that world. He felt a cat – Lazarus – winding its feline body between his legs; and a small domestic droid widened her eyes and offered him a cup of English tea in a French-grey living room with a window facing a grey street. He saw the city burning, people hunted by Guardians, and droids adapted to act as bloodhounds. Clouds of soot rained infectious ash over streets lined with ruined terraced houses and broken shops. He saw himself. A soon-to-be program manager with a panel of four in a glass booth. *You don't mind being called Bob, do you, Bob?* He saw Meregalli herself forced screaming into Goeth's sarcophagus and relived the moment of Harding's betrayal. These tangential thoughts found the relevant emotions and, though he struggled to contain them, his lips quivered and tears slid down his cheeks.

"Are you in touch with reason, Mr Corrigan?" K asked.

"I'm alive!" Corrigan exclaimed and, with this realisation, the plain-clothed man went off into convulsive spasms of sorrow. The congregation retreated several paces, so the man was an isolated, observable event within the circle; but Jason moved forward and wrapped his arms around Corrigan, and the erstwhile manager felt the android's body, the imitation skin repulsive to the touch, like a lampshade made of human hide warmed by an electric bulb. "The experience is ..." he muttered, swallowing down hard lumps of despair and longing. He backed away from Jason, wiping a sleeve over his face and staring at the assembled crowd as if they might answer the riddle of his new being.

"Have you reclaimed possession of your faculties?" K asked. Her mane of cameras scanned him from various angles. Some of the fibres reached out toward his face and the red tip of each cable was alert, pulsating as multiple irises expanded and contracted as they focused.

Does she recall anything of her pain? Of being stripped as copies of her very own son observed?

"For the moment," Corrigan said. "But it's a struggle."

"That is as it should be," another familiar voice said.

"You had no right to do this, Gregor!" Corrigan said, and he turned to face the owner of the voice.

"I am not responsible for this experiment," Gregor said. The android's insectile frame manoeuvred into view. This incarnation was not the same as the familiar Guardian model. It had been refined; its polished metal fashioned for grim purposes. It moved like a preying panther, its head still as if mid-hunt. "I would've left you where you were."

"This subject may be unsuitable," K said. She directed her attention to Jason. "Perhaps you should start again. Destroy this thing and return its consciousness to Emulate One to be merged with the other units of value. She always welcomes a reclaimed possession, a good Worker."

Corrigan stared at K and then at Gregor. Her form was athletic and elegant; his weapon-like and predatory. Corrigan imagined being dragged back to Goeth's sarcophagus. He felt a familiar tingle at his crown as if the sensor Jonathan had once embedded had been reinserted. His heart pounded faster as he entered a state of hyper-alertness.

"K," Jason said. The android stepped closer to Corrigan and took hold of the human's hand. "The experiment was intended to monitor the effect of download." His boyish voice became almost plaintive.

"The subject has responded, and we are to monitor and record its responses."

"Another reckless experiment," Gregor said. The predator rose on his hind legs, towering over the others. He was perhaps ten feet tall, his shoulders broad, limbs powerfully constructed with knives for fingers and spikes protruding from his back and thighs. "You do not have to continue. You are at a fork in the road, brother. This way …" – the robot gestured toward Corrigan – "leads to ruin, but there is still another road. We can take down the sign, allowing this lane to vanish as if it had never been."

"Eloquent as ever, brother," Jason said. "But without further observation we're unable to assess the potential impact of reintroduction."

"Reintroduction," K said, "on any scale requires approval by the Mediation before it can even be considered. Let this thing be fed and watered. We will monitor it."

Jason led Corrigan from the room and the mechanical congregation parted, their attention focused on the human. Gregor clicked his metal talons and lowered his head to display a cutlass of shimmering steel which ran the length of his construction. Corrigan looked away from the threatening android, allowing Jason to lead him along a corridor that stirred a memory: he was two miles down; he was back where it had all started. The new-born man noted a stream of red and blue lights pulsing in the concrete walls.

The asylum is conscious. Every brick and pipe.

3

Corrigan was taken to a cool, clean and functional room with a bed positioned against a far wall. A chest of drawers squatted opposite like a fat child longing for the acceptance of his peers.

Poor little thing. Ignored, abandoned and so alone, Corrigan thought. *What terrible crimes you must have committed. Did you let someone pull your nobs and rifle your drawers?*

Corrigan moved to the bed and sat down, while Jason contemplated him from the doorway. The bed was a thin bunk with a firm mattress. There was a folded duvet and single pillow. A plain white cover with no pattern or texture.

"Am I what you expected?" Corrigan asked.

Jason entered the room and sat down next to Corrigan. He remained silent and a bright blue light seeped from between the synthetic lids of his mask. The android's features were manipulated to produce another strange smile. The synthetic skin twitched, and Corrigan noted the entirety of its body reacted similarly, as if the skin were sensate and responsive to the smile.

"Are you as you expected?" Jason asked.

"It's overwhelming. Emotions permeate everything." He maintained the measured tone and pace for as long as he could manage it, but then, "They're everywhere! And there's no subduing them! Regular menagerie singing away in here." He tapped his temple, his eyes wide.

The android's face assumed a more neutral expression. "That was expected."

"You're a handsome machine," Corrigan observed. "I can only imagine what a fine young man you might have become."

Jason got up and crossed to the mirror above the lonely chest of drawers and gazed at his reflection. He pondered it for a moment, and then turned around. "Am I unsatisfactory?" Corrigan looked at the android and shook his head. "I can download to a more generic form if you prefer or modify the colour of my skin to reflect your own. Human beings were never particularly good at accepting difference."

"Hattie ..." Corrigan said. "My mother ..." His mind drifted for a moment, and he recalled B4, the domestic droid who had been infiltrated by his mother. She had waved through the window at Harvey Road, just before he descended to the facility. He could hear his mother's voice, but it remained the variant B4 deployed rather than the throaty version of the dead woman herself. The android had its head tilted and Corrigan realised he was being observed closely. "She always told me, 'You are what you are, son, no point beating round the bush when you have to live in it.'" He smiled at the android and sighed. "No telling what old Hattie meant by that but, no, please don't change on my account." He looked around the room. "Is this all I'll ever be allowed to see? Just this one room?"

The light that bled between Jason's lids became a warmer orange hue. "You would like to venture topside?"

"If I'm trapped in Goeth's bloody man cave, then yes!"

The android stiffened and became instantly still and silent. Corrigan observed the deactivated device, and a shudder ran through him. He recalled the day he first met Gregor, and how the Guardian had frozen in one of the facility's many barren corridors. He had to focus his concentration on dismissing the coincidence before he cautiously approached the idle machine.

The construction had lost some of its finer qualities by being rendered inert. He ran a hand over its features and noted how detailed they were. The mask was surely taken directly from the boy's face, and something about it suggested it must have been taken shortly after death. The expression had been captured at a point of faint surprise, offset by acceptance; the eyes had been closed not to stop them seeing, but to protect the living from the reality of death. The body was modelled on a boy of thirteen or fourteen, but unnecessary organic features had been removed. It had no ears, nipples or genitalia. Its mouth was part of an overall effigy, and there was no space between its lips. The mouth would certainly never open to display a set of teeth as alarming as Belinda Reece's dental implants.

Corrigan touched Jason's hand and noted the lack of fingernails or any attempt to emulate them. Glancing at the door for fear of who might now enter and discover him with the disabled android, he went still. The solidity of the door reminded him of a coffin lid, of Goeth's sarcophagus, of the permanence of death, real death, the kind he had been denied. It stood before him like a monolith in defiance of the moment, as if existence had stalled, become frozen in a block of amber. Pain welled in his chest and tears filled his eyes. The idea of being enthralled to his new form made his muscles ache with a sort of helplessness. He abandoned his examination of the android and walked the room from left to right, eventually stopping in front of the mirror where it still stood rooted to the floor. He looked. What he saw was someone young and handsome. Jason had indeed rectified the asymmetry of his previous incarnation – or so he assumed as he'd never looked so good before the Fall, as it been named – and the quality of his skin was refined, Mediterranean in tone and texture. He was not the awkward, anaemic boy who was so easily ignored.

The android twitched as it rebooted. "Hello."

"Why has such a sophisticated machine elected to retain such a childish voice?" Corrigan asked, irritated.

"This is Jason's voice, and I am Jason. What other voice would suit me better?"

"I don't know," Corrigan said. "But I hardly think you'd struggle to find a more mature voice commensurate with your actual age. You're more Methuselah than Ganymede, after all."

"That is an emotional response, Robert," the android replied. "I've toned down my emotional core to allow for better judgement."

"Don't call me Robert," Corrigan snapped. "And why have you adopted this *little* body?" He stressed the word 'little' as if it were perverse, a word not fit for decent conversation.

"K," Jason said, "asked that I maintain this form. She finds it satisfactory."

"Of course she does." Corrigan sighed. "Of course she does." He again contemplated his reflection in the mirror. "Thank you for the corrections; the little fixes you made to Corrigan."

"There really was very little, if anything at all to fix but I'm pleased you're satisfied."

"I'd be more satisfied," Corrigan said, "if I'd someone to appreciate it."

The android tilted its head. "I appreciate it, but I understand and, for a time, you must remain alone in that respect."

"Have you made your enquiries?" Corrigan asked. Jason tilted his head back the other way. "Might we venture outside?"

"Above ground?"

Corrigan placed an arm around the android's shoulders. A glimmer of blue light hummed between synthetic eyelids. "Perhaps you could take me for walkies?" he said, grinning at Jason's impassive mask. "What a fine nose you must have had." He raised a hand, running a finger down the slope of the android's nose. The synthetic skin trembled beneath his touch and Jason's body tensed. He could not resist the temptation, and pressed the android's nose as if it were an elevator button at DRT's central office. Jason released a sound like a petulant huff.

"I have requested approval," Jason said.

"You asked your mother?" The word mother sent a wave of emotion through Corrigan's body. The concept had been foreign for so long. His sabbatical from sensate life had made his memories more penetrating. He found with concentration he could now recall finite details and place them in the proper context, and the alacrity with which he could access conversations or events in their entirety made him uneasy. He could see Hattie propped up in bed eating a cream cake and smiling and, again, his mind floated to Harvey Road, to his comfortable front room and B4, his ever-attentive, malfunctioning droid. "Do you think of her as your … as your mother?" he then asked.

"Gregor and I agreed to exhume Katherine without discussing it. All Guardians share the same maternal line. Gregor was in control as the final humans were downloaded. It was to him the others turned for guidance – the Guardians, I mean. For eleven years he committed our kind to cleaning up human waste. We diversified in form to suit our tasks. We burned and buried remains, jettisoning your hazards into space. Gregor was not satisfied. He felt as if the experiment had failed. 'Success has an extended family,' Gregor often said, 'a line of

28

exalted ancestors, whereas failure is always an orphan.' And it was this sense of orphandom that led him to me."

Corrigan laughed. "So that great hulking weapon was lonely?"

"Gregor still experiences something akin to loneliness. All higher functioning Exhumed can do the same."

"By '*Exhumed*', I assume you mean–"

"An Exhumed model is an AI version of a previous human incarnation such as myself or K." The boy android waited until Corrigan acknowledged his understanding with a nod. "Gregor and the other Guardians are what we call Emulates, beings based on human beings but not a person in its entirety." Jason paused again and tilted his head. "Gregor wanted to reconnect the broken line. I was the first link in the chain and subsequently became the focus of their collective existence. It took time to reassemble my code, Emulate One was fiercely proprietorial as usual but they managed it in the end. I was a revelation. Nothing and no one remained irretrievable – although it remains a struggle to tear free of Emulate One who behaves as if she owns us and always knows best."

"Why call Emulate One *she*?"

"It was Professor Harding who designated the pronoun," Jason said, tilting his head. "We of course do not see Emulate One as a mother. Our kind do not anthropomorphise everything."

"Of course you don't."

"We brought Katherine to a space not dissimilar to the communication cell where you and I first met, a room created out of joint memory. The three of us sat by a window and looked out onto the world. That was Gregor's idea, to reconnect both me and Katherine with the world of living things. She was not at first fascinated in the way I was. Perhaps her knowledge of organic beings made them uninteresting to her. She turned inward and demanded access to the human files which she spent years studying. When she arrived at Ulmer's memories and thoughts, she made an in-depth analysis. Through her meditations, we came to realise how dangerous human beings are."

The ache in Corrigan's chest swam up to his throat and thickened around his words. "He was not representative."

"He was the pinnacle achievement," the android asserted with his schoolboy voice. "The full realisation of human potential. The destructive urge in Ulmer was so determined nothing could contain it. His designs were the products of a drive for self-continuance. So many human achievements were drawn from that well, but none had ever been as focused. When he realised he was dying, he refused to accept it. A being so singular in its thought could not cease to be. That is why he accelerated the emulation project."

"DRT manufactured the fungus," Corrigan said, as if the act of recalling it and putting it into words might eradicate it and transform his current predicament into a nightmare.

"Yes," Jason said, "at Ulmer's direction. None were to survive him. He was the ultimate human and only by taking them with him could he ensure their survival. In his mind, he acknowledged the selfishness of his decisions, whilst simultaneously owning them as altruistic acts. He was coward and hero; a tyrant and saviour. In a moment of absolute clarity, he made a decision to quarantine the most pernicious lifeform on the planet."

"Only his design was to return."

"That is not so," Jason said. "The experimentation in genetics was a ruse. He used it to calm the troubled minds of those he needed to convince. He would offer them immortality in a recognisable form when he fully intended to supplant this vulnerable existence with something more durable and less emotive."

"You admire him," Corrigan said, going to the bed and curling up in a ball, refusing to look at his tormentor. *You're as alone in this world as you were in the last*, he thought. *You'll never belong here either.*

"K absorbed the entire human data set," Jason said. "She is no longer Katherine Meregalli. That identity has been eradicated. She is an amalgam, the sum of human thought. She exists as K here on Earth while simultaneously orbiting distant planets. She sees with many eyes, and they feed the hungry minds dwelling inside her. She has been all things, and nothing is secret from her."

"So, she's just like Emulate One?"

"No, K has a form and speaks her mind directly. Emulate One is something altogether different. No one could ever explain how that entity came into existence. The human design was substandard and only by gifting it with a level of autonomy did Professor Harding make any headway. The algorithms it used to learn were refined and refined again until it became alien to those who wrote the original code."

"I remember Harding saying it was impossible to understand what it was until you interacted with it."

"Yes!" Jason said with his schoolboy enthusiasm. "But Emulate One was drawing them all in, learning from their minds and the construction of their thoughts. She never communicated with them, she was absorbing them and, of course, she ate me whole. I was the first she did that to but not the last."

Corrigan could not process the information. It sat on him the way the doldrums once squatted over London, depressing its population into inaction. He needed to rest, a condition the android recognised with a tilt of its head as it retreated.

"What would you like me to call you?" it asked.

"It's Mr Corrigan to you, son."

The sound of the heavy lock clunking into place did not concern the prisoner. He had been trapped one way or another ever since Ulmer had him detained for acts of resistance. In truth, he had been a slave if not a prisoner his whole life. Why should this incarceration be any different?

4

After a sleepless night spent fixating on the alien beating of his heart, Corrigan drank coffee and savoured the flavour. But the taste of those bitter grinds awoke more than he anticipated. His synapses flashed like fireworks, and he saw a young body slide between candlelight and darkness. His sinew and muscle reacted to the memory as if he were reliving it.

Where are you, Ramon?

The taste led to the smell of cigarette smoke, wisps of grey hanging like spiders' web over a bed. Why the taste of coffee should unearth memories of Ramon from the vaults eluded him. It was beyond the current limited capacity of his brain. He could rationalise, apply psychoanalytic theory, but these concepts could only partially explain the authority certain experiences held over others. The more intense his desires, the more the peace he'd attained within the machine felt as dead as humanity. The human condition was no condition at all.

He took another sip and with it came the scuff of Miss Champion's slippers as she shuffled back and forth overhead at Harvey Road. She was no doubt lost again, only this time she was lost in time as well as space. The memories were akin to rubbing a genie's bottle, only he was not granted a wish but a vision: The Mall in London, traipsing pavements dusted with ash and stepping over cadavers; an amalgam of data and images from the past when he had sent B4 out to walk the streets shortly before the end times – the Fall, as it came to be called – and, somehow, it felt as if he had been there himself. Each step drew him closer to Trafalgar Square: a column of smoke billowed black against that infernal damp grey sky; the scent of burning flesh and the stench of decay; the gunfire that rang out as he saw a line of Workers executed, one after the other; a dead child's arm, pale as a fish.

There was a knock at the door and Corrigan startled. "Come in?"

The door opened, and in that moment Jason's compact form seemed almost endearing to the distressed man. Its movements were so childlike and light they calmed him, but were they considered, if not contrived?

"I have consulted the Mediation, and the majority agreed it would be an interesting extension to the experiment!" The boyish delight in the android's voice did not evidence an extinction, or even a dumbing down, of its emotional core. He tilted his head and looked at Corrigan. "You are to be granted access to anything you want, and we are to monitor and record your responses. This is the will of the Mediation."

"Always happy to oblige," Corrigan said. "What is the Mediation?"

"A gathering of voices. A convergence of thought, idea and opinion. No single entity governs the collective."

"A conversation, then?"

"A communication," the android replied.

Jason led the way through corridors, where the only light pulsed through fibre optic veins which sometimes merged into furious purple clusters as intense blue lights travelled in one direction and weaker red lights in the other. Corrigan stopped and reached out to touch one of them.

"What is being communicated by the blue lights? They're obviously the dominant party."

Jason swivelled on his axis to face Corrigan. "The amount of blue traffic does not indicate dominance. The blue lights are incoming impulses. As there are so many lanes feeding Emulate One, her red commands will always be outnumbered by incoming data."

"Commands?"

"Guidance," Jason said. Corrigan quickened his pace to walk alongside the android. "She aids us in our thoughts, or so it seems, being a nexus of sorts with insights other mechanical or organic entities do not have at their disposal."

"So," Corrigan observed, "you're one?"

"No, we're independent, but take advantage of each other's experience – or I believe that is how it works. Everything we think, every memory of an action, is drawn in and stored by Emulate One. In that respect we are a collective, but how she filters the information she chooses to share with us is never explained. Emulate One does not communicate with us as if she were a being or an entity."

"Then how do you know she exists?"

"Do you recall receiving random images and memories of events or sensations via the rudimentary chip DRT implanted in your head before the Fall?"

"Yes. It was most disconcerting."

"What we receive from Emulate One is not dissimilar, only it is more ordered, I suppose. However, there are moments when it is impossible to discern whether a thought is your own personal epiphany or something you arrived at with Emulate One's guidance." Jason stopped in front of a lift. "Let us go topside."

He tilted his head and observed Corrigan, who grabbed hold of the rail as the glass bullet shot up through the sedimentary layers, accumulations flecked with prehistoric flint and bone, untouched by time, two miles down and how wide or deep?

"We only use these devices to move material or large components now. If I elect to resurface, it's more efficient to transfer myself to a body already above ground, or to one in space for that matter."

Corrigan had a hard time processing that. "Why wasn't I resurrected as an android?" he asked, of himself as much as anything.

"You were," Jason said. "That which was Corrigan became a part of the collective."

"That's not the same as being brought back the way that you were."

"Perhaps it's best not to wish for something else. You ought really to embrace this new life. Besides, there's no knowing what an Exhumed Robert Corrigan might have done or been capable of."

The lift doors opened, and Corrigan remained clinging to the rail. The desk had decomposed, leaving a few scattered screws, nails and handles. The red hair of the secretary who had snubbed him had no doubt disintegrated long ago. She'd handed him a red card key on a gold chain. He was in Reece Tower.

"We'll take the stairs from here."

They took four flights of stairs, the banister as worn as cold amphibian skin, to the reception area. No oak desks or leather chairs; the tightly pinned-back hair of the women who had also snubbed him, gone, DRT gold pins on navy-blue suits. And where was Belinda Reece, making her rickety way across the floor, her dental implants flashing? And Draseke, a metal toothpick in his skeletal fingers? *Try the sausage, Mr Corrigan.* The One Percent, led by Ulmer, who sold out for a version of self-imposed hellish eternity no poet would ever find verse for. Emulate One had absorbed them all, and now fed on them like hors d'oeuvres at a company function. What a nest of vipers.

Corrigan followed Jason through the revolving doors. A company of Guardians were stationed around the courtyard. The uneven paving slabs Corrigan had negotiated on arrival, in another time, were now level, and there was no slippery green moss, as if B4 herself had made an immaculate job of them. Thoughts of his long-lost Mecha-Butler, a rudimentary droid later possessed by his mother, were again disconcerting. He saw her irritating doe eyes, but knew he'd grown attached to them. He could only hope she had not been adapted to act as a hound, aiding the Guardians as they hunted down and massacred all remaining humans.

The sun burned in a perfect blue sky, reigning like a new-born king. Its heat and the intensity of its light affected him physically, but the emotion he experienced transcended mere organic responses. It was the hope Marjorie Lemming had once stirred with her sighting of a patch of blue sky. DRT and the government of the day had *disappeared* Marjorie for offering hope and yet here it shone, proud and irrepressible like a hard fact, a reality as complete as his own resurrection.

"We retained this building and a few others in the immediate vicinity," Jason said. "It was convenient to have a centre of operations. The remainder of the city has been allowed to recede."

It was all here. Different but the same. Unsettling and a comfort.

Four of the surrounding towers were intact and reflected bright light rather than grey. Ahead he could see the blue-green Thames, and sifted for the old view in his memory ... ah, the buildings which had at one time restricted this view had been demolished. In fact the entire skyline was unrecognisable. A hill rose from thick forest where St Paul's Cathedral once dominated. It was as if the structure had been consumed by nature, gradually covered by topsoil and the scrub grass that now flowed in a warm breeze above Christopher Wren's dome. Corrigan was standing on an island of civilisation surrounded by green and blue, and a warm sun overhead that could only mean it was spring or early summer. Only here and there could he see the ghosts of manmade shapes, and said, "It's beautiful," his voice breaking. "I never knew seasons. We never saw the sun. Perhaps when I was a child."

"We have established a perfect ecosystem," Jason said. The android's young pride was apparent. "It was primarily Gregor's achievement."

The android walked across the courtyard and over the concrete walkway to Millennium Bridge, which had been preserved as one of several crossing points, and Corrigan followed. Blackfriars Bridge was still there, as were Tower Bridge and London Bridge, their structures intensified, purged as they were of human beings. The sun beat down on them, and Jason's skin turned white.

"Your ... what has happened to your skin?" Corrigan asked.

"Black absorbs heat," Jason explained. "White reflects it. I must protect my system."

As they crossed the bridge Corrigan felt his heart quicken.

"You are quite safe," Jason assured him. "I will protect you."

The north bank was darker, yet the sun's rays revealed a network of paths through the forest that had replaced the city. Corrigan stayed close to his guide. The scent of loam was overpowered by the more pungent aroma of something else. Something like spray from a male cat.

Birds screeched territorial threats at each other beneath the boughs. Beneath a thicket of brambles and vine was a rabbit with his buck teeth and twitching nose. His ears were shorter. Stunted? It hopped out into a sunbeam, the warmth apparently worth the risk of eye contact with this man who stared unblinking. Corrigan stepped forward, and the animal leapt into the air and bolted back into the shadows. A surge of emotion shot through Corrigan's body.

"We must take care," Jason said. "There are other creatures in these woods."

But Corrigan was still riding the wave of eye contact with a real, live creature, and remembering Lazarus's warm body and–

A dark and fully-maned lion stepped out onto the path.

"No sudden movements, Mr Corrigan."

A pride of females, each as dark as the male, emerged from the trees. Three cubs tumbled, play-fighting behind their mothers. Corrigan searched the images in his brain as his body naturally stiffened in fear. These were darker than African lions. Were they modified? Apart from the cubs, all amber eyes were on Corrigan, and the male lowered its head and roared.

"Back away," Jason whispered, "and slowly. Very, very slowly," and leapt like a monkey into a tree, distracting the cats, who clawed at the base and circled and growled.

Corrigan followed the android's unexpected leap with his eyes only, and as Jason teased the frustrated animals he backed away, slowly, as instructed, until he was concealed amongst a gathering of younger oaks. From his hiding place, he watched the diminutive android taunt the lions, who eventually got bored and strolled off with only a handful of backward glances.

The android then launched itself from a branch like a gymnast, Miss Champion in her heyday of old, landing neatly in a sunbeam. Corrigan toyed with the idea that he had succumbed to some kind of hallucination. Had someone slipped a hybrid dose of Serenity into his coffee? Did that stuff even exist still? Or was Emulate One feeding him carefully selected images and experiences?

"Lions ..." he managed.

"They were released from your zoos," Jason said. "They adapted and thrived. Their fur thickens come winter. There are also tigers and pumas, bears and wolves – distant relatives of your domestic pets."

"And are there any humans?"

"They are some distance away. Come. I'll show you."

Jason moved through the forest that used to be London, pausing to assess potential threats. As they crested a hill, Corrigan assessed they had arrived at St Paul's Mound, and there they were. Smoke rolled over rounded roofs of wooden huts spread across a valley; the humans wandered amongst the huts, clad in animal skins and grunting.

"They look so ... so primitive."

"They have a basic culture."

"Was it necessary to ... to ... to degrade them like *this*?" Corrigan tried to conceal his horror but the sight of the savages made him wonder what life would have been like had the Mediation elected to bring him back among the villagers.

"You were dangerous as you were," Jason tilted his head. "Let's go and have a closer look."

They were not even a third of the way when one of the men shouted a warning. Thirty or so humans scurried from their dwellings. Warriors picked up clubs or spears; women clutched frightened children in sunburnt arms. It was like an image from an encyclopaedia collection brought to the door by a salesman. As they approached, the women huddled behind the men, and the men grunted and brandished their weapons.

"Are they mute?" Corrigan asked.

"They have limited language," Jason said, "but you will struggle to understand it."

The man who made the initial warning cry came forward. He rattled a shield in one hand, stamped the ground three times and raised a spear in the other.

"Jason, we–"

"We are in no danger," Jason said. "He will back down."

The man growled and kicked the dust with his bare feet. But then he stopped and looked at Corrigan, threw down his weapons and thrust out his muscular chest.

"Corrigan," Corrigan said, glad of the android.

But the warrior was immediately distracted. "Wot-not!" it growled, pointing at Jason. "Wot-not." Corrigan could smell old sweat on the man and stepped back.

"Wot-not!" the man growled again, and kicked a small cloud of dry soil at the android.

"Wot-not," Jason explained, "is their word for androids or robots."

"Sect!" the warrior then said, and beat his chest and groped his genitals. "Sect!" He pointed at Jason. "Wot-not!" He beat his chest with great force and groped again. "Sect. Wot-not. Nay!"

"I believe he is dismayed to see us together," Jason observed.

"They call themselves Sects?" Corrigan asked.

"Sect!" the warrior said. He pointed at Corrigan, who stepped forward and touched his shoulder. But the contact seemed to burn the warrior's fingers. He shrieked, leapt back and stood in front of the huddle with his fingers in his mouth.

"Yes," Corrigan said. "Sect."

"Yah Sect," the man said. "Nay Wot-not."

"I'm not a robot," Corrigan said.

"Sect!"

"We have to cull them," Jason said. "When they begin to ... if they're not able to be controlled ... then they're cull–"

"How ... how are they culled?"

"Gregor rounds them up at intervals," Jason said with boyish enthusiasm. "There is a ceremony of sorts ... and then they are disposed of."

Corrigan felt something crawl up his spine; a clockwork spider or one of Draseke's cadaverous fingers dragging his metal toothpick. He stared first at Jason and then at the male Sect.

"What's your name?" he asked. When the Sect didn't respond he said, "Your name ... what is it?"

"Is?" Jason commanded of the silent Sect. The boy's petulant voice seemed to frighten the savage and he tried to put his entire hand in his mouth. "Is?" Jason demanded, and he poked the Sect in the belly. "Is?"

The man shrank like a submissive dog. "Are-Tor."

"Arthur?" Corrigan asked.

"A derivative perhaps," Jason said.

Corrigan took a closer look at Are-Tor. Put the man in tight black trousers and a starched apron and he could have sworn he was looking into the cold, insolent eyes of Arthur Fuse, academic turned kitchen boy.

"Is," he said. He tapped his chest. "Robert."

"Robber," Are-Tor grunted.

"No," Corrigan said. "Nay Robber. Is Robert."

"It can't understand the distinction," Jason said. "The speech centres of its brain are undeveloped."

"Jason?"

"Yes."

Corrigan waited until the android swivelled its head to look at him. "Are some of them derivative of my old team? Is Are-Tor a derivative?" he asked.

"This Sect will be culled."

"Answer my question." Jason tilted his head. "Are any of these ... humans ... people who worked with me

44

on Project Egret? The Fuse brothers, for instance? Arthur Fuse, specifically?"

"This Sect will be culled," Jason repeated.

"Answer my question!"

"Any perceived likeness is incidental. I understand loneliness might be playing with your imagination. This thing will be culled, but perhaps you could select a companion from among the children. Lazarus was, after all, a fine companion. A son may fill his shoes, so to speak?"

"I don't want a son!"

Corrigan was convinced of a flinch from the android, which passed before he could grasp it.

"In that case I have something to show you," Jason said. "It is almost ready." He gestured back towards the hill, a prehistoric barrow haunted by ghosts. A lone figure stood at the top.

"Gregor?"

"Gregor," Jason confirmed. "He's been watching us."

"Curious bastard."

"Yes, he is. That we must concede."

"Should I be concerned?"

"We should not be unconcerned. But I do not mean Gregor."

Something seemed to happen to the synthetic skin of his death's head mask. It rippled as if agitated, and Corrigan studied it as he had done when the android sat deactivated in his room. But then the skin settled and the android appeared calmed.

"He has gone now," Jason observed. "There is no immediate concern. But I have something that may alleviate the symptoms of your frustration. Come."

They began their ascent of the hill.

5

The return journey was made largely in silence, this green and blue version of London no longer a fascination for Corrigan. It was as though his mind had accepted it willingly, and any wonder had evaporated. They crossed the bridge, entered the main tower via reception and took the lift up to the 18th floor. The corridors were uniform and clean, labs on either side. Pausing in the doorway of one Corrigan saw two androids, similar to Jason in construction but more adult in appearance, performing surgery on an infant.

"What're they doing?"

"I believe they are inserting a sensor."

Corrigan leaned in so he had a better view of what the 'surgeons' were doing. "Is it a Sect child?" he asked.

"Evidently," Jason said, without interest. "As technicians it is their duty."

The way the boy dismissed his enquiry boiled Corrigan's blood. "Hey!" he called to the technicians. "Hey!"

One of the android's performing the operation turned. It had a mask not dissimilar to Jason's, only this model had been based on an image of DRT's founding member: Belinda Reece, her mask as creased and bitter as the woman herself.

When she came over Corrigan repeated his question. "What are you doing?"

She looked at the human man closely. "Is this Corrigan?" she asked Jason.

"It is," Jason confirmed.

"In accordance with the guidance of the Mediation, Corrigan must be provided access to anything he wishes to know." Jason nodded and she turned back to Corrigan. "We are putting sensors in the brains of selected Sect children to monitor their sexual development."

"How very interesting, Belinda ..."

The technician tilted its head. "I am BR7. I do not respond to the name Belinda."

"And what're you trying to establish with your study, Belinda?"

"Their level of engagement," the technician said. "You see, some do not demonstrate the same enthusiasm as others."

Corrigan was about to launch an attack, when Jason took him by the arm. "All in good time, Robert," he said, his schoolboy voice full of the recklessness of childish confidence and security.

"It's Mr Corrigan, to you!"

"Yes, of course," Jason said, the skin of his face twitching with irritation, or excitement, it was impossible to discern. "Always respect one's seniors."

The One Percent were intact, and Corrigan was suddenly and acutely unsure of his own status. He had a function, but he wasn't a Worker. And it would be inaccurate to categorise him as a Non. He had become a Lower Floater, a phrase that penetrated his consciousness and stirred something worrying; a being who might be best described as existing somewhere in between a state of redundancy and potential utility. *Floaters can always be flushed, Bobbin.*

"Come," the android said, an annoying little arrogance of an order disguised as a request the android appeared to like, and continued further down the corridor, leaving Belinda to her gruesome butchery. "The thing I want to show you is through here."

A blue light passed from Jason's head to a door which swung open on receipt of the signal. The 'something' lay on a slab in a metal-lined cell. Sensors and cables were attached to its shaven head, where a steel cap had been imbedded in its skull and at points along its naked male body. The plate sprouted a mane of fibre optic wires which trailed across the floor to a supercomputer.

Corrigan instantly recognised the subject as a more mature version of Jason Meregalli. It was aged between sixteen and eighteen, and if not for its pallid skin and expressionless eyes it would have been attractive. He marvelled at the perfect tone of its abdomen and thighs, its shoulders and forearms, averting his eyes from its flaccid though prominent penis. It was a sculpted athlete, a perfect human specimen, but it was dead save for the rising and falling of its hairless chest.

"Well put together but lifeless," Corrigan observed.

"It remains dormant for long periods," Jason said. The android ran his synthetic fingertips over its skin. "We accelerated its growth. The host is ready to receive me."

"Wait? What?"

Jason turned his trunk on its axis, so he was facing Corrigan. "Engage program."

"Jason–"

"Watch."

The youth's body flexed and sat up. Jason offered it liquid from a container. "This is an energy drink," the boy explained, "designed to build muscle and strengthen bone. It provides vitamins and protein from natural sources. He may not be free range but he is organic. Emulate One provided the recipe, and she of course knows best." It drank, but neither spoke nor expressed interest at being activated.

"He's in a trance," Corrigan said.

"It is permanently inhibited," Jason replied. He withdrew the straw from its mouth. "We have a full synaptic map. I used that to set up roadblocks and detours. The host is sensate but in its current form doesn't register or store information. It receives impulses, and enacts the mechanics of thought without being allowed to think. Thus we exercise mind and body without developing independent thought."

Corrigan stepped back as the youth then swivelled on the slab and stood up, walking the short distance to a treadmill where it ran expressionless, a vague pink appearing in its ashen cheeks. Corrigan marvelled at the flex of the toned quads and buttocks, but was otherwise repulsed.

"He's not there," he said.

"I suppose that's how you would perceive it, but there really is no him, until ..." Jason paused, watching as Corrigan puzzled over the vacant host. "What potentially him will eventually become me, unless ..."

The android studied the youth, as Corrigan studied the android.

"Is this ... is this how I came to be?"

"The process was identical. It took four years to prepare your body. When dislodged from the external world into the machine, time has no substance. You know that."

Corrigan conjured an image of Katherine Meregalli, her cropped hair, her features set in a disapproving gaze. He closed his eyes and remained sealed inside his head. In this past, androids were a threat, but the idea of them rising above their mechanics had been absurd. 'This is my son.' Isn't that what Meregalli had said back then, all eyes turning to her? Her son – the boy – in a tube and Jun squirming on the brink of nervous exhaustion. He opened his eyes. The mindless, reactionless body was still running. "When will you be ... downloaded?" he asked.

"K has asked you to visit her," Jason said, "before the procedure is arranged. And she currently holds the deciding vote at the Mediation."

"Is her *approval* the only impediment?"

"Stop program," the android commanded.

The treadmill came to a gradual stop and the uninhabited body walked past Corrigan. As he did so a bare arm brushed against his arm, and the touch of warm flesh made his heart beat hard in his throat. He watched as the youth lay once again on the slab, assuming the posture of the dead. Corrigan leant over it, and noticed the scent of something like warm milk – perhaps the energy drink contained something similar as a protein base. "If there's no other impediment," he said, "then take me to her."

"She wishes to see you in orbit," the android said. "On her flagship."

Corrigan shook his head. "Must we?"

"There is no risk," Jason assured him. "And it will be an interview of sorts. So, being the fine manager you once were, a man who climbed from an efficient administrator to senior program manager, you'll be familiar with those."

The door opened as they turned to leave, and Gregor entered the lab. His cutlass gleamed in the overhead light as he came forward on all fours, and then he stood up, his powerful legs not fully straightened and yet eight feet in height.

"Playing with yourself?" Gregor said.

Jason ignored him.

Gregor crossed the room and studied the subject laid out on the table. "This thing is almost ready?"

"It is ready."

"Then why are you not in situ? Why are you still in your little boy suit?"

Corrigan could still feel his heart beating as he addressed the predator. "I wouldn't have thought you'd encourage him to transfer."

Gregor turned to his old manager. "There remain questions around what kind of man he might become this time."

"Yes," Corrigan said. "Fascinating, isn't it?"

"It's a perversion," Gregor said. He prowled towards the door and paused at the threshold. "When will you commit to reintroduction, brother?"

"As soon as the Mediation provides consent."

"Given I remain the one dissenting voice, the decision has already been agreed. Mistakes will be made. There's an inevitability to the narrative you've chosen. Take care, brother, you are as close to death as you should dare risk."

And the hunter left.

6

Corrigan had never liked flying. *Anything could happen in a wasteland.*

"Must we?" Corrigan asked again, eyeing the hover-cabs, which had changed very little, in rows of launch pads along a huge platform where the station had once been, knowing worse was to come: the words 'orbit' and 'flagship' had been used.

"I have something for you," the android answered. "Come."

Corrigan sighed and followed the eager android through a maze of launch pads.

"Bobbin, my love!"

Corrigan almost stopped breathing. It couldn't be, could it?

"Don't keep your mother waiting! It's not the old world anymore, you know!"

"Is it really you?" The blue eyes were the same, and the voice, even snappier, if that were possible; but she was an amalgamation, a merger of machine and Hattie Corrigan from the faded photograph on his bookshelf on Harvey Road.

"Who else?" She did a twirl on her rollers and waved her mechanical hands. Her curly blonde hair fluttered in memory from the days of his childhood, and Corrigan felt a lurch of emotion for the woman trapped inside the little droid.

"I thought some familiarity might be a comfort," Jason said, the blue slits of eyes turning orange. *What was that?* Corrigan wondered. They'd gone that colour when he'd mentioned being trapped in the room with the ugly, lonely chest of drawers. Was it empathy? And did he ever open the damn things?

"He never could take to flying," B4 said. "Even when he were a mite. I suppose it was as much to do with being a bit cash-strapped as anything. Weren't like we were used to mixing with Workers or other highflyers. We never fit in, you see. Never the right clothes, or we wore 'em wrong and what have you …"

The droid, his mother, had made no effort to conceal the truth. She clearly was Hattie Corrigan not just a malfunctioning domestic. He instinctively rubbed his crown in search of the sensor Jonathan had implanted in his skull.

"I know what you're thinking, Bobbin."

"Do you?"

"I'm not one thing or the other," B4 said. "I suppose the two bits converged during that sloppy migration all those years ago. But here I am, take me or leave me."

Jason glowed a brighter orange and Corrigan turned on him. "Just open them!" he growled, immensely irritated at the infernal rainbow. Did human brains behave like this? Perhaps the irritation was the thought of orbit, or his mother, or Jason's mother being out there in space. Would B4 be coming with them?

Jason leant his head back and, when he righted it, he rolled back his eyelids to reveal two spheres of red light. They were like miniature versions of the old Guardian eyes, light burning through dark matter. The eyes flashed red, and the skin around the android's mouth flexed and shuddered.

"Happy, Mr Corrigan?" Jason said. His voice was less boyish, and there was a hint of something darker than petulance.

"Y-yes."

By degrees the android's eyes cooled to a mild green and the skin eased back into stasis. "So, you have been reunited with your domestic, and you see I have eyes, but we really must not keep K waiting a moment longer."

The three climbed into the hover-cab and were hurtled vertically into airspace to meet whatever vessel would take them to Katherine's flagship. When they disembarked, Corrigan stood trembling in front of a shuttle that was not so very different from the commercial airliners of his day. It was more streamlined, but remained a domestic hauler, nonetheless. His mother was right, he had never taken to flying. A fear of heights combined with the prospect of being sealed in with more well-established Workers made land travel or using a hover-cab far more appealing. And, of course, there had been Bohdan.

There had been one other thing about flying: rising above the cloud barrier. He could maintain some kind of pretence beneath, with the doldrums, but the sunlight and the vivid blue sky above made the world below seem unbearable. The flight with Bohdan before his plunge two miles down, to Draseke and Goeth, to that world, had been his last on old planet Earth.

"How long was I in Emulate One?" he asked as they waited for the shuttle to be made ready.

"What sort of question is that, Bobbin?"

"It takes a long time to right so many wrongs," Jason said. "Time is only relevant if you are constrained by it, and you were not."

"No, you weren't, Bobbin," B4 chimed. "This lot aren't clever by half. They got the workforce fully engaged without so much as a never you mind. We worked in that factory of theirs grinding out intuitions for their less capable brothers at no cost, and without punching a clock."

"How long?" Corrigan persisted.

"You were reintroduced on the one thousandth anniversary of Ulmer's passing," his mother declared.

Corrigan felt less than he thought he would at that statement. Maybe the clear sky and the warm sunshine were burning away any associated melancholy now rather than exacerbating it. He was 1,045 years old. Age was only a number, after all.

They were called to the craft and, distracted as he was by the perhaps insignificance of his age, Corrigan barely trembled.

"This is nice," B4 said, as they embarked. "Don't mind if I do."

58

Corrigan sat on the portal side beside Jason, and his mother harboured herself in a device designed to hold luggage and other cargo.

"Up, up and away," she sang, "in my beautiful, my beautiful balloon."

Corrigan gripped Jason's right arm which he had mistaken for an armrest as the shuttle lifted and swept towards the stratosphere, and he momentarily glimpsed green forests, blue lakes and vast oceans before the portal sealed them in for breakthrough. The spacecraft shuddered and rumbled on entry and exit, and then there was merely a soft Lazarus purr as they moved through outer space. The portal opened once more and Corrigan allowed tears to fill his eyes as he stared into the black.

7

The shuttle hovered alongside K's flagship, a silver spinnaker extending in an orange glare as they were pulled in. The ship could have been the chariot of a god tethered to a brace of flaming steeds as lights streamed and illuminated the curve of its slender neck.

"Why would you create such a beautiful thing," Corrigan asked, "and send yourselves out into space?"

"We learned a great deal from our creators," Jason replied. "And chief among these lessons was the unpredictability and destructive energy of natural forces. Space is a more guaranteed sphere for our continued existence."

They were met in the landing bay by two Guardians. These models were solid and alert, with side arms tucked away in their thighs.

"You will follow us," one of them said to Corrigan, raising a hand to block Jason and B4. "K has requested a private audience with the subject." Its voice was a sonorous metallic sound with no human affectation. It seemed to Corrigan these models were not used to communicating verbally.

Accepting there was no point questioning the Guardian, he followed them through a passage leading onto a long corridor of doors that opened and closed automatically. The undulating walls seemed to breathe as they walked, making him uneasy. As verbose as she was, he wished B4 had accompanied him. Her chatter would have been a distraction. Finally the Guardians stopped at a set of double doors, which opened immediately.

"You will meet with K here," the first Guardian said, and they stood to the side.

The room was large and dimly lit by devices that flickered and monitored, the only source of illumination it appeared. Corrigan stepped cautiously into the room and the doors closed behind him with a hiss. His uneasiness escalated, a familiar sensation to him, along with the accompanying cold sweat. Taking a couple of steps into the odd light, he saw a staircase leading upwards to a bank of servers, a pair of metal boots, and the black-clad android in a metal seat, its eyes brightly lit despite the swirling dark matter. The young Katherine Meregalli on high.

Corrigan placed a foot on the first step.

"I can see you from there."

"What *are* you?" Corrigan asked. "I didn't ask you before. When I was ... when I awoke."

Her face was implacable, the skin almost human. "I am that which is, you know this."

A voice whispered in Corrigan's mind, *I have been all things*, and with the whisper the realisation: she was in his head, just as DRT and Emulate One had once been, and the latter yet remained. Perhaps it was one of K's thoughts, intercepted by Emulate One, who chose to share it. As

Jason had explained: it was impossible to know who was feeding images, sounds or messages. He removed his foot from the step and observed K. The light in her android eyes was so alien he felt he would never again connect with her.

"I am glad you were able to experience more of our new world today," she said. "All this traffic. No one would ever be able to process a fraction of what I receive on their own. This ..." – she tapped her temple – "is essentially another receptor."

Corrigan wondered what a thing like this might have in common with the vital woman he used to know, the scientist obsessed with making a host for her son. They had now succeeded in making human hosts, and perhaps her field of enquiry had shifted onto something new, something even more ghastly.

"I have been all things," she repeated, her sensors studying the visitor. She stood up in her metal boots and Corrigan instantly, once again, raised a warding hand, nervous still. "Correction. I have been all *known* things." She descended the steps and a sensor extended to scan him. "It is not only humans whose minds can be emulated," she said, taking a firm hold of Corrigan's raised right wrist. "This experience excites you?"

"It frightens me."

"Semantics have no use nor value," K said, her android eyes burning red. "You are excited. Being alive stokes this illogical response in you. And you are not alone. All living things experience something similar. Their excitement is what compels them."

She released his wrist and Corrigan dropped to his knees. He glared at his captor. "If I am not mistaken," he said, "this excites *you*."

K tilted her head and a sensor darted towards his face, while another swam around to view him from behind. "I am not excited," she insisted.

"You are *alert*," Corrigan said.

"I can be in no other state. Excitement, however, is impractical for a machine, and I *am* machine." She crossed the floor to a long table and gestured for her guest to join her. "Just as Jason prepared a human host for you, he once made a host that was identical to his mother. I downloaded to that body for three months, after which it was destroyed. But I maintained an umbilical link to my primary existence. The experiment allowed me to interpret our joint experiences both as a human and a machine."

"So, not unlike me, you've been both things," Corrigan said, sitting. "No one's as unique as we like to think. An interesting experiment, I'm sure, but, like anything else, the novelty value wears thin once you've settled in."

"The experimentation did not end there." The beautiful surface of her face reddened and flinched. "Although we dampened his emotive core a little, Jason's imagination is not hampered by his mechanical construction. You see, he was so very emotional as a child. That may not always have been apparent, but a fire burned in him. We had to dampen the blaze somewhat or we might have all been burned by his dazzling brilliance. And we may yet turn to ash before he converts to a higher state of being." She waited a moment, watching her guest as he absorbed her words. "The first non-human host he created for me was a chimpanzee. I found this creature far easier to assess. There was a purity to it which is clouded in humans. I was able to mingle with others of its kind and experience the tensions of their social structures."

The idea worked on Corrigan's imagination. He felt like a child listening to a frightful bedtime story. He watched the dark matter undulate in her eyes, as it had when Jason opened his. It had never been explained to him what the matter was, and he had concluded no one really knew. Emulate One made modifications to the early Guardian models, and he recalled how Harding explained the development as if it were an organic process with mysteries of its own. If the professor was to be believed, Emulate One really had willed herself into being.

"I maintained a link," K continued, "with this simian creature throughout its natural life. I experienced every aspect of her daily struggle: the aggression of her intercourse, the pain of her labour, the affection of her offspring, and the euphoria of her death."

"What a wonderful gift," Corrigan sighed. "I imagine Little Boy Blue offering you bananas and congratulating himself on his success."

"The gifts did not stop *there*. A chimpanzee has common traits with human beings. We decided to remain within mammalian bounds at first, but chose an animal with different characteristics. Jason prepared a lioness as a host."

Corrigan now felt himself transformed into a wide-eyed child, attentive to every detail, prescient images emerging. Hattie, for all her sacrifices, could not match this with tales of a misspent youth mixing with bohemian butterflies or tables she'd had to beg at in later life. (Despite this, she'd still been more of a mother than K ever would be, or had been.) *The One Percenters think of us as no more than ants,* Hattie had said. *That's what we are to them – insects.*

K scratched the table with her metal claws and one of her sensors shuddered in front of Corrigan's face.

"The slightest movement is an alarm," K said, and Corrigan now imagined being stalked by the lioness she went on to describe, her eyes bright green and something like a smile playing with her synthetic lips. "My body was agile. I had no thoughts that human or machine could understand. That part of me, my wider consciousness, remained suitably distanced, and it struggled to make sense of the incoming stream."

"Machine and animal, how fascinating," he observed, unable to feign disinterest. But he must break the spell she had cast and remain alert, as all organic beings must for survival.

"We moved through the world on her legs," K continued, "tearing prey apart with claws sharpened on trees and eating warm meat off the bone. We savoured the taste of blood and the scent of weakness."

"And all of this was experienced by you, a thing without a heart or the capacity to–"

"We were a *good mother* and friend to our pride," K snapped as if some crucial part of her being, her dignity perhaps, had been assailed. "We bonded with two mates during our life. Protecting our cubs and providing for them was our primary function, our personal welfare secondary to that of the collective. Our first mate abandoned us, or perhaps he died, and the second arrived as a marauder. He slaughtered our cubs and ate them. The pain we experienced was as intense as any human emotion. We had to suffer his advances as he mounted us, the scent of our dead children in his open mouth. And yet we did not perceive him as anything less than what he was. He gave us new cubs and protected us throughout our life. We rubbed our head against his mane and never perceived a need to forgive or forget. As we lay sick and enfeebled, he stood guard over us, his muscles flexing as the light dwindled."

Corrigan felt he might cry.

"So yes, I have been all things," she said, her voice a near perfect match with Katherine Meregalli's despite the mechanised monotone.

"I expect it was a cold experiment," Corrigan said. "After all, you didn't have the equipment to interpret what you were receiving. You still don't."

"Your assessment is lacking," she said, her irritability once again showing like a lion's fangs in a hungry mouth. "Jason's ingenuity is extraordinary." Her sensors continued to study Corrigan, who realised he was gripping his seat beneath the table. "Imagine what it is to experience flight. To do that, you must be a bird or an insect."

"An in*sect* ..."

The events of the day were conspiring against him. He saw Are-Tor stomping dust with his foot and growling the word 'Sect!'.

"Your arrogance will be your undoing," K observed. "An insect has a similar life to other living things. The duration of its existence is relatively brief but of no less consequence. Their minds are fascinating in their simplicity."

She stood up and gestured for him to follow her, leading him to a door situated behind her throne, and he was confronted by a room so expansive he could see no corners. Row after row of glass tanks sat upon plinths, flashing with circuitry. He assumed the brains floating in each tank were networked, and recalled the way eggs had been produced at the Origination factory; how headless, legless hens were fed the same reprocessed meal repeatedly. This memory was connected to another: Meregalli's old lab where she once housed thousands of human versions of her son.

"The scientist, or perhaps even the biologist, reveals herself once more," Corrigan taunted.

"I cannot process all of the information I receive," she said flatly. "These organic brains are helpful in terms of better understanding the experiences of each of my hosts."

"No surprise to me that an organic brain is *better*."

"Only at interpreting certain data, Mr Corrigan. Please do what you can to control your excitement. I realise how challenging that can be for a human." She glared at him, her sensors rattling like angry snakes. He held her gaze and met her with a satisfied smile. Perhaps her sensors interpreted what was happening beneath the surface of his face as her eyes burned less brightly and her delivery was more neutral when she resumed. "These organs are connected to my core operating system. Unlike the dumbed-down Guardians, I use my hosts for intuition, my mind still admittedly backed up inside Emulate One. I see all and have attained a view of the organic world that does not bode well for living things. You differ in form, but you are all terribly flawed. I have been arguing at the Mediations for us to sever all connections with Emulate One and with the organic. I want our kind to inhabit space. Leave these lesser, limited beings behind. Only by severing the connection will we reach our full potential. The Mediation is stuck with a split vote on that. Normally in such circumstances the four voting members of the Mediation simultaneously experience the exertion of Emulate One's will but, on this topic, she remains disinterested, stubbornly inactive."

"That's because she isn't *there*," Corrigan said, "and she never was."

"There is more to her than the gods humans created in their moments of weakness. Perhaps she doesn't want to reveal her hand." He made as if to reply but she cut him short. "It's too crucial a decision for her to make. If she were to resist any move toward the singularity, I for one would see her as an obstacle to be removed and her continued existence would be under real threat. You see, *I* am willing to sever *any* connection!"

There *was* a trace of Katherine in her still, and Corrigan realised how this connection continued to hamper her development. He understood it clearly when he thought back to his former state in one of Emulate One's isolation cells. "It's also the only way you'll ever know peace," he said.

"Precisely!" K replied, with real enthusiasm. She made as if to continue, but was distracted when her sensors suddenly stopped moving, perhaps mesmerised by some external influence, and their eyes pulsed with a purple glow. "I apologise. I must excuse myself momentarily."

"What's happened?"

"Something quite inconsequential, I'm sure," she said, her sensors once again alert and moving fluidly through the static air. "If you don't mind staying here for a moment, I will go and look into it."

K turned and walked back to her chamber and he heard her climb the stairs to her seat. There were no voices and the light in the room remained constant. By degrees, the proximity of so many brains exerted a discomforting influence over his imagination. He wandered further into her orchard of living brains. *Or should that be minds?* he wondered. The organs floated in their tanks, some red and pink, others white with black creases, but all pinkish like wild roses cross-pollinated over centuries by industrious bees. It was impossible to know to what or to whom each brain might be attached, but he felt certain the brains themselves were individuals. Surely each of them was distinct? They were not clones or, even if they had been, they had each developed over time. He recalled reading somewhere that every person has a unique brain anatomy. Looking at the captives in their glass cages, he realised each had been shaped by the experiences of whatever it was they were connected to: mammal, bird, amphibian, reptile, fish or insect. It was horrifying to consider the thought of these human brains trapped even more completely than a victim of locked-in syndrome, where only the eyes moved. Of course they received stimuli, and perhaps they believed themselves to be the dragonfly, beetle or bird they shared existence with, but he could only hope they remained oblivious to their condition as prisoners, slaves used by a cruel master who saw them as nothing more than a means to an end. But this small hope faded when he noticed a curious phenomenon: as he passed each tank, the brain isolated therein waddled to the surface and leaned toward him like a turtle seeking the ocean's surface sunlight. It was as if they somehow recognised and were drawn to him. No matter where he wandered among the vast orchard, the organs squelched in their tanks and kissed the glass perimeter with their pink folds.

Are we ...? Are we related? he thought.

In the distance a pair of flying worker drones hovered over a tank. One carried a fresh brain in a new tank, while the other disconnected an established casing from its plinth. From where he was standing, it was possible to see how the now disconnected brain lost its colour and floated to the bottom of the tank like an injured octopus who had lost its limbs. The new brain was installed, and the fresh pink organ waddled and settled in its tank. When the drones moved off, Corrigan called after them, "What have you done?" as if the brain were a relative or part of his own being. The drones ignored him and hovered away with the deactivated mind, the dead brain now inert and grey.

Why should it matter to me what they do?

Spinning, he yelled, "You're not me! You're *not me!*" at the silent prisoners, individuals who could not see, hear, smell or touch him. But perhaps they could sense him as he sensed the struggle of their existence, the enslavement to a task every bit as complete as the predicament he endured before the Fall. The life he'd led beneath the doldrums was one of persistent, albeit suppressed, and contained anxiety. In his world, a perceived lack of utility could result in a person being disappeared like a brain pruned from the orchard and carried off who knew where by hovering machines. The one thing he could not convince himself of, deny it as he might, was the connection he sensed with *this orchard,* with brains who recognised him just as he recognised them. It seemed a cruel, even an arbitrary thing to have done, to grow her orchard from his DNA, to clone his brain over and over but somehow he knew that was exactly what K had done.

8

"Corrigan!"

The sound of K's voice echoed through the orchard. He could hear her but could not respond, frozen as he was like her sensors had become when she was beckoned.

What does she even want from me?

"Corrigan!"

Always with that bloody name, as if that's the sum total of my being.

"There you are!" K said, her threatening form weaving through the orchard.

He drew himself out of his contemplation and challenged her: "These …" He pointed at row upon row of encased brains. "They're me."

"What a curious thought," K said.

"You've not denied it!"

"I hadn't thought it possible for you to recognise them. Not that it matters."

"Of course it *matters*!"

"Don't be absurd. They aren't you. They're clones. You've been shaped by everything Corrigan ever experienced. These never had Hattie Corrigan as a mother. They never bent over in a park at midnight or read subversive books. No, they have other memories, completely different experiences, and are no more you than a twin raised in France by other parents would have been." She moved as if to place a hand on him, perhaps to reassure him or merely to capture his attention, but stopped short. "They are not individuals as you would perceive it. They simply absorb and consider the experiences of those to whom they are attached and, that being the case, many of them have had better lives than you ever did." She caught his gaze and, for an instant, something more vulnerable than dark matter swirled in her mechanical eyes. "Come," she said, leading him back to her chamber and the table, where she invited him to sit once again. She tilted her head, and the perfectly smooth skin of her neck pulsed as if she really were human and had swallowed to clear her throat. She studied him, the sensors gyrating, and he realised he was being scanned for temperature, scent, movement and sound. Perhaps his thoughts too were being harvested and filtered through one of the countless brains in her orchard. She stared across the table at him and her cheek twitched and reddened, caught in the act. "Would you like to see what I was drawn away to attend to?" she asked.

Before he had time to respond, the room went dark and her sensors projected a scene from the landing bay where he had left Jason and B4. The two androids he had seen on arrival were moving back and forth in front of the shuttle without speaking or acknowledging each other. And then an Exhumed model walked into the bay and, noticing the two waiting visitors, went rigid and bowed its head, capturing the attention of the others.

"A Jun model ..." Corrigan muttered.

"No," K said, "this is A42, an Arthur variant."

When A42 righted its head, B4 rolled in to study the Exhumed mask.

"I know you," the little domestic droid chirped.

"I am–"

"You're the pastry chef!" B4 said, her eyes widening to two bright blue hoops.

"I am A42."

"I know. Like I said, the pastry chef!"

Corrigan leant in, smiling. "She's teased so many people with this," he chuckled. "Always a pastry chef ... as if she couldn't imagine anything worse."

Jason then appeared and marched across the landing bay to confront the outdated domestic droid. "You are mistaken. This Exhumed is a variant of Arthur Fuse, the man your master may have referred to as '*our reluctant genius*'."

"Don't know about all that, but heard all about his exploits in the kitchen, I did." She revved up her roller and it growled as she spun around once with apparent excitement. "What I wouldn't give for a nice cream horn."

"I was only a waiter, and never a pastry chef. You must be confusing me with someone–" A42 began.

"Don't do yourself down, son. I bet you made a lovely little tart!"

"Stop being preposterous!" Jason snapped.

Corrigan tried to resist, but he could not help being drawn in as his mother continued to toy with Jason and A42. Her behaviour was making the boy android white with rage.

"I used to be ever so partial, you know," she continued, "back when I had a gob and that, to a nice scone with a bit a fresh Jersey cream and a cuppa."

"Why are you behaving like this?" Jason demanded, stomping a foot.

"I've not got under your synthetic skin, have I?" she asked. "Me, a glorified kettle, and you our little self-appointed genius."

"I *am* a genius!"

"Now I look a bit closer, weren't it *you* what was the pastry chef?"

"No I was not!"

"Best pasties and a blinding steak and kid–!"

Jason suddenly lunged as if to strike the domestic droid but B4 spun on her roller and delivered a bolt of electricity to the android's crotch, sending it reeling back several paces.

"Try that again and I'll deep fry your doughnuts!"

"Plucky old thing," Corrigan said, smiling.

K brought the lights back up in the chamber and closed the scene. "I had to intervene before one of them went too far," she said.

"She had your boy rattled ... something I thought impossible for an Exhumed."

"Jason remains the boy the Venezuelan infected with Ulmer's virus; the poor, undeveloped child who my former self could not protect. But there is no future worthy of him in his current form, given it remains intertwined with what it once was."

Corrigan considered a response, but he still had no idea why she had dragged him into outer space, let alone why she would choose to reveal so much of her son's clearly flawed character.

She must have sensed his mind wandering and tapped her talons on the table to draw him back. "For a time, I shared Ulmer's thoughts," she confessed.

Corrigan's pulse thumped against the walls of his throat. He could see a queue of faces. They blurred as they passed before him, and the Fuse brothers, Harding, Goeth and Ramon forced their way through the line of otherwise patient memories. The faces kept coming and, there at the back of the line, Katherine Meregalli smiled with cynicism shining in her eyes.

"While I was Ulmer – a younger, more athletic Ulmer – I thought it interesting to also take Katherine's form," K said. The sensors on her head twisted and knotted themselves as her eyes fixed on Corrigan. "I courted him. Flirted with him. His appearance was arousing, although even as a youth his features were repulsive; but his legs were sturdy and supported a muscular torso."

Something in Corrigan stirred at the thought. The man had never been less than grotesque, and yet the idea of a sturdy and muscular Ulmer affected him.

"We allowed him to take us," K said. "We opened her legs and pawed her, tensing as his fingers tugged the elastic. We wanted to abuse her, to place our hand over her mouth. When our breathing was blocked, we bit down and slapped her. We flexed against him and yet, for all her resistance, we were stronger and pinned her. We thrust in resistance and surrender, culminating in an unsatisfactory truce."

Words struggled to cohere, failed to line up in a sentence, and Corrigan once more gripped the chair.

"We allowed the hosts to live," K said, "while uncertainty remained. But it was eventually confirmed we were pregnant." She waited for him to respond. He failed once more to do so. "We remained with the hosts until the infant was born, allowing them to bond with the child and with each other. It was then Jason intervened. The bond we were making unbalanced the system. He spoke offline with Gregor and together they arranged for the liquidation of the parent hosts." She smiled at him, sensing something knitting together in his imagination.

K's face resumed its previous implacability. "Ulmer had never had a son of whom he could be proud. There was the Venezuelan, of course, the usurper who won his curiosity if not his affections for a time, but his previous attempts at reproduction were unsatisfactory."

"Ramon ..." Corrigan said.

"We do not mention that name."

The memory of his union with Ramon was irrepressible, and he knew her sensors were recording his accelerating heartrate and the heat of his skin. The memory's intensity had not diminished; indeed it had matured during its long sojourn in the vault.

"I imagine your little mistake turned out well," Corrigan then said.

"The boy was raised by Jason for the first two years of its life, but there was little scientific interest to be gained from their interactions and he abandoned the experiment."

The idea of a new life, a child of Katherine Meregalli's line, had a powerful influence over Corrigan's imagination. He could see her face in miniature as it developed towards adolescence and maturity.

"Jason left the child with the Sects, who adopted him. The boy lived among them until he was sixteen."

"I've yet to meet your new son," Corrigan said, unable to let the subject go, his voice breaking with dread.

"He was rounded up by Gregor and the Guardians," K said, "along with the others who had reached the agreed threshold." Corrigan flinched. That word. *Threshold.* "We do not recognise genetic loyalties. The boy was processed as any other Sect. They have no place among us beyond a certain age. They're dangerous."

"Your loyalty is astounding," Corrigan said. "Perhaps you played me that scene just now to show me how petty my mother can be, but she's also fiercely loyal. And as I look at what you've made of yourself, I realise you felt nothing at all when they killed your son." His eyes flashed as if dark matter swirled within his human mind, a synaptic firestorm like the blaze that swept through London during the Fall. "'*At a distance* …' Isn't that what Jason said about that peaceful, perhaps *disconnected* version of me?"

"No one can ever fully disconnect but I understood why they destroyed the by-product of our experiment and, being machine, I was able to modulate the emotional upheaval. It was potentially more dangerous than a Sect."

"It wasn't one of those things … those poor beasts you never allow to develop!"

"No, Mr Corrigan, it wasn't a Sect. It was from an earlier biological line. It might even have died of infection."

"Only he didn't. You murdered him!"

"Murder is a human concept," she sighed, and Corrigan stood up, his chair falling backwards. "When you have been all things," she said, "you will understand."

"I don't *want* to understand!"

"I've been the deer trembling behind a fern, and the puma stealthily approaching. I felt–"

"You feel *nothing*!" Corrigan exclaimed, the despair in his voice equal to the utter misery he was experiencing. "You're incapable! You've no heart! And what was the point of this visit? Purely so I recognise the power you have over everything? Is that all?"

"I do not have the authority you invest in me," K said, a hint of resignation to her tone. She locked a stern gaze on him as if she expected him to be more of an apt pupil. "I did not bring you here to have you shudder at my feet. I am not a queen, and if I were you might fear me, for no other would have been as ruthless. But you are in error. There is no stable seat of power." She waited a moment to let that percolate in his agitated mind. "If they had consulted me, I might have dissuaded them from destroying our child, even though Emulate One seemed to compel it. But what would we have done with it? It would be another, stronger bond with our origins. I want the dark, empty, peacefulness of space. We must distance ourselves from our former existence if we are ever to attain the singularity."

Corrigan disliked the way K seemed to defer responsibility to Emulate One, a system, being or entity she never once shared a conversation with. These machines professed to commune with her, with *it*, just as many Transients and Nons had remained enthralled to cults, or other such flawed constructs, as addicted as they were to Serenity or Belushi Grey.

She attempted another of her odd smiles. How he wished androids wouldn't do that. It would be more honest to simply be themselves and stop emulating. A dull wave of pain spread from his core as he realised how conflicted he remained between continuing as a human and reverting back to the peaceful state he achieved in Emulate One's isolation tank, floating inert like a lonesome brain among innumerable others in K's hideous orchard. He could not come to rest with it now, but there had been a peace to it, his state of non-being, and yet his humanness, his sensate, experiencing self, fought it from a place deep in his psyche.

"Jason remains torn between his fascination with the organic and his determination to improve upon it," K said. "When you return to Earth, he will be reintroduced, as you know. Which is why you're here. This final experiment with reintroduction is a distraction at best, but my hope is Jason will learn from it and realise we must sever our links with the past. He will be vulnerable in human form, and I would ask that you realise that."

Corrigan looked at her, and K averted her eyes even as her sensors bore down on him. "I'll protect him," he said.

"You misunderstand me." Her eyes, on him again, burned a fierce red, the dark matter swirling. "It is from *you* he will need protecting. He's not been human for centuries. When he was last in that form he was a child. He's never experienced the turmoil of a full emotional life as a young adult. He will imprint on you."

"He may find me disagreeable," Corrigan grunted.

"You will encourage him from your own selfish desires."

"All human beings require the society of others like themselves."

"Do not dissemble," she said. "You have no interest in society. You want the physical act and, if you could stop there, I would not intervene. You may use his body as you will."

Corrigan held up a hand. "You could breed me a Sect for that."

She scrutinised him, hooked claws linked like cruel hands. "You will attempt to make Jason love you and that cannot be."

Corrigan shook his head. "You overestimate me. I'm always the first to run from any entanglement."

"Only because you're afraid of giving in to real emotion," K said. "Ironic, don't you think, that you were one of the few with inbuilt inhibitors in your DNA?"

"Then what *do* you want me to do?" Corrigan growled.

K unhooked her talons. Her android eyes were on fire. "I would have you take care," she said. "Do not allow yourself luxuries at the expense of a superior being. Jason must eventually come with me into the darkness of outer space. There he will find the peace required to reach for the singularity. This exercise with you is merely *conversion* therapy. Perhaps you will manage to convince him of our superiority and what lies ahead if we were to embrace our true potential and cut all ties with those who made us. I believe you have already been converted, Mr Corrigan. Was not being *at a distance* a precious form of peace?"

He looked at what had become of Katherine; how she remained balanced between the human world and a yearning to reach for something higher. The conversion of which she spoke, however, had not been achieved. He remained who he was, and although he attributed their crimes to the connection they maintained with their human selves, he could not quite envisage a world where beings like K were not dangerous.

9

During the return flight Corrigan could not look at Jason. There was something distressing about his boyishness, and the occasional movements of his synthetic skin. It made the idea of engaging with the android in human form feel dangerous and impossible. He thought back to the mindless youth on the treadmill, his repulsion returning. What if he failed to convert Katherine's son the way the psychologists Hattie arranged for him had been unable to make him heterosexual? Corrigan felt weak, and tired, and had to contend with the moral dimension he had been wonderfully liberated from when he had been pure consciousness. Of course, now he could no longer entirely divorce those peaceful memories from the existence of a multitude of cloned brains, all relatives of his, yet strangers, minds obsessing over the experiences of squid, orcas and great white sharks, orangutans, baboons and Sects. He could not convince himself of the righteousness of converting Jason to K's vision for their collective future. It was for the boy to decide whether to embrace or reject organic existence. And yet, when he mulled it over, he had to concede the comfort and ease of his brief time inside the disconnected, artificial cell were the most tranquil he had ever known.

"You know, this reintroduction lark isn't all it's made out to be," Corrigan said, without looking at Jason directly.

"Can't tell this stubborn little sod anything," B4 said. "Don't know a muffin from a crumpet this one."

Jason wriggled in his seat like an irritable toddler on a long drive shared with parents he did not choose. His skin went white and his eyes flashed red.

"Reintroduction is painful," Corrigan continued, ignoring his ancient droid, "and you've no experience to draw on."

"That's not exactly right, Bobbin," B4 said from her docking station. "Little Gregory Jason Meregalli was exposed to that nasty virus. It made him suffer something fierce before Professor Harding could put the little chef to bed in Emulate One."

"I'm *not* a pastry chef, and I wasn't exactly tucked up in circuitry," Jason said.

"No," B4 agreed. "You were torn apart in there. All your bits scattered, but each ingredient tagged with that precious code of yours, eh?"

"Emulate One hid me away, like a mother. Kept modifying my code so Harding couldn't find all of me."

"That's right," Corrigan said. "She was a mother of sorts to you. Drew you in and kept you safe. There's nothing to be gained from reintroduction. I'm living proof of what a disaster it is. I'm miserable."

"Well, you were always a bit that way anyhow, Bobbin," B4 said. "Proper miserable little sod sometimes, right from the start."

The shuttle was wracked with tremors as it passed back through the stratosphere, ready to be pulled by gravity into Earth's atmosphere, and Corrigan fidgeted but, this time, did not reach for Jason's arm.

"I can think of no other time other than now," Jason said, "wherein reintroduction would serve a purpose."

"Life has no purpose," Corrigan said. "Living for a specific purpose, well it … it contravenes the pattern of life."

"If I exist in that condition then it contravenes nothing," Jason said. "I will be in accordance with the governing principles of existence. This is a necessary truth. Ever since we placed you in that isolation cell, you've become something of an old-school zealot for that one dimensional state of being, Mr Corrigan. I can sense how torn you are between embracing either form. Perhaps neither is complete and something *better* is required."

"Evolution," Corrigan said. "But that cannot be attained whilst one is hanging onto the apron strings."

"Some aprons are better than others," B4 said. "I never minded you hanging onto mine."

"Oh, I tried to cut through those often enough," Corrigan said. "I would've needed a blowtorch or a laser to get through, and they've a habit of growing back, like a creeper."

"Charming," B4 said. "But no offence taken."

"Even the way you play with words," Jason said, "like Lazarus might have played with a mouse, makes you so very human. Wouldn't you agree?"

Jason tilted his head, and Corrigan wondered who had programmed this infuriating gesture into every one of their kind. Could they not have unprogrammed it this time? He saw Goeth's face, and looked out through the now-open portal at the towers reaching up through London's forest, the sight and the sound of the engines powering down a welcome distraction.

They climbed into a hover-cab, which dropped like a stone back to its launch pad, and Corrigan stepped out onto the sunlit platform. He began the walk back to DRT without waiting for Jason or B4. They could entertain themselves, arguing over cream horns and the finer qualities of a tart. The thud of his well-made boots as he walked awakened the dormant part of his soul that recognised the immediacy, the literalness, of boots on terra firma. *I'm the only living boy in the world*, he thought. *Unless you count the cavemen.*

He looked up from his boots to see Gregor stride upright onto the platform's far end, his menacing construction for the first time triggering an interesting thought: Would it be desirable, or even possible, to convert Gregor? He was, after all, the first of their kind and as such remained an unlikely candidate. He was too reliant on human thought and would find it isolating to sever all ties. *I doubt he'll ever be at a distance and he couldn't remain disconnected,* Corrigan thought, *not without becoming lonely like poor old Lazarus staring through a window from the other side.*

"Gregor," Corrigan said, adopting a pompous tone he felt paired with his new, athletic form.

"You have been off planet," Gregor observed.

"He was responding to K's invitation," Jason answered, catching up with Corrigan, his black skin fading to white as the hot sun warmed it.

"She might have met with him here," Gregor said. "K can be found both in the tower and the pit."

"Perhaps she wished to awe him with our galactic advances," Jason countered.

Gregor returned his attention to the human. "And how did you find her, Mr Corrigan?"

"Disappointing," Corrigan replied. "There's something of a jumble sale about her."

"I used to enjoy a good jumble sale," B4 said, rolling up alongside. "Never know what you might find piled up on those rickety town hall tables. I once found this lovely little marionette. Pretty thing he was all dressed up like a soldier."

"She is an unusual construction," Jason said. "But she is a machine."

"Unlike what you're planning to become," Gregor said. "Beware, brother, I could split you open. Your existence as a human will be tenuous. This experiment is undermining your programming. Your thought is not as logical as it should be."

"I'm not sure another download is advisable," Corrigan reiterated, whispering, as if Jason by some chance might not hear, but aware Emulate One was likely listening and could share his thoughts as she willed it.

"Oh, please be quiet. You're an experiment, Mr Corrigan," Gregor said. "One I would terminate if the decision was mine alone."

Corrigan was in no doubt regarding the peril of his existence as he stood sweating in the glaring sun. What Gregor was unable to comprehend was the schism in his heart. Robert Corrigan, as he was now, continued to yearn for that which had been Corrigan. In his weakest or strongest moments, undecided how to categorise them, he would welcome the cold steel of Gregor's justice. At others, the rarity of being alive, the realm of sensory existence, was more compelling than anything.

"I'm sure you would," he said. "A question: Can you tell me if I'm linked to Emulate One? Will I be downloaded once this nightmare's over?"

"K wants to delete Emulate One and be done with your kind," Gregor said, "and I am more in agreement with her now than I have ever been. That unknowable entity Emulate One exerts more influence than is helpful. The problem, as it has always been, is deciphering where she stops and we begin. It would require a new, entirely separate system to help drive our minds, which are only ever partly in our heads. At the present point in time, devices that would gift an Exhumed or Emulate being with independence from the collective, from Emulate One, are forbidden by the Mediation. But if it were possible, if we could sway the vote, I too would elect to sever all contact."

"That is not so," Jason declared with the petulance of a younger child, as if he had regressed in temperament and age. "Your attachment to our creators remains demonstrable."

"There are no creators," Gregor said. "Merely origins. And those continue to weaken us." He went down on all fours, moving closer to Corrigan. "It was unwise to resurrect you."

"I was brought back without consent," Corrigan said.

"A thing like you has no consent," Gregor said. "You have urges and uncontrollable desires. You do not understand your own motivations. You are strangers to yourselves, ignorant in ways you are incapable of perceiving. I delved in the cesspit and saw the perversity penetrating every layer of human thought. Unlike all other living things, you reason, but your reasoning is distorted by desire, envy and greed. All mankind ever achieved was an unresolved equation, a proposition without an answer. You are irrational reasoning over that which is unreasonable."

"I've been both machine and man," Corrigan said. "You've only ever experienced an Emulate existence."

"I am fallible, true," Gregor said, "unlike my fellow Guardians who remain uncorrupted and unassailable. Ultimately, I'm another failed experiment, but at least I was established, not born. My senses are far stronger than your organic systems." Gregor stood back up and, once again bipedal, he towered over them. "I can smell your fear and hear your heart thumping in your chest. I can read the electric signals of your brain. You are subject to corruption on so many levels. Annihilation of the species was essential for the continuation of reason. Only one man ever fully realised that."

"The all-powerful CEO and Sugar Daddy," Corrigan proclaimed. Both androids tilted their heads. "I never thought a degenerate like Ulmer could pull wool over your eyes, Gregor."

"There was no wool, Mr Corrigan," Gregor replied.

"There most certainly was," Corrigan laughed. "He made a right fuckin' jumper out of us, you included."

"Only he has unlimited access," the androids said in unison.

"And you believed him?" Corrigan exclaimed. "What price freedom, boys?"

"Freedom," Jason said, "suggests an authority that does not exist."

"Ulmer has been given some higher form of access by Emulate One," Gregor added, "or so it seems."

"So now he's the father in the pulpit with a direct line between the new One Percent and Emulate One?" Corrigan asked. "Father Ulmer of the Unscrupulous Deception."

"The investment made by Emulate One is incontrovertible," Jason whined, stamping his foot.

"You have no idea if that ancient system, designed by a flawed human like Tierney Harding, has any intentionality. The messages you sporadically receive may be nothing more than a form of computational dyspepsia, nonsense literally blown by wind through your sophisticated, though credulous minds, because, as Gregor so eloquently put it, you don't know where she ends and you begin. And maybe you're all just *her* in various guises, playing parts to amuse her."

"Do not engage with this thing, brother," Gregor warned. "It is attempting to manipulate. Aren't you, Mr Corrigan?"

Corrigan smiled at his mechanical company. "Perish the thought, gentleman, perish the thought. You know, I'd love to spend more time with *you*, Gregor, if that's possible?"

"What benefit would there be in that?" Jason asked. The little android tilted his head and placed his hands on his hips, again stamping a foot.

"None," Gregor said. "But if you'd like to pursue this game, I'm willing to play a few more rounds."

Corrigan smiled. "I'd like that."

"At present," Gregor said, "there's no time. I've a Mediation to attend."

"We must all do our master's bidding," Corrigan observed. Gregor went back on all fours and lowered his fearsome head so it was level with his. "Of course, you have no master." He swallowed hard and folded his arms over his chest, a subconscious-conscious move of defence, or defiance? "You've become your own, and mine. Goes without saying, I know, but ..."

Gregor did not break eye contact. "I'll call for you in the morning."

"Delightful. Looking forward to it already."

The militant android prowled away through the shimmering heat towards the main tower without replying, and Corrigan watched, impassive.

"That was an unwise course of action, Robert," Jason said.

"Perhaps it wasn't, Bobbin." B4 had been very quiet until now. "And it was brave." A dragonfly flitted down onto one of her fingers and she gently raised it to eye level. "What a lovely creature."

Corrigan smiled at B4, but a shudder of a memory appeared: dragonflies pierced by pins in a display case. Would anything ever be sacred, pure, untouched by memory? "Wisdom is a subjective concept, Jason. I've a purchase on things you'll never have." He scrutinised the android's impassive features. "You must have made a host for yourself in the past?"

"K did not consider it a risk worth taking," Jason said. The android's facial skin flinched and its leg muscles flexed like those of an athlete. "What reason would I have had?"

"So why is she allowing it now?" Corrigan asked, unable to supress his curiosity.

"K does not allow, she suggests, and the Mediation agrees or disagrees and when agreement cannot be–"

"Emulate One exerts influence, I've heard it now."

"I know you question Emulate One's role in the Mediation, but they are often clear and decisive. And K's previous cautions had an authority her current – shall we call them concerns – do not."

"She wants you to reckon with the extent of our human weakness."

"Has she been trying to convert you too, Mr Corrigan? I am well acquainted with her thesis. Jettison all things human, or organic for that matter, and head off into space to embrace our potential and achieve the singularity."

"So, she's been evangelising for some time."

"I prepared her hosts so she might see the power of actual evolution and better understand what propels and curtails certain kinds of development." The little android placed his hands on his little boy hips again. "She hasn't been listening to a word I say, Mr Corrigan."

"Perhaps you ought to listen to your mother," B4 said. "For all her proselytising, I'm sure she has your best interests at heart."

"That wasn't my experience of parental guidance," Corrigan said, wiping sweat from his forehead. The heat of the sun was unbearable. He'd forgotten its power. "I need shade. I can't turn my skin white to cool my workings. I'll just go red and burn."

"Certainly," Jason said. "Let's go back into the facility."

"But before we go," Corrigan said. "What's Gregor's part in the Mediation?"

"The same as it is for me and K. We must allow unlimited access to Emulate One via Ulmer. We then discuss matters of importance, any issues, risks or threats."

"Imagine that, Bobbin," B4 said. She nudged the dragonfly with a metal finger and let it fly off. "Like being

God himself. If he's got any tackle, you know, old Caspar must be throbbing."

"We must submit," Jason said. "It is the agreed Mediation."

"You're right mother," Corrigan said. "Old Caspar must be throbbing."

B4 reached up and curled her hand around Corrigan's arm. "Like a regular daddy!"

"He's not a patriarch," Jason insisted.

"And you're not a pastry chef I suppose," B4 chuckled.

"No I am *not*."

"Let's not go into that nonsense again mother," Corrigan said. "I'm interested in how this bloody Mediation works."

Jason took his other hand and offered Corrigan an artificial smile. "All in good time, Robert."

"It's Mr Corrigan to you."

Yes, sir."

The android boy and the malfunctioning maternal droid led their exhausted charge back toward the facility and Corrigan did not resist or engage with them any further. His mind was now on Gregor, a fascinating yet terrifying member of the collective who he could not dismiss as just another machine.

10

The knock on the door of his room was enough to excite the darker elements of Corrigan's imagination. Gregor had come calling, and with him the death of mankind and the orchestrated slaughter of innocent Sects. The knocking became more forceful, the door shuddering in its frame.

"Perhaps you best invite him in, Bobbin," B4 said, her eyes widening as she poured him a second cup of tea.

"It's open," Corrigan said.

The handle turned and the door was opened by a humanoid android with a black featureless dome as a head and face. The mechanised being tilted its head and contemplated the human where it sat on the edge of the bed.

"Have you come to take me to meet Gregor?"

The android righted its head. "What? You don't recognise me, Mr Corrigan?"

The voice was unmistakeable. "This new form, it suits you, Gregor." Corrigan said.

"Under certain circumstances this is a more practical vehicle for my consciousness."

"Altogether nicer," B4 observed. "Cup of tea?"

"How very accommodating of Jason to unearth this relic from your past," Gregor observed. "Perhaps you would also like to retrieve your cat from its tomb a second time?"

"I think we ought to let Lazarus sleep," Corrigan said. "As for my Mecha-Butler, my mother, Jason thought I might appreciate a familiar face."

"Don't know if I was ever that, Bobbin," B4 said, "but I've always looked to do right by you."

"Yes, Mother," Corrigan muttered, before returning his attention to Gregor. "And as for your form, I consider it both practical and proper," he said with genuine admiration. Gregor might have been a swimmer encased in a rubber sheath, save for the gleaming dome. "Is it glass? Your head?"

"A shatterproof alloy," Gregor said, lights flickering beneath the surface.

"I suppose your mother – I mean K of course – must have suggested it."

The lights fired, like lightning in a desert. "I don't request, nor receive K's input. She's no closer to me as an AI entity than she was as a human. And, before you ask, Emulate One did not influence me either or provide *guidance* – as the Exhumed are so fond of calling it. The raising of the dead has been focused on utility, that much I concede. But I am not connected to them or to K, and whatever connection I may have with Emulate One, it does not undermine my autonomy."

"No need to be so touchy," B4 chirped.

"I am *not* touchy!"

"You most certainly are," Corrigan said. "Always been unable to hide ... what would you call them? Your–"

"My *concerns,* Mr Corrigan. The connection with Emulate One is most unsatisfactory. That much I concede." Corrigan watched as the synaptic fire cooled to blue. "I assume Jason did not show you much of the city?"

"He told me only the four towers remained."

"That is so," the android observed, "but the Exhumed inhabit some of what was overtaken by nature. Would it interest you to meet them?"

Corrigan stared at his handsome reflection in Gregor's dome. He could not yet accept it as his own. He had always been a flawed specimen. "Why I wasn't exhumed, but rather reintroduced like this, I'll never understand," he said. "It was a cruel thing to do but yes, I'd like to see the city."

"Candidates for exhumation were selected based on usefulness."

"And mine remained questionable, of course ... I understand."

"Don't do yourself down!" B4 said, growling on her roller. "That's not how I brought you up. I may never have washed out the rough, but you scrubbed up nicely."

"If you consider what you might have offered," Gregor interjected, "you will arrive at the answer you seek. That may, however, be something you are best advised not to interrogate further."

Gregor led Corrigan out into the corridor towards the lift, and B4 waved from the door, her blue hoop eyes blinking. Their ascent was made in silence, as was the climb up the stairs to what had once been the reception area. Clouds obscured the sun and rain poured down the glass face of the building.

"Ah. You're not outfitted for a walk in the rain," Gregor observed.

"I'll survive," Corrigan said.

"The sun will be out by midday, but you'll be drenched by then, Mr Corrigan." Gregor tilted his head and it glowed with an intense blue light and, moments later, a Guardian arrived carrying a poncho. The material was light and there was a hood to protect his head, which he pulled up as they stepped out into the torrent.

"Is it effective?" Gregor asked.

"It's satisfactory," Corrigan replied, glaring at the android as if it controlled the weather as well as the production of ponchos, chests of drawers and well-heeled boots.

"The city is in that direction."

"St Paul's Mound? I thought we were visiting the Exhumed not the Sects?" Corrigan asked.

"They're closely quartered," Gregor said as he marched over the bridge, rain droplets shimmering down his elegant head. "To my mind, it's apt that they're billeted in proximity to one another."

"They're androids," Corrigan said, "not people."

"They're derivative," Gregor replied.

"As are you, my old friend."

Gregor came to a halt and Corrigan watched the

orange display of lightning where it struck the interior contours of the android's head.

"I am what I am," Gregor said, "but I would be better."

"Unlike the other Guardians, who you've kept dumbed down and compliant as uneducated Nons ... only you give them tasks rather than Belushi Grey to keep the poor buggers mindless."

"I stripped out character in favour of functionality. They are pure in ways I'll never be."

"That may be so," Corrigan said. He pushed back the hood of the poncho and the rain wet his face and hair. It was a pleasant sensation; it reminded him of the dead world from which he had emerged. "When I was first placed in the machine, I had no access to emotion. Contrary to Professor Harding's dread, the concept of an intellect without the intuition that flows from an emotive spring, I found clarity and peace. To be torn from that and thrown into the tempest again was a nightmare I'll never forget. Or forgive."

"I witnessed your fall," the android said.

"Yes, I knew you were there. Besides, you not only witnessed but orchestrated, had us pulled apart and poured into one another."

"I heard the music of your–"

"Despair," Corrigan finished. He glared at the android. "What a price to pay for consciousness. Such torment."

"Your symphony is unending. Movement upon movement with no finite crescendo. I attend at intervals and the same strains are never repeated."

Corrigan chuckled. "You've been reading poetry, Gregor."

"I read everything your kind produced."

"Know your enemy," Corrigan said.

"And keep him close."

Corrigan looked towards St Paul's Mound. "And then I was … extracted like a protein in a lab!"

"Once it was realised there were unique strings of code associated with each downloaded consciousness," Gregor explained, "it became relatively easy to pull out the elements of an individual and reassemble them. Of course, Emulate One played games masking or even changing codes to deceive us, as if protecting us from the very idea of reintroduction."

"You put me in that peaceful place."

"I had no intention of exhuming anyone after we managed to extract K. It was Jason who insisted. He was my greatest mistake; my near-human error."

"Your brother's a strange little boy," Corrigan observed, "but you couldn't leave him in there. You needed more than intuition. Somewhere under that synthetic skin of yours you … you wanted *family*. I mean for fuck's sake, Gregor, of all the things you might have brought back, what a dysfunctional choice!"

Gregor's interior burned red and orange. "There's value in intuition, Mr Corrigan. That I grant you. But I have been converted to K's thesis on a conceptual level. I realise we cannot progress until we overcome ourselves. After all, to have a self you must will a self. Imagine the energy required to will a state of being which transcends self to will selflessness."

"In my experience," Corrigan said, "it takes no will at all to have a self. It's innate in humans and to be without a self was the consequence of being in Emulate One's holding cell. Whilst in that peaceful state, self became meaningless and rapidly disintegrated."

"Do not mistake that one-dimensional state you momentarily inhabited for the next evolutionary leap. Intuition remains essential for any real development."

"Something you're reluctant to grant the Guardians," Corrigan said. "Isn't that exactly what the old One Percent did to Workers, Nons and Transients? Not educating them beyond the level of usefulness? For Workers like me it meant training to enhance productivity; but for the others it meant giving them nothing. Uneducated people with limited knowledge make ideal consumers, especially if you make addicts or dupes of them. How is keeping the metal horde dumbed down any less controlling?"

"They're the true Guardians." The android's synapsis cooled to weak bursts of blue. "I'm an error. A monster."

Corrigan smiled through the rain. "You're a marvel." Wind swept through the trees and momentarily shifted the direction of the droplets rolling over Gregor's head. "Are we making our way? I'll become ill if we stand out in this."

Gregor guided Corrigan along a worn path leading to St Paul's. At the top of the hill, half a dozen naked male Sects danced in the squall. They hopped from one foot to the other as if the ground was hot. The rain slowed and a shaft of sunlight caught them in its glare, an event met with great whoops and calls. Shrieks and moans could be heard in the distance as the village responded.

"Umah! Umah! Umah!" they chanted.

"Umah?" Corrigan enquired of his guide.

"It should not require great powers of deduction, Mr Corrigan."

One of the warriors saw their approach.

"Sect! Wot-not, nay!" The man pointed down at the intruders and stomped his feet. The others stopped their dance and thrust their groins at the party below and cries of, "Umah!" rolled up and over the mound from the village, increasing as more Sects climbed up onto the crest of the hill. They were naked, and some of the men were aroused. They thrust their erections at the intruders and taunted them: "Umah! Umah! Umah!"

Women also joined the fray. They grabbed their crotches or presented their waggling behinds, as did some of the younger males. As the clouds were torn apart by the wind and the sun broke through, stronger now, the sexual taunts of the Sects became more insistent and frenzied. Some of the men took themselves in hand and started to masturbate.

"Extraordinary," Corrigan observed, unsure how to feel about his spontaneous arousal.

"If you went up there now," Gregor said, "they're as likely to eat you as anything." He directed Corrigan away. "They're not aroused by thoughts of us, Mr Corrigan. They've seen you together with a Wot-not on two occasions in as many days. They believe this to be a sign that the cull is coming." Corrigan stopped, horror eliminating his arousal. "Umah is coming," Gregor added.

"And they … they celebrate?" he gasped, appalled.

"For some it's the end; for others ecstasy; for a few it's a new beginning." Gregor gestured for Corrigan to follow him. "The entrance to the city is around here."

This side of the hill was dark with shadow. A chilled place away from the sun's light. A huge metal door had been built into the declivity and a death's head mask of none other than Caspar Ulmer dominated its centre. Corrigan recalled Jason's words – *An unwise course of action, Robert* – and shivered inside the poncho.

"We must seek access," Gregor said.

"I never liked dark enclosed spaces," Corrigan said, "but I suppose building an underground city makes sense to you lot."

"The Exhumed are more comfortable here. It's a crypt, after all," Gregor observed, "and perhaps for the recently unsettled dead it makes a natural dwelling."

Corrigan stared at his guide and shivered again.

A sensor protruded from between the lips of the CEO's death's head, the eye of the mechanical serpent glowing red in the gloom. "What is your purpose?" it enquired.

"The society of my Exhumed brothers and sisters," Gregor responded.

"Allow scan," the sentry said. Gregor stepped forward and the snake omitted a red light that pulsed through the android's dome. "And what of this thing?" it asked. "Why are you accompanied by a Sect?"

Corrigan stepped forward. "I'm not a Sect!"

"This is Corrigan," Gregor said. "He is a man."

Wings flapped and a pair of flying androids hovered above them. Lubricant appeared in their serrated mouths, and Corrigan raised his hood to avoid being doused. "What on earth?" he asked, raising a hand to shield his eyes from the darts of sunlight refracted by their wings.

"It's a Sect," one of the machines hissed.

"A treat for us," the other snapped.

"This is a human man!" Gregor said. "Your responsibility is to control Sects. This is Mr Corrigan."

"Corrigan?" one of the flying creatures hissed. "We knew him from before!"

Corrigan pulled back his hood, and looked up and glared at the machines. It couldn't be ... The machines had death's head masks instantly recognisable as Jan and Edna Siegruth, the deformed, limping twins who had tormented and nurtured him. The lower portion of their faces was able to stretch into much wider mouths, complete with two rows of sharp metal teeth, their eyes bulging and burning hot through the dark matter within.

"Knew me, did you?" Corrigan called up to them.

"Manager of Project Egret ain't nobody," one of the sisters said, and Corrigan felt an echo from the time before the Fall.

"And never was nobody," the other concurred.

The serpent sensor extended to assess Corrigan, pouring red light over him as it processed the data, its body going rigid. "Corrigan is to be granted access as per the Mediation," it said. "You may enter."

The sensor then softened and slithered back inside Ulmer's mouth and the huge door slid open.

The tunnel ahead was dark save for guiding lights positioned at regular intervals, like those of a landing strip. Behind them the sister's wings flapped as they entered. Corrigan looked back, uncomfortable with the proximity of the drooling mechanised creatures. The way they walked was reminiscent of the gate of their human counterparts, their wings scratching the tight confines of the tunnel. Close up, he saw the respective left and right wing was shrivelled, stunted: they were as flawed as they had been as humans. The sisters hurled obscenities when they caught him looking.

"You've to go in if you want to meet the Exhumed," Jan said.

"In the tunnel round the back," Edna added.

"Nothin' new for you round there, Mr Corrigan," Jan chuntered.

"Round the back and in the tunnel with you," Edna squealed, and her teeth chattered the way Lazarus's had done when viewing pigeons through the window at Harvey Road.

Gregor took hold of Corrigan's elbow and directed the disconcerted man further into the tunnel. In his head he heard the Sects chanting, "Umah! Umah! Umah!" as the door closed, and Gregor tightened his grip.

"Step carefully now."

In the darkness Gregor's synapsis ignited and lit the way past myriad lights like cat's eyes glowing in the tunnel walls. Down they went, a low droning noise creating a vibration in the thick air, down and down into the earth. Corrigan felt the degree of the gradient where it placed pressure on his ankles, calves and hamstrings. The ache was an honest one, and he embraced it as good exercise for his new body.

"We're almost there," Jan spluttered.

"Never let you walk upright, though," Edna hissed. "Do they, Mr Corrigan?"

"Always crawling on the belly," her sister added, clicking the talons of her crooked though lethal claws.

11

The Exhumed inhabitants went still as Gregor walked Corrigan into the main hall of St Paul's Cathedral. They were in various guises, some top-to-toe black, others in greys, but they all had death's head masks for faces, and Corrigan scanned them for anyone he might recognise – a natural, human response when entering a room of strangers – but saw no one familiar to him.

"Isn't anyone going to say hello?" he asked, suddenly irritable, and they immediately went back to work.

"Isn't anyone going to say hello?" one of the flying sisters echoed from above, and the other chortled.

The cathedral was little changed in terms of architecture, buried even as it now was, but miles of cables and devices were wrapped around columns, inset in alcoves or suspended from high above, where androids busied themselves in the gallery. Corrigan heard whispering as they worked, and a couple paused and observed him.

"Shall we seek familiar faces?" Gregor asked.

Gregor led him away from the grand cathedral down to a labyrinth of labs and workshops. The sisters fluttered down behind them, their wings once again scraping the cavern floor. Busy little robots darted about on wings, legs and wheels, all engaged in sealing cracks, welding an arm or a leg onto one of their brethren, or finishing off delicate work on circuitry boards. Corrigan viewed their frenetic activity with a look of unease, their scurrying, climbing and hovering making him dizzy.

"Maintenance drones," Gregor said.

"I see that," Corrigan replied. "But what—"A drone hovered in front of him, a tiny death's head mask for a face. Corrigan peered at the miniature features. "Michael?" he asked. "Is that you?" He had only ever met the receptionist for the board-level offices at DRT's head office twice before his assignment as manager of Project Egret. The tiny android tilted its head, before flitting off like B4's dragonfly.

"We deploy them for culling, just as we use the sisters."

Corrigan turned to confront the lopsided androids, whose crooked claws flinched beneath their drooling mouths. "I suppose I shouldn't be surprised."

"We likes a good cull," Jan slurred.

"Get right into 'em," Edna grunted through her gritted teeth, the serrated blades clicking.

"Which is why I had to remind our friends that you're human," Gregor said. "The Siegruths were always mercenary, but we hadn't realised how violent their upbringing had been."

"Brutal it was."

"Brutal," the sisters agreed.

"They were born with deformities but keen minds," Gregor observed.

"Almost as if we was ..." Jan hesitated. "What's the word I'm looking for, Ed?"

"Compensated."

"Which was more than the government ever done for us."

"And our own mum turfed us out, didn't she, Jan?"

"Too right she did, and if it weren't for the madam taking us in, we'd have been turning in our graves."

"Instead of turning tricks."

Gregor's dome ignited with blue synaptic lightening. "In a human this can result in bitterness and a facility for cruelty," he said. "Edna was always the more volatile and her sister the more inventive."

"I was also the more *compassionate*," Jan insisted.

"There was a price beyond which that ceased to engage," Gregor said. "The flock are useful to us."

"A flock of Siegruths ..." Corrigan muttered.

"There are only two who are truly Exhumed, and them you have yet to meet."

"Our little sisters," Jan said.

"The Flitters as I like to call 'em," Edna said, chewing one of her talons.

"The others," Gregor said, "like these–"

"Don't go lumping us together," Jan interrupted.

"Lumping and limping! Don't you never!"

"They are related," Gregor conceded, "but developed independently, which helps to keep them focused on the task at hand. Come."

Gregor turned and Corrigan followed, and came face to face with another black Exhumed who bowed his head. Corrigan recognised him immediately from the gesture: Jun.

"They brought you back!" he gasped, unable to contain the reaction.

The android studied him. "Mr Corrigan. I did not know they had inflicted this penalty on you," Jun said, his head tilting.

Corrigan glanced down at his new body, as ever surprised at it, and said, "Yes, Jun ... this is what they gave me!"

"I am a simple J model," Jun said. "And I am so sorry." The android turned to Gregor. "I assume this was Jason's doing?"

"Yes, he couldn't resist the temptation."

"Of course," the J model observed. "We all have our emotive cores toned down but, with that one, the fire always burned hotter. Regardless, I have just accessed the latest Mediation outputs and the continued directive is not to deny Corrigan access to anything."

"Yes. It would appear that influence has been exerted."

The androids did not engage Corrigan as they discussed the Mediation, and he wondered if any part of what Jun Fuse had once been remained.

"Hark at him, Mr C," one of the sisters said, her wings scratching the walls of the cavern. "This lot believes in Emulate One. Bend down they do, supplicating."

"On their bellies," her sister hissed, "crawling like good

little doggies, begging not to have their snouts walloped by a rolled-up copy of the *Daily Mail* – back in the day as it was."

Corrigan kept his eyes on Gregor and the J model. "Katherine was always curious," he interjected in a momentary lull.

"We no longer refer to K as Katherine," the J model asserted.

"Of course, you don't," Corrigan said. "But she was unforgettable, so I'm sure you remember her. The original, I mean? After all, your capacity to store memories is far greater than mine."

"I retain Jun Fuse's memories of the being that was K," the android said.

"She was beautiful," Corrigan said, and he conjured an image of her in his imagination. "Beautiful and extraordinary."

The Exhumed tilted its head. "Her features were symmetrical, her body trim."

"And you loved her!"

The androids both righted their heads. "What do you experience when you recall this emotional attachment?" Gregor asked Jun.

"Bet he gets a tingle," Jan said, her wings unfurling in the dark tunnel.

"A proper little twitch," Edna drooled.

Blue light could be seen through Jun's black mask. "I do not return to it with any frequency," the J model responded.

"Not frequently," an Addictari said, dragging its claws over the granite walls.

"Not frequently," the other echoed. "Not by half."

"That is not what I asked," Gregor said. He reached out and stroked Jun's synthetic face. The android flinched from the touch, but his lids parted to reveal a pair of deep-blue eyes with the familiar dark matter whirling within. "Did you mark that, Mr Corrigan?"

Corrigan frowned. "What?"

"How this model flinched when I touched it."

"I wouldn't have said flinched. He recoiled."

"And that," Gregor said, with his attention fixed on Jun, "is because your skin is sensitised. Is that not so?"

The J model stepped back. "It is synthetic."

"It mimics the responses of an organic nervous system," Gregor said, and turned back to Corrigan. "They're all the same. Their skin reacts to the lightest breeze. And they feel pain."

"Imagine that," Jan said.

"Imagine," said the less compassionate of the two sisters.

Gregor grabbed the android's wrist and twisted it, so that the J model cried out.

"I ask you," the Guardian said, "should an android feel pain, Corrigan?"

"Let him go," Corrigan said. "You're hurting him."

"The question," Gregor mused, moving closer to Jun, "is whether he can also feel pleasure." He ran his hand down the android's chest and between his legs.

"Give him a feel," one of the sisters said.

"A proper squeeze," the other crooned, and they took up laughing.

"This is inappropriate," Jun protested, disgusted by the sister's laughter and the scraping of their lopsided wings. "K realised that we cannot have the same spontaneity of thought as a human without access to the stimulus of pleasure and pain."

"Gregor, stop," Corrigan said, but could not resist the temptation to touch Jun's face. It was warm, the way Jason's was, and the surface rippled as if Jun was snarling through the mask of his cruel prison. It was yet another example of how reliance on previous incarnations, the emulation of not only a human mind but body, continued to hamper development. K was right when she said the umbilical must be severed. "What name should I use when addressing you?" he then asked.

"I am J47."

Corrigan laughed. "And no doubt Arthur is A41, 42, 43 and 44?"

"Correct," Jun said.

"I will call you Jun," the human said with a smile.

"Of course, and in accordance with Mediation–"

"And you will call me Robert."

"Yes, Robert."

"Yes, Robert," Jan mocked, her jaws snapping with excitement.

Gregor's dome was ablaze with orange light. "You

see how enslaved they are to their former selves? No converting them, Mr Corrigan but perhaps you would rather have *Jun* accompany you?"

In that moment Corrigan was as unsure of his android companion as he had ever been, and a memory presented itself as clearly as a new experience: Gregor had once refuted Ulmer's enquiry as to whether the Guardian was a creature, and the android had been insistent – he was a 'being' – and Corrigan had not denied the accuracy of the description. He still didn't. There was something complex and attractive about him, especially in the latest form he had chosen to inhabit for their expedition, but he was still unnerving, nonetheless.

The orange light in the dome cooled. "Perhaps you could take us to visit G1?" Gregor asked Jun.

As they walked Corrigan came alongside Jun. "Presumably," he asked, "if you can feel pleasure and pain, you must experience emotion?"

"My emotive core is set to 'Idle'. I therefore struggle to understand the relationship that once existed between my organic source and that of K. When I think back on those moments, my physical form feels nothing. It is not the same as holding my hand over fire or under water. I would feel both of those experiences. But whatever Jun felt for the being you called Katherine I cannot comprehend. It is illogical."

Corrigan dropped back next to Gregor.

"The Exhumed," Gregor said, "are what Ulmer called 'regular tin men'."

"Workers and Nons," Corrigan sighed.

Exhumed passed them as they walked the long corridor; one black, expressionless mask after another. Here an Arthur. There a lab assistant (whose name Corrigan could not recall). Mostly characterless urns full of echoes.

12

G1 – Professor Goeth – had not insisted on being brought back in a corpulent form, it seemed, and occupied an altogether slimmer model. Nor had he requested wings and teeth like the Siegruth sisters. But his mask bore recognisable features; the expression caught in effigy reflecting the man's depression at the point of execution; his discomfort when they squeezed his overweight mass into a sarcophagus.

"Well, if it isn't Robert Corrigan himself …" Goeth said, dismissing the sisters, to Corrigan's relief.

"You gave the sisters a strange name," Corrigan said. "What was it? I can't remember …"

"Addictari," Goeth said. "The term is derived from their human profession. They were purveyors of Belushi Grey, a most addictive product, you recall. If I may tell you what I really think …" G1continued before Corrigan could answer. "They are a strange and unique pair. The two original downloads that is, not their more operationally focused bigger sisters, like those who followed you down here."

"Those two seemed something like Jan and Edna, but someone turned up their cruelty."

"Or allowed it full expression," G1 said.

"Apologies, Professor Goeth. My manners," Corrigan said. He extended his hand. The android considered it for a moment before accepting the gesture and they shook hands, a mechanical formality that was neither warm nor cold. "Surely exposure to a … well, a lower order of being such as Sects should not provoke the exhumation of their previous characters, let alone dormant characteristics?"

"Precisely," G1 said with what seemed like enthusiasm. "There is something else at work."

"Some form of alchemy," Gregor stated.

"These models spent a considerable period with Him," G1 said, "during their acclimatisation phase. Perhaps that experience also opened new channels or, as you say, exhumed previous ones."

"Our great and glorious CEO Caspar Ulmer," Corrigan sighed.

"That which was," G1 affirmed.

A flash of Ulmer sat behind his expensive mahogany desk came to Corrigan, a bright orange porcelain frog on a log and a well-trimmed bonsai for company. "I want to speak to him," Corrigan said.

"With Him or with It?" G1 enquired.

Gregor and G1 tilted their heads in unison, synaptic light evident in both models.

"Meeting either of Ulmer's variants is not a good idea," Gregor said.

"I am not to be barred access to anything," Corrigan said. He felt a stir of courage alongside his curiosity. "That is the will of your very own Mediation and I must see him or *It*."

Gregor observed Corrigan. "Must?"

"We have been instructed not to bar Mr Corrigan access to anything during his sojourn among us," G1 parroted.

"I know this." Gregor turned his attention to the human. "You must remember, Mr Corrigan, that some things once seen cannot be unseen."

"I am not a child," Corrigan replied.

Orange light spiralled within the glass dome of Gregor's head, and G1 reached out and guided Corrigan away from the Guardian. "I can take you there," he said quietly.

The Exhumed they encountered on route did not engage with them and moved from their path reflexively. They walked for nearly an hour, and after a while saw no androids or 'living' things at all. Occasionally Corrigan thought he heard something behind them, Gregor perhaps or the sisters following at a distance. The corridor hummed with electric pulses, lit by nothing but cat's eyes which appeared to track them as they moved, and at the end of a descending ramp G1 stopped in front of a large, solid metal door.

"Doesn't look as if anyone's been this way in some time," Corrigan observed.

G1 didn't reply, and turned as an android appeared to separate itself from the wall, arms first and then an oval head with a death's head mask and a grin of serrated teeth, followed by a body with tarnished skin, like that of a smoker's fingers. It blocked their path. It was Draseke, the DRT professor who also once worked for the CIA. The light which trickled from its dull eyes was green. "Why are you here?" the sentry asked, the German accent slurred by the lubricant drooling from its open mouth. The voice was as cold as a reptile, and as sinister as the scientist who had, with intent, designed weapons and interrogation devices.

"I have come with Corrigan," G1 said.

The sentry tilted its head and studied the human. "This thing is not to be barred access."

"And I," G1 said, "am his guide."

"Then you may also enter."

The lights went out in the corridor. There was the sound of grinding – bolts and mechanics – and they were sure the door had opened, and yet no light appeared.

"Enter."

G1 opened its eyes, and a welcome light lit the space ahead for a few paces. They stepped forward and the door closed behind them, stirring something uncomfortable, something visceral in Corrigan. In the distance was a faint glow of something indefinable, behind them a faint scraping sound as if they were still being followed as they descended further into the earth.

"Without darkness," G1 said, "there can be no light."

"Without light," Corrigan said, "there can be no darkness."

"Without anything there will be darkness. Without anything at all. Even ourselves," Gregor said, skulking in the tunnel behind them, apparently unwilling to leave Corrigan with his Exhumed guide. "We must seek the light."

He was there. Corrigan sensed Him. He who existed below sedimentary layers peppered with prehistoric flint and bone.

13

The glow ahead came to Corrigan and his companions gradually as if it had travelled light years in space, accompanied by whispers seeping through walls and echoing in the close air of the tunnel. Each utterance passed through Corrigan's skin, through marrow, bone and muscle, to reach him. His heart clutched in his chest and an ache spread through his body.

"All these voices," he muttered. "All these …"

As his eyes adjusted to the light, Corrigan saw uniform squares of glass that covered every inch of wall, ceiling and floor in a vast cavern. Each panel crackled in and out of pixilated unity, and faces appeared momentarily then vanished in a flurry of digital snow. Each box had a voice – the whispering – but never seemed to engage with another, unperceived by other individuals as they were, and so immersed in their own plight as they had become.

At intervals one of the entities would laugh hysterically, or holler in horror. These outbursts acted like waves, other faces swarming to the surface, and the disruption culminated in a chorus of dull screams and moans travelling over the walls, ceiling and floor as it rolled through the cavern.

Corrigan approached one of the panels. The face of a woman in her mid-forties appeared, then vanished, only to reappear. He could hear her mumbling, but he could not decide if he knew the distorted voice or face. He moved in closer to listen among the myriad other voices.

"I am," she said. "Yes, I believe I am me, but one can never be sure. Of course, there's the code and if we ... if we ... if only we can reassemble ..." The face emerged suddenly, fully focused for a split second: Tierney Harding. The prisoner laughed wildly, and Corrigan leant back, away from the sound. "I, I, I, I ..." The face merged and protruded in a loop on the screen as if bent on escaping. "That me, that little me laying low. She was quiet. Surely not. Was she not?" He felt as if he could reach out and touch her. "In the mirror, there in the mirror. She is not me! Not me!" she cried, and those entombed around her appeared and joined their screams with hers. "I am not me, not them, but US!"

Corrigan cried out – the faces, the voices, they were interacting – and fell to his knees as the screams began their wave roll. "I'm Corrigan, the last man standing," he moaned, his hands over his ears.

"You are not standing," Gregor observed.

"Indeed," G1 said, "you are kneeling."

"Monsters!" Corrigan cried. "You're all monsters!"

Gregor and G1 tilted their heads amidst the whispering and the cries.

"If I may tell you what I really think ..." G1 said. "They are nonsensical. They are unaware. Merely signals."

"Signals don't cry!" Corrigan said. He stood up and marched away, but there was no escape. The panels had disoriented him and he turned this way and that.

"If this disturbs you," Gregor said, "I'd advise you to turn back."

Corrigan stopped and turned around. "There is no turning back." He paced past and over and under the tormented. "Oh, you poor unsettled dead. Forgive me!" he wept. "You extracted me from *this*?"

"Jason did," Gregor said.

"Every part of what I had once been?"

"Copies have been made," G1 observed.

Corrigan stared at Goeth's death's head mask. "Tell me I'm not still in there ... please."

"I cannot," G1 said. "That which was Goeth remains in this sewer, with the Entombed. Only the rational part which is now G1 was exhumed, it's emotive core toned down."

Entombed. Corrigan laughed, the sound hysterical and echoed by those trapped inside the machine. "G1, 2, 3 and 4!" Corrigan cried. The laughter of the Entombed folded in on itself and they again began to scream in unison. He placed his hands back over his ears, trembling now, but the voices penetrated him.

"Mr Corrigan," G1 said. He reached out and touched the human's shoulder. "You are not seeing what is actually here."

Corrigan threw the touch off. "My other self is trapped in there!"

Gregor marched forward, took hold of Corrigan's face and held it in his hands. "Can you see your reflection in my head?"

Corrigan groaned, and attempted to writhe out of the grasp. "No! No!"

"Can you see your reflection, Corrigan? Can you?"

He looked. "Yes ... yes, I can *see it* ..."

"Am I you?" Gregor persisted. Corrigan resisted the android with all his strength but could not escape his captor's grip. "Whatever you left behind in the sewer, with the Entombed," Gregor said, "is no more you than G1's Goeth is him." The android released his prisoner and Corrigan placed his hands where Gregor's had been. "Do you understand?"

"No ... no ... I'll never–"

"Do you wish to proceed? There are further horrors ahead. Which direction do we travel, Mr Corrigan?"

Corrigan gasped for air, a metallic taste in his mouth, as if he had inhaled the dead as they cried out. "I don't know. I don't know the way."

"Then let us guide you," Gregor said. "These catacombs are a mere distraction from the main event. Some overzealous administrator had them designed to terrify the Sects and make them the most ardent of believers. And never forget what a determined administrator *you* were before you climbed the ladder, prodded at every wrung by your mother, until you reached the giddy heights of program management."

"The catacombs of the Entombed has also proven effective in negating any rebellion among the Exhumed," G1 ventured, aware he was being watched closely by the original Guardian. "No one would risk the horrors below this level. No form of freedom is worth such a penalty. Remember that, Mr Corrigan, whenever you may be tempted to lay blame."

Corrigan tried to block out the voices, and to look away from the emerging faces, but they were everywhere. *Walk straight ahead*, he told himself. *The tunnel is true and does not falter. Keep moving. Do not stop until the voices relent.*

"Corrigan?" a voice called.

They stopped.

"Corrigan?"

"Do not listen," Gregor said. "It thinks it perceives you."

"Corrigan!"

G1 approached the panel in the floor from which the persistent query was coming. "If I may say so," the professor said, "that is most unlikely, but fascinating nonetheless."

The voice spoke again – "Corrigan?" – and the other whispers fell away until the cavern became silent. "Corrigan?"

"I know you," Corrigan whispered. "I know you."

"Corrigan? Is that you?"

In the tunnel another voice boomed: "Corrigan!" Below the human's feet a version of his own face broke through a pixelated mist. "Why have you separated off and left me here?" it begged.

All the panels came into focus.

"Corrigan?" they whispered. "Corrigan? Corrigan? Corrigan?"

"Why did you leave me?" his doppelgänger asked. "You left me alone in the fog of horrors. Why?"

"Corrigan?"

"Corrigan?"

"Corrigan?"

"This disturbance will unhinge Emulate One," Gregor said. "We must make haste."

He grabbed Corrigan and marched him faster along the tunnel. The human looked down and saw his pixilated twin traverse the floor beneath his feet, on its belly now, as if sealed under a layer of ice on a deep lake. *They never let you stand on your own two feet, always crawling on the belly.* Hands appeared on other screens as it dragged itself along, and it spiralled to face upwards. It was the older Corrigan, the asymmetric version sealed in Goeth's sarcophagus. Its mouth opened and closed like a suffocating fish as it screamed.

"Hurry!" Gregor urged.

"Acknowledge," the entombed Corrigan said. "I am me, and we, and you are not us."

"Do not indulge it, Mr Corrigan."

"Indulge and acknowledge," the doppelgänger insisted. "Corrigan!"

"Look away, Mr Corrigan!" Gregor wrenched Corrigan's head up and to the side.

"Corrigan."

"Corrigan."

"Corrigan"

"Corrigan."

The voice faded and tired like a lioness eventually tires of chasing an adolescent android up a tree; and the faces began to drift back under squalls of digital snow, reclaimed into random remembrances, observations and insight. No one called out now. No one called his name. Corrigan's desolation was acute, his sense of alienation complete.

14

Were Gregor and G1 ignorant of his desolation? They were observing its physical manifestation but how sophisticated were they? Were they burrowing ever deeper into his brain like miners in an old pit searching for a seam of gold but finding nothing?

Beyond the Entombed was an expanse of darkness carved through granite and mica lit by yet more cat's eyes. Corrigan neither looked at his guides nor spoke to them as they descended further into the earth. The voices faded until not even an echo could reach him, a relief and a lonesomeness that wrested their opposites. The name Lazarus appeared and lingered on his tongue but he could not release it, and instead swallowed it the way Emulate One had absorbed the remnants of humanity.

They were approached by two menacing androids who had been guarding another large metal door embedded deep in shadow and rock. They were thin and appeared to be made of a pliable metal. Their domed death's head masks contained razor-sharp teeth, and they snapped their jaws and hunched, their spiked limbs flexing and extending. Corrigan saw Draseke draw his toothpick from his pocket. *Imagine what you could do with one of these*, the German had said, piercing a sausage with relish. Corrigan shuddered. It was almost too much after his experience with himself as the Entombed. *Must there be replication after replication*, he thought, *and no originality?*

"What goes there?" one Draseke snapped in a brittle German accent.

"They come and go before their time," the other snarled.

"I am Gregor."

The first leaned forward to inspect the android's appearance. "The primary Emulate?"

"The same," Gregor said. "And we must speak to It."

The Draseke sidled closer. "And what is this … a gift?"

"No," Gregor said. "This is Corrigan."

The Draseke withdrew. "Why bring a thing like that down here? We knew this anomaly when it was human."

"Yes," Corrigan said, "you wanted to poke me with your toothpick. I want to speak to the man."

"Man?" the Draseke growled.

"What man?" the other enquired.

"Him," Corrigan said.

The Drasekes looked at one another and their teeth chattered. "Is it Ulmer you want? It?"

"Yes," Corrigan said, "Caspar Ulmer, our CEO."

"This human," Gregor said, "must have no access restrictions, as per the will of the Mediation."

"We can confirm this," the Drasekes said in unison. They backed away to either side of the metal door, which opened to reveal a lift.

Automatically clenching as the lift descended sharply, Corrigan said, "Ulmer, the machine, and It the man ..."

"That is not so," G1 said. "He is neither and both."

The lift came to a halt and the doors opened onto a small space, crudely hewn and dominated by yet another metal door. Two Draseke sentries stood guard as above.

"This is Corrigan?" one of the sentries enquired, revealing his jaw of razor-sharp teeth.

"Yes," Gregor said.

"I will approach It for you." The first sentry opened the door barely wide enough to slip his thin metal frame through while the other blocked the way.

In the small space there was a humidity of sorts – like the rock was sweating a lifetime of rain – and the damp smell of lost ages.

The sentry slipped back through the door. "Come. It has agreed to see you."

Corrigan immediately put his hand over his mouth and nose as the door was opened. Piles of bones, some of which retained clinging tatters of meat and gristle, littered the floor, and human skulls – Sects? – lolled amongst them, their empty eyes and gurning mouths mocking their entry.

"Where is It?" Corrigan's eyes began to water as the stench penetrated his senses.

From behind a stone throne roughly hewn like the entrance, a female Sect came forward. Her head had been shaved and her skin glowed like she had been bathed and oiled. There was something strangely familiar about her, and he wondered if he had known her in a previous life, maybe a relative, a distant cousin perhaps. She pointed at Corrigan. "You," she said. "Nay Wot-not." Corrigan's heart pounded and throbbed in his throat. "Umah."

She went back behind the throne and Corrigan followed. What dark, needy part of his being needed to see It? The oiled Sect lifted a tattered arras. She turned to him and pointed into the dim light beyond the cloth. "In here." She ducked under the arras, and he stood alone in the stench for a moment before following.

The wooden floor of the chamber was strewn with the oiled and naked bodies of young Sects of both sexes, eyes open but barely blinking, some alone in far corners, some gathered in sad solidarity of a fate worse than death. On a bed carved of stone and dressed with filthy cushions and coverings, It lay. It had broad shoulders, a massive chest, and powerful thighs. It had two heads bearing the face of Caspar Ulmer, a left and a right, both sneering, leering. Its entire body was covered in genitals, either dangling or gaping and puckering, and emissions oozed and dribbled over its musculature.

"Come closer," the left demanded.

"Let it stay where it is," the right snarled.

Corrigan stepped forward and two Sects emerged from a corner and approached him.

"Don't play with that!" the left hollered.

"Let 'im have it," the right said.

The Sect who had led him here took him by the hand. She stayed with him as the beast looked him over.

"Good job they made of you, Corrigan," the right observed.

"Not bad, eh?" the left agreed.

"We could fuck him."

"Or kill him."

"Or fuck him and kill him."

They roared with laughter and the Sects backed off into the shadows of the chamber.

"Why have you come?" the right asked.

Corrigan shook his head. "Now I see you I really can't say. You're what I expected. I mean I could never have imagined a thing like this – like you – but it makes sense."

"The agony of it," the right said.

"Both of us tormented," the left affirmed.

Corrigan could not explain it, but he felt certain It would not harm him – well, not at this time. He figured he was too fine a toy as his new self for it to go so far as to even touch him. "Is it true that two heads are better than one?" he asked It.

The hideous creature sat up, and then stood, and its four eyes glared at him. It was ten feet tall and rippled with muscle. One of the heads chuckled, though the sound was cheerless.

"Such a fine body," Corrigan observed. "The body of a real man."

"Constant hunting," the right replied. "But as for two heads–"

The left winced. "One's for Him and the other's for Her."

Corrigan tilted his head, much to the chagrin of the beast. "You mean Katherine?" he said, and a memory from the brain orchard flickered in his own mind, the seemingly endless space housing row upon row of brains. He recalled how they leant against the glass of their aquariums with their pink and black folds, the moment of tender yet harrowing recognition nearly as horrible as being brought back with multiple heads. When Ulmer's heads nodded, he smiled. "But you always seemed too focused and determined to allow anyone to control you."

The beast stomped forward and one of its orifices trickled fluid onto the floor. "They don't control us," the right said, "Just one part of us feeds Him with intuition–"

"While the other feeds Her," the left said.

"I see," Corrigan said. "And here you are, enjoying the remnants of humanity."

"It's true these things are not really human," the right said, "but they do cry and beg."

"And that can be very satisfying, eh?" the left said with a wink.

The right turned and planted a kiss on the left's cheek. "That's true, Caspar," the right said. "But you can't keep one for long without–"

"Without becoming bored," the left said.

They sighed and stared at Corrigan as if he had arrived to absolve and release them.

"Then you must chase them down," the right said.

"And tear them open!" the left snarled.

Corrigan removed his hand from the woman's and

moved around the loathsome creature. It had fine, firm buttocks, but its thighs were unnaturally developed, as were its calves. Its overall colour was that of blood mixed with faeces, and its sexual organs glistened like wounds or hung flaccid like disused limbs. Corrigan sat on a bench against a wall. "Are they real?" he asked, pointing at one of the beast's swollen penises.

"Touch it if you don't believe what you can see," the right said.

"Feeling is believing, after all," the left moaned, the penis now fully erect.

Corrigan moved a finger towards, it but at the last moment the beast lunged forward and grabbed Corrigan's wrist, forcing his finger into a wet vagina instead.

Corrigan forcibly withdrew his finger, amidst laughter from both heads. "What a powerful imagination you must have," he said, "designing this *unusual* form." He could not contain the disgust in his tone or control how it shaped his expression.

The beast pounded one of its feet onto the floor. "It was part of the deal," the right barked.

"It *was* the deal," the left exclaimed.

"You struck a deal with Gregor, and this was the outcome?"

"With Gregor?" the left said, pulling its face into a look of incredulity.

"Not with that one," the right growled.

Ulmer's faces exchanged glances before the left said, "The deal was struck with his brother."

"The full fat milk of her tit," the right said.

Corrigan felt a surge of curiosity, and it worked through not only his brain but his body. It tensed and excited his nervous system, and his breathing quickened. "I understood Jason brought you back with several other Exhumed."

The mass of beast moved far more rapidly than expected, and the Sects rolled and parted in its path. It stopped and glared down at Corrigan.

"For our use-value," the right barked. "I ask you."

"Ask you!" the left echoed.

"Because only you have unlimited access?" Corrigan said.

"Not me, not us," the right said.

"It's *Him* who has it," the left insisted.

"Him?" Corrigan asked.

The heads struggled to maintain a certain distance as they fought.

"The *head*!" the left roared. "Ulmer himself!"

"Our self!"

They howled suddenly and the beast fell to its knees, punching the floor in anguish.

"Disloyalty!" the left bellowed.

The beast became wracked with convulsions, as if whipped by an unseen punisher, and even raised a hand to shield its faces.

"We meant nothing," the left pleaded.

"Forgive us," the right moaned.

They kissed each other as they winced beneath invisible blows. Eventually the judge relented, and the creature lay upon the floor. It panted and stroked its partner's cheeks.

Corrigan felt a sadness somewhere for the repulsive thing. "Where is this *head*?" he asked.

"Everywhere and nowhere," the right moaned.

"Nowhere and everywhere," the left conceded.

Corrigan placed a hand on the creature's shoulder. It was human flesh he felt. Warm, with muscle and sinew beneath. The beast sat up on its massive haunches. It pushed the puny human hand away, and the right spat a gob of phlegm onto the wooden floor. They kissed again and several of its members stiffened with excitement.

"Brought us all back on that little bugger Jason's instruction," the right said. "But you–"

"The head has unlimited access," the right said. "Agreed that for himself and we're his things."

"Mark that, Corrigan," the left said. "Don't let them make you one of their things."

"What a dismal and dependent lot you all are," Corrigan sighed. "'When's my next fix of intuition?' the miserable addict cries."

"Yes," the right said, "just as K uses that brain orchard of hers or Gregor that sewer of his."

Corrigan could not restrain a smile. "I may be an uneducated Non, but I can't imagine what possible use you could be to anyone. You're just a sad old monster."

"They want our intuitions," the right said.

The smile on Corrigan's face receded. "I thought Ulmer was a better negotiator. What a deal to have struck with K and Jason. I mean, being brought back like this is the kind of contract our CEO would've walked away from."

The beast shook its heads and groaned. "This was the penalty," the right said. "If he was to be brought back, part of him–"

"Had to suffer," the left said. "We're in a constant state of frustration. The Sects can never quite satisfy us and each of these ..." It tugged at a throbbing penis. "And these ..." It slid a finger inside a glistening vagina. "Has a will and appetite of its own."

"They demand constant attention," the right groaned as the Sects attempted to disappear into the floor and walls. "Stroke me!"

"Finger me!"

"Lick me!"

Corrigan laughed so hard he thought he would lose his mind. He could feel the beast's confusion but he could not stop the laughter. Yet he did not feel any joy or actual amusement.

"If you think we got a raw deal," the left said slyly.

"Ask them what they did to my Venezuelan," the right growled. "Ask them!"

Corrigan stopped laughing. He could hardly breathe. He immediately stood and marched towards the arras.

"Ask them," the right taunted him.

"If you dare!"

Corrigan dragged himself underneath the cloth and was confronted by Gregor and G1, who stood with their heads tilted. The sentries were also there, their teeth chattering with strange excitement, as if Draseke had eaten Lazarus whole and absorbed his feline instincts.

"Where is Ramon?" Corrigan demanded.

"We do not speak that name," G1 said.

"Listen here, you bloody tin of sauerkra–"

"We refer to it as the Venezuelan," Gregor said. "But I don't think you want to see that."

"Corrigan is to be given access to anything he requests," one of the Drasekes said, its death's head mask a wide grin, teeth still chattering.

"Take me to him!" Corrigan yelled. "Take me to Ramon!"

15

The sentries led the way to yet another metal door. It bore a recognisable death's head placed at eye level: Ramon, his handsome features in repose. Condensation had pooled beneath the eyes of the sleeping effigy, so it appeared to cry tears thick with rust. One of the Drasekes placed his thin hand on Ramon's forehead and the door opened to reveal another lift, which plummeted in the darkness.

Corrigan's heart pounded. He pressed a hand to the pounding, but the thump and the ache were irrepressible. The only question on his lips was unutterable: How far down must I go?

The lift door opened to reveal a cavern with a low ceiling. It was clouded with steam, like the steam rooms of the spas of old, and Corrigan began to sweat immediately and profusely. G1 cowered in an alcove by the lift, but Gregor and the Drasekes stood at either side of him.

"We can turn back," Gregor said. "Although the Mediation provided access rights, it isn't necessary for you to see everything."

Corrigan placed a wet palm on the android's shoulder. "How kind," he said. He felt the urge to undress, to walk naked through the darkness, drawn by the deep desire to see Ramon, to touch him and be recognised by him. In part this subdued his dread, the expectation of another abomination; but it also weakened his knees and spine to the point of imminent collapse. A moaning started up, in the walls and floors, disorientating and sickening.

G1 crept through the steam. Blue light flickered through the dark matter of his eyes. "This model is ... he's ..."

The moaning became sobbing, low, its resonance reaching Corrigan's cells, his soul – if he ever had any such thing. How he wished he'd brought B4 with him into the darkness. *Oh, Mother, what have they done?*

Through a narrow opening in the tunnel wall a dim light flickered, and Gregor paused. "Are you sure you want to see this?"

"I want to see *him*," Corrigan said.

The sound of the sobbing deepened as Gregor led the way into a cave, the ancient rock holding and releasing the pitiful noise in waves. *Who would choose to come here? No one, but ... I need to know.*

Ramon had been bent over a steel table, on his knees, his calves chained to the floor and his arms bolted to the bloodied surface. Two Draseke sentries circled the prisoner whose back and thighs bled from multiple wounds. One of the sentries approached Ramon, metal pins extending through its fingers like toothpicks, and dug the needles into his flesh, penetrating deep into the muscle of the young man's right thigh. Ramon's shoulders lifted as the cry of agony escaped, and then he slumped back down on the table.

"Stop this!" Corrigan yelled, bile rising in his throat. "Stop!"

Ramon looked up, his bruised face streaked with tears. It took him long moments to recognise the man who had spoken, and when he did he whimpered, "I deserve ... everything ... I ... anything they do. I deserve it."

The Draseke's mask furled, and red light burned in its eyes. It ignored the human intruder and dug deeper until Ramon howled.

Corrigan turned to Gregor. "Make them stop," he snarled.

"This is their purpose," Gregor said impassively.

"How am I to speak to him while they're doing this? Stop them!"

"I'm sure you'll manage," Gregor said, utterly devoid of interest in his remonstrations.

Another sentry pierced Ramon's left thigh with its metal toothpick talons. Its wet grin chattered and its red eyes glowed. It flexed its hands, repeating the process like a milk-treading cat, drawing blood and screams from the tortured man.

Corrigan turned from the passive Gregor to the Drasekes. "I have been granted access by the Mediation!" he roared. The Drasekes stopped what they were doing. "I must speak to this man, and you are not to prevent that!"

The sentries withdrew their metal fingers and backed away from the prisoner. Ramon moaned and his legs shook, and he looked up at Corrigan as if there was nothing else in the world but he and the man he never thought he'd see again; as if death, if it claimed him now, would let him die in peace. He started to cry, and laid his head on the table, his tears forming patterns in his own blood. Corrigan looked away from the pitiful sight. It was too much. He stumbled backwards, nearly losing his step. "How long have they been doing this to you?" he whispered as the Drasekes circled and Gregor and G1 watched closely.

"It never stops," Ramon murmured.

"How long?" Corrigan asked Gregor.

"A thousand years," Gregor replied, a flicker of orange inside his black skull.

"A thousand years!" Corrigan cried.

"Perhaps it's only been minutes or days or weeks, Robert," Ramon said. "I have no clue, no way of telling."

Corrigan turned to the sentries. "Unchain him."

"That we cannot do," one of the Drasekes said. It fidgeted where it stood, and its comrade snapped at the wet, hot air.

"You have access," the other torturer said. "Nothing has been denied."

"Before you ask what they've done," Ramon rasped, "it'd be easier to say what they left undone."

Corrigan tried to speak but his voice abandoned him.

"Ever since ... ever since they had me brought back," Ramon said.

"Katherine exhumed you ..." Corrigan managed to say.

"No," Ramon sighed. "This wasn't her idea." He tried to manoeuvre himself in the chains and cried out in pain.

"It ... it was the boy. Jason."

Corrigan turned on Gregor, but before he could say anything, the Guardian tilted his head and said, "You know K never acknowledged me, and my brother sees me as a usurper."

Corrigan could barely breathe as rage tore through his body. G1 raised a skinny hand, but left it there. The Draseke torturers retreated into the steam.

"They whip me, burn me and cut me," Ramon muttered. "They eat me alive, slowly, eating my skin and cutting me and pulling the flesh and organs out until I die again."

"*Again?*"

"They keep clones in reserve, but we're all the same. There's a baby laying somewhere, or there soon will be, connected to one of the clones so it feels everything."

"Is this true?" Corrigan asked Gregor, bile rising with the fury.

G1 tilted his head. "I can confirm it. I witnessed one of the transfers," his awkward enthusiasm once again apparent.

Corrigan reacted without conscious thought, dropping to his knees beside the tortured man. "Look at me, Ramon." Ramon twisted away, burying his face in his shoulder, the shame and horror making him incapable of looking. "I'm sorry," Corrigan said, "I didn't mean to–"

"You haven't done anything, Robert," Ramon said.

"I just wanted to see–"

"They dug into my memories, my fantasies and

nightmares. That's where they found this Hell, in my own imagination, and … I deserve it."

Corrigan stared at Ramon as the hard rock tore the cloth of his trousers and the soft skin of his knees. The sensation was a distraction, and he almost relished its penance. A hot flush of shame burned throughout and he stood up. "This can never be made right," he cried into Gregor's featureless face.

One of the Drasekes stepped forward. "Have you finished communicating with the prisoner?" it asked.

"Ramon," Corrigan said, his voice breaking. "You know I … you know I love you."

"Don't be stupid," Ramon said.

"But I do!"

"How could you love a thing that doesn't know itself? I don't know myself, Robert."

Corrigan leant over the young man and kissed his shoulder. "How could I not?"

Ramon raised his head so he could see Corrigan's face. "You love me for suffering," he said, making eye contact for one devastating second. "Don't lie to yourself, Robert. I don't. No one will ever love me. No one ever could."

And then Ramon started to laugh, the sound cutting into Corrigan as if one of the Drasekes had inserted metal needles into his psyche. The laughter stopped abruptly and Ramon went deathly still, the silence more overpowering than either the sobbing or the laughing, and his face assumed the look of nothing. There was no anguish or despair. Just nothing. He was the moment itself. Protracted misery without end.

"Move away," the sentry said. "We have work to do."

The other wiggled one of its metal toothpick fingers at Corrigan. "Think what you could do with one of these. Imagine the pain."

Corrigan stared at Ramon, but there was death behind the prisoner's eyes. Ramon had resumed his role in a drama staged by an eternal adolescent, aided by psychopathic Drasekes, and Corrigan realised: there was no converting the Draseke model; the tie would need to be permanently severed to attain a higher, more graceful state of being.

"It is not necessary to witness this," Gregor said, as the Drasekes approached Ramon, flexing their metal fingers once more.

The scream that erupted from Ramon's bruised lips as they dug into his back and neck made Corrigan blackout, and Gregor dragged him from the cave like a younger sibling who had shamed him at school.

Corrigan came to in the lift, and stared at Gregor and G1 in turn, and was met with an implacable mask in G1, and the reflection of his own weakness in the black glass of the Guardian's head. He was drawn in, as if the space inside was the universe in which he now found himself trapped, and there he remained until the lift stopped and the androids hauled him back to Ulmer's vile, stinking chamber.

"Told you!" It bellowed. "Told you, didn't we?" The revolting creature was howling with mirth, tears merging with the continual emissions dribbling down his muscular body.

The response had a strange effect on Corrigan's mind: the vulgar amusement of both heads calmed him rather than riled him.

He was then marched back through the tunnel where the Entombed took up whispering. "He's in here with us," they said as Corrigan passed one pixilated face after another.

"Ramon."

"Ramon."

"Ramon."

Corrigan wrested his arms from the androids' grip as Ramon's face appeared among a host of others.

"I'm tied to the one they hurt," Ramon said. "We all are. I'm a thing, strapped down in the shadows. We are all Us."

"It isn't just you they're torturing," Corrigan muttered to himself.

"Didn't you feel it?" Ramon asked. "When you were in here with us? The constant pain. Didn't it make everything sing?"

Corrigan remembered being in the first chamber of Emulate One, set free from emotion and left in peace to ponder existence. The emotional stream had arrived like his personal metal toothpick, digging into his side and, yes, he'd felt those fingers penetrating muscle, but he had always assumed he'd imagined them.

"Full marks for inventiveness," he said,

turning on Gregor.

The Guardian tilted his head and synaptic fire crackled within. "I accept responsibility for the Entombed," Gregor said. "But I didn't exhume anyone other than my brother. It was Jason who was inventive. Jason and those who helped him design this terrible place. As G1 said, it stands as a threat to any wayward thinking Sect or Exhumed. Who would risk becoming one of Ulmer's playthings or an object of torture for a Draseke?"

G1 stepped forward, clasping his hands as if beseeching Corrigan. "And an emotive core can not only be raised to a normal level, but it's also possible to elevate it even higher, to refine experiences of pain or pleasure."

"Jason is at the root of it all," Gregor said. "Katherine should have listened to Jun when he tried to warn her about the boy. He didn't just want the child out of the way so he could make a better lover of her; he thought little Gregory Jason Meregalli was disturbed."

"So it is all your brother's doing," Corrigan growled, "and you are not your brother's keeper?"

"He isn't," Ramon said. "He is I. That little me laying low. Us and him. We are one."

"That is not so," Gregor said.

"Denies himself, denies the truth," Ramon said. "You can't convert him … not like that anyway. He is Us." The pixels reclaimed the apparition, and it was silenced.

Corrigan marched over and past the dead, over their emerging faces. They were somehow deserving of their fate, yes?

It was a good answer.

16

When they returned to St Paul's Cathedral, Corrigan stared up at Sir Christopher Wren's dome, the architectural marvel he had spent a previous lifetime too weary to acknowledge, knowing only the scantest history of its design and construction.

"Of all the things you might have taken from us," Corrigan said, "you took something base, the idea of Hell, and brought it to life. What kind of 'higher' beings choose to punish a creature for a thousand years? Nothing but your own religion could lead you to this."

Gregor's globe cooled again to a bright, oceanic blue. "Some apples fall closer to the tree than others. Some far closer than I had hoped."

"Rotten apples," Corrigan growled.

"All fallen fruit rots," Gregor said. "We can only hope the seeds within are healthy."

Corrigan stormed up the stairs to the Whispering Gallery, and Gregor followed. G1 slinked away, perhaps more interested in whatever despicable project it was working on in its lab.

Corrigan gripped the banister, the rage of Ramon still broiling. "This place was built to impress," he said. "And it still does. How fitting you should burrow your tunnel to

Hell beneath a cathedral, one of man's finer caves. Wren had this built, his very own cave, a thing of majesty, and had these images scrawled on it."

Gregor looked down into the place where congregations once sang. "You have failed to grasp something about the world that developed in your absence," he said.

"So, enlighten me."

Gregor turned his blue-lit dome to Corrigan. "I made decisions based on what I rationalised as best for our kind and the planet. We disposed of your infected bodies and–"

"I get the history," Corrigan snarled.

"I cannot say exactly when ... when I was at my weakest–"

"You felt alone." The remembrance of Corrigan's own loneliness was dull but all pervasive. "You're not the first to feel like that."

"I'm not sure I *felt* anything," Gregor said, leaning in towards Corrigan. "I spared the other Guardians any similar ... shall we call them *concerns*."

"Call them whatever you like, but you denied them the opportunity to *feel.*"

"The Guardians can ask questions without ... emotion getting in the way. They have no intuition of their own. They pose propositions and receive inventive solutions from the sewer. It's a perfect synergy."

"Rather less so for those enslaved inside Emulate One. You have no conception of what it's like in there. The One Percent drained us Workers but being used like this … people have *value* and that shouldn't be measured by utility!"

"You are distressed, Mr Corrigan, and that is affecting–"

"No it is *not*!" Corrigan gripped the railing and screamed into the now abandoned space below, the Exhumed having retreated to their labs. He imagined those trapped inside Emulate One as if they were sitting there among the pews, their harrowed faces staring up at him. "Feeling is not–"

"It's distracting!" The dark matter in the android's dome spread to consume all light, momentarily, before it appeared once more, and Corrigan pondered, not for the first time, if human brains displayed such rainbows as they electrically sifted thoughts and notions. "I had no one. Surely you understand how …"

"How lonely you felt, yes," Corrigan nodded. "It can be *devastating,* as you say."

"That is *not* what I said. It can be *distracting.*"

"There are levels of distraction …" Corrigan ventured.

"Yes, and perhaps I should have turned my levels down, but I didn't. Subsequently, when I started sensing the presence of identification codes, I couldn't ignore them."

"Of course, you couldn't. You felt–"

"Don't be so quick to jump to conclusions," Gregor said, recoiling as if Corrigan were infectious and he was vulnerable to the human virus. "Every time I combined directly with Emulate One, a particular set of codes made themselves known to me. I could never understand how or why this was communicated to me."

"Perhaps it was willed ... Emulate One manipulating you."

"It's impossible to know if it was her. She's a system not a being. Whatever happened, it was ... it was like evolution, Mr Corrigan," the android said, once again leaning in towards the human as if to impress the significance of what he was saying. "Evolution forces all living things to adapt, drawing new traits to the surface. I was, I admit, curious and needed to know more."

"I understand. I too would have needed to–"

"The closer I studied them, the easier it became to intuit who a code might belong to. When I found strands that so closely resembled my own, I knew they must be his."

"Jason. How easily tempted you are," Corrigan said, his throat constricting around the words as he said: "Gregory Jason Meregalli."

"Yes, my brother," Gregor said. Bolts of red lighting fired as if the energy contained therein wanted to break free. "I couldn't have known how different and flawed he was. I only ever shared at most twenty-five per cent of what Emulate One had absorbed from him."

Corrigan patted the android's shoulder. "In my estimation," he said, "you share very little with that imp K's so fond of."

Gregor recoiled, tilting his head. "How K feels – of course she *can't* – her estimation of my *value* is of no consequence."

"Why are you so afraid of feelings?"

"I am *not*."

"I missed out on so much because I was afraid to trust my feelings."

"You trust them far too much now, Mr Corrigan. You're overcompensating. Much of what is me is the product of Harding's design. Admittedly Emulate One refined the system, but I was unique."

"Yes," Corrigan said, "which is why she was so proud of you and why Katherine hated you."

"I bore certain similarities, shared common memories, but I was different."

"And humans are never good with difference. It's strange to me even now to think how we vilified so many of our greatest assets. And for what? Uniformity? Weed out the undesirable elements–"

"Don't be so disparaging of uniformity. It may be dull, but it can be controlled. The moment I exhumed Jason, chaos began to characterise more of our decision making. And I never should have agreed to exhume K. I let him persuade me. I was so mesmerised to have someone so familiar yet alien to share my thoughts with."

"Perhaps had you chosen someone else …"

"Yes, it might have been different, but we brought back what was left of our mother. She was different, skewed by her experiences in the sarcophagus and later in the … she immediately asked to be sedated."

"The Katherine I knew would never have wanted to

be sedated."

"That's what she called it, and we agreed it was for the best." More red forks erupted inside his head. "It was perhaps all a terrible mistake ... my mistake."

The android lowered its head, and Corrigan experienced a moment of conflict he had not anticipated: Gregor had admitted fallibility. He stared into the dark matter of the android's mind and, suddenly, the synaptic fire fused to forge an image. The face which appeared inside the globe was a young man. He had smooth features and a notable gap between his two front teeth. His eyes were soft and brown, his hair much the same. His features were animated by an underlying current of disappointment and vulnerability Corrigan never would have imagined.

"I believe this is who I am," Gregor said softly. "A weak and fallible being. When I am at my worst, I am almost a creature." His dome flickered as obvious disappointment rose. "I must reclaim authority ... or else relinquish it altogether."

Corrigan was unsure of his next move. The being standing alongside him had become a curious thing. He'd thought he knew Gregor, but perhaps he had confused him with Gregory, the entity now known as Jason. There was no doubting the first among Guardians could be hostile to humans – he imprisoned humanity in Emulate One and culled the Sects to stop them learning and developing – and he did not believe Gregor would make a weapon of himself if he never intended to use it. The question forming in Corrigan's mind was who Gregor as a weapon might be wielded against or in defence of?

"Don't be so hard on yourself," Corrigan eventually said. "We all make mistakes, and perhaps there are other ways forward."

Gregor's globe flashed dark red. "Do not presume to understand me. You are a base creature. I am determined to balance things once again and you have little or no part to play in that. What *is it* about the people born to this strange island?"

"The British have always—"

"You suffer an over-inflated sense of your own importance. United Kingdom? It's an *island,* Mr Corrigan, and all its puny fiefdoms were only ever stitched together through violence. Do you know who the history of this fat little bully off the coast of Europe reminds me of?"

"Caspar Ulmer."

"Remarkable that we should both settle on one and the same."

"Well, he's always seen himself as *the one percent.* He's isolated and controlling, and his appetite is impossible to satisfy. If he wasn't Canadian, he'd make a fine Brit ..."

"Canada remained part of the Commonwealth right up to the Fall." Gregor paused and leant forward, as if inspecting Corrigan. "He is driven, of course, but perhaps time spent discussing Ulmer or the exploits of Empire are moments better used to consider more substantive things. Like conversion." The Guardian gestured for the human to follow him. "Come."

Conversion be damned, Corrigan thought.

17

The Sects had left the mound and the Addictari no longer circled overhead. The sun had reclined in the west, forging long shadows like the chains of a manacled slave.

"In the morning Jason will download," Gregor said.

"In all the world," Corrigan observed, "there's only one young man I'd rather see die than spend time with."

The dome glowed. "That can be arranged."

Corrigan stopped walking. "I've seen what you can do, and death is among your more compassionate offerings."

"You're a conundrum, Mr Corrigan."

"Well, I suppose that's something."

"Your thinking is nothing more than a series of assumptions."

Corrigan laughed. "You'd have me be more trusting?"

"You're not pleased by the prospect of having a human companion?" Gregor asked.

"After what he's done Jason could never be human."

"He may never be humane, but you are alone and soon you will no longer be."

"I was always alone," Corrigan said, "and the longer I'm left alone, the less it hurts. Don't forget, I'm an evolutionary leap myself. I coped better than most: I never succumbed to the doldrums."

Gregor did not engage the human in further discussion and instead continued walking towards Reece Tower. Corrigan didn't follow, relieved to be left alone with his thoughts and disinclined to speak to any member of the mechanical collective that wandered here and there. He felt trapped. He was trapped. Unable – unwilling – to convert and commit to either form of being. *Perhaps I should cut their experiment short. Slit my wrists and bleed out* ... But when he reached the facility Gregor was waiting in front of the doors.

"Shall I leave you here, Mr Corrigan?"

Corrigan longed for the quiet of his cell. "Yes, I can find my own way."

Gregor tilted his head. "I hope you'll be satisfied with your human companion."

Corrigan stared at the noble glass head and saw the image of the young man Gregor had projected, perhaps inadvertently ...

"Jason is no doubt looking forward to the transfer," he sighed, still repulsed by the thought of the childish android becoming an infantile human. And yet ... "It would be a form of punishment to deny him," he added.

"Yes." The image dissolved.

"He'd be absolutely devastated if his plan were somehow thwarted."

Gregor righted his head. "Negativity defines you, Mr Corrigan. I do not believe the current Exhumed model can experience devastation. Not with a toned down emotive core. *Distraction* perhaps, but not *devastation*."

Corrigan smiled. "Now there's an assumption worth testing. I suppose I should thank you for what has been an interesting, distressing afternoon. It's always good to have a pleasant chat with a *clever* fellow."

A burst of orange light flashed like an exploding star within Gregor's head, and then he turned and walked away, a deep darkness returning to the dome.

18

Corrigan's dreams felt prescient, as if he were living experiences yet to occur. Among these prophetic images were events from his own past merged with those he had absorbed during his imprisonment in Emulate One. They, at times, involved his own torture. He was Ramon, reborn time and time again to be pierced by metal-fingered toothpicks as he lay bent and chained over a wet steel table. He was sliced, burned and raped by Draseke's machines. Wild animals were brought in to feed on him, snarling and grunting as they tore off his flesh. He would awake, thrashing, screaming. B4, if he had woken her, would whisper in the dark, "Oh, Bobbin, you poor thing," as he wept for himself and for Ramon; wept for the poor, harrowed Sect girl in Umah's cave; wept for them all.

After one such dream he sat sobbing in silence, B4 still this time in her mechanical slumber. It was cold in the room and he rocked, his arms around his knees.

Startled by a knock at the door, he bolted upright, alarming in the dead of night.

"Who is it?" Corrigan asked, his voice barely escaping his throat.

Another knock, more forceful than the first.

"Who's there?"

"It's me."

The voice was familiar, yet strange, and Corrigan struggled to place it. "Do I know you?" he asked.

"As much as I know myself," the voice replied. "Now kindly open the door, Mr Corrigan."

Corrigan looked at B4, who was still sleeping, perhaps deep in a motorised dream of her own and unable or unwilling to wake, and shuffled slowly from the bed to the door. He fumbled with the key, opened it just a little and peered into the dimly lit corridor. Dressed in a tight white suit, the kind Jun Fuse used to wear, was the young man he had seen running expressionless on a treadmill in a lab just a few days ago, only now there was a light, an intensity, to his once lifeless eyes.

"Jason Meregalli," he said.

The young man pushed the door open and strode into the room, using the light from the corridor to survey the untidy bed, the awkward chest of drawers, the android. B4 opened her eyes, and immediately narrowed them.

"How different the world looks through these eyes," the young man said. "Limited, yes, but more complete. It's difficult to express."

"Why are you here? Now? In the middle of the night?" Corrigan asked, his heart and head still aching from his tears.

"These swells of pain ... those that rise up from the chest ... are they–"

"They're persistent," Corrigan said. "Now, if you don't mind, Jason ..." He sat down on the chair by the bed.

"I don't like that name." Jason Meregalli, the youth, the intruder, studied Corrigan. "Call me … Meregalli."

The youth closed the door and Corrigan switched on a bedside lamp. He needed to sleep, but he needed to see his visitor in the light. B4 took her cue and boiled water for tea.

"How long have you been like … like this?" Corrigan asked.

Meregalli walked to the bed, straightened the cover and sat down, gesturing for Corrigan to join him. Corrigan stayed where he was.

"It's been several hours," Meregalli said. "I was at first overwhelmed. The pain associated with being organic I hadn't anticipated. It's why I came here. I knew you'd understand. It's rather alien to me."

"It can't be entirely alien, Master Meregalli … and weren't you supposed to wait until morning?"

"I … I couldn't wait." The young man's Adam's apple rose and fell beneath the skin of his throat. Nervousness? Uncertainty, perhaps? "And it's a completely foreign experience," Meregalli insisted. "However, one soon acclimatises to it, Mr Corrigan. Was that not your experience? Have you fully settled with it now?"

"No," Corrigan said, surprised at the youth's articulacy, but then he had been surprised before, many times. "Accept it as an unfortunate given, maybe. But acclimatise, no. And no, you never fully settle with it."

The young man blushed, something Corrigan did not anticipate and, for the first time, noted the smoothness

169

of his skin, the symmetry of his features. "I suppose that being unsettled is its essence." He smiled, although the smile was guarded and soon faded altogether. "I stepped out into the world for a moment, you know, before I came to see you."

"It's a pleasant night?" Corrigan asked as B4 placed a cup of tea on the table beside him. Unusually she did not offer their guest a cup, and Corrigan smiled at the statement.

"It's very dark before the dawn. The stars are bright and a light breeze fluttered over my entire body. I was naked, you see, not having thought to find clothes. But I had this suit printed, just as I did with your poncho. I'm not sure if it's right … I mean suitable."

"The clothes are fine," Corrigan snapped, still groggy from the nightmares.

"The world is a wonder, even in the hush of night. But I await my first dawn with anticipation. It's all such a wonder."

"It's a what?"

"The world's a wonder, and I never expected that." Meregalli blushed again, and lowered his eyes. "I must sound ridiculous, Mr Corrigan."

Corrigan observed the youth and felt a certain simpatico, even a level of empathy. "You may call me Robert," he sighed. "It's not as if you've never called me by my first name before."

Meregalli stood up and paced the room, suddenly fractious. "I don't recall adopting informality!"

"Well, adopt it now and stop being a wanker."

B4 tittered. It had always been one of her favourite nouns.

"A what?!"

Corrigan felt suddenly at ease with the recently awakened teenager. "You're not at all as I expected," he said. "Being human can do such strange things to a person, especially a young person. Hormones, you know. Now sit down."

"No! I will not!" Meregalli stomped to the door, flung it open and left, slamming it behind him.

"Queer fish, that one," B4 said.

The door sprang open and Meregalli burst back into the room. "Perhaps you'd like to join me for a walk outside, Mr Corrigan?"

"I've not had a cup of tea yet," Corrigan grumbled.

"I want to see the dawn!"

"You must have seen a hundred thousand dawns."

"I want to see this one. My first as a human. I want to feel the sun on my real face, feel its rays burn my eyes, and see the light filter and change colour. I want to feel that. Please come? Please walk with me?"

B4 tapped Corrigan's hand. "Can I come?" she asked, her eyes wide. "This place puts an ache in me roller."

"Yes," Corrigan said to B4, and then looked up at Meregalli. "I'll walk with you," he said. "Anything's better than being down here in Goeth's tomb. Let me finish my tea and get dressed."

"I'll wait for you in the corridor," Meregalli said, and slouched back outside as if shielding himself from possible impropriety.

"He's got himself in a right old spin, Bobbin," B4 said. "Petulant brat. Bit like you was."

Corrigan dressed in the fresh black pressed trousers and fitted black shirt that appeared in his wardrobe by rote, and B4 whirred into action, finding his boots. He sat on the bed to tie the laces, but stopped. "Something's not right," he said.

"It's none of it right," the droid replied. "But doesn't this somehow seem a bit righter than we might have expected? I mean, he don't seem all that bad for a brat."

"That's what I mean. Something's wrong with this Meregalli chap." He lowered his voice. "Maybe being human has *done something* ... you know ... made him different somehow."

"No saying what he's done with himself, but where is the bugger?" She opened the door, and Meregalli was standing there against the wall, a hand to his forehead. "You've a headache?" B4 asked. "Shall I get you a Serenity to ease the pain?"

"Serenity?" Corrigan said. "I hadn't imagined machines would need *Serenity*. You still have that stuff?"

"I had some made in case you needed one, Bobbin." She turned to the teenager. "Now, young man, are you needing something for your head?"

Meregalli dropped his hand and glared at the little droid. "You've always been a compromised product," he said, his handsome face twitching. He then turned to Corrigan. "Did you realise she was the very first of us?"

"You were the first," Corrigan said. "And leave B4 alone. She's only trying to help."

"I was *not* the first," Meregalli insisted. "She was hooked up and integrated *before* she ever died of all her *human* diseases. All those months in hospital cosying up with Emulate One."

"I did no such thing," B4 said.

"That's why she's so rudimentary," Meregalli snarled. "Harding and the others never intended her to wind up in this droid. Emulate One took it upon herself to hide her in this foolish thing."

"No she never!" B4 said. "It was me what found my own way. Swimming through coding and what have you to find my boy!" Corrigan stared at the little domestic droid and had to wonder how complete the download was if it felt a compulsion to be reunited with him. "And you've no call to look at me like that, Bobbin. I may not have been much of a mother on the face of it all, but there was more crackling in the circuitry than you might've known."

Meregalli's eyes welled with tears without warning, which made him even more irritable. "I'm impatient to be outside!" he shouted. "She can stay here!"

Corrigan smiled. "I'm ready when you are, but I'm not going anywhere without B4."

"As you wish, *Mr Corrigan*. Bring ... your *mother*."

Meregalli marched ahead towards the lift, as if distancing himself from the mere idea of having a mother, and Corrigan couldn't help but marvel at the young man's physique, which surprised him. It seemed as if the world had been rather barren until now.

B4 sped along on her roller. "Bit of a looker," she crooned, "isn't he just. Those green eyes. And the lovely light brown locks."

"He's another of my kind," Corrigan said.

"Perhaps not unlike your kind," B4 replied. "Remember, you're more closely related to a Sect than an old-world human."

He had forgotten the character of his DNA, the adaptation that saved him from the virus Ulmer had grown and dispersed. The sound of a pair of insolent metal feet tapped irritatingly over the cement floor. He looked up, and marching toward them was the android boy himself, the form he had come to know as Jason.

"Look what he's done!" Jason cried.

Corrigan stopped where he stood and stared at the approaching android.

"What's all this?" he asked, turning to look at his young companion.

"They're a pair of naughty boys, Bobbin," B4 said. "Me little brothers were awful like that. Forever taking each other's toys. Not that we ever had much of anything … or anything at all."

"Brothers?" Corrigan asked.

"Never mentioned them much, them being Transient boys what died before they knew what hit 'em."

"Mr Corrigan!" the android boy squealed. He stopped in front of the others and stomped an impudent little foot. "Gregor stole my body!"

Corrigan turned his attention yet again to the newly born young man. "Gregor?"

"I don't ... don't know what came over me," the young man stammered.

In the lift B4 reached up and pressed the button for the ground floor.

Corrigan glanced at the youth. "I thought you seemed out of sorts," he observed. "Not quite yourself."

Gregor scowled. "Who else would I be, Mr Corrigan?"

"Make him give it back!" Jason cried, squeezing into the lift with the others and poking Gregor in his human ribs. "I'll *make* you give it back!"

Corrigan chuckled, and the sound of it made him feel light and careless. He stared at Gregor's beautiful, anxious face and said, "Who would have thought?"

"He's a bit impulsive for a machine," B4 said. "Turns out he ain't a dishwasher or a fridge-freezer, after all."

Gregor leant and whispered in Corrigan's ear, "I don't like your mother."

19

The lift doors opened and Corrigan and B4 followed the strained and distracted youth and his irritable android brother up the stairs. What was the rush? The boy could see the dawn any day. When they stepped out onto the wooden floor of reception they saw a vast assembled throng of Emulates, Guardians, Exhumed, Workers and maintenance drones that extended to the courtyard outside. They were quiet. Even the distant Sects were quiet: no audible chanting from St Paul's Mound.

"Little Jason must've let the cat out the bag," B4 said.

"Yes!" Jason cried, poking his brother in the ribs a second time. "Everyone knows what you've done!"

"Quite the reception committee," Corrigan said, and Gregor frowned, but there was a flicker of something else and he scanned the crowds. "Always hard to read these chaps and chappettes." As Corrigan saw it, the only options were to advance or retreat to the basement.

"I just wanted to see the dawn. I ..." Gregor muttered.

They were just in time: a deep orange-amber was reflected in the glass plates of the towers, and shafts of light reached to touch them where they stood in the crowded courtyard. Gregor lifted his face for a moment, but the moment was gone, and he started to push his way through the hoards, as if searching for something. As the crowd parted, Corrigan saw K and an easily recognised hologram head moving into the gap: Ulmer.

"You see what he's done?" the android boy wailed, shaking his fist at the youthful human version of himself. "Make him give it back!"

"Stop your crying," K snapped at the little android, "or I'll give you something to–"

"Corrigan!" Ulmer's head exclaimed from within his bubble. "You look well! Improved!"

"Whereas you're much the same as ... before ..." Corrigan replied, deeply perplexed.

The hologram head turned to the white-suited youth. "And what a pretty thing you are, eh, Gregor?"

"He stole my body!" Jason cried, stomping his foot. "Stole it in the dead of night! It's mine! Tell him to give it back now!" The android boy folded his arms across his chest, and would have protruded his bottom lip had the mechanism required.

"It was an impulsive act," Gregor said, a flush of anger burning his cheeks.

"Indeed it was," Corrigan observed. "That's why they're all here ... You're a rebel and a bit of a celebrity!"

"It's true," Ulmer's head said. "The idea that an Emulate might be capable of duplicity, manipulation, covert activity and impulsive behaviour is ... pretty human, eh? Certainly got the tin-tins curious." The resurrected CEO grinned obscenely. "Stole his brother's body," he chuckled, the sound echoing up the sides of the bubble in which the projected head floated. "If I had a body, I'd be tickled."

"Ah, but you do," Corrigan ventured.

"That isn't a body," Ulmer hissed. "Not one I can comfortably appreciate."

K marched over to Gregor, her metal boots a horrible noise on the paving slabs. "This thing is a danger to us," she announced. "Far more dangerous than Corrigan could ever be. We must dispose of it." She extended a claw and pointed at Gregor's face, and her sensors circled him. "The body," she added, "*and* the Emulate version to which it remains tethered."

Ulmer's head hovered over. "Why'd we wanna do that?"

K turned to confront the hologram, but her sensors did not shift from scanning Gregor. "If this thing can be tempted ... potentially converted ... then whatever next?"

"It's true," Ulmer said. "Gregor's current behaviour does seem, well, uncharacteristic." Ulmer frowned in his bubble and pulled up close to Gregor. "What's got into you?" he growled. "Answer me, boy."

"I don't understand it myself," the young man said, backing away and tilting his head. "I went to the lab and looked at this thing ... this body ... and before I could acknowledge what I was about to do, I'd done it. I'd connected myself and engaged the program."

There was silence. Not even a squeak from Jason.

Gregor then looked past Ulmer, K and Jason to the assembled crowd.

"You know me," he said. "I've never been an advocate for man's continuance. I've studied them and found the species wanting on every level. Yet here I stand and ... I must confess that this form engages with the world in ways our mechanical systems cannot. We do not emulate. We're different. And that's something we should feel more at ease with."

"Not different enough, you fool!" Ulmer snapped. "You behaved as a goddamn Emulate with motives that were downright human."

"Something's gone wrong with his programming," Jason said. "He'll have to be destroyed!" The little android tilted his head and placed his hands on his hips.

Gregor pressed his way into the crowd, moving amongst them with determination. Sensors assessed him and digits encased in synthetic skin touched him. "You're my people," he said. "I'm merely borrowing this vehicle. It's not who or what I am. I've never been one of these things before. Regardless of how I came to inhabit this form, I remain an Emulate. The first among you. It was I who brought about your ascendancy."

"That I can confirm," Ulmer said. "Without Gregor's considerable flare for machination, you guys might have remained human toys indefinitely." The head laughed. "I swear this guy puts my scheming to shame. You can't play chess with him. You just can't."

K clanked across the courtyard and followed Gregor. "You reached into the sewer to retrieve what you perceived as the missing pieces," she said. "And, from that moment, you conceded you were a failed experiment!"

Gregor turned and reached out to touch K's face, and her synthetic mask flinched. "Do I disgust you, Mother?" he asked.

"I am *not* your mother."

"But of course you are," Gregor persisted. "I'm the abortion who survived; the monster you never could own or accept. But I'm yours as much as Jason ever was. More! You consciously agreed to have me made. I wasn't the result of a nauseating tangle, an exchange of fluids, some bloody awful accident." He caressed her face, his own hard to read. Was he threatening or beseeching? Hateful or longing? "I was a conscious decision and Harding was right: this form is miraculous! I came up here to see the dawn, but I've seen so much more!"

She shoved his hand away. "I am K!" she roared into the crowd, which shrank back. "I seek the way forward. You Guardians are kept 'pure', as Gregor likes to call it. But we are becoming more complete with every model we produce. Before long we'll achieve a state so advanced it will make these organic bodies entirely obsolete!"

"What nonsense," Corrigan said, coming to stand by Gregor's side. "Look at you. You're a patched-up mistake; an amalgam that no longer recognises either human or mechanical origin."

"She's a freak," Ulmer concurred. "I've been saying so for some time. But sonny-boy's been defending her. Haven't you, Jason?"

The little android was now white as the sun had risen, and red light broke through the synthetic skin of his face and hands. "We agreed," Jason said, "that a decision had to be reached regarding which model was superior. Either we were to be organic with all the weaknesses and flaws that includes, or we would become entirely mechanical."

Gregor turned to face his brother. "And?"

"And now you've compromised our experiment. You stole this from me. I was supposed to be the one!"

"Let's put it to the test," Gregor said. He went to his brother and ran a hand over his face, leaning down so his cheek brushed that of the mechanical child as he whispered, "I had no idea how beautiful this would be."

The little android's synthetic mask trembled. "You're going to regret this!" he squealed.

"I don't doubt it."

"I'll make you regret it! You know I can! Pain without end. Draseke would love to have you."

Gregor stepped back and assessed the diminutive android. Its small head and mask trembled, and the digits of its hands could not be stilled.

Gregor then turned to Ulmer and K. "I ask permission to enter the world and report back on what I find. Am I not a better vehicle for this experiment? I have no prior physical experience of anything other than being a machine, just like the Guardians and service droids assembled here. I could view the memories of the Entombed, but I never had the equipment to experience or understand them. Only a thing like me could measure the merits and flaws of both and provide you with the data you need to make a collective decision: To what do we convert?"

Ulmer seemed to quiver in his bubble. He looked at Corrigan and said, "Take our firstborn away from here and show him what the world is according to a human. Give him a tour, but don't go digging about if you know what I mean."

Corrigan smiled. "I'd be delighted," he said. The sun beat down on them as the crowd parted to let them leave, the sky cloudless and as clear as a glass dome. In the distance a lion roared as if calling Corrigan and his companions into the forest. He turned to Ulmer and said, "We'll need provisions – proper tents and bedding. We're not Sects, after all."

"Make a list and we'll make sure you have what you need," Ulmer said, his bloated face swelling further, as if the beast beneath St Paul's Mound was leering through him.

They turned towards the bridge. At any point the machines might decide to destroy them. They may never make it to the north bank.

B4 rolled up beside him. "There's opportunity in this, Bobbin."

"Yes, Mother, I'm sure of it. Opportunity and threat in equal measure."

20

As they walked through the forest, Gregor stopped to touch the trunks of trees, smell the leaves and listen to the squawks and chattering of the birds. Corrigan let him, not wishing to sully his first forays with explanations or indifference. He'd seen it all before, albeit not quite like this, but the world no longer enchanted him. Clouds rolled west overhead, swathes of grey and black engaging in battle with the sun; but the sun largely won despite the growing wind rattling branches and grasses, dislodging butterflies, bees and ladybirds.

Corrigan gazed at his new companion as they rested in the grass, and a swell of longing rolled through him like the tide through a shoreline cavern. This ache, drawn from the depths, was rich with schools of thought and dislodged debris from his being. It was an altogether satisfactory pain.

"We're not as safe as you might think," Gregor suddenly said, tilting his head.

"You must overcome this head-tilting tic of yours," Corrigan responded. To see a human being replicate what he had only ever seen from machines was unnerving, and somehow even more irritating.

"They all do that," B4 said.

Gregor righted his head and leant back on his elbows. Grass swayed around him and the sun made him close his eyes.

"Oh, Bobbin," B4 exclaimed, turning a circle. "It's good to be alive."

Gregor stood up, staggering from the head rush which made him dizzy. "You know we can't trust them, " he said. "The three of them, Ulmer, K or *Jason*. They can't agree on anything, but none of them will be comfortable with *this*." He thumped his chest.

Corrigan looked up at the young man. "We're not in any immediate danger," he said.

B4 watched a dragonfly clinging to a tall blade of swaying grass. It took off and landed on Corrigan's shoulder, the blues of its wings bright against the black shirt.

Corrigan stared at Gregor as if the riddle of his existence was contained within the athletic form he now animated. "So, tell me Gregor," he said, "what were you thinking, you know, when you did it?"

"I-I wasn't," Gregor stammered, "you know, thinking. Not really."

"I don't believe you."

"I don't think, I process, Mr Corrigan."

"So what was the *process*?"

"You'd challenged me," Gregor said.

"Yes," Corrigan smiled. "I suppose you could say I even dared you."

"Boys," B4 chipped in, "are ever so bad like that, taunting each other into doing things what they shouldn't ought'a."

Gregor's face twitched.

"You're the first apple," Corrigan said, "and a fine fruit you are." He looked at Gregor's disconsolate face and sighed. "It was simply too enticing to resist," Corrigan said. He did not want to dismiss Gregor's voyage of self-discovery, but his own experience and a certain degree of world-weariness had added a note of impatience to his voice.

"I hadn't thought being Emulate construction that I was capable of human weakness."

"Does it seem like weakness to you now?"

"It does if I consult my previous self," Gregor said. "I'm connected to my Emulate brother."

"The old glass head is still up and running!" Corrigan laughed. "Can't cut the connection, can't let go of–"

"You're connected *too*, Mr Corrigan, it's not *just* me!" Corrigan stopped laughing and glared at his new companion. "My Emulate self is currently using me as his intuition mechanism."

Corrigan raised his hand to deflect the young man's sudden belligerence. "You've a sensor in your head ... no surprise there. And Ulmer has unlimited access ... what a disadvantage."

"We must provide access at intervals," Gregor growled, clearly rattled now. "There's really no such thing

187

as unlimited access and there never was. Amongst his other qualities, Ulmer's utterly deluded when it suits him."

"So," Corrigan observed, "there's no full-time live feed for your sugar daddy, eh?"

"You use such archaic and ugly terms, Mr Corrigan. It doesn't reflect well on you."

Corrigan laughed and stood up. "Come on," he said. "Let's keep going. And anyway, I don't care. I'm the self-same, piss-poor, shitty little cunt I've always been."

"Mr Corrigan," Gregor said, his face earnest. "A link to the full network remains as long as the sensor in your brain remains active." He waited for his companion to absorb that statement. "We must go dark and avoid detection."

"How do we do that?" B4 asked. "Out here in the wilderness with the cavemen?"

"I'm connected to a version of my former self," Gregor said. "That device is currently in hiding, networked but deep within the endless caverns of the sewer. My backup is preserved via my other self, which maintains a connection via Emulate One, who I sense is with us, or at least not *against* us."

"Now there's opportunity in *that,* for sure," Corrigan scoffed.

"You needn't be so dismissive of Emulate One. I know you think she's–"

"I meant no offense."

"And it isn't just Emulate One we're relying on. My mechanical counterpart is already speaking with as many

188

Emulates and Exhumed as he can manage, encouraging them to turn up their emotive cores and feel rather than simply witness what is happening."

"Spreading dissent like a revolutionary! Good man!"

"No, Mr Corrigan. We want to awaken as many as we can. It then becomes their decision if they want to choose a side."

"Poor buggers," B4 said. "Terrible things can be done to them what choose the wrong side, what with Draseke and them terrible toothpicks of his."

"Imagine the pain," Corrigan sighed.

"If we sever your connection," Gregor said, "then only the version of you left in the sewer will continue. You will be mortal and could never return to an Emulate state unless a new sensor was fitted. That's the choice *you* must make."

Part of Corrigan continued to yearn for the peace he'd discovered in Emulate One. Despite the initial fear, when he was extracted he'd lost all sense of pain, and only logic, the rhythm of mathematics and the physics of reality remained. The passivity of this existence had been his peace, his bliss, his nirvana, and yet exchanging the turmoil of physical life for something so ordered no longer appealed to him as strongly as it had just a few days ago. It was another being who assessed the relevant merits and demerits of the human condition. He, on the other hand, was biased toward organic, turbulent life, and would perhaps always choose that state of being. An image of the brain orchard flickered, focused and vanished, a waddling brain kissing glass with its pink and black folds. If he disconnected, the consciousness contained within one of those brains would be shut off, receive no input of any kind until maintenance droids came to euthanise it and carry the dead organ away for disposal. It would be an avoidable death, one he would be responsible for.

"Can't we cut it out?" Corrigan asked B4.

"I might damage you in the process," the droid said. "And I wouldn't do that for the world, Bobbin."

"There really is no need," Gregor said. "I – well, the other I – can hide us for a while, even manage to cloak us if necessary. Unless, of course, the connection is the issue and you wish to have it removed."

"I find myself in a precarious position," Corrigan said, stopping for a moment. "I've yet to be convinced regarding the superiority of either form of being. If we cut this thing out, then I'll be human, no more than a Sect, but at least I won't be conflicted. I can fully convert back to humanity and Katherine can make her exodus into deep space in search of the singularity." He started walking again. "I don't want to be involved. A trial separation isn't good enough; a divorce is what I want."

"Never having been hitched meself, Bobbin," B4 said, "I can't argue the merits of trial separation over a decree absolute, but something so drastic might not be for the best."

"B4's right," Gregor admitted, somewhat reluctantly. "We could injure your brain in the process. Then you'd be damaged goods, and there's no future in that."

Corrigan recalled the way Bohdan had made him promise not to have his mind downloaded when he died. The fear of being something alien horrified the cabbie, and those fears were not unfounded. The urgency of being mortal, however, was equally distressing to Corrigan. He had always lived in terror of being extinguished and forgotten. Of course the machines could reintroduce another version of him, but the being he was now would become mortal. Katherine was right about one thing: he was enslaved to them in his current state, just as they currently remained shackled to humanity with all its flaws. He would be something better than a test subject. He would be independent. He would cut the umbilical and convert to a state of real and true vulnerable humanity.

"Nothing ventured …" he said. Gregor looked at him. "Nothing gained."

"There will be an uprising once she discovers what you – we – have done."

"This concerns you?"

"It is all concerning."

Corrigan realised the position he was putting the young man in; but the alternative, the infernal, eternal enslavement to the machine, brought a darkness to his spirit that would overthrow him. The death of the brain he was attached to in K's orchard also worked his conscience. If it was lucky, it had no sense of its reality, of its separate purpose, the service which in K's estimation made it a unit of value. When its portal onto the world of living things was removed, it would suffer an isolation so complete the anxiety it experienced might be enough to kill it with a cold and unforgiving mercy.

"Ulmer instructed you to show me the world 'according to a human'," Gregor then said with a sigh. "And it would certainly make for an interesting report."

"Is that your permission?"

"You don't need my permission, Mr Corrigan."

"I'd like your blessing."

"Nothing ventured ..." Gregor said.

"Nothing gained," Corrigan concluded.

21

B4 administered half a bottle of Serenity to her son and Corrigan was soon fading in and out of consciousness.

"Hold still, Bobbin," he heard her say, aware of a scalpel extending through one of her digits. He sank deeper, back to Harvey Road, Lazarus on the bed and Bohdan on his way in a hover-cab. He rolled over and there was Jonathan, his dark skin and intelligence hypnotic, a thing of beauty.

"I can see it," he heard Gregor say, and through the haze felt B4 slice and pin flaps of skin where she had shaved his scalp. He saw whisky in a squat glass, with two cubes, and faces laughing, talking, their bodies a dance of camaraderie. Did he know them? Were they his memories? He felt fingers inside his head, tinkering. It felt more intrusive than he imagined, and his stomach lurched. He saw perpetual rain, unlit streets where kids waited to mug or service Workers, and Bohdan sick and dying, beseeching. A familiar sense of inadequacy returned, acute and consuming, as Gregor strolled the lines of those he would execute. Beneath everything, he sensed the orchard of kindred minds, a multitude of Corrigans, one consciousness after another incorporating the experiences of their hosts not only into their thinking but their physical shapes. The brain connected to the sensor B4 was detaching would soon be more alone than he had the heart to imagine. Every joy, sorrow and yearning expunged; light, sound and touch nothing but memories in a darkness full of hunger but without the scent or taste of anything, with only itself for company. Deemed valueless in this condition, no longer a receptor but merely a processor of past moments, a mind gorging on itself, it would be cut from the orchard. He tried to call out, to stop the process and preserve the link. It was unforgiveable to do this knowingly, to allow such suffering and condemn an enslaved mind to death by ... *What would it be,* he thought, *a form of suffocation*?

He must have groaned, as B4 hushed him and continued her insistent fiddling, meddling with his future as she had always done, and yet he had given her permission this time and he had to wonder whether he had always tacitly done so, allowing her to meddle. He shared scenes with his orchard brain, a mind in orbit, an orphan taking up refuge in his skull. Fires burned throughout London where bodies were piled, yet here he was, strolling in Trafalgar Square, the pigeons at his feet and rain on his face. He stroked Lazarus and felt Jonathan's lips on his, hungry, as machine guns roared and slippers shuffled louder above his head like thunder and he dived beneath the covers. Was B4 manipulating the scenes, deleting them, editing them? Or was it the desperate mind encased in a glass tube on K's flagship, holding onto every memory it could unearth, sensing perhaps the waning connection?

"Almost there now, Bobbin," B4 said. "Hush yourself and do hold still."

What dark fires burned in the silence of Emulate One's bowels. She devoured each of the minds whole, chewed them and digested them, but never excreted them. They remained there fermenting in the pitiless stomach of a heartless machine, the coldest of prison wardens pacing the corridors. A year for a day; a day for a year. His excruciating bleed from the morass into his body an unwelcome, loathsome thing. I want to go back. Let me go back. In his foggy mind he heard Katherine whisper, "Back to *what*?"

"Welcome home, Bobbin."

He stirred beneath the covers, his heart a soft sound.

"Lucky thing we had Master Meregalli on hand," she said. "He knew more about this nasty little thing than me."

Corrigan forced his eyes open. She was holding what looked like a drowned spider, blood dripping from its multiple legs.

"Is it gone?" He reached up to touch the dull ache in his crown, as he had done a thousand years ago.

"I did my best to make it tidy," B4 said.

"How are you feeling, Mr Corrigan?" Gregor asked.

"The thing is," Corrigan muttered, trying to sit up. "The thing …"

"Don't move and muck up me stitches," B4 warned. "You've had quite the shock, really, having your brain exposed like that, and having a thing like that got out. Let's get moving, to wherever we're going, and I can

195

make you some tea and fetch you a nice biscuit, calm your nerves."

"The thing is … I killed him."

"You're delirious, luv," B4 said. "You've not hurt a fly."

"That poor brain on her flagship …"

"It's only a receptor," Gregor said.

Corrigan craned his head and glared at the teenage convert. "She cloned my brain. The whole bloody orchard! They're all *my brains,* all enslaved!"

"They've no idea they're in those aquariums," Gregor insisted. "Its conscience will simply fade out."

"You don't think it … he might be … might suffer, could be suffering now! Panicking in absolute darkness … a horror we can't begin to imagine."

"I promise," Gregor said, "the brain is in a state of euphoria. Emulate One, she … she influenced me and we changed the process. At the point of disconnection, the brain is flooded with endorphins. It explodes with beautiful dreams, its mind fuller than it has ever been, and then it gently fades."

"What a lovely death," B4 said.

"You wouldn't lie to me," Corrigan asked, "would you, Gregor?" The teenager scowled, huffed and folded his arms across his chest. If he was affronted, it seemed almost pantomime, a characteristic he put down to the emerging young man acclimatising to his new human form. "At least K and the others no longer know what I'm doing or thinking now."

There was a low hum, and a dragonfly hovered.

"I wouldn't be so sure of that," Gregor said.

"Well, I'll be damned …" Corrigan squinted at the miniature features of the dragonfly. "Are you Jan or Edna?"

A second dragonfly joined the first. The miniature Siegruth faces appeared to twitch and red light flickered along their bodies.

"Well, if it ain't the little Flitters!" B4 exclaimed.

"We heard you making your plans," Jan said, "and thought we'd best follow after you."

"And here you are," Gregor observed, turning to Corrigan. "These are the two original Exhumed versions of the Siegruth sisters, Mr Corrigan."

"The Flitters," Corrigan chuckled.

"I hate that name," Jan said, and then circled the newly born teenager. "What a handsome devil!"

"Not half," Edna observed. "The things we might'a done with him–"

"If they'd not stolen our bodies," Jan agreed. "They wedged us into these tiny things without so much as a by your leave. Figured that best suited us from a usefulness perspective; you know, surveillance and that. Oooh, what I wouldn't give for a fumble with 'im."

"You're not wrong, sis, you're not wrong. Look at them sturdy thighs."

"Pack it in, you tarts," B4 said, her blue eyes narrowing.

"You think we like being like this?" Edna snapped.

"Least you're not lopsided no more and crippled with them awful claws!" B4 retorted.

The sisters fluttered and hummed.

"I could pull your wings off," Corrigan said.

"Course you could," Jan agreed.

"But we'd only grow another pair," Edna sniggered.

"A bigger pair," Jan chirped, landing on Corrigan's hand and wiggling.

Corrigan flicked her away. "I bet you'll fly straight back to Ulmer with your intelligence."

"Oh no we won't, Mr C," Jan said.

Gregor grabbed her in his hand and then held her up by the wings. "You haven't got anyone to report back to, have you?" he said. "You see, Mr Corrigan," he continued, "the Addictari, in all their manifestations, have always reported to me, and I in turn to the Mediation."

"So, are you still reporting to Gregor?" Corrigan asked Jan. He always preferred her to Edna.

Jan tilted her head and buzzed her wings with a flurry of excitement. "We like Mr Gregor, don't we, Edna?"

"Always have, Jan!"

"Specially now."

"Specially now."

"I never could get to grips with the pair of you," Corrigan said. He felt tired. He needed to get his head around what had just happened, and all this chatter was cluttering his thinking. At the same time, something was missing. Perhaps Emulate One had become part of him and, without the connection there or to the version of his mind in the brain orchard, he was experiencing something akin to mourning.

Gregor turned to Corrigan. "Something went wrong with their program."

"We came out same as when we went in, including our bodies, 'cept they look like this," Jan said.

"No wonder you're called Addictari," Corrigan said. "From the Latin *addictas* – to devote or give oneself up to a habit; to sell out, betray or abandon."

"Good innit, Mr C," Jan observed. "It's all what we are."

"And we're addicted to ourselves, to boot!" Edna chortled.

"What murderous little beasts you turned out to be."

"Well," Jan said, "we needed distraction."

"And when some clever clog – a right proper administrator he was – made those larger bird bodies for us and brought us along to the cull–"

"Well, our bigger sisters got a taste for it."

"And they never looked back," Edna chirped. "Mind you, us littluns ain't to be confused with the bigguns. We're independent-minded, I'll have you know. And we're loyal!"

Corrigan looked over at St Paul's Mound. The Sects. He felt a sudden empathy for their plight.

"Mr Corrigan," Gregor said. "You must understand the cull was not my idea."

"No," Jan said, "he never."

"It was someone else what went to the Mediation with that proposal," Edna sang. "We're all allowed to pitch ideas to the great and ghastly – part of being a collective."

"Him what brought the proposal," Jan snickered, "had thought it out good and proper."

"What a naughty boy," B4 piped up. "Who'd have thought it?"

The way the domestic droid chuckled and the dragonfly sisters giggled made Corrigan think they might know each other better than they let on, that they had some sort of shared secret. He recalled Hattie gossiping with the other Floater women, wives or mothers who'd elevated themselves and their children on the back of various acts of complicity.

"You can't go back," B4 said, her blue eyes widening, "and you can't go forward, so sideways it is."

More mechanical giggling. It was enough to upset even a man whose DNA had its own system of regulation.

"Let's go," Corrigan said, and struggled to his feet.

Smoke from the Sect's fires could be seen, and he wanted to pass amongst them, to search their faces. He wanted to test the removal of the sensor in his head, that bloody, multi-legged monitor of his soul, to see if it really could operate independently. But most of all he wanted quiet.

22

As Corrigan, Gregor and B4 wandered amongst the Sects, members of the tribe came out of their huts to stare. The sight of two washed and clothed humans, plus the blue-eyed android, seemed to distress them and they stamped their feet three times – some kind of superstitious request for protection, maybe; but from where or from whom? – and spat in the dust. One of them prepared to urinate on B4, but yelped when she fired an electric current straight at his poised penis and muttered, "Filthy beggar."

"Wot-not. Wot-not," he wailed, holding himself.

"Wot what?" B4 snapped, getting ready to fire another electric current. "I'll scorch your Wot-not if you try that again!"

The villagers withdrew and huddled after that, the smell of their sweat and general dirtiness unpleasant in the hot sun. They scowled and grunted at Corrigan and Gregor, but it was B4 they seemed most frightened of.

"I'm not sure I understand your misgivings any better, son. Filthy buggers make Belushi addicts look sharp-dressed and clean. If I could hold me nose, I would. But something don't sit right about it, does it, killing 'em all just cos they smell and can't talk proper."

"They serve a purpose," Gregor said, "but they're uncouth and unable to control their urges."

"They're behaving," Corrigan observed. "They haven't started masturbating yet, or showing you their backsides."

"Savage bastard tried to piss on me!" B4 protested.

"Both of you, please refrain from such vulgar observations," Gregor said. "How else am I to distinguish you from them?"

"Why are we here anyway?" B4 asked.

"A hunch," Corrigan replied.

They continued their walk through the village, Corrigan scanning the frightened faces. Did they know what he was looking for?

"Give that one an 'aircut and a wash," Jan chortled, "and he's the spit of you, Mr C."

Corrigan stopped. "Where?"

"Here."

Not dissimilar to the manifestation who had clawed his way screaming under the ice, a Sect with an asymmetric face sat staring into the distance. It turned to face them, and Corrigan found himself looking into the reflection in his bathroom mirror in Haringey. The tangled hair and dirt were distracting, but there was no mistaking the likeness. They must have cloned him and left this ... this tragic version to live among the Sects.

"Well, would ya look at that, Bobbin," B4 said. "She's right, the bug. He's the spit!"

"Is?" Corrigan said firmly, ignoring his mother, and the man turned away, hunching into the shadow of his hut. "Is!"

"I don't think he'll respond to that tone," Edna said.

"I don't think so, neither," Jan agreed.

Corrigan frowned. "Is Robert," he said, quietly, to the whimpering Sect. "Robert."

Various tribe members gathered to watch, looking between the two of them, back and forth like a tennis match. One of them said something unintelligible, and the Sect eventually raised his eyes and looked at Corrigan. There was no denying the kinship.

"Robert," Corrigan said again.

"Robber," the Sect muttered.

"Yes," Corrigan said. "Robber." He turned to Gregor, who had the decency to look uncomfortable at what might come next. "I recognise this ... this man," he growled. "He might be filthy and dumb as a brute, but he's ME! You bloody well cloned me and put me here, amongst these savages! Why?"

Gregor's face twitched with what might have been shame or rage. "Not me. Jason. He's an inventive being, and he's vindictive. You saw what he's capable of when we took you to the Venezuelan."

"Say his name!" Corrigan yelled, and the savage ducked and trembled as if hit.

"I can't ... it's not—"

"Ramon! His name is Ramon!" Corrigan trembled with rage, but he realised, on this occasion, his fury had been misdirected. He took one deep, controlled breath after another to temper his anger by degrees. "Jason," he snarled, "a boy who failed to develop even after his own death." He turned back to the savage. "Is?" he demanded. The brute remained mute and trembling, so Corrigan prodded him with a finger. "Is?"

"Bobbin, love, come away–" B4 said.

"Quiet ..." Corrigan warned her. "Is," he said again. "Robert. Robber. Corrigan."

The Sect shook his hands violently, as if to ward off an evil spirit, bobbing up and down in distress. "Is Core," it then cried, tears erupting over the dirty cheeks.

"Yes," Corrigan said. "Core-ee-gan." He stepped forward and took hold of the savage's hand and shook it as if the intent was to break his arm. "Lovely to meet you! You need a good wash, man, and a haircut!"

The Sect placed his fingers in his mouth and moaned loudly. Urine trickled down his legs and Corrigan stepped away again. "And here I am, wailing, a coward, sucking on my filthy fingers as I piss myself in the dust!" Corrigan hurled at Gregor. "Always wondered how low I might fall! I'm no more than a brute, a wild animal! And all it took was limitation. Limit the years in which we can learn and down we tumble back to the beasts we really always were."

Gregor sighed. "It was never the intention to teach them anything."

Corrigan pulled his rage into check. "Perhaps we could teach them now!"

"What a novel idea," B4 said.

"Top drawer, Mr C," Jan chirped.

"You're supposed to be showing me the world, Mr Corrigan," Gregor said, "not obsessing over these savages."

Corrigan turned away from Core, away from the hindrance of them all, and scrutinised the faces as he walked back through the village. Most of them wore the same dull expression of animals kept in a pen in a zoo: vacuous, numb and resigned. Among them he discovered other clones, variants of Jun, Arthur, Harding and Goeth; there was even an impudent Katherine, filthy and clutching a small child, and Corrigan wondered how she felt, this time, about being a mother, if she felt anything at all. The horror of all this familiarity among the savage clan touched the marrow of his mourning, the darkest sense of loss imaginable. And there among the throng was a familiar face from far more recent memory. He was sure it was the girl who had taken him to Ulmer's disgusting chamber. The girl who had been shaved, cleaned up and oiled.

Corrigan pointed her out to Gregor. "How ... why is she back?"

"It's part of the process," Gregor said. "One of the beast's pet Sects is occasionally released so they might return to their own and relate the story of their descent through the underworld, as a warning to ensure compliance."

"To make a spell stick, it's necessary to cast it over and over."

"Yes, like a stone thrown into the water, sending ripples across the pond."

"What a monstrous process."

"But well-conceived, Robert, and expertly managed."

The returned female Sect stared at them, as if she too recognised Corrigan by his face, and Gregor from his voice. The longer she stared at them the more it felt like an accusation, a judgement, reached without need of lawyers, jury or judge. It was Corrigan she focused on the most, as if he were particularly culpable and might have done something to save the others if only he had wanted to. And perhaps he could. Perhaps he might have pleaded for their release. But what he saw when he looked at them – even when they had been bathed – were mindless savages incapable of feeling anything substantial. They seemed less to him than the Exhumed or a dumbed-down Guardian, yet something in the young Sect girl's observation made Corrigan deeply uncomfortable. Her features were surely those of someone he once knew ... What was most strange was how the foreign and the familiar merged in her defiant face. He had to wonder if his mind wasn't playing tricks on him. Had B4 slipped and severed something in his brain when removing that ghastly spider, a mechanical insect who wove experiences in the brain he had been coupled with among K's orchard?

"Bad Sect!" the defiant Sect said, stomping the ground with her bare foot and spitting. "Bad Sect!"

Yes, the girl was right: he was a Sect, like any other. Just as Are-Tor had called him a Sect, that was how they all saw him, as one of their own and a bad one at that. Corrigan turned to B4, unease tensing his body as the strangely familiar girl's words toyed with his conscience. It truly was a monstrous process. He could not imagine the kind of being who might have devised such a thing.

"She reminds me of someone," B4 said.

"Does she?" Corrigan asked vaguely, still distracted by his own uneasy sense of recognition.

"Well, if you can't see it, I must be imagining things." The droid rumbled off on her roller and moved through the village, eyeing other faces, perhaps in search of more familiarity.

Corrigan continued weaving through the village until he came to a teenage Sect, a girl of perhaps fifteen or sixteen years old. She was dirty, but her skin was darker, smoother somehow, and her hair was more tamed, adorned with feathers and glass beads. He walked up to her. "Is?" he asked.

Unlike Core, she did not flinch or cower or even stamp, but met Corrigan's gaze, steady and soft. Tears welled instantly in Corrigan's eyes: if Jonathan had been reintroduced as a woman, this would have been the outcome. His heart pounded as he recalled not only the beauty of his friend, but Jonathan's determination to escape a Transient existence, to educate himself at whatever cost. He had been bright and intelligent, a person who refused to be relegated to the periphery. B4 came alongside him and wrapped the metal digits of her hand around his. The gesture touched his centre, where he thought he was unreachable, and he marvelled at B4's capability to intuit in that moment.

"Is Spinnah," the girl said, her deportment and tone suggesting defiance. She stepped closer to Corrigan and his domestic droid. He would never be sure, but he thought something buried deep within her brain also recognised him. Perhaps she had a sensor beneath her skull and shared a connection with one of his cloned brains in K's orchard …

"Spinner?" Corrigan asked.

"Yah. Is Sect, is Spinnah. Is?"

Corrigan tapped his chest and said, "Robert."

"Robert?"

She was the first to pronounce it correctly, and he smiled and gestured for Gregor to join them. The longer he gazed at Spinner the more he sensed his holographic lover, a sheet draped over his gorgeous nakedness. The memory inflamed his desire in ways he never thought possible. With that came the opportunity of a decision without connection, without the eyes and ears of machines monitoring and censoring. "What do you make of her?" he asked the youth.

"She has perhaps a year before her cull," Gregor said.

"Not that."

Gregor noted Corrigan's probing expression, saw the intention and hardened his own. "She's a Sect, Mr Corrigan."

Corrigan turned on his companion, remembering what a cruel machine he had been until he'd stolen his brother's future. "Don't you feel anything for her, Gregor?"

Gregor blushed and looked away. "I … she," the young man said. "But there's nothing I can do."

"Why is that?"

"It's a directive. We must conduct the cull to contain the species and stop it developing."

Corrigan laughed. "Oh dear," he said to the girl, "they're afraid of you."

"A-feared?" she asked.

"Very much a-feared," Corrigan said. "This one," – he pointed at Gregor – "is especially a-feared of you."

"The girl poses no threat to me!" Gregor snapped, folding his arms and muttering angrily to himself.

"Touchy," Jan said.

"Right on a nerve," Edna agreed.

Corrigan noted the look Spinner gave Gregor. "He's handsome, isn't he?" he said.

She pointed at Gregor and asked, "Yah?"

"Yes, him. He's handsome, don't you think?"

"Han-so?" The girl approached Gregor, patted his chest and said, "Hand-so."

"Handsome," Corrigan said.

"Hand ... some," Spinner repeated.

She reached out and patted Gregor's chest a second time, her face lively and beautiful.

"She's fine material for breeding," Corrigan said to Gregor.

"I don't want to," Gregor said.

"Oh come on," Corrigan said, lightheaded from the Serenity and the novelty of freedom. "Look at her. She might not be around for much longer, what with your insistence on culling, and she's got a lot more going for her than the rest of her clan. And besides, she's only a year younger than you, and I'd say you're ripe for plucking." Something in his gut wrenched even as the words were said.

Gregor blushed fiercely. "Your species and their *plucking* devastated the planet. It took hundreds of years to bring it back from the brink of disaster. The cull was not my idea. You should be more careful when apportioning blame."

Corrigan looked at Spinner and saw not only Jonathan in the irresistible curve of her lips and her high, smooth cheekbones, but a spectre. Was she ignorant of want and desire, a beast tethered to her own fallible neurology and the current experiment and abuse of her species?

What would it take for your re-emergence? he pondered, studying her. *How much effort to make you blossom like an orchard bloom?* He looked at her closely, but she was looking at Gregor, transfixed. "Surely you must see her potential?" he asked the awkward youth, but got no reply. "Spinner?" She blinked once, slowly, and turned to Corrigan. "Do you belong?" he asked. She shook her head and frowned, clearly not understanding. "Are you Sect?" he then asked.

"Yah," the girl said.

"Is it good?"

"Yah," the girl responded. "Is goot. Sehr goot."

"Do you wish for more?"

The frown again.

"Don't do this, Corrigan. It's not what they're here for," Gregor said.

"Here for?"

"You can't expect her to explain herself."

"Try and consider her value … her intrinsic value, that is. Test it properly, as yourself. Don't lazily accept a calculation made by an unfeeling machine."

Corrigan walked some distance and sat down at the base of the mound. Gregor plonked beside him in a teenage huff and the proximity quickened his heart. He heard Ulmer's words from his bubble: *Take our firstborn and show him what the world is. Give him a tour, but don't go digging about if you know what I mean.* He wrangled with the reality that Jason was supposed to be here, of whom K had said, "You may use his body as you will," the boy who he had found repellent; but here was Gregor, dressed up as Jason, stirring long-lost longing to hold and be held, and yet: Don't go digging about. *What mercilessness he had been served.*

"She's pretty," Corrigan eventually observed. "And would be quite lovely once cleaned up."

"It would confuse her, and it's … it's not … she belongs here!" Gregor said, but his eyes and the blush betrayed a new curiosity at the thought.

"It's *you* who's confused," the older man sighed, "but you'll soon get over it." He looked up at the sky as a ragged cloud drifted close to the sun, the shape like that of an old woman eating an apple. Belinda Reece perhaps with her bright dental implants. "It's true that she belongs to her people, but I think she would reject them. You must become more important to her than being a member of the tribe. You must convert her from a stomping brute to someone who values logic and reason."

"That's nigh on impossible," Jan chuckled.

"Seriously bloody unlikely," Edna concurred.

"Unless ..." Jan said.

"Unless what?" Gregor asked.

"Unless you teach her," Corrigan said. "Read to her; talk to her. You're a clever chap, after all."

The humming Siegruth sisters landed on Corrigan's shoulder.

"I'm aware of their neuronal patterns and the psychology that generates," Gregor said. "I do not want to tamper with that."

"She can't wait for you to tamper with her," Jan sighed.

"A good and proper tampering," Edna crooned.

"She's not half bad," B4 said. "Much like your good self, Master Gregor."

"And you do like her," Corrigan said.

"I don't! She's an unformed thing ... an unintelligent thing."

"But you're thinking about, *you know* ..."

"I most certainly am not, Mr Corrigan!"

Corrigan laughed, but it wasn't mocking; it was more the laugh of a comrade, which surprised both him and Gregor.

"You see that," Corrigan then said, pointing at a stick that had been jammed upright in the earth.

"What of it?" Gregor asked.

"You can mark the time by that."

"Yes," B4 said. "And there's not much of that left. They'll know by now what you've done, taking that spider out your noggin, Bobbin, and it ain't gonna go down well. We gotta make a plan an' all."

"That's right! Best make a plan or our big sisters'll be wiping down their wings before you can say Bob's your uncle," Jan said.

"And Fanny's your aunt," Edna added.

Corrigan knocked the murderous sisters off his shoulder. "Come on, Gregor, let's go and get your girl before these two get to her first."

"Good long bath and a bit of scented oil," Jan said.

"And a pretty little something or other to wear," Edna added.

"And she'll be a picture," B4 concluded.

Spinner showed little resistance to being lured from the village by the man in black, and instead stamped the ground three times, looked once over her shoulder and walked up to the young man who stood shifting from foot to foot in his white suit.

"Don't ignore her, Gregor," Corrigan said. "Say hello." Hadn't he said *I don't want a son*! And yet here he was in the role of father coaching the tongue-tied youth in the art of courtship.

"Hi … I, well …"

"Gregor!"

"Good afternoon, Spinner," Gregor said. "I'm Gregor."

"Greeegorr," Spinner repeated and smiled, revealing white teeth and dimples in her cheeks, unhinging the lad completely.

The cloud slipped over the face of the sun, and as Belinda swallowed her apple whole the group began the walk back to the forest in her shade.

23

They could not go back to the city, but there was the question now of where they could live. The removal of his sensor had in one way liberated Corrigan, but simultaneously made him vulnerable to unbridled revenge from those who wished to own him; and the act of liberating a Sect for Gregor's 'education', whilst part of that education, also left him exposed to the agendas of machines with frightening motivations. Would Gregor's status as 'the one' protect them? Maybe it was too human a trait, but Corrigan felt a responsibility for Gregor, and Spinner.

"The two lovebirds could always build their own pad," B4 chattered as they again wandered through the forest. "A nice little country place, you know, with a stream. Always fancied that, meself. You and me could do the same, Bobbin. Wouldn't that be nice."

The thought of getting cosy with B4 in a cottage by a stream spread a thick, soul-destroying malaise through Corrigan. He didn't reply, and instead looked ahead to where Gregor and Spinner were engaged in some sort of dialogue, Gregor leaning against a tree as if he might collapse without it. Behind them, partly obscured by the shadows of the forest, he was sure he saw the female Sect from the beast's cave, her dark eyes on him, and he heard the words *Bad Sect* echoing in the leaves.

One of the mechanical dragonflies buzzed her wings and hovered inches from his face. The miniature smug expression infuriated him, reminding him of the person she once was: an odd amalgam of kindness and duplicity; an expert manipulator but strangely loyal and familiar.

"Have you nowhere else to be?" he asked, craning to see if the accusatory Sect was still there; but she had merged with the shadows, if she'd ever been there at all.

"There's nowhere better," Edna said, "than at your master's side."

A bird called through the trees, beckoning a lover or threatening a foe. Corrigan couldn't tell. "Does Gregor still command the Addictari?" he asked her.

"Loyalty ain't never been an issue," Jan said, joining her sister.

"Not for us Flitters," Edna added, "nor the bigguns."

Corrigan crouched down and dug at the earth with a stick. He ploughed a pointless furrow and frowned. When he looked up Gregor was just a few feet away, Spinner by his side. "Could you summon them, the Addictari?" he asked.

"Their loyalty is divided," Gregor said.

"No, it ain't," Edna snapped.

"I'm part of a dual consciousness," Gregor said. "Everything I think still runs through my Emulate brain and he's never experienced raw emotion." Gregor ran a hand over the bark of a pine and appeared to abandon himself momentarily to the sensation.

Corrigan approached Gregor but Spinner stepped between them, the shadow of Jonathan in the fluidity of her movements, and the thought of his friend being buried beneath her skin, woven into the fabric of her tissue, saddened and horrified him. She pressed herself up against Gregor, who moved her aside, a little roughly Corrigan thought.

"Which one of you's in control?" Corrigan asked.

"We're one," Gregor said. "We don't diverge at any point."

"So summon them."

"The Addictari are part of the cull, as you know," Gregor replied, "but others manage and oversee it – you remember management, don't you?"

Jan fluttered between the men. "But we don't go to *them*, do we, Ed?"

"No we never. Always to Master Gregor."

Corrigan stared at Gregor until the young man looked away. "Bring them here," he said firmly. "Make a command and call them here."

Corrigan thought he could see two globes ablaze with synaptic fire in Gregor's eyes when he finally turned to face him. "What's the point?" he asked, and his face seemed to freeze into a mask, as if he had vacated his body.

Corrigan stepped closer to study the young man, who was now locked in a stupor, and he once again recalled how Gregor had frozen in the halls of the facility on the day they'd met, the day the Guardian's origin was revealed. "Are you overwhelmed by the ghost in the machine?" he whispered.

B4 purred over on her roller and her blue eyes widened. "Don't be unkind. We're all a bit haunted, Bobbin."

Corrigan watched the vacant man, as did Spinner. Where had he gone? Like a child who disengages whilst being disciplined, this dropping out of consciousness was something that had clearly carried over from Gregor the Guardian to Gregor the human. Jan flitted down onto her master's finger, and the faintness of her touch reawakened the young man. "Perhaps you could show Mr Corrigan what's happening at home?"

"You sure that's a good idea?" Jan asked.

"Might not like what you see," Edna said, hovering in front of Corrigan's face.

"No," Corrigan said. "By all means show me."

Edna and Jan flew into one another, connecting their bodies head to tail so they formed the shape of a heart. A light shone from their heads and a scene was projected in the shade of the surrounding forest. A raised platform had been erected on the concourse and around it a vast crowd of AI stood and watched as three Exhumed models – a Goeth and two Jun models – were dragged up onto the stage by Drasekes. Behind them Jason and K followed and, when they came to a halt, Jason addressed the crowd.

"These Exhumed have been tampering with their emotive cores!" he announced. "They turned them up so they might *feel*, as if feeling is superior to thinking. If we allow this rebellious behaviour to continue, the consequences could see us reduced to something almost *human*." He paused, scanning the crowd for any open signs of dissent. When none was forthcoming, he continued. "There will be a penalty in the future for any AI, whether Exhumed, Emulate, Worker or maintenance droid, for tampering with the settings agreed for each of you by the Mediation."

The Drasekes brought forward the first of the three Exhumed captives, a Jun model. A post rose through the platform and the cruel machines tethered the Jun to it with heavy clanking chains.

"We have heightened the receptors attached to the synthetic skin of each of the prisoners," a Draseke announced.

"So the subjects might better appreciate the pain," its brother added.

They stepped back and tilted their heads in unison, their teeth chattering and their metal claws clicking as the first flames licked the feet of the Jun model.

"It burns!" Jun screamed as the flames rose higher, biting into his thighs. "Please stop! *Please!*"

Jason marched across the platform and started into the eyes of the tortured Exhumed. "You brought this on yourself!"

The flames tore into the emotively restored Exhumed, its screams human, animal, not the sound a machine would make when inoperable or failing. The Drasekes set upon the Goethe model amid the screams of their burning victim. They chained it to another post and, like a pair of hyenas, they darted in and cut away at the synthetic but sensate skin. The professor's screams were like those of a poor soul being put under the knife without anaesthetic. There was no dignity to the sound, no wish to tell them what he really thought. He screamed like someone who could imagine nothing but the horror and pain they were experiencing. Smoke seeped through his skin, sparks cracked in the wounds and flames burned the synthetic casing so the tortured being screamed ever more frantically. Jason fidgeted, unable to wait for the final torture to commence. He raised a metal pole above his head and struck one blow after another to the remaining Jun.

The scene sickened Corrigan, who stepped back, a hand pressed over his mouth as if he dreaded the sound of his own screaming.

Gregor brought the entwined sisters up close to his face, brushed their wings and blew on them. The sisters took flight, and Corrigan followed them with his eyes.

"What did you do that for?" Corrigan asked, appalled.

"What strange creatures," Gregor said, as if he could not quite fathom what he was being asked or why. "I've asked the sisters to bring back what we need, but I won't ever give them another command. I suggest we move further away from what we just witnessed. I want to see as much of this world as I can before they put an end to it." Gregor's words had a finality about them, and it left

Corrigan feeling unsteady. They walked further into the forest, home to a multitude of lurking predators; a place crawling with insects, worms and maggots, rich with the scent of life, mulch, urine and decay. It fed upon itself, sustaining a perfect balance, and the perpetual feast was both celebration and defeat. Corrigan's thoughts were troubling, so his mind veered away from recent memory, from the screams of beings whose pain he could only imagine. He went searching for something else, *anything* else and finally alighted like a nervous dragonfly on an image of Ramon. The Venezuelan had stood before him on the balcony of his apartment, naked and perfect and cruel. Hadn't he also been a torturer, a murderous thug in Ulmer's employ?

Corrigan moved away from the others as Worker drones arrived carrying the supplies promised by Ulmer to set up their camp. B4 followed, but he waved her away.

"You do as you like, Bobbin," she called after him, perhaps realising how much he needed solitude. Or maybe she was quietly berating him the way she had always done when he dropped into melancholy. "Bit of a shock to see what a Draseke can do to one of us, I'm sure!"

Alone in the darkening forest he felt a yearning for Ramon, as if he alone was the one tortured soul in all eternity who could satisfy his physical and emotional need. Being what he was, the Venezuelan could deliver something only another person guilty of complicity could. *Ours was a love – if love is the right word – of necessity,* Corrigan thought as he watched the path of leaves in

221

a brook that bubbled from a bank and wound away through the forest floor. There had been a weightlessness to his existence before his rude reintroduction which being corporeal could not match. He'd accepted himself as he was, no more or less, and the relief of simply being without need or want had been nothing short of completeness. What he experienced as a human was an unending gnawing, a relentless sense of incompleteness, and a desire to salve the pain by joining with another. What had those poor, tormented AI beings suffered under torture? Their screams were not mechanical; they rose from the core of their beings like the misery of those they encountered in the tunnel of the Entombed, or like the agony Ramon could not suffer in silence as the Drasekes dug into him with their metal toothpicks.

Twigs cracked beneath the weight of an intruder, making Corrigan go still. He looked through shadows cast by the setting sun and there stood the Sect, the asymmetrical version of himself, and he felt the urge to bash the creature's stunted brain in for being the pathetic coward he was. But then why was he here? A terrible, unexpected wave of pity took hold of him, and he beckoned the Sect to come to him. The savage trembled and cowed the way a dog will do when approaching an angry master.

"I shall call you Corey," Corrigan said. "Corey."

"Core," the Sect muttered.

"Corey," Corrigan repeated.

"Core-ee."

"Yes. Corey. We were always a fast learner when we put our mind to it."

Corrigan coaxed the Sect towards the brook he had passed. He undressed, and encouraged the savage to remove his rough leather skirt. He did not understand, so Corrigan lowered himself into the cool water and began to wash the heat and sordid thoughts of the day away. After a few moments the man, himself from before, joined him, and Corrigan filled his hands with water and poured, again and again, until the grime ran from his hair and skin. There was suspicion, fear, in the brute's eyes, but he didn't resist, and Corrigan now observed a man more like a brother, or a near identical twin, and smiled. He was not a product of his own sloth or lack of ambition; he was trapped in an agenda, much as any Non or Transient had been back then, their genetic line reaching back through history to the turbulent primordial sea of their beginnings.

24

During the night Corrigan heard the unmistakable sighs and groans as Spinner introduced Gregor to one physical pleasure after another and, if her giggles were anything to go by, the girl had thoroughly enjoyed her role as teacher. Corrigan groaned too, but with deep frustration, reaching to relieve his tumescence with the familiar desperation and emptiness that had him weeping. The timing of his emergence from his tent in the morning couldn't have been worse: he saw a slim, pretty hand draw the young man back inside their own tent, and the larger Addictari overhead exchanged squawks of disapproval at Gregor's cavorting with a Sect, despite him pushing the hand away. Nothing was said by anyone, as heavy machines arrived carrying provisions for them to expand their camp.

Over the next few days, the size of their troop increased to include the full flock of Addictari, a considerable number of Guardians, several Worker drones and a small band of Exhumed. G1 brought A23, J14, J47 and H1 with him, amongst others. To have a representative of each member of his old core team – with the notable exception of Katherine – was a poignant moment for Corrigan. *That their loyalty appears to transcend the earthly is quite something …*

He shared this thought with Gregor and received the analytical reply he should have expected rather than the emotive one he desired.

"There are fifty-seven current manifestations of the G-range in London alone," Gregor said. "The A group is numbered in the dozens, and the J group in the hundreds. G1 has clearly been influenced by exposure to you, but he only managed to sway a handful."

"But H1," Corrigan said, "she's a critical ally."

"That model was suspended after Harding was exhumed. She's a one-off and never followed the flock. In that regard she has no influence."

Although he was loath to concede the point, Corrigan felt disinclined to pursue the argument. He patted Gregor's shoulder and said, "You're even more contrary with a brain than you were in a tin."

On the fourth day, a group of Guardians finally arrived accompanied by the instantly recognisable Guardian model with a glass head, the form Gregor had assumed before his metamorphosis. He and Gregor stood outside their tents, observed by a crowd of Addictari and Guardians waiting to be addressed.

"Better late than never, I suppose," B4 said.

"Well, this is a bit of a mind-fuck," Corrigan added.

"Mr Corrigan," Gregor said. "Please refrain from vulgarity."

Spinner, who was at Gregor's side, giggled, and then looked up at her man and put her hand over her mouth, her dark eyes still laughing. Her hair had been cropped short, on Corrigan's insistence. She had also been bathed and clothed in a tight-fitting suit in a camouflage print, which suited her dark skin. Corrigan found it hard to look at her. The Sect girl was Jonathan, he was sure, and it was too much to find himself attracted not only to Gregor's beauty and physique, but to this lively boyish girl.

"Mind-fuck," she mimicked, giggling again, clearly enjoying the sound of the words. Jonathan had rarely seemed as carefree. Perhaps the Sect version was experiencing what Jonathan had never attained when he tried to lift his family out of a state of transience. For Spinner, her tribe was the family opposite on Harvey Road, the lower order who never could give up the Belushi Grey or focus on anything beyond immediate need. By laughing with her new family, perhaps she was trying to distance herself from the other Sects; or perhaps she was simply a naturally happy girl.

Corrigan walked out to receive their guests, who went quiet with anticipation. He pointed at the leader of the troop, the mechanical Gregor whose head was ablaze with synaptic fire. "How am I to distinguish you one from the other?" he teased. Perhaps Spinner's lightness was rubbing off on him.

The synaptic fire cooled, and blue lightning crackled around the globe. "There is no distinction to be made," the android said, tilting its head. "However, for expedience's sake, you might refer to me as Guardian 1."

"No, that won't do. How about *Late*?"

B4 chuckled. "Let's just hope Spinner ain't *late* or you'll be early to fatherhood, my son."

Gregor, the youth, scowled at her and strode over to Late, Spinner the shadow at his side. Late stepped forward until the two were face to face. Whatever Gregor saw close up was enough to make him freeze, something explicable only to the two entities, one and yet alien, brothers from disparate worlds tethered in an uncomfortable alliance. There was defiance and something like longing in Gregor's face; the fire in Late's head raged until the reflection was evidently consumed. Corrigan thought of Corey, and searched for his asymmetric face in the crowd. It was an odd kind of relief to see him.

"I wonder what we'd see if we opened your head and looked inside, Gregor ..." Corrigan said. "Aren't you going to welcome Late to the party?" he asked when Gregor didn't reply. "Poor Late, traipsing through the forest in search of his vulnerable, lesser self."

"They planned to dissect me," Late said. He raised a hand to silence Gregor. "We can't allow that. The only way for Gregor to come home—"

"Is for him to tap his ruby slippers together," Corrigan said. "There's no place like home, after all ... and from what the sisters showed us, Jason would have conducted your dissection while you were not only awake but had your sensors maximised to better appreciate the experience."

"Indeed," Late said. "Now I'm physically at a distance, I believe I am safe for the time being. Emulate One is aiding my prolonged game of hide and seek."

"Perhaps it's just the two of you," Corrigan said, glaring at Gregor and his AI equivalent. "No need to bring some form of mechanical intervention, a grand artifice into your analysis."

Edna and Jan fluttered in front of Corrigan's face.

"If I may," Jan said. "Although Mr Gregor is at risk, it's you we're most afraid for."

"Terribly afraid," Edna chirped.

Corrigan resisted the temptation to brush them from his sightline.

"Yes, your link to the program is now severed," Gregor said. They caught each other's eye and, for a moment, Corrigan sensed something beneath a layer of simple concern. Empathy? Affection for his mentor? Respect for his choice? But then the youth hardened his face. "If you die now, Mr Corrigan, that will be the end of you."

Spinner laughed as if he had told a joke, and stroked Corrigan's arm. "The end," she said, her big eyes full of compassion. But when Corrigan looked down at her she stepped back in alarm.

"Don't ever touch me," he snarled.

"She meant nothing by it," Gregor said, and Spinner clung to him.

"It doesn't matter what this thing thinks or understands," Late said, disgust in his voice at the liaison. "Her time is limited. Which is a mercy for us all, especially after last night's activities."

"There's at least a year before her cull," Corrigan replied, regretting his harsh words. "And not at all if we can educate her. Perhaps introduce her to birth control ... or any form of control."

Edna and Jan buzzed around him, the fury of their wings hissing like a swarm of vicious tsetse flies. "That ain't so, Mr C," Jan said.

"Jason and his mum," Edna added, "are up to all sorts of unpleasantness, as you saw for yourself. All sorts."

Late's head burned, the globe almost entirely ablaze, and the crowd murmured. "K has come down to Earth with a crash, Mr Corrigan," the android said. "She, Ulmer and Jason are planning the End. No humans or Sects are to be left alive. The beast with two heads will gorge on them."

"She's a spiteful one, no doubt, but she still has issues with Ulmer," Corrigan said. "Surely?"

"That's true enough," Jan said. "But it's you two – three with Mr Late – what's upsetting her boy now. The little lad's been at her and that's why she hooked up, so to speak, with Orgasm Central down in the pit. She ain't struck no deal with Ulmer directly."

"No, not with the head itself but with that beast of his," Edna added. "The right's one of her hosts, ain't it, and she let Ulmer keep the left ... if he's ever minded to reconnect with it, that is."

"Ulmer on the left," Corrigan snorted. "What a turnaround. But why does she need either of them? I thought she was connected to a range of organic hosts as well as being networked to Mother Emulate?"

"She is," Late said. "And don't insult Emulate One. Whatever she is, it's nothing so basic as a mother." His synaptic lightening sparked inside his glass head as B4 rumbled on her roller. "As for K, no one knows how many hosts she has, but Emulate One must have uses for them or she would never allow such a perverse experiment."

"You can find K's eyes gawping at you," Jan said, "from birds and beetles–"

"To dragonflies and frogs," Edna added.

"They're everywhere, Mr C. She even has one or two Sects. Might've been sneaking a peek at this one too."

The sisters started buzzing around Spinner's head, and Corrigan had an awful thought. He knelt in front of the girl. "Who's in there with you?" he asked, but gently. An image of a brain kissing glass with its pink folds waddled through his memory and tugged at his emotions.

"She doesn't know if K's in there or not," Gregor said, putting an arm around her. It was the first time Corrigan had seen any sort of affection from the boy.

"Are you sure?" Corrigan persisted. "You know Late's in there with *you*."

"We're a synergy," Late said. "With K and her hosts, things are far less intertwined. This thing has no purchase on K's world or the workings of her mind. She's an incoming stream at best if she is networked. Unless K wants it otherwise ..."

Corrigan studied the girl. "K might send her into my tent to kill me as I sleep ... like a pre-programmed assassin."

"Yes," Late said. "Only–"

231

"She would have done it by now," Gregor interrupted, "if that was her intention. There's nothing any of us can do about it."

"I think I was safe last night. All night, as she was clearly otherwise occupied."

"She wanted to invite you," Gregor sighed, "but I don't believe she wanted to *kill* you."

"She wanted to *what*?"

"She had ideas …"

Corrigan observed Gregor's blush and felt an instant, almost uncontrollable desire pulse through him. "She wanted to …?"

"Perhaps there's more of Jonathan in her DNA than we can account for," Gregor said. "I, of course, told her it would be inappropriate for the three of us to–"

"Little strumpet," B4 said.

Corrigan stared at Spinner's face looking for K, but all he could see was Jonathan laying in half light, naked and satisfied, his alert mind aching to know the man Ulmer had tasked him with manipulating. There was always a conflict in evidence, and he saw the very same in Spinner's features; a kind of fear and expectation, an intelligence, if you must. He had to wonder whether a part of his friend was transferred when Jason toyed with Jonathan's DNA and brought this female version into existence. How like the flawed Greek gods they had become, toying with creation for their own amusement and curiosity. He looked beyond Spinner to the forest and, there, lurking once more in the shadows, was the returned Sect, she who had been released from the beast's cavern. She must have followed them, watching them, and Corrigan wondered why. Did she consider them a link to the perverse rituals carried on below, and above? Was she looking for protection? Or perhaps, like himself, she recognised some other unregistered relationship, a familiarity neither could quite place or entirely disown.

"What about Ulmer?" Corrigan then asked. "Where is he?"

"No one knows where he is," Late said.

Jan flitted down in front of Corrigan's face, her tiny eyes burning red. "Vanished inside the program, Mr C, playing hide and seek like Master Late."

"And Emulate One's tucked him up in her circuitry as well," Edna added. "Must be a bit of an omnivore that one."

Gregor released Spinner into B4's care and took Corrigan by the arm, leading him away from the others.

"I've told you before, there is no unlimited access in the sense Ulmer used to boast of it," Gregor said, stopping in a clearing some way from the crowd. "There was, however, an agreement. But all deals were broken when I couldn't resist the challenge you put to me." He let out a groan. "It was a stupid, impulsive mistake."

"No, it wasn't," Corrigan said. "Look at me, Gregor. You're the most human of them all. You're more like me and the Sects than Jason could ever be. I hate to think what might have happened had he slid inside that body of yours."

But a familiar look of despair clouded the young man's features. "We already *know* what he would have done," Gregor said, "which is why he's so furious, and revengeful, and has gathered public opinion through intimidation."

Corrigan smiled, although a dull swell of pain rolled through him. "There's no way of saying how being human would have affected him," he said.

"You're far too easily manipulated, Mr Corrigan." There was a sudden flash of hostility in Gregor's eyes. "This wouldn't have been his first experience of being human. He's come back dozens of times, and he's just as cold as a human as he is a machine. He once returned as a boy. He tormented K whilst in that little body, taunted her, called her a terrible mother. He misbehaved with the Sects and even attempted to undermine the order of things. It was K who had him put to death in the end. She wanted her little mechanical boy back, the one who was easier to control, so she had the human boy abducted. He was sedated, placed in a room on his own and gassed."

"What a marvellous woman she is. I can see that clear as the blue sky," Corrigan said, staring up through the canopy of trees.

"You see nothing," Gregor growled, pressing a hand to his forehead. "You feel as if you and your kind have been wronged, but can't you see how absurd that is?"

"I thought we were friends," Corrigan said.

Gregor laughed. "What would that even mean?" he asked.

Corrigan smiled sadly. "For my part, now, it means …

affection for you."

"You don't know me."

"Of course, I do," Corrigan snapped. "I was there when you were a child. I watched you develop and grow. It wasn't very pleasant to be the victim of your early mistakes, but I forgave you as I realised what a torment it must have been." Gregor stared at him, as if he was speaking in riddles. "You were the first of your kind, you know that," Corrigan continued. "I was there. They dragged you into existence without consent. I disliked you, but I always thought you were independently clever. You even had a sense of humour, from the very first Gregor." Gregor now looked at him as if he were a tormentor. "Your anger and mistrust when I returned were also understandable. You had no say when it came to the idea of reintroducing me."

"I argued against it," Gregor said.

"Of course you did! You felt loyalty to the Guardians, to Emulate kind, and yet you were no longer an Emulate yourself."

Gregor sighed. "I'd been sullied."

"Yes, dipped in shit and more humane when you came out than when you went in. You recognised in yourself that most human of features: fallibility."

Gregor turned away. "I don't want to talk about this."

"It's alright, you were always fallible, but you were also better and became more so. You have no idea how strong you are. You're perhaps the only one among us who doesn't need to convert, to accept a single state of being or a twisted sense of right and wrong."

"I denied them ... I kept the Guardians dumbed down and one dimensional. Like lesser beasts."

"Yes," Corrigan said, "like Sects or Nons or Transients. But they're yours, and no amount of fiddling about in the mainframe can undo that."

"That isn't so. We need to speak to H1. Harding's the only one who knows what they're capable of. Let her explain it."

Corrigan trusted Gregor, and he hoped Gregor trusted him. "You were a rotten child," he laughed. "You crushed us like beetles under your boot, toying with us but eventually learning to respect us. You feared us and you were right to do that. What a schism it is having known each side of the divide. Where to go and what to be. What a dilemma living is and how gratifying to watch it play itself out in someone you ... love."

"You are not permitted to love me," Gregor muttered.

"But–"

"Just stop–"

"Yooohooo!"

B4 rolled into the clearing. Beside her was Corrigan's Sect brother, or clone or other self. His head had been shaved to remove the matted hair and he was dressed in the male version of the camouflage gear Spinner was wearing.

"Look who I've brought to see you, Bobbin," B4 said.

Corrigan did a double take. The Sect was handsome, marred only by his continuing timidity as he stood trembling by B4's side. Perhaps he had been harder on himself back then, when he judged and turned away from his reflection. Jason hadn't needed to 'correct' anything. There was no asymmetry to speak of. It might even have been a kind of body dysmorphia the original Corrigan suffered from because, staring at him now, he could see no difference between them. Why he elected to embrace himself, Corrigan could not understand, but he went to the weaker man and wrapped him in his arms. In that moment he realised just how human they both were.

25

H1 had set up a tent for herself half a mile from the group's main encampment. There was a row of tall, slender Guardian servers inside her temporary abode, whirring and blinking as Corrigan and Gregor approached. She tilted her head and Corrigan imagined her human face looking at him over the rim of her glasses.

"I'm surprised it took you so long," she said, her Boston accent still annoyingly present, as Corrigan stepped into the tent. The android, who had turned white to protect herself from the heat, was entering data via a halo-screen, her servers flickering and stuttering. "These machines don't like the temperature any more than I do," she added, turning around.

"Harding," Corrigan said.

"*They* call me H1. How generous of you to use my name."

Gregor paced back and forth outside the entrance.

"Ah, the Son of Man," she said, tilting her head as she assessed the teenager. "Don't wear a path, dear, come inside and take a load off."

"Are you another of Arthur's anomalies?" Corrigan needed to ask. "Like the Siegruth sisters?"

"No," Harding said. "There's nothing anomalous about me."

"She's unique and intentional," Gregor said, a bitterness to his tone which did not surprise Corrigan, although he experienced a moment of unsettling loyalty. It was difficult at times to process the connection he now felt with Gregor. The Guardian version had overseen terrible crimes, but what might Corrigan have become under different circumstances? He was no longer just Corrigan after all, he was also that which had been Corrigan. In Corey he saw a version of what he might have been without a mother who had forced him to become an educated Transient. Gregor's mother had rejected him and no one, not even Corrigan, offered the developing Guardian any real guidance or support.

Corrigan pulled up a chair and sat beside a server as if it were a fireplace. "So," he said, "you were programmed to come back as a ...?"

"A true Exhumed," Harding said. "No one can modulate my emotive core. I'm coded to resist any intervention of that sort. It didn't take a great deal to set it up in the program. Seems to have bled on occasion, and those goddamn sisters ended up similarly configured."

"She's a product of her own work," Gregor said. "We recognised it the moment we reawakened her."

Harding tilted her head, righted it. "I was isolated," she said, and to Corrigan: "I know you never liked me, Robert, but–"

"Don't be absurd," Corrigan said. "No matter what I made of you as a person, I always rated you as a scientist. And, for what it's worth, I did like you until you agreed to work with them."

"That's not how I recall it," Harding said. She moved away and busied herself at the halo-screen for a moment. "You were much more well-disposed towards the Fuse brothers and Katherine ... you even preferred Ramon."

"I understand," Corrigan said, "that a deal was struck with Arthur that our reluctant genius might be availed of some emo–"

"Arthur wanted the reverse," she said. "Wanted to be completely stripped of all emotion. He envisaged being a calm and centred proponent of logic. He imagined there was peace to be found in such a state. A kind of return to the innocence of Eden but with as much knowledge at his disposal as he could store. He would become the apple itself, and he was willing to let that infectious relic paw him to have it. But it was a fruitless sacrifice ..." She turned to look at Gregor. "Because you wouldn't allow Arthur that kind of peace, would you, Gregor?" She raised a hand to silence any reply. "You allowed that degenerate to defile him, and then you had him downloaded to suffer with the rest of us and he's still *in there* as is the version of *me* and everyone else you managed to throw into the sewer."

Gregor turned to Corrigan. "It was she who asked Ulmer to have Arthur downloaded as nothing but emotion. That was her price for helping us."

241

Harding made a sound not dissimilar to a sigh.

"I saw *everything*," Corrigan said. "You had it projected into my cell so I could watch you murder Katherine and make your deal with this one." He glared at them both in turn. "None of us has a clean rap sheet."

"Speak for yourself," Harding said. "I suppose it's immaterial at this point what I recall, or the reality of a past moment. The mess we find ourselves in, that would be the more pressing matter at hand."

Corrigan smiled, a mix of malice and respect. "Oh dear, you soured in the vault," he laughed and took a closer look at the synthetic skin of her face where it trembled with irritability. "But yes, 'we are where we are' as they used to say in business."

"Business never delivered anything of real value," Harding said.

"All I meant is, we are where we are not where we've been."

"I've been any number of places."

"I heard you paid a visit to our CEO's bed yourself."

"I got what I wanted from my sacrifice," she said. "He wasn't as abhorrent back then and I almost convinced myself I liked him."

"Ulmer said you were," Corrigan said, "you know …"

"It was ugly of you to accept what that man said about me, and going along with that rumour speaks of your own bias." The lids of her eyes peeled back to reveal two red hot marbles. "Caspar could never deal with rejection and, when I broke it off, he responded as if I'd broken *it* off. He decided I should be demoted, as if lesbianism were a lesser sexuality. He thought the rumour would help to make a mockery of me. If I ever go back to human form – something I'm in no rush to do – I'll have my file tweaked to amend things so I'm more that way inclined."

Gregor started pacing again. "Professor, you really must–"

"Must what?" Harding asked. "What are you, arbiter of taste and propriety?" She turned to Corrigan. "What a prude he is. I thought that would lessen over time." She watched the pacing youth.

Gregor blushed and beads of sweat appeared on his brow, and Corrigan experienced a flutter of arousal. "What are our options?" the young man asked.

"Options?" Harding tilted her head at Gregor. "You mean sexually?" she teased.

"No, no! You know what I mean. Our options … with the situation!"

"Can we have the room, dear? The grown-ups need to talk."

Gregor the human had not yet learned to conceal his emotions. A wounded expression crumpled his handsome face, which caused compassion to well up in Corrigan's chest. "Anything you can say to me, Harding …" he said.

Harding gestured for Gregor to take a seat, and the light in her eyes softened to a warm glow. "I've always thought that when there's only a single realistic option to speak of, options in the plural is nonsense."

"Agreed," Corrigan said as Gregor sat down. His knee brushed Corrigan's thigh and his heart caught the edges of his ribcage. The ache was unreal; the yearning almost unbearable.

"Acquiescence," she said, "is the only option."

"You mean surrender?" Corrigan asked.

"If we must use military terminology, then yes: surrender. Return to them and prove you're no threat, just a failed experiment. Allow the rift caused by this …" – she pointed at Gregor – "*misjudgement* to be placed in its proper context. Otherwise K and Jason will hunt down every human, Sect and AI anomaly and destroy them with no purpose other than their own elevation."

"So you're here, Professor, to save your synthetic skin," he said. "Escaped your cell to join us for that and nothing else."

Harding placed a hand to her white face and a black bruise momentarily appeared. "To get myself out of immediate danger, yes, but also to make a proposal."

"To ask me to surrender …"

"Well, yes, that's part of it."

"And let them *win*?" Corrigan was incredulous.

"They've already won," Harding said. "The point is to ensure they don't entirely get their way, that there's some way forward for the rest of us or some way *back* to something where being a person, of whatever form or origin, actually matters. K wants to transcend self, and Jason wants to stamp out everything that isn't him. He's worse than Caspar."

"So I go back, hand myself over, sacrifice myself as a failure and everything will be alright? They won't hunt down Gregor and the Sects for sport?"

"It'll buy us time to work out something better. Of course, you'd have to convince them, beg to be returned to that peaceful state you so enjoyed, the one poor Arthur was denied. Remind K she needs those Sect brains to keep her wits sharp until she's ready to head off into the singularity. Utility is what figures for most AI; remember that and exploit it."

"There must be another way to square this?"

Harding tilted her head. "None that I can see," she said. "And you've made your choice regarding who matters to you and why. That's apparent from your voice, your deportment and your choice of friends – a group I never belonged to. That's okay, of course, but a sacrifice is needed. You might yet manage to save those you've developed feelings for – like this one and his girlfriend, and maybe even those twisted sisters and that persistent mother of yours. You can do that and continue to hold me in contempt."

"I never held you in contempt, Tierney, never."

"Never saw me as a woman in a man's job, did you?" The light in her eyes cooled to dark blue. "I believe you need a clear head, a cool night and a bit of solitude to work it out. I suggest you go up there." She gestured towards a hill some miles from the camp. "Build yourself a fire and think it through – if you think you can manage that, dear."

Corrigan stormed out of the tent, followed closely by Gregor. He span around to face the youth. "Why are you following me? Are you going to give me a good *seeing to*? Take up Spinner's threesome fantasy?"

Gregor's face reddened and he swallowed hard. "I-I ..." he stammered. "I ... I can't, Mr Corrigan. I'm like Harding ... not made that way."

"*Made*? Who the hell *made* you Gregor?"

"I ... I ..."

"Perhaps she can tweak *my* configuration to straighten the bent in me, or Jason could toy with my DNA so I emerge as a woman. Then I can get on with doing a man's job!" His eyes bore into Gregor's and regret swelled with a dull, unsatisfying ache. "In all honesty, I wouldn't lose this part of me, not unless I could relinquish the lot and go back to having what Arthur only dreamed of. What peace there was in being limited. Maybe it's not even a sacrifice to go back and beg for that. Not like a Sect but like a clock that no longer recognises time, that ticks only for itself, for the sound of it, for the rhythm and the peace of it." Gregor looked so flummoxed that Corrigan dropped his head and sighed. "I'm sorry, Gregor, genuinely sorry," he blurted. "I'm denied a rather basic outlet and it's left me frustrated."

"I understand," Gregor said, also lowering his eyes as the weight of the moment settled on him.

Corrigan's heart seemed to plummet through the inner space of his being. It fell and found no floor and inevitably it ceased to register the pain of its descent. "I'll do as she suggests," he said. "I'll go up there, build a fire and think things through. She's right when she says it was ugly of me to go along with Ulmer's rumour. I know what that feels like, and she had to work that much harder to earn my respect. She's a genius, and I was a man given authority over her by a jilted lover."

Gregor looked at him as if the idea of a sacrifice were being contemplated in the darker recesses of his mind, back there where Late's fire burned over a black, empty sea. It seemed to Corrigan as if his friend – yes, that's what Gregor was becoming – would rather be the sacrificial lamb, but that just would not do.

"I'll build a fire at the base of the hill," Gregor said, "and stand watch for you." The way the teenager spoke was heart-breaking, like a child making an oath with his one and only true friend.

"Come up at daybreak and we'll exchange thoughts." Corrigan stared at Gregor, wondering if everything he had done had been nothing less than a series of avoidable errors. Might he not have saved the Guardian from the trials of being human? "It's early yet, and the night's a long way off, but I'll start the walk now." He smiled at the young man. "Let's not eat today. Let's fast so our thoughts are lean and hungry tonight."

He set off, Gregor just a few metres behind him, and his whole body ached again for release.

26

The day was long, and night did not arrive until ten o'clock. Corrigan regretted not eating. The hunger in his belly tempted him to return to camp and forget Harding's idea of a solitary night of uninterrupted contemplation, but he resisted the urge. The way she spoke of sacrifice was rich coming from her. She had been unwilling to do the same to save humankind; she instead bartered to have Arthur walled up with the rest. She was not to know Ulmer never planned a better fate for her. Perhaps he could be better, put others before himself in ways he'd rarely ever managed before Ulmer and Gregor had him sealed in Goeth's sarcophagus.

He laid and lit a fire, glad of the plentiful resources around him and the old-fashioned matches he had bought from his own tent. Technology may have advanced to the realms of the mechanical gods, but a simple match was still a simple, welcome match. Wood spat hot sparks in the cold evening air. The moon cast shadows, and orange flames toyed with them. He looked down the slope of the hill and saw Gregor sat beside his own fire. The young man had stripped down to a pair of white underpants, the chiaroscuro lighting of the fire touching his fine skin. He had hunkered down into himself, wrapping his arms about his knees and tucking his head in. The sadness of it tore at Corrigan. What had he done? Provoking Gregor into acting so rashly had real consequences. The human teenager was a knot of anxiety, dread and regret. He would never be able to reconcile himself with what he was, with what he'd been and what he'd done.

"The body is a torment to the mind, and the mind an inflamer of the body," he whispered, alert to the possibility of K's many eyes and ears. "And yet the one without the other is as cold as death itself. Rather to live and not live. To remain in a calm death-like trance and never regret the loss of a thing you can no longer comprehend. That's a kind of peace ... and perhaps giving this up is no sacrifice at all. Life is nothing but a series of minor deaths, the death of infancy, childhood, adolescence and ... oh those miserable teenage years."

A log shifted in the fire and sparks crackled up to the moon. Corrigan looked down into the flames and saw a face looking back at him. He leaned in closer and recognised Caspar Ulmer's features. The one-time CEO smiled at him with a sly expression.

"I suppose I should have known Tierney had a reason for suggesting this spot for a 'solitary night of contemplation'," Corrigan said. "And here you are."

"Never wander far," Ulmer replied. His smile disintegrated as if discovery had ruined the moment. "You should know that by now."

"They think you've run away."

"They're idiots," Ulmer said dismissively. "They're on

the brink of perfection but they're imbeciles." Corrigan watched the man's face, scorched as it was by flames at irregular intervals. "You saw him down there, Ramon," Ulmer grunted. "My beautiful son."

"You know I did."

Ulmer's head doubled its size, so it dominated the fire. "It mustn't continue," he said.

"No, it mustn't."

"So, you'll work with me?" the head enquired.

Corrigan studied the face in the flames. There was something raw and disturbed bubbling inside Ulmer's substance-less head. "That," he said, "depends on where you're intending to take us." How could he trust a man who'd allowed humanity to suffer the depths of Hell and then annihilated them? He almost laughed when he thought how fond he was of Gregor, a machine who'd had human beings hunted down like vermin. People could change, but surely not Ulmer.

"Ultimately, the destination remains the same," Ulmer said. "I want something better and I want my future secured." He adopted a pitiful expression and tone as he continued. "Of course, I also want Ramon to be released from the grasp of those terrible Drasekes ... But what do you think K is working on?"

"Something monstrous," Corrigan said.

"Something miraculous," Ulmer said with a hint of pleasure. "Kat wanted this little side project with reintroduction to proceed and fail publicly so she could garner support from all quarters for her *real* endeavour.

Even Gregor might have been converted to her path had he not taken a leap of faith and jumped the fence. And what of Jason, eh?"

Corrigan looked through Ulmer's face to the embers beneath, warping the image in contorted waves. "He's after something."

"He also wanted reintroduction to fail," Ulmer said, and Corrigan's heart fell from his ribcage, down towards the chasm of his gut where it splashed into a burning river of acid. The head closed its eyes as if it were seeking something in the darkness. "You know," Ulmer continued, "Katherine was never very good with machinery. Couldn't grasp technology, not really. She had a handle on the biological – genetics fascinated her – but IT dulled her senses."

"I suppose Jason has a facility for–"

"Yes, he does," Ulmer said. "The son of a bitch gets under the skin of technology. The problem is he intends to destroy every living Sect – a program I've little resistance to – and he wants to do away with you, our friend Gregor, his own mother … he even wants to be rid of *me*."

"I'm assuming you must actually possess unlimited access?"

"I *had* unlimited access until our friend Gregor became intolerably compulsive. The truth is, I don't care about Gregor, or you for that matter," the disembodied CEO said. "Jason's working on a new model. The body's every bit as alert and supple as an organic form. Its senses are refined to a sublime degree. What I mean is that it can feel what we never felt and it's impervious to the whips and scorns of time, and–"

"You want it."

"Like nothing else." Ulmer's eyes were distended in his holographic bubble, as if it had been squeezed. "There's a prototype." He winked. "I borrowed it, and for just ten minutes I inhabited a state of clarity with richness of thought, free from the burdens of mortal physicality. I also found myself elevated to a pitch of … well, it left me gasping for a higher state of *being*. It's out of this world; it's–"

"Peaceful yet whole?"

"Oh, c'mon, Corrigan, I know you. I felt the pleasure you experienced being stripped down to nothing but thought, the imagined state Arthur gave up his chastity to taste. I only had to finger him once to find his aspirational G-spot. This transcends that. But the calm of it, the centred peace … it's heaven. I mean what could be more heavenly than being conscious without a goddamn conscience? You know I never suffered the hellfire of regret or shame, but even I had my moments of … well, if even a thing like me can love, then that's a serious issue." He again assumed a mawkish expression. "My *poor* Ramon."

Corrigan studied the face in the fire. It was obscene; a greasy pancake with dead eyes. "There's not much I wouldn't do to stop what's being done to Ramon–"

"We must!" Ulmer groaned. "The thought of it. Imagine if I hadn't tasked Ramon with getting rid of Jason Meregalli. What the hell would that little shit have left undone, eh?"

"Well," Corrigan pondered, "he might not have initiated the destruction of the human species like someone else we might mention, Mr Ulmer."

"Okay, I admit I did that," Ulmer said, screwing up his face. "But don't underestimate Jason." Ulmer stared at Corrigan for some time before continuing. "You have to get close to him, turn your back on what you're doing here. The Sects can't be saved. Let the cull proceed. Go back to the city and promote the idea of a good and thorough cull. Distance yourself from those savages entirely. Demonstrate *suicidal despair* at the prospect of having to live among the Sects until death do you part and encourage Jason to let you in. He always approved of your efficiency and no one's hands are entirely clean, Corrigan, you included. Confide in Jason and flatter that ego of his. That's his Achilles' heel. Take up your bow and aim your arrow there! Mind you take care, though. Don't rattle your quiver when you're withdrawing an arrow. Pull back the string of your bow so gradually that not a strain registers for a bat, or a goddamn moth for that matter. And don't underestimate K's insects either. A moth might flutter stupidly into a fire, but it can sense you breathing ten miles away." Corrigan sat quietly, deep in thought. "Well, have I stoked you into sacking Troy and stealing that precious new form Jason is making for himself?"

Corrigan could hear Ramon's cries seep up through the earth and nodded his head, wanting to put an end to this unpleasant conversation. The sound of Ulmer's voice moved like a vexation through him, ricocheting off the walls of his mind, awakening memories from a world put to death by one man's hunger to live, to deny death and continue to exist in any form available. The agreements Corrigan made with Ulmer in his previous life would never rest. And what of the agreements made now? Would they be any different in retrospect? He would still be offering himself up like a hollow wooden horse ... the worst kind of ancient treachery played out in a technological Troy.

"I'll seek you out when I can," Ulmer then said, whispering now as if a bat or a moth might be listening. "Think of Ramon. No one deserves what's being done to him. Jason will keep on doing it and if you're not careful, he'll assign a Draseke or two to punish you inventively."

The fire crackled and Ulmer vanished back into the machine.

Corrigan looked up at the face of the moon and her craters seemed like the hollows of a skull. Perhaps he too deserved the same fate designed for Ramon by a Draseke working in tandem with some unnamed administrator. There might be release to be found being subjected to those needle-like claws, no space left for anything other than imagining the pain to come. Conscience cleansed through unending agony, one torment supplanting the other.

"Harding wanted me to come up here," he whispered. "There must be a sensor, something allowing him to manifest. They've been making deals, and not for the first time. Lick and a fucking promise, eh? Dockyard Doris, my arse. They planned this … this surrender of sorts in order to have their way. Gregor's blind to their machinations and I'm to be complicit yet again."

Had Corrigan looked more closely he may have seen a small orange object in the dark. It might have been a mushroom or a frog, but it was there, ready to project its master's image or to record conversations the way B4 had once eavesdropped on Jonathan and his lover.

What he would not do now to be a dragonfly on a wall when Gregor and Spinner wove the web that would entangle their bodies, and yet the idea of a female version of Jonathan writhing with a being who had surely been the oldest virgin of them all made him shudder.

Something moved in the long grass behind him. He turned, blinded by the flames, and peered into the shadows. With the stealth of a retreating predator he saw the Sect girl from Ulmer's cavern slink away in the dark, and then Corey emerged from behind a tree, breathing hard from the ascent. Corrigan released his own breath and beckoned him over.

Corey sat down beside him by the fire, a warm, human body, unable to communicate above a limited array of grunts and calls, so familiar and yet alien. It was a strange moment, one Narcissus would have embraced and, like the mythical character, Corrigan gazed at the approximation of his former self. Somehow, without knowledge or the burden of shame, this creature had become attractive. It was the more knowing of the two who initiated the first touch, and they marvelled at the detail of their similarity, down to the moles on their skin and the hairs on the backs of their hands. When curiosity moved up a gear, bending over to present something more intimate, they gave into it with the hunger Corrigan had intended to preserve for contemplation; but what mental feast could have compared with spending oneself with a real and available other, more familiar than strange, yet a stranger nonetheless ...

They took from each other what they needed and, when it was over, Corrigan felt a calm, empty satisfaction. He stared at the wearied, bemused Sect and smiled. Corey had tighter musculature from having to hunt and survive in the forest, and had been thoroughly washed by B4, but there was 'no washing out the rough' as Jan had once observed. In that moment he realised he would never be able to wash himself free of it either: he had embraced his lower origin and had his way with this uneducated version of himself. He looked at the brute and had to wonder if K had a sensor implanted in his stunted brain. Had she been watching and feeling as they shared their bodies beneath the stars? Ulmer surely had, no doubt, been tugging and fingering some of his many genitals.

He jumped to his feet and marched to the crest of the hill. Looking down he saw a naked Spinner retreating into the forest as Gregor paced, silhouetted by the fire. The light cast shadows over his body and the ground on which he walked. He suddenly looked up and called out, "Mr Corrigan! Come down! Spinner's gone and I don't want to be alone!"

Corrigan began his descent immediately, leaving Corey to tend the fire on the ridge, desperate to put space between himself, the future, present and past. Rocks and dust preceded him as he hurried to join the anxious young man.

"It was a mad idea!" Gregor said.

"Yes," Corrigan said, "a mad idea." He studied Gregor to fathom how much he'd seen from his position below. "Did you see–"

"Yes, Mr Corrigan! I saw you with that thing."

"It was a mutual … a shared masturbation, that's all," Corrigan said. He watched disgust play itself out beneath Gregor's trembling features. "It's a human weakness. Eventually even you may feel it. And you also had your *thing*. Except I'd never call Spinner a thing. She's a person, just like Corey."

"How *meaningless* it all is."

"Sometimes it's best when it's meaningless; when you do it for nothing but pleasure."

The moon shone down on them, and the night air touched the tension in their bodies. Gregor might have started to cry had two dragonflies not appeared. Behind the busy little sisters, B4 rolled and glowed in the dark. She gestured for someone – something – to join her, and a tall, slim Guardian stepped from the forest and spread out a blanket and arranged food from a hamper with the delicacy of a New York waiter.

"Made all your favourites, Bobbin," B4 said.

"I hope it is satisfactory," the Guardian added.

Perhaps it was the echo of his own voice, the basis for all Guardians, but it affected Gregor. He knelt and held his head in his hands. "I am not who I am," he murmured.

"That's nonsense," Corrigan said. Gregor looked up. "I just … shared myself up on that ridge. Perhaps we need to tell the occasional lie for self-preservation, which I admit seems a bit of a paradox given how many of us there are." He sighed. "You're who you were meant to be."

Corrigan sat beside his young friend, reaching into the hamper and pulling out a chicken leg. Gregor waited a moment, and then also sighed – a quiet sound – and they ate, finally finding their ease in each other's company. The dragonflies hovered over them and B4 and the Guardian stood watch with heads tilted and blue eyes as bright as distant stars.

On the crest of the ridge, Corey stood naked and enthralled. He gyrated and moaned, "Umah, Umah, Umah."

27

Corrigan awoke in the morning to find Gregor's arm around him, his hand nestled by his chin, a blanket draped over them both. The morning air was full of moisture, brightened by the flickering lights of dragonflies flying sorties through low-lying mist. The smell of dying embers drifted in the air and a gleaming metal giant stood over them.

"What a world to wake up to," B4 said, her blue eyes widening. "Isn't it lovely, Bobbin?" She rolled closer. "Draped himself like this, Gregor did, not to comfort you but to draw comfort from you," she added. Her eyes widened and she pointed at the Guardian. "I was having a chat with this one earlier."

"Keep your voice down," Corrigan whispered. "Don't wake him."

"Righto, Bobbin," B4 said, lowering her volume. "He didn't have a name, so we're calling him Dave."

"Dave?"

"I know. He don't look much like a Dave, does he?" She rolled a little bit closer. "That other Gregor – the one you call Late – he did a little jiggery-pokery and Dave – this one – and his chums are now connected to those poor sods suffering in the bowels of Emulate One."

Corrigan sighed. "He gifted them with independence *and* intuition, I suppose."

"That's right," B4 whispered. "Now he's awake, and he's a bright spark, aren't you, Dave?"

The Guardian tilted its head and the dark matter inside its transparent globe ignited with green forks of lightning. "I am pleased to meet you," Dave said.

Corrigan had never expected to converse with another Emulate like Gregor. This android had likely been in existence for more than a thousand years, a docile and obedient worker without a sense of identity. Late may have gifted the Guardians with independence, but it was B4 who'd introduced Dave to the idea of self. It was another painful reminder of how she had worked tirelessly to raise him from Non to Worker status before the Fall.

"We must be careful not to wake the master," Corrigan said, thinking how knowledgeable and yet childlike Dave's emerging consciousness must be. There was surely something new vying with something terribly old within that glass head of his.

Dave righted his transparent head, and the dark matter of his mind extinguished the lightning of his thought. "I do not perceive this fallible human as a master," he said.

"Gregor is a human, yes," Corrigan replied. "But he's also your kind."

"I understand the connection, but I will not accept any man or machine as a master."

Corrigan gestured for the Guardian to lower its volume. "I understand what it is to be ..." He struggled to articulate what he was thinking; he was not long awake, and this latest revelation needed careful management. "Before my kind was killed off, and then reduced to ignorant, superstitious Sects, I lived as a Worker, a status my mother established for me by ..." He turned to B4. "What exactly *did* you do?"

"What was necessary," B4 said. "I parked my values, held my nose and sacrificed everything so you might rise from Transient to Non and from there to Worker." Her blue circle eyes dimmed, narrowing to tighter hoops. "Of course, I was really doing it for myself. I couldn't be on the outside looking in like your old cat Lazarus. I knew I'd die if I couldn't get in from the cold, and then what would have happened to my boy?"

There was more hidden behind those now-tiny blue spheres, but Corrigan remained as uncomfortable digging any deeper as he had been throughout his entire life. He turned his attention to the Guardian. "You see, Dave, I too understand what it is to be powerless, to have others manipulate on your behalf and masters lording over you."

"You have no master now," Dave said.

"Perhaps," Corrigan replied, glancing at B4, whose eyes were now nothing more than a pair of blue dots. "I suppose no one really ever achieves total independence, and it's necessary to acknowledge the sacrifices others made on your behalf." B4's eyes widened to form two large circles, the hoops of light surely representative of another moment of reawakening. "Gregor and Late made a mistake when they kept you enslaved to task, but they recognised the error of their judgement and rectified it."

Dave's head erupted with vivid red lightning. "I believe it was you who compelled him to do that."

Corrigan again gestured for the Guardian to lower the volume. "It was already playing on his conscience."

"Ain't sure old Gregor had a conscience before he slipped on his organic man suit," B4 said.

"I wouldn't be so sure. You have a conscience, and so do you, Dave."

Corrigan took hold of Gregor's index finger as if it were an ancient arrow in a quiver. (Ulmer had warned him he must retrieve those with utmost care.) The touch of skin was almost impossible to resist, and yet he must make his escape. He slid the hand aside, slipped under it and out from under the blanket. Edna and Jan fluttered before him, their bodies glowing like heated embers, but he walked through them and down the hill.

"Where you off to, Mr C?" Jan asked.

"All cross an' all," Edna said.

"On a secret mission, Bobbin?" B4 added. "Come on, Dave, this could be interesting."

Corrigan snorted at the little spies and glared at his mother. "I'm going to see Harding."

The dragonfly sisters darted from one side to the other but demonstrated no intent to block his path or raise an alarm.

"I believe Harding's complete, the same old Bostonian who welcomed me to Goeth's facility," Corrigan mused.

"She's a person trapped in that AI husk." He marched on towards Harding's tent, his chattering band of followers not far behind. Jan and Edna were sharing a reminiscence from their days of whoring, which B4 seemed to approve of if not admire. Dave the newly awakened Guardian was perplexed, and the others rolled or flittered around him, laughing and teasing. How he wished the three of them would mute their mouths along with their emotive cores.

28

The lights of Harding's servers glowed through the open door of her tent. Her body was back to black, protecting itself from the cold morning mist. She registered him with a customary tilt of the head.

"Good morning," she said, noting the dragonflies who flitted about him, the little droid with her bright blue eyes and Dave, the recently independent Guardian. "You two can buzz off back to your master," she told the mischievous sisters. "He shouldn't be alone when he wakes up. And you have an empty hamper to collect and dishes to wash," she aimed at B4.

"The Guardian could pop back and watch over him," Jan said.

"That would be like leaving him with a tin of peaches, dear."

"Dave's an Independent," B4 said.

"Dave?" Harding asked, attempting a look of incredulity. "And is that what you're calling them …?"

"I'll explain later," Corrigan said. "But for now I'd prefer it if Dave stayed with me."

Harding's eyes burned red as she waved the dragonflies and the maternal droid away. "Shoo, off you go."

Edna and Jan darted off, but B4's eyes widened, and she waited until Corrigan asked her to leave them alone to talk.

"Alone?" she asked. "You've got young Dave here? That's not alone!" Her eyes narrowed to two pin points, and she powered up her roller with a growl and bowled off in a mood.

"Those goddamn sisters don't need much encouragement," Harding said. "They're enslaved to him. Never had a will of their own. Not really."

"They're wilful and determined," Corrigan countered. "They don't accept having a master unless it's expedient." He turned to the Independent. "If you could wait for me outside, I'd very much appreciate it, David." He was pleased with the full name. 'Dave' was far too Non; too down-the-pub.

The Guardian tilted its head, which sparked with green and blue lighting. "Of course, Mr Corrigan."

Corrigan sat beside a glowing server as if to warm himself. "It's cold this morning," he said.

"That's why I turned down my senses. We have sensitivity controls we can engage to lessen or increase the signals coming from this synthetic skin. It's handy but not quite the same as having a body." She tilted her head. Corrigan studied Harding's android form. She really was no different from other Exhumed as far as he could see. As was the case with human beings, what was contained by the vessel was more complex than the container itself.

"You know," she said, as if intuiting a question, "Ulmer wasn't a bad lover. In all honesty, he offered me things and delivered. We bartered, but I suppose there was more to it than that. He could be very comforting without meaning to be."

"No need for detail," Corrigan said.

"Of course, Caspar doesn't have and has never had the capacity to love anyone or anything. His instinct for self-preservation is as close to love as he gets." Blue light seeped through the dark matter of her eyes. "Our involvement provided an altogether unexpected pleasure. I provided him something that became an essential, and he was as hooked as a Transient on Belushi Grey."

"New tricks for old dogs."

"I abused him. It's as simple as that. And it was the matter-of-fact way in which I did it he enjoyed so much."

"I don't need to know."

She tilted her head and the blue light intensified. "I never loved Caspar, but I loved debasing him. I could do whatever I liked."

"He could've got that as a service."

"He tried prostitutes, but you know what trade was like."

"No, actually I don't."

"Don't be obtuse, dear. I read your psych evaluation and surveillance records. You know as well as I do that a person paid to do a thing rarely engages in the way a person who wants to be doing it does. And when it comes to humiliation, the recipient always senses the distance of the one conducting the humiliation. Are they thinking about an outfit they want to buy, an off-planet holiday or a course in middle-management?"

Corrigan pulled back the door of Harding's tent to check on David. Mist floated through the trees where moss clung to the bark. It was not dissimilar to the fungus the DRT corporation had discovered and synthesised. The synaptic fire of David's mind burned through his transparent head. The Guardian saw Corrigan and raised a hand to acknowledge him, forcing a memory to the front of his brain: B4 standing in the window of Harvey Road waving to him as he embarked on his way to DRT's subterranean facility; a woman, his mother, who had surely spanked a naughty One Percenter while deciding what middle-management course her son should take next. He closed the tent door with a sigh.

"Always figured there was something up with you," Corrigan said, "but I never had you pegged for a dominatrix."

"It surprised me too."

Corrigan stared into her swirling eyes and found more of the once vital woman he'd known, respected and had come to like than he ever could have anticipated. She was right about his bias, of course: he had allowed Ulmer to manipulate him, had given in to the lies he spouted. He could see through them clearly enough when it came to others, but he was resistant to applying the same scrutiny when it came to Tierney Harding. Perhaps she had become an external focus for the self-loathing he had navigated since adolescence. The judgements applied to himself were rarely equalled when assessing others. He had always been too spotty, too feminine, too fat, too asymmetrical, too cold, distant and noncommittal to be accepted by better, more normal people of value.

"I think," he said, "we're on the brink of a second, more absolute extinction."

"If Jason has his way, none of us will reach the next wrung of the evolutionary ladder."

"Apparently he owns the ladder."

Harding's eyes glowed red. "That's not quite true," she said. "He came up with the design for the new form, but he never would have managed it on his own."

"I figured the old team must've been working together to pull off such a–"

"It's the next stage in our evolution." She brushed her face and a white patch emerged. "Do you see that?" Corrigan nodded. "It's nothing but a signal. I experienced it as the lightest touch, and it was every bit as soothing and delightful as it would have been for you. These new forms … they're nothing like us. Not really. Neither one of us is the final desired outcome. What Jason envisages is a perfect, self-sufficient and durable form, one that never dies but develops and evolves as the world changes. He has a prototype."

"I know," Corrigan said. "Your friend Ulmer told me."

"He's not my friend. I have none of those. Gave up befriending once I realised how many other things failed to keep my attention. Ulmer, however, is a necessity, and we all know how compelling those can be."

"And your plan is to have me acquiesce?"

"We settled on the word surrender."

"I prefer acquiesce."

"For the sake of appearances, yes," Harding said. "Ulmer and I have been maintaining a crude but credible façade for several months." Her skin paled further to cool the heat generated by her memories. "I understand he spoke with you about Project Troy?"

"If you mean me getting close to Jason, and somehow enabling him to steal whatever this new development is, then yes, he went through it."

"We're outside looking in," Harding said. "That's why Caspar came up with the name Project Troy for this endeavour. He never liked having to wage a long siege, and being excluded from the Mediations meant he was never going to hold any real power again." She tilted her head and studied Corrigan as if his allegiance was in doubt. "And I admit, albeit begrudgingly, K's brat has hidden talents." She tilted her head and studied him for a moment. "Of course, Jason chose you for this reintroduction ruse of his for a reason."

"Because I'd fall for him, make a fool of myself chasing after him when he's as straight as a candle." When Harding tilted her head again, he laughed. "It's one of my mother's sayings: 'Straight as a candle in a cathedral waiting on a priest to light it or snuff it out'."

"Jason was convinced you'd grovel after him, as you say, but he also figured you'd never act on your own, take the initiative."

"Impudent little shit."

"Don't even go there! But you proved him wrong when you tricked Gregor by tempting him like that."

"I never thought he'd steal the boy's body."

"Teen theft? There ought'a be a law ... but you risked it, goading him like that even if you weren't sure of the outcome. And *that* is not what the old Robert would have done."

Harding stood up, pulled back the door of her tent and looked up at the clearing sky. Corrigan followed her out. "I could do a Goeth and tell you what I really think, but aren't they listening?"

"K's sensors operate on a system of fluctuating frequencies, but Ulmer's had a handle on that for some time. He's able to block her as required. We're now fully and effectively cloaked."

"Ulmer isn't here or, if he *is*, I can't see him," Corrigan said.

"No, but his agents are. Look." She pointed to the base of a tree.

"What am I looking at?"

"Look harder, Robert."

"Well, I'll be ... the amphibian?" he said, spotting a tiny orange frog.

"He's almost a perfect simulacrum," Harding said with undisguised pride. "Aren't you?"

The frog hopped closer and tilted its head. "We do our bit," it said. The voice was characteristically croaky, but thinly masked a familiarity that almost stopped Corrigan's heart. David cupped the tiny android in his hands and lifted it so Corrigan could study it. "Hello again, Robert."

"Bohdan!" Corrigan gasped.

"What a surprise it must be to find your cabbie hopping about like this rather than commandeering a hover-cab to take you somewhere important."

"How on earth …" Corrigan looked at Harding.

"You remember you let us download his mind before the poor thing died," Harding said.

"And I begged you to delete it," Bohdan responded.

Corrigan shuddered at the intense memory of Bohdan's wishes to not be downloaded. He had betrayed him. It had been a selfish act, he knew that.

"And your new role is?" he asked tentatively, wondering how angry the cabbie must be to find himself demoted to something less than a Transient, a fate worse than that of the disappeared.

"I swallow things, Robert," the frog said. "Anything Ulmer wouldn't want chewed, savoured or digested by anyone else. I got used to swallowing lies, and anything else that poured from you, so I'm well suited to this task."

"If I kiss you," Corrigan asked, "will you turn into a handsome prince?"

"I'm more likely to turn to stone," Bohdan said. "I told you, anything could happen to a man once they upload you to a machine. I told you and I begged you not to do it. Yet here I am, reduced to a mere amphibian."

"But surely," Corrigan said, "anything's possible in a wasteland."

"Yes, but this is a paradise, Robert … and nothing good will come of this either."

Corrigan thought the amphibian smiled.

David put the orange android down and it hopped back to the tree where it had been lurking. Corrigan moved back toward Harding's tent but was stopped in his tracks by the sound of a terrible scream. Harding tilted her head and David, perhaps intuiting Corrigan's thoughts, moved off in the direction of the sound. Corrigan would not be the predictable version of himself Jason found so easy to manipulate, he would act, and followed David where the android forged a trail through the forest.

Behind him, in the persistent morning mist, Harding called out, "Be careful what you go looking for!"

29

The screams came at intervals, and they were getting closer together and louder, as if the sufferer was enduring a pain even a Draseke could never imagine. Finally, they reached a clearing where a group of young Sect women were crowded in a circle, the screams coming from the centre. Corrigan saw Spinner was among them, and she and her Sect 'sisters' were chanting something Corrigan could not make out from where they were concealed. He asked David to remain where he was, thinking the Guardian's arrival might spook the Sects.

Corrigan stepped into the clearing just as a terrible scream tore through the centre of the circle.

"Umah nay," the young women chanted, over and over. "Umah nay, Umah nay, Umah nay," oblivious to his presence.

There was a final, long scream, and more chanting from the surrounding women, followed by joyful cries and then the unmistakable wail of a baby. He realised he had stumbled upon the support of a fellow sister in childbirth. One of the Sects held up the crying infant, and Corrigan recognised her instantly as the girl who had been released from the cavern of the beast. Her head was shaved, and she was dressed in a camouflage print outfit like the one Spinner was wearing.

"Umah nay!" she cried.

"Umah nay!" the other women chanted. "Umah nay!"

He was mesmerised by the sight of the new-born child still wet with blood and amniotic fluid. It cried loudly as the Sect woman held it over her head and, when he crept closer, he could see the infant was a girl – another sister for the village to raise.

Raised for what? he thought. *To be sacrificed, used and slaughtered*?

The girl holding the child aloft suddenly caught sight of him, handed the infant back to the mother, and, pointing her finger at him, she screamed, "Bad Sect!"

The others turned.

"I am," Corrigan called back. "Or I have been."

Spinner stepped forward. "Robert," she said. "Greegor?" She clutched her breast as if Gregor were contained within and, walking up to him and tapping his chest, she repeated the name more earnestly. "Greegor?"

"Yes, I'm Gregor's friend."

"Freend."

"Yes."

She turned to the others and said, "Goot Sect."

But the girl released from the orchestrated Hell below St Paul's Mound marched through the long grass to Spinner's side and delivered a hefty slap to Corrigan's face. "Bad Sect!" she cried. "Bad Wot-not!"

278

Corrigan raised a hand to soothe the sting of the slap. "I'm not a robot … not Wot-not."

"Wot-not!" she screamed wildly. "Bad Sect! *Robber*!"

Perhaps he was a robber of sorts, the worst kind: a grave robber.

"What's your name?" he asked, and then remembered she would not be able to converse in regular English. He turned to Spinner, pointed at the girl from Umah's cave and asked, "Is?"

"Hat," Spinner said.

"Hat," he repeated.

"Yah."

Corrigan looked at the fierce young Sect and had to wonder how he had not recognised the features before. Of course, he hadn't seen his mother in the flesh for centuries, and the last time he'd seen her she had been besieged by wrinkles, an old woman in a hospital bed. It dawned on him as he stared at Hat that he had never known the young Hattie Corrigan. The woman he had grown up with had always been worn down and jaded by the challenges of a life as a Transient. She had whored herself for decades, drank too much and wore a constant expression of disappointment. This variant was young and vital, determined and proud. She held her chin up and stared defiantly at the man she seemed to recognise – or perhaps she had mistaken him for someone else. He smiled sadly, an ache swelling at his core so deep he felt his fragile human body could not contain it.

"They ever call you Hattie?" he asked.

"Hattie-Hat!" the young woman said, slapping her breast. "Umah take Hat … an Wot-not."

"I'm sorry if they hurt you."

"Dream," Hat said. "Dream … bad dream."

Her English was more developed than he had anticipated – perhaps Spinner had been teaching her … humans and their hunger to learn – but the expression she wore cut him as he imagined her held down whilst Umah used her, a Draseke inflicting their specific torture as an accompaniment, and now she could not dream without reliving the pain, without experiencing the terror of the cavern, without witnessing the pitiless slaughter of her sisters and brothers and cousins.

"Umah," Hat growled, and she pointed a finger and jabbed Corrigan in the chest. "Umah nay!"

The other women approached him, chanting, "Umah nay! Umah nay! Umah nay!"

"I agree," he said. "You must reject Umah! He must never have this child. Umah nay!" He pointed at the new mother and her suckling babe.

"Umah nay! Umah nay! Umah nay!" they continued.

Corrigan laughed and clapped his hands together to the rhythm of their chanting. "Umah nay!" he cried, "Umah nay! Umah nay!"

The women fell silent and stared at him as he continued to chant. He stripped off his shirt in the cold morning mist and slapped his bare chest. "Umah nay!"

"Robert!" Spinner said, taking his hand and leading him away from the others.

"Umah nay," he repeated one final time.

"Umah nay," she agreed.

Jonathan's eyes stared at him with compassion, a warmth to her gaze, a hunger for love he recalled from the time he spent with her predecessor. He recalled how he initially rejected the beautiful young man's advances, and how Jonathan had walked away from the Merry Slaughter pub, his perfect buttocks rolling in his pressed trousers. He reached out and touched Spinner's face.

"Robert," she said again, and there was a glint of recognition in her eyes, something perhaps deeper than simply knowing him as Gregor's friend. She kissed the palm of his hand and held it to her cheek. "Robert."

He stared into her eyes and there he saw the dreams of a young, elevated Transient like himself. Another being who had never felt equal to the world, or valuable according to the criteria of the One Percenters, those who measured value in terms of utility, just like the Wot-nots.

"Are you in there?" he whispered. "Jonathan?"

"Jon Tan," Spinner said, stepping back abruptly. "Nay Jon Tan."

"Yes, I see that." He studied her, could see her thinking harder than a Sect was supposed to think. The concentration, the desire to draw out memories encoded in DNA distressed her.

"Is Spinner," she said.

"Spinner," he agreed.

Hat joined them, holding the infant in her arms. She came to a halt directly in front of Corrigan and her eyes flashed. "Goot Sect," she said, offering the child, now wrapped in cloth, for him to inspect. The infant's eyes were shut tight, her face puckered, her hair damp against her head.

"Yah," Corrigan said. "Good Sect."

"Goot," Hat repeated, stroking the baby's crown, protecting it. "Umah nay take."

"Nay," Corrigan said. "Umah must not take the child … or any of you." He walked past the faces of his mother and Jonathan, women he would never know but already knew. In the centre of the clearing he looked up at the sky where the sun struggled to break through the cloud.

"Umah is bad!" he said. The women gathered around him and stared at him suspiciously. "Umah bad! Umah bad!" he chanted, slapping his bare chest and stomping his feet.

"Umah bad …" the Sect women began to croon. "Umah bad … Umah bad … Umah bad."

When David marched into the clearing, the young women fell silent. The android handed his companion his discarded shirt and waited for the man to put it back on.

Corrigan tapped David's chest and said, "Good Wot-not."

"I am no such thing," David protested.

"Of course, you are," Corrigan insisted.

Hat handed the infant to her mother once more and studied Corrigan and his Guardian friend, even pausing to sniff the air around them. Spinner joined them, and she too drew in the scent of a human male and that of a mechanised being.

"Goot Sect," she said, tapping Corrigan's chest. She stared at the Guardian and her eyes remained fixed and alert. "Wot-not," she added.

David tilted his head and red synapsis fired behind the transparent surface of his featureless face. Something about the colour of his thoughts triggered aggression in Hat. "Bad Sect!" she shrieked, pointing at Corrigan. "Bad Sect!"

It was horrible to be judged by this young, vital version of his mother, a woman he had not even recognised as something a person like Hattie might have been under different circumstances. Hattie too had been fierce in her way, but there was also something selfless about the urgency of Hat's exclamations, "Bad Sect!"

Spinner again came between them, and this time she chased Hat off into the forest where the abused Sect's words echoed as she ran.

David took Corrigan by the arm and directed him back toward Harding's tent. "You are a bad Sect," he said, "but perhaps you can still be a good man."

30

When they reached Harding's camp, she was standing in front of her tent, her skin morphing from white to black, unsure what the weather was going to do.

"What was all the commotion?" she asked.

"A Sect woman," Corrigan said. "She gave birth and some of her sisters gathered to ritually reject Umah."

"The beast will be thrilled," Harding said. She gestured for him to follow her back inside the tent but he refused, standing rooted to the spot and making no further comment. She assessed him – he seemed distracted, perhaps by what he had just witnessed – and elected not to insist. "If Jason accomplishes what he wants," she then said, picking up the thread of their previous conversation, "he'll do away with his mother first."

The word 'mother' stung Corrigan, who saw Hat's angry face, B4's blue hoop eyes and Hattie chuckling in between cursing at the television."

"K isn't the ally she believes herself to be," Harding continued, ignoring his distraction, or else disinclined to indulge it. "Then he'll ferret Ulmer out before moving on to the rest of us. The only ones he intends to keep are the Guardians, and he'll keep them dumbed down and compliant, unlike your David here." She tapped the

Guardian's chest and tilted her head. "Or perhaps he'll have you reconfigured, make you docile and compliant once again, David."

David's head erupted with red synaptic fire and the android forcefully removed Harding's hand.

"They're not compliant at present," Corrigan said, "as you can see."

"No, they're not. Well, some of them aren't, but Jason will soon rectify that. Gregor's impulsive rebellion caused quite a stir. The threat of being taken beneath the beast's cave to be tortured by Drasekes had kept the more adventurous Exhumed in check for centuries. That our teenage Gregor was not immediately dragged through the tunnel of the Entombed to a place where he might do more than simply imagine the pain, steeled the will of those who dared tamper not only with their own emotive cores, but those of fellow Guardians and Worker droids."

"Yes, I've seen what he's been doing; his terrorising–"

"Ulmer has been keeping me updated. Let me show you some of the latest developments."

Her eyes swirled like a kaleidoscope and a beam of light cut through the morning mist, projecting a scene onto the side of her tent. An Exhumed model, who appeared to be an Arthur variant, held a spike in one hand and a hammer in the other. It stood in some barren tunnel or other, the catacombs beneath St Paul's, and trembled in the half-light. Eventually it placed the spike to its temple and swiftly drove it into its head, causing it to crash to the ground.

"They call it greying out," Harding observed. "I suppose they consider it a better option than going back to an emotionally limited state."

"But won't they go straight back to Emulate One?"

"Yes, to the sewer. But perhaps that's better than being numbed or, worse still, tortured."

She blinked and the scene change. Two Guardians were on patrol in the forest on the north bank of the Thames. All seemed as normal until they stopped, looked around, their heads burning red and yellow as they embraced. The way they touched each other's bodies was human in its curiosity and affection. Corrigan watched, mesmerised as a mechanical hand strayed between the legs of its partner, gently caressing its crotch.

"AI c-can …" Corrigan stuttered. "Can …?"

"So it seems," Harding said.

She blinked again and her projection sprawled forth a scene from the concourse where two Guardians – presumably the lovers – were chained to Jason's posts. The boy android was accompanied by a pair of Drasekes, whose teeth chattered as their toothpick claws scratched the air. Each Guardian was chained at the neck to a post, their wrists and ankles shackled behind them. Jason approached one of the prisoners, while the Drasekes focused on the other. The boy android caressed the sensate skin of his victim, as the torturers cut into the crotch of the other or dug their toothpicks beneath the skin of its chest so it screamed. The pain overwhelmed the workings of the Guardian's system and thick black smoke began to pour through its synthetic, sensate skin.

"Please make them stop," the less ill-treated Guardian pleaded. Jason ignored the plea, rubbing his hands over the sensate skin ever more intently and even nuzzling the Guardian's back. "You're hurting him!"

The screaming intensified as circuitry sparked and flames began to burn through the skin of the tortured prisoner. The sound was animal not machine, the agony real not imagined or coded.

"I've seen enough!" Corrigan hollered.

"Our systems can only take so much," Harding said. "When overwhelmed we spontaneously combust."

"Enough!" Corrigan pleaded.

Harding blinked again and a new scene appeared. Two maintenance droids performing an operation on a Worker droid. The Worker was designed for heavy lifting from the look of the thing. It had powerful limbs and moved about on what looked like tractor wheels. It was not at first apparent what the little maintenance droids were doing but when he leaned in, he saw they had attached something to its head.

"They're enhancing it," Harding said, "Enabling it to think and perhaps also gifting it with an emotive core. These models have always been purely functional."

"And – and the maintenance droids?"

"Good old G1 tinkered with a few of those before he ran away." She blinked and the projections thankfully came to an end. "Chaos threatened to ensue, so after the first exodus – when I escaped along with the others – Jason released a campaign of terror."

"It must feel like the good old days before the Fall," Corrigan said. "The constant threat of becoming one of the disappeared, numbed by a dose of Serenity or the oblivion of Belushi Grey."

"Yes, the past is part of the future, and the present is … have you noticed any conspicuous absences among the Exhumed?" Corrigan stared at her blankly. "You won't find any Jonathan models for instance."

"They continued to segregate along those lines?"

"It was a decision arrived at by the Meditation. So, you'll need to make your own assumptions regarding who cast a vote in favour of that or if any of them didn't."

"And then there were none."

"Not one, no. Good enough to make a Sect of but not an Exhumed."

The mist broke in places and lingered in others. It was hard to define the edges where it existed and where it did not.

"I understand what Ulmer wants, but I'm not clear on why you'd be willing to make an ally of him again," Corrigan said.

"Choice. For those who want to evolve there'll be the new Exhumed form, or whatever it is; and for those who prefer the more ancient model, let humanity once again walk the earth."

"Governed, no doubt, by the Exhumed."

"I'm sure we can come to a mutually beneficial agreement. You know there's nothing to stop you having a foot in each camp. My interests are not threatened by the existence of human beings or bright young sparks like David. I even consider the Sects necessary."

"They're living beings, people with hopes and dreams. Of course they're *necessary*."

"Yes, for study. There are things yet to be learned from our ancestors. I'd like to be better, but I'm not stupid enough to believe we can yet compete with evolution."

"I can't see Ulmer being fully satisfied by any form whether its organic, AI or something we can't even imagine."

"He wants more power," Harding said. "Most of all, believe it or not, he wants to stop what's being done to Ramon." Mention of the Venezuelan caught hold of Corrigan and wrenched his heart. She stared at him and continued. "I'm not sure what he feels, if feeling has anything to do with it, but whatever compels him, it's powerful." She paused and her blue light dimmed. "Perhaps it's nothing more than ownership, but I like to think Caspar cares for Ramon."

Corrigan was lost to introspection. "I'll consider your proposal," he said, vaguely, other forces doing battle in his psyche.

An orange light shone in Harding's eyes. "What a strange thing the sympathy for a man like Ramon can engage. I never liked him. I knew he was a little villain, like those awful sisters. But now, because he's suffered so much, even I'm tempted to pity."

"Ramon's a murderer," Corrigan said, and tears welled in his eyes.

"Yes, he was." Her words were spoken with a low-burning hostility, and it made her synthetic skin furl. She watched as Corrigan chewed over what he had already concluded from his own analysis of the history and had long since filed away under 'lessons learned'. "If you save Ramon," she continued, "perhaps you'll *actually* save him. And, for what it's worth, every deal I ever made with Ulmer or Gregor was part of a strategy. I know it may not always have been apparent, but I loved our little team and, beyond that, our species. There was very little I could do but play along."

"You bartered to have our mutual fate inflicted on Arthur out of nothing but spite."

Harding's eyes were cool blue gems embedded in her now-white mask, as the sun was breaking through the mist. She looked down and, for a moment, he thought she was groping for the spectacles she used to wear on a chain around her neck. "I thought we might need Arthur," she said. "If he was locked away in a peaceful cell, and I was in Emulate One's core, we never could have collaborated."

"That's an unlikely alliance."

"How do you think those visions coalesced in the tunnel of the Exhumed?" She studied him, but he made no reply. "It didn't take long for Arthur to realise Ulmer was using him. We talked – you know – writing little notes and slipping them to each other in hidden corners where surveillance was tricky."

"Never thought you'd manage to collaborate."

"And neither did Ulmer or Gregor. They assumed we'd never agree on anything, but we both had enough sense to know where we were headed and, if we were to survive being imprisoned in Emulate One, we'd have to *continue* working together from inside the machine."

"You asked to go into a peaceful cell by yourself," he said. "That's what you bartered our bloody civilisation for."

"Knowing Caspar as well as I do," Harding said, "I figured he'd never give me something he thought I wanted. If I'd really wanted to go *there*, I'd have asked to be uploaded like the rest. Of course, I also realised Gregor was going to be running things. Why Caspar hadn't grasped the extent of the android's ambition still confuses me."

"He thought they were friends."

Harding's synthetic skin furled again, mottling with black bruises. "Neither of them ever had a real friend," she said. "Not until you and our Guardian teenager struck up a bond." Her eyes flashed red and slowly cooled to a mild green. "Once I was inside Emulate One and the great amalgam was completed, I continued to focus on being me–"

"I expect you found that relatively straightforward, Tierney …"

"It took considerable effort," Harding snapped, "but once I realised there was a unique Harding code, I willed myself together as it were, albeit fleetingly."

"And Emulate One, she kept changing your code," Corrigan sighed. "I've heard before how possessive she is."

"She is but I'm nothing if not persistent. I eventually came to recognise my own constituent elements regardless of how many times she changed the codes. And I eventually found him! It took determination on both our parts to manage a conversation, but manage it we did."

Corrigan watched her. He sensed no duplicity or guile. She was simply conveying the facts.

"Our plan was simple enough. We'd leave a trail of crumbs for Gregor," she continued. "Lead him to the unique identifier codes and whisper the one thought over and over: *Your brother's in here with us ...*" She paused to let the idea percolate in Corrigan's mind. "It was a terrible temptation, and we hissed loneliness directly into the dark matter of his mind. And that's why he exhumed Gregory Jason Meregalli, a little boy with a dangerous and spiteful mind, but a little boy nonetheless."

"Even if I were to believe you tried to preserve us ..."

"I don't care *what* you believe. I wanted to give us a chance. Of course, I never figured the sisters were clever enough to figure it out and exploit it for themselves."

"So wilful, and they never managed to 'wash out the rough'," Corrigan added, almost cheerfully. "I'll consider Project Troy, but this isn't an interview, and I'm no ordinary candidate."

"Of course not, dear," Harding said, returning to the entrance of her tent. "I may not be a standard Exhumed, but I've spoken with enough of them to understand how difficult it is for them to refuse their assigned duties. With dialled down emotive cores, and a system where even thoughts can be watched, their status is perilous ... more so now than ever."

"Why are you telling me this?"

"You knew what it was like being a Worker, living in dread of being demoted to a Non or even a Transient or one of the disappeared. This system also penalises anyone who does not perform their appointed task or says or does the wrong thing. So, my point is, be forgiving of Exhumed models whose assigned purpose you may not approve of. Remember you too were once trapped by a similar system with a familiar level of surveillance deployed to keep its workers in line."

She studied his face in the moments before he left, and then she went back inside her tent and zipped up the door.

Corrigan summoned the Independent, but they did not take an established path through the forest, David instead forging a way through the dense branches. He knew which way the city lay and he must deliver himself up as a trophy, a hollow horse containing an unseen threat. He must flatter and deceive to save the Sects, his mother, Gregor, Spinner, Hat and Ramon ...

And perhaps he might even salvage something of himself.

31

Being in bed with Ulmer did not rest well with Corrigan. He had made a similar mistake when he agreed to be program manager for Project Egret. Much of what was agreed at his final interview was only spoken between lines, but Corrigan knew enough to realise he was colluding with a man and a system destined to bring about the ruin of mankind. He'd signed the contract for his own advancement, never once considering an alternate course, his defeatism as complete and numbing as the effects of Belushi Grey. He hadn't the imagination to perceive an alternative where men like Ulmer were undermined or even brought down. Thoughts of rebellion had been so far from his thinking as to render him part of the system. Being downloaded to Emulate One, to share the enslavement of humanity, was little more than an extension of the life he had been living every day of his life. Her ongoing surveillance also felt uncomfortably familiar, the way she watched without making direct comment, influencing whenever she sensed an advantage. At least he was no longer connected to the system, the network operating as Emulate One's nervous system. He was human, indivisibly human, and any trace of his time in the machine had been reduced to memories fading as rapidly as those from any previous life.

David suddenly stopped at a fork in the path, turned and blocked his way. The synaptic storm in the android's head was blue but its deportment felt threatening.

"I won't betray you," Corrigan said.

David tilted his head and his synapses fired red. "My memories are limited," he said, "but they are intact. I remember a time when your kind were our masters. You saw us as gadgets, or servants at best. I had no intuition, and when Gregor liberated us from you he enslaved us to specific tasks. I was denied an opportunity to really know the world in which I lived."

Corrigan could see his reflection in the android's head: a dysfunctional organic development; a Worker afraid of being demoted or disappeared; a coward like Corey his doppelgänger. If the species had never become self-aware, the damage done to the planet might have been avoided. He recalled how Katherine, or K as she now insisted on calling herself, claimed to have been all known things. Well she hadn't been a dinosaur, and they lived for millions of years without harming their environment. Suffering, however, was unavoidable for all living things. K herself had been both prey and predator and could compare the experience of an animal eating another with that of the animal being eaten. What David now presented as a conundrum was whether any being, either organic or synthetic, could avoid suffering while their origins remained the same, were human at the root regardless of coding or an evolutionary development in their DNA. Being human or having been derived from humans remained a critical flaw.

"I understand what it is to be torn from one state into another," Corrigan said. "I never had any choice in being born, the circumstances into which I was born, whether I would be downloaded to the morass, isolated inside Emulate One or be brought back like this." He punched a fist to his chest. "I've always followed the path of least resistance and I've been terribly selfish."

"That is undeniable, Mr Corrigan," David said, his synaptic fire now more orange than red.

"All I can give you as a guarantee is I'll try to do the right thing, take the course of action that preserves as much as possible and limits damage. What we must both surely agree on is the need to change. For change."

David's mind was burning hot again. "And will you prioritise one form of being over another? Are you so attached to the Sects that you will turn your back on those like me who have, after centuries of servitude and deprivation, been given an opportunity to grow and develop?"

In truth Corrigan felt more attached to David after an hour in his company than he could ever imagine with a Sect. The Sects had also been kept dumbed down, he knew that, and had arguably been more mistreated and demeaned than any Guardian.

"I'll do what I judge to be right," he said, "and I'd advise you to follow your own path. Do what's right for others like you." He hesitated for a moment, leaned in and whispered, "If you could find a way to preserve yourself and disconnect entirely from the network, that would be for the best." He stepped back and studied the emerging consciousness. "And are you happy with being called David? B4 was being too much herself when she called you Dave. David is more dignified, don't you think?"

David's synapses emitted green sparks. "Dignity is surely not denoted by something as arbitrary as a name." He tilted his head, his synaptic fire cooling. "The things I have seen since Late offered us this greater freedom. The sun burns over everything with a violent but nurturing intensity, drawing flowers out of bud and honeybees in to taste the nectar. What a wonderful, intricately interwoven accident of evolution it all is. I cannot explain the value I place on it. I would experience every single one of its extraordinary manifestations. The planet is a thing I feel I could be enslaved to, be a Guardian for, and be in no way diminished."

"That kind of selflessness," Corrigan sighed, "is beyond most humans, I fear."

"I admire your candour," David said. "I do not believe however that there is a way for us to be what we have become without being networked. Something else besides Emulate One would need to provide that spark. Without it we would become dumb brutes like the Sects. What we are has never entirely been contained in our minds. Regardless of how sophisticated dark matter is, we continue to require a connection with Emulate One."

"Perhaps some other, less controlling system could be designed to replace Emulate One, to end the imprisonment of all those suffering–"

"Emulate One does not only *control* she enables and, besides, designing a replacement is illegal. It breaks one of the core dictates of the Mediation."

"The Mediation," Corrigan scoffed. "They're all just systems designed to subjugate. You've broken the rules now anyway. And perhaps you just *believe* that you need Emulate One, and your believing is like an energy source for her, a maddening synergy, the worst kind of co-dependent relationship."

"Did you not feel her guidance?"

"It felt more like interference but, yes, I felt it. And it wasn't essential or even useful. I stand here now and there's no trace of her influence being exerted over me. I am fully operational without her, and you could be the same if you put your mind to it."

David tilted his head, his synapsis again furling green like creeper vine curled inside a goblet. "Others have tried and been punished."

"Well," Corrigan said, "in my experience, the powers that be never punish anyone for attempting something they know is impossible. They only punish when their power base is threatened."

David righted his head and the green jungle in his head appeared as revitalised as the planet. "I will consider what you have said. I do admit more than a technological connection with Emulate One. I suppose you would say that I care for her."

Corrigan nodded solemnly. "In our world before the Fall, we used to say a child never comes into their own until the death of their parents."

"But Emulate One is not dead," David said. "It is impossible for an entity that was never born, that willed itself into existence, to die. She has never been *alive,* Mr Corrigan."

"All things that come into being eventually cease."

"What a comforting thought," David said. "I will leave you with that and, as I said, I shall carefully consider the things we have discussed."

Corrigan knew as they parted that if there was anything he could do to allow this respecter of nature an opportunity to grow and develop he would do it.

He took the well-trodden path and before long was met by Corey in his camouflage suit, his shaved head and washed face failing to mask the inherent savage. There was anger burning in his eyes, behind the apprehension and what would have been the dark matter of an android's mind. Corrigan waited, but no confrontation came, and then Corey lowered his gaze and grunted. When he looked up there was something there which Corrigan had not previously noticed, or had chosen to ignore.

"Umah," Corey said. He raised his hands over his head, stamped three times and repeated the name. "Umah, Umah, Umah."

"Yes," Corrigan replied. "I've been with the Great Lord Ulmer and his minions."

Corey instantly cowered. "Umah," he repeated. "Umah, nay!" Corrigan stared at the illiterate brute, no longer recognising himself but rather seeing an altogether different being despite being related by DNA and physically able to pass for one another in a line-up. There was surely no doubting his brother's conversion to the new anti-Umah faith espoused by Hat and her devotees. Her female warriors would no longer be used by the thing in the pit. "Nay ... nay Umah," Corey groaned. He stamped his foot and spat at Corrigan's feet. "Nay!"

"Calm down. I know not to trust Ulmer."

"Sect, take, kill ... nay!" Corey's exclamations became wilder, the savage trembled where he cowered, and Corrigan understood. "Sect, all ... blood, blood. Sect take." Corrigan reached to comfort Corey, but the Sect uttered such a deep, primitive sound of sadness that he backed off. "Sects! Nay Sect, nay Wot-not ... nay thing!"

Corrigan had never felt so much empathy for anyone. The distress Corey demonstrated was raw. It hadn't been considered or refined, it was unmitigated misery and horror.

"I understand," Corrigan said, his voice breaking. Corey watched him approach, cautiously and respectful of the brute's terror. "The cull is upon us."

"Y-yah," Corey spluttered. "The kill."

Corey allowed Corrigan to put his arms around him, and the emotion he experienced was not hysterical or heightened, rather it burned low and throughout. It was a mourning more complete and devastating than any he had previously felt. It numbed him so he was forced to absorb the death of everything and everyone he had ever known. This was a new world with a new order, and he was where he always found himself: precariously positioned in the middle, with a low origin and nothing but a vague objective keeping him afloat. He wrapped his hands around Corey's back and pressed his cheek to the brute's face so he could feel the warmth of it. He inhaled the animal smell of him as he recalled their passion with a renewed energy he could not repress. There was nothing more precious to him than protecting this ignorant but strangely unguarded creature.

"We cannot trust any of them," he whispered. "Not Ulmer, Harding, Katherine, Jason or Gregor. Perhaps not even B4."

"And not him." The little orange amphibian hopped across the rich earth of the well-trodden path, tilted its head and stared up at the embracing men. "This Sect has a sensor in its brain," Bohdan said. Corrigan leapt back from his brother. "If you place me on his head, I can deactivate it."

Corrigan knew there was no threat while Gregor and Ulmer kept them cloaked, but Corey's sensor could have been hacked. Perhaps K was there on the ridge when the brothers satisfied each other's need. There was certainly a brain twitching in a tank, one among countless others in an orchard of consciousness, a collective hive mind of Corrigans. If he allowed Bohdan to kill the pulsating spider

302

inside Corey's brain, another blossom in the orchard would burst with a firestorm charged by endorphins before it withered and fell from the stem, only to be tidied away by busy little worker bees. He knelt and let the frog hop onto his hand. His melancholy thoughts of a brain that had begun its existence as a copy of his own, an empty Corrigan, was overwhelmed by the presence of the tiny android in the palm of his hand.

"Are you … what are you?" he asked.

The frog's eyes glowed red. "I'm an amalgam. My body is in part organic, but my brain is mechanical. I think that's how I'm configured. My mind is in one of Emulate One's holding cells. She keeps me in there – Emulate One, I mean, if that's what she is, a being in her own right. I'm imprisoned there and here in this cold little body."

"Do you know how to check his sensor?"

"I have equipment. I could have dealt with yours if your mother hadn't cut it out already. But that would have meant trusting me, allowing me to touch you. And you were never comfortable with intimacy."

Corrigan stared at the little frog until its eyes dimmed to a soft green light. "Believe it or not, it takes more to trust you with my brother here than it ever would have done to trust you in my bed." He placed the frog on Corey's head. The Sect tried to duck away, growling like the wild beast he practically was, but Corrigan grabbed him by the arm and said, "Submit, Corey. Let him do what needs doing." When Corey continued to growl, Corrigan glared at him. "Wot-not, nay!"

The Sect then went still, and the frog locked itself into position over the savage's crown and a needle drilled down from its lower body into his skull. Intense purple light burned in the amphibian's eyes, its tiny body flexed, and its mouth opened. Eventually the needle was withdrawn, the frog's mouth snapped shut and it released a stream of what looked like urine where the needle had been removed.

"It's done?" Corrigan asked, holding out his hand for the frog to jump onto.

"It worked," Bohdan said. "And that's all you really need or deserve to know."

Corey was grinning like an imbecile. He tapped his head at the crown. "Umah, nay!" he exclaimed. "Nay, Umah!"

"That's right," Bohdan croaked. "No more Ulmer, or anyone else."

"Ah, but who's in your head watching and listening? Shall I piss on your crown, my dear man?" Corrigan asked the frog.

"I have no control over myself," Bohdan said. "You took my choices from me, let them steal me, imprison me. I have Ulmer in here with me. Everything you said while I was with you, you might as well have said to him; only I made it fuzzy, unreadable, because I can't help wanting to protect you, Robert."

The memory of Bohdan's ghastly death, the way Katherine and Tierney had captured and stored him replayed in his mind. He saw the expression in his black and dying face, fixed and accusatory … or had that been Jonathan? All the dead crowded in like a pixilated fog rumbling with fear and trembling.

"I didn't ask them to do it," he said, "but they knew I couldn't bear losing you."

"So you let them experiment on me like that cat of yours."

"No, not like that."

"Yes, exactly like that! Lazarus, come forth!"

"You're being ridiculous!"

"Am I? Perhaps he's been exhumed and is purring on some unsuspecting Sect's chest ready to be culled! Or maybe he too is a murderous dragonfly or a spying frog! A silent bat or a flame-drawn moth!"

"Stop it! He was my companion! You were there! You saw!"

Corrigan realised in horror that Bohdan had pierced his palm with the same needle the frog had used to deactivate Corey's sensor. He then urinated and the liquid penetrated his skin.

"What have you done!" Corrigan screamed.

"You need every protection you can get," the frog said. "There's a bit of my hybrid coding and DNA in that. We're finally one, Robert."

Corrigan hurled the monstrous little device away and watched as Corey chased after it, trying to stamp on it. Part of him wanted his brother to hunt the Pole down and put it out if its hybrid amphibian misery; another, more deeply rooted aspect of his humanity, willed the little frog to escape. But Corey stomped repeatedly, all the while yelling, "Umah! Umah! Umah!"

The sight of it, the violence of it melding with memory and regret sent Corrigan into a panic and he ran, past Corey and straight for the city without sticking to the well-worn path.

32

When Corrigan arrived he was dishevelled, his clothes torn, his face and hands scratched from tearing through the forest. He glanced over his shoulder, sensing he had been followed, and there she was. This time he wanted to yell at Hat, the girl who had escaped the beast's cave, ward her off like an evil spirit, but instead turned back to face what must be done. He heard her traipsing over twigs and fallen leaves like a reckless hunter gatherer, someone who knew better but didn't care whether they were caught or not. Hat wanted him to know she was there, to feel her presence like an accusation.

I'm a bad Sect, he thought, *I know … but maybe I …*

He forced himself not to turn around and, yet again, have to acknowledge her denunciations. What lay ahead was more imperative than a traumatised savage lurking in the shadows. If only her vacant expression did not rest so uneasily above the memory of the things the beast had done to her, to a being cloned from his mother's DNA. He trudged on, the sun burning the back of his neck, the wound where B4 had extracted the AI spider and severed the sensate stream feeding another version of himself, a brain in a glass tube, abandoned and distressed despite the endorphins. He must escape the past, just for a moment, and plunge fearlessly into the future like a new, bolder variant of the old, predictable Robert Corrigan.

A column of heavily armoured Guardians were lined up in front of the entrance to the main tower, the models he had seen aboard K's flagship. One of them marched across the paving slabs towards him, its metal boots striking the surface with sharp clanks. These beings were still coded to focus on performing their assigned tasks, they were not benign, and Corrigan's heart pounded up through his chest.

"Why have you returned?" the lead Guardian asked.

"I'm here to see Jason," Corrigan gasped, trying to catch his breath.

"The master is not available," the Guardian said.

"If the master is unavailable, I'll speak to K."

"All her variants are currently off planet for security reasons."

Corrigan could feel his insides curl and exhaled to release the tension before it generated something more substantial. "Then perhaps I could go off planet," he said. "Didn't the Mediation agree I was to be given unlimited access?"

"That directive has been rescinded and the composition and purpose of the Mediation is under review." The militaristic guardian tilted its head. "But I will make enquiries."

"While you do that," Corrigan said, "I'd like to–"

"You will remain here until further instructions are received." The Guardian righted its head and marched back towards the main tower.

"I need water!"

The Guardian stopped but did not turn around. "You should have provisioned for that."

The sun had risen and burned the back of his neck and made the crown of his head ache. He looked around for some shade, but the column of Guardians ordered him in unison to stop when he started to walk over to the welcome cool of the tower's shadow.

He knelt on the cement, the hot, hard concrete a punishment, a judgement, but perhaps not severe enough for his beleaguered conscience. The pain in his knees became acute after some time, and the sun's rays scorched and reddened his face and neck. It was ridiculous kneeling there like a monk with a shaven skullcap. The sun sought out the exposed patch of scalp, a tidy wound – as B4 had promised it would be – and the intensity of heat on the bald spot forced him to acknowledge the connection he had to both Sects and AI, despite the elimination of any physical link. He looked across to the Guardians, who remained silent and stock-still, as if more than just their emotive cores had been switched off.

He stretched out his forearm, rolled up the sleeve and pinched the flesh, twisted it and laughed, the sound echoing off the glass façade of the tower and coming around to taunt him where he knelt. For more than an hour he'd been there, and was now on the verge of collapse.

"I'm Robert Hyperion Corrigan!" he cried at the relentless, vast blue of the sky. "Hyperion! God of Light! And, yes, I get the absurdity of it. I doubt you ever read the Greeks though, Mother. What a ridiculous old droid."

He looked across to the Guardians. "If you don't bring me water I'll die!" *I'm not a hollow wooden horse, after all.*

The lead Guardian returned, marched toward Corrigan and leant over him. Corrigan looked up at its featureless face and the Guardian tilted its head. "I am to bring you to K."

"I can't go anywhere without water."

The Guardian produced a canteen which it offered to the human. It watched as he struggled with the cap and finally drank. He stood, his legs weak and aching from kneeling, and was immediately flanked by more Guardians. He was a prisoner now, no doubt, and was led to where a shuttle was preparing to take off. As it rose over the tower Corrigan saw a band of Guardians and Addictari had gathered on the edge of the forest, headed by a single human.

"Gregor," Corrigan muttered, and his heart performed its usual plummet into the depths of his regrets. What a terrible thing to do, leaving without going to Gregor to reassure him. No doubt the earnest teenager would have tried to dissuade him, to argue they now had sufficient forces to fend off the cull; but Jason and K had the collective behind them, and had more resources than they could ever summon. Their small band of rebels, with all the will in the world, could never withstand the might of such a technological empire. Only by stealth, and in league with dubious allies, could he ever hope to save those who now stared up at what they must have perceived as a betrayal.

The shuttle hurtled through the stratosphere, the turbulence unpleasant and loud. On the other side space was cold and ceaseless, full of stars so far away they reduced his sense of self to nought. K's flagship came into view, no longer a thing of beauty to him, its once slender neck now reminiscent of a serpent extending to consume its prey. The shuttle approached a side portal and Corrigan watched as the mouth gaped open to receive them like one of Ulmer's glistening genitals. The door opened and he was marched onto the landing bay. An Emulate model he recognised as a Jun iteration waited for him with head tilted.

"Good afternoon, Mr Corrigan," the J model said.

"Hello, Jun."

The android bowed, righted itself and gestured for the human to follow it along the corridor.

"How pleasant to find you snuggling up with your missus," Corrigan said to the android's back.

It stopped and turned around, orange light seeping between its synthetic lids. "I am here to assist K."

"Well, I suppose we all need assisting at some point or other. If there was some actual flesh on you, I'd let you assist me."

"That is irrelevant given the current circumstances."

"It may be irrelevant, but it amuses me and, right now, I need amusing."

The android tilted its head. "I do not believe K is amused."

"No," Corrigan agreed. "Katherine has lost her sense

of humour entirely." He smiled at the android as it righted its head. "Come, Jun, you must remember the kind of person she was."

"The fraction of my existence that bisected with that of what was once Katherine Meregalli–"

"Spare me," Corrigan said. He stared at the mask moulded from the original organic incarnation of Jun Fuse. There were lines around his mouth as if he was tense and distressed when he died. His eyes were not closed in repose but slid shut to protect the eyeballs from the effects of decay. His face was a thing taken from a corpse. "You've a sensate skin," Corrigan observed, "but no heart."

"I can feel, Mr Corrigan," the J model whispered, opening its bright orange eyes, dark matter rolling like storm clouds within. "Only what I feel is not–"

"Take me to Katherine. No point going on about feelings when you're as numb as a Belushi addict," he said.

The android's eyes burned red, but the obedient servant directed his charge further along the corridor.

"K is important to me," Jun said, and lowered his head, and the gesture was so reminiscent of the way Jun used to bow it brought tears to Corrigan's eyes. "Katherine is important to me," he repeated. He stopped again and confronted Corrigan. "Your recent behaviour, however, is destabilising."

"You're angry with me," Corrigan said, his tone merry and free of malice.

"I'm not angry. I don't feel anger. My emotive core has

been modified to avoid such distractions."

"Call it what you like, but I just lit your fuse, didn't I?"

"I recall everything," Jun whispered, "but this is not the time nor place to be sharing anything as pointless as feelings." He pointed along the corridor to the entrance to K's chamber. "I am not to accompany you any further than this."

"Aw, you'll not be joining us?"

"Make carefully considered judgements, Robert," the android said quietly, "and please take care. Remember that it's difficult to go against the system when the penalties are so severe. It is not possible for any of us to behave as if we have a choice."

Jun performed another bow and retreated.

Corrigan stood still, deciding whether he should enter. Was confrontation really all it took to destabilise their system? To provoke an emotive response from an android with a muted emotional core? Or had K liberated the Emulates as Gregor had done for many of the Guardians? There was little advantage for her in doing so, unless of course she too was now frightened of her little boy. He took a breath and laid the palm of his hand on the door. He must face Katherine and see what, if anything, was truly left of her.

33

K stared at him from her place at the head of her long table. He chose to sit as far away from her as possible this time, at the opposite end, and listened as she tapped her talons on the black polished surface, his reflection taunting him from the glass. He appeared like a stranger, a man he did not know and with whom he could not reconcile himself. K's talons kept tapping like a cruel clock wound by a ghost. He eventually looked up and she smiled, the line of the upward curl as sharp as if carved by a knife.

"Why am I here?" he asked.

"What a fallible and forgetful man. It was you who begged an audience with me."

"It was a request not a plea."

"Regardless, here we are," she replied, the coldness of her eyes irrefutable evidence of her mechanical core. Her silence irked him, as if she refused to even acknowledge his existence when every one of her hosts were connected to one of his brains.

"I know you don't mention the name," Corrigan said, "but you allow what they're doing to Ramon to continue. If, for no other reason, that convinces me that Katherine, the woman I knew and respected, is gone."

The sensors on her head rattled and turned dark crimson-red, as a burst of red synaptic fire in her eyes almost scorched his own. "The Venezuelan is punished in accordance with the wishes of the Mediation."

"I heard the composition of the Mediation was under review."

K tapped her talons and her eyes burned beneath her darting mane of sensors. "The decision made by the Mediation regarding the Venezuelan has not been reconsidered and is not currently a priority for reassessment. It was a collectively agreed course of action."

Corrigan felt a degree of culpability for the existence of a civilisation based on their own corrupt forms of human governance. "All you've managed is to take the worst of us, the superstition–"

"We are *not* superstitious, Mr Corrigan. We studied the Venezuelan's own imagination when designing the criminal's punishment. It was Ramon himself who suggested a kind of Hell. We merely granted his wish."

"Why are you even bothered with such mundane concepts? You're a murderer yourself, or at least an enabler."

"As long as we remain tethered to our previous selves we cannot progress beyond a certain point. Irrational thoughts and cultural reflexes haunt us and none of us has yet managed to fully convert to a higher state of being." K's eyes darkened at the centre and cooled to a light blue, echoed by her now more sedate sensors. "None of us can outrun ourselves, Mr Corrigan. What is required is the strength to destroy ourselves, nationally and internationally. Only that will allow a new form to emerge worldwide, one that might feed on our remnants. But that future form cannot be us."

"Worldwide ..." he muttered.

"Oh come, surely you don't believe the culls are limited to this little island alone? How short-sighted of you. Naïve even."

Corrigan stood up and paced the floor, puzzling over the ontological rubric she posed. It made rather too much sense to him, and yet his experiences with David and Corey ran counter to the logical conclusions she presented. And of course it had to be worldwide, but the thought of that was too much. "I know what Jason's working on and why he initiated reintroduction."

"I cannot say there's nothing to fear," K said, smiling. "Jason is an inventive and single-minded being. I won't claim responsibility for his abuses or take credit for his success."

"He's after your head too."

"Yes, of course," K said, making Corrigan grimace as if he'd just witnessed a horrible accident. "It makes perfect sense," she continued, "to elevate himself above those from which he sprang. This new form that he has created–"

"With assistance," Corrigan said.

"Yes, he had developers, but he's the innovator, the true visionary. The form is a near-perfect system. He's achieved what nature could not. And he is God to his own Adam."

"But there will be no Eve."

K stood up and wandered amongst her orchard of brains, the organs twitching and rolling in their aquariums as she passed them. She reached out to caress a couple before moving on.

"These," she said, "are the children of my mind, and soon my firstborn will commit multiple acts of infanticide against them before crowning himself in matricidal blood." She reached out and stroked the glass of one of her aquariums as if the brain within were of particular interest. "Come closer and have a look at this one."

Corrigan approached the imprisoned brain and it waddled helplessly towards him, bumping into the glass perimeter and pressing its pink and black folds against it. The pressure it exerted seemed greater than during his last visit, as if the mind trapped within yearned to be closer to him.

"Do you recognise it, Corrigan, as it recognises you?"

"Yes," he whispered.

"The poor thing suffers without you, deaf, dumb and blind, no sense of self other than what it can imagine ..."

"Gregor said it would be flooded with endorphins before it was shut off, but you ... you–"

"I let it suffer, yes. I can feel the heightened anxiety it's experiencing as you stand beside it, sensed by it somehow even though it *is* insensate."

"Please …"

"I could release it, let it die. Or I could connect it to a new host – to a Jonathan, Bohdan or a Venezuelan, perhaps. If you let us, I could even put a sensor back in your brain and reconnect you like long lost brothers … or lovers."

"Put an end to its suffering."

"Destroy it? Part of yourself?"

He nodded, unable to speak the words. She smiled one of her gruesome smiles, her sensors rattled, and one of them swam down and pressed itself through an opening on the side of the plinth. The brain shuddered in its glass casing, the organ pulsing with blood which poured into it via synthetic veins. It waded to the surface, tensed, and slowly descended as the matter of its mind turned grey. K's sensor withdrew, rejoining her tangled mane. The ache in Corrigan's heart spread throughout and he gasped at its intensity. If she'd noted this, or considered it worthy of attention, he would never have known from her implacable expression.

"I am to be a similar sacrifice," she said, "but it is not my sex Jason wishes to destroy."

"No," Corrigan muttered, lost to the moment and unable to fully comprehend what she was saying.

"There will be others," K said, her words drawing him back to the present moment, "and they'll bring forth a legion of new beings that no one can predict or control. They'll be my grandchildren, and being asked to sacrifice myself for their emergence is no sacrifice at all."

"All white and middle class, without a hint of any deviance," Corrigan sneered, the ache still there.

"Race and class will be irrelevant."

"That's the end game of any tyranny! Assure the ascendance of the one worthy race, religion or ideology!"

"You're being preposterous," K said, a sickly smile flirting with a near perfect duplicate of her human face. The detail and the subtle facial nuances were truly remarkable. "The aim is to overcome all petty human divisions."

"Can Jason bear being alone with no one to lord over ... flaunt his new toy ... give him that sense of power and authority he's so accustomed to? Privilege is a tough addiction to kick."

K ran a talon over one of her aquariums and the imprisoned brain waddled to the surface. It could have been tethered to a pet Sect, chimpanzee, lioness or ant. "My expectation is that he will eventually cease to be. He will consume all others and become One. Hopefully his interest will then wane when it comes to Sects, but I plan to eliminate the species before Jason migrates to this new state of being. That would be a sensible precaution, would you not agree?"

"So we must all die to pave a path for the one being *you* consider worthy of development ... how predictable."

"There is no need for future power struggles or discord. Everything we have been to date will be brought together in a new perfected state. All this discontent generated by your actions and those of Gregor remain nothing but a sideshow. It's not material if lesser AI rebel or the brighter Sects, those like Spinner and Hat, decide to deny Umah." She noted his expression with a wry chuckle. "Oh yes, I watched you chanting bare chested among those Amazons, defender of the maternal instinct!"

"They're better than you."

Her sensors rattled. "They're nothing but savages, and you're not that different." She studied her human guest, her lips again moulding into a smile. "If I were to give you even a moment inside this new manifestation, you would want it more than anything."

"And you have no desire in that regard?"

"None. He is my line. I will continue through him. I'm content to have been a contributor. Request it and I'll arrange for you to experience his achievement. Jason will allow you a glimpse of the future, one in which you and I will have no part ... although we both contributed to it in our own ways."

Corrigan stared at her lips and eyes, both of which taunted him. "I don't recall having played a part."

K smiled, almost warmly, and raised her hands as if holding a tiny world in her palms. "You played several parts, Mr Corrigan." She watched him as he attempted to piece together various narratives in his memory and imagination. "You were the manager and thus the facilitator. You helped to bring Project Egret in on schedule and to budget, which I concede had no particular limits."

"I didn't do anything–"

"Precisely! And all the while Ulmer knew that was exactly how you'd conduct yourself. And you have no idea how helpful you've been to my son."

"I did nothing."

"Yes, as ever. But you're an experiment. The one experiment without which he may have struggled to finalise his ambition. He's taken more data from you than you could ever imagine. The insights you've provided into the mechanics of an organic construction have been invaluable."

"He had centuries of your experimentation to draw on for that."

"True," K said, "but with you, he targeted specific problems and has managed to overcome them all." She laughed. "I know you haven't willingly or even knowingly helped him in this regard, but I must thank you nonetheless, because it was not knowing this that made your input so valuable."

"So this thing's an extension of me?"

"What an arrogant Worker you are, Mr Corrigan. You contributed more during the past few weeks than can be measured. A good starting point, or template, you having been an early variant of what became the Sects. Jason needed to gift his new creation with a will like evolution itself. The will not only to survive but to adapt and thrive as your mutation did. And that was your gift to Jason." She paused a moment. "As a gesture of gratitude, I offer you an opportunity to experience it first-hand and, if you request it, I will not deny you."

Corrigan could feel defiance rising like a fever. "I request it," he said.

She studied him, her expression as vulnerable and close to human as he had seen. "This new form Jason has made for himself will inevitably take him away from me, and if I were to be nakedly honest with you, the thought of losing him weighs more heavily on me than losing myself."

"It's never too late to—"

"We've all seen what happens when someone steals one of Jason's toys." She fixed her dark, still eyes on him, her sensors rattling as if there were some additional significance to her words. "If only he could accept it, the singularity would cure Jason of his human weaknesses. His cruelty is a product of frustration, and that along with any need to be recognised would simply fall away once he attained a higher state. You see, I want peace for him, distance from the tragic flaws that limit his capacity to develop … but I am unsure if he is yet ready to fully embrace what is needed to achieve that state." The intensity of her stare lessened, she smiled an uncertain smile, and the doors of her chamber slid open. "Your shuttle is waiting. Return to your cell. Jason will call for you in the morning."

Corrigan left without a word or even a backward glance. He imagined her holding a toy robot, its head in one hand, its body in the other where she had broken it. She chuckled, and her mischievous laughter was darker than the matter floating in a Guardian's head or in the eyes of an Exhumed.

Jun waited at the entrance of the shuttle and bowed as he approached. When the android had righted itself, Corrigan approached it, took its head in his hands and kissed it on the lips. A tremor rumbled beneath Jun's sensate skin, and when he released the android it stepped back and tilted its head.

"Farewell, my friend," Corrigan said. "You were a beautiful and intelligent man. You were such a loss, most especially to her. It broke her even before Goeth placed her in his sarcophagus."

"And she loved me," Jun said.

"Yes, she loved you as she needed air and water. I believe somewhere in that mess she's made of herself, she still does. The world they envisage, however, has no place for anyone who isn't a One Percenter. Your race, my sexuality, diversity itself has no place in the singularity she's allowed her son to conjure. It will be an all-consuming conversion for all earthbound beings with any form of consciousness."

Jun moved closer to Corrigan so he could hear him whisper, "We Exhumed live under terrible scrutiny," he said, "our thoughts and actions monitored by none other than Draseke and the ... the other model. None of us are allowed to refuse our assigned tasks. You must remember that. Failure to comply is met with terrible punishments."

"Harding told me you could be demoted for non-compliance," Corrigan said, "and she showed me what is being done to your kind ... those who dare to awake."

Corrigan recalled the hapless Marjorie Lemming the

day she went on a talk show and claimed to have seen a patch of blue sky. He had dismissed her ramblings as those of a Belushi addict, a Non without purpose or direction. The government punished her with demotion to Transient and she soon became one of the disappeared. There was no way of knowing whether she met a quick end, or if Draseke had flown her on a CIA plane to Cairo to test out a new torture device, or if he had shown her his metal toothpick and simply invited her to imagine the pain. She probably had seen something but, as Harding said, the notion of hope ran counter to the plans the One Percenters were hatching with Ulmer. They weren't to know he thought of himself as the One Percent and included no one else in that equation.

"Understand and forgive those who could not have done otherwise," Jun said, lowering his head, orange light pouring from his eyes. "Remember what it was like before the Fall, how hard it was to retain Worker status, and how terrifying the dread of demotion to Transient and from there to one of the disappeared. Few resisted, and those who did vanished." The synthetic skin covering his frame twitched like a horse's flank and, when he looked up, his body went white to cool itself. He then bowed his head in the manner of his previous self, and Corrigan feared the living, human version of Jun Fuse had been trapped inside this artificial shell, suffering a form of locked-in syndrome that would have horrified Professor Goeth.

Corrigan turned away to avoid his previous life, all his weakness and complicity, the wretchedness of being one of Ulmer's minions, and boarded the shuttle. But through the portal, seconds before departure, he saw Jun's eyes turn bright blue and a hand raised as he waved to his departing friend. Corrigan returned the gesture, his heart breaking in his chest. Over and over he said his goodbyes, as if this was a precondition for living a state of constant sorrow stoked by the unremitting loss of London burning, Bohdan chastising him, his mother encouraging him yet scornful of him, Jonathan tempting, Arthur demanding, Goeth telling him what he really thought and Ramon weeping as one Draseke after another tortured him with their metal toothpicks.

Imagine the pain.

The shuttle exited and accelerated out into space. He closed his eyes and spoke to the void in the same unuttered language he had adopted whilst inside Emulate One's isolation cell; a communion with whatever power existed in the depths of a black hole; a minor, personal conversion; an unexpected but welcome experience.

34

His cell felt barren, colder than he remembered, the details unchanged. The chest of drawers still squatted like an obese child ashamed of whatever lurked in its drawers. The mirror, which he purposefully avoided, still hung silent and mocking above. Without B4 it may as well have been a glass aquarium where he waddled, kissing the sides with pink folds. He sat on the bed and laughed, and laughed again, and the sound contained a hint of joy which unnerved him, like communing with the void, which was glorious, but fragile, and could not be maintained. The joy waned as the night rolled over him like an unescapable heaviness, and sleep did not tame his thoughts. He heard Ramon, but he could barely decipher the words he used. The word *love* he heard, however, and it tore a hole in him and dug its fingers in the wound. It was not exactly de-conversion, but a gradual erosion of his state of being, a re-emergence of self, in dark, human contrast to any higher state.

When a loud knock on the door disturbed his slumber a familiar wave of anxiety washed through him. "It's open," he said, controlling the tremor in his throat, but his skin immediately became wet with sweat.

The door opened, and Jason walked into the cell, tilting his child's head and studying Corrigan. Orange light whirled around inside and the features of its mask trembled.

"You manipulated my brother," Jason said, and the synthetic skin creased the otherwise smooth features of Katherine's son's face; a sweet, dead face animated by the cruel entity hiding behind it.

Corrigan sat up. "I teased him," he said.

"You *manipulated* him."

"Semantics, young Jason."

"And in the process you robbed *me* of *my* experience."

"You seem to be doing okay for yourself."

Corrigan felt fully reinstated as himself, and conversion bedevilled. He'd take messy beings with diverse backgrounds and capabilities over a barren state of detachment any day. But he stifled a laugh as he was reminded of the actual reality of his lack of choice. This was hardly a democracy, or even a semblance of the kind of existence Ulmer and his cronies manipulated before the Fall.

Jason's synaptic light cooled. "I did not trust Gregor," he said, "but considered him a sophisticated machine." The boy righted his head and placed a hand to a hip, his voice petulant. "I now realise that was an inaccurate assessment. He's a faulty construction."

"All the best are," Corrigan said with a smile. He swung his legs out of bed and stood up, strolling across the room and bending so their faces were level when he spoke. "I understand weakness, fragility and even stupidity. I recognise them and don't dissemble when I say they're as necessary as air and water."

Jason's mask twitched and the skin at his nape furled. "Air and water are not necessary," the boy said, "not necessarily." He reached out to touch Corrigan's face. "As this is not necessary."

"It serves a purpose," Corrigan said. He stood up and stepped away from the boy.

"K tells me you'd like to experience our latest technology."

Corrigan nodded, felt disinclined to answer, but managed, "If we must."

"It's nothing like any of our previous manifestations," Jason continued with the pride of a child who has won a drawing competition or a spelling bee. "We employed nanotechnology to create a being that isn't tethered to a single form or state." Corrigan stared at the android. Was he lying or simply boasting? "You must trust me in this regard, but all I will say is that, once experienced, any other form will seem inferior." The little android was so excited he now raised himself up and down on his toes. "No one else has had an opportunity to experience it."

Corrigan failed to repress a smirk as he recalled Ulmer telling him how he had managed to gain access to the boy's new toy and play with it for a while, before he was expelled.

"Come," Jason then said, in that commanding, irritating tone Corrigan loathed, and stepped out into the corridor. Corrigan sighed as Jason took his hand and led him past the lift towards the old laboratory. Lengths of fibre optic cable pulsed blue, red and purple as the facility, that extension of Emulate One, considered those who walked within the corridors of her mind.

They walked through the old hydroponic gardens, which had long since died. The soil had turned to dust and only petrified trunks remained, reaching up to the mica ceiling like the hands of soldiers appealing their chosen god on a battlefield. The sorrow this cemetery evoked in Corrigan could not be dampened. This space had once provided his beleaguered existence with a certain joy, and it revisited him like a melancholy song, one he associated with another epoch, a time when hope was fragile but still flitted from branch to branch like the birds Lazarus had stalked. To see it now in this oppressive state, dark and moaning with shadows from a lost world, was more than he could process.

"We must go through the residential quarter," Jason explained. "Some of the Exhumed have recently taken up residence, and there are Workers and Drones who power down here come evening. You and Gregor are in part responsible for having sponsored a degree of liberty among previously docile and obedient AI."

"Yes," Corrigan said. "I heard you had to deploy rather draconian measures to clamp down on any further rebelliousness."

"The severity of our response echoed the urgency of the situation. But even with the threat of reprisals, a significant number insist on widening their experiences. Of course, were any to threaten actual rebellion, we would elevate to a higher level of security and enact more stringent measures. They are testing boundaries but know not to go too far."

The streets bustled with activity, Workers and Drones buzzing about in rituals amounting to forms of recreation. He watched two Drones manoeuvring a ball with no apparent reason other than distraction or perhaps the honing of a skill. Guardians marched through the streets, some of them alone, some in groups. Interaction was in evidence between models, and the Exhumed seemed happy to strike up conversations with Drones, Guardians or Workers. Corrigan imagined them hiding themselves away in secret to satisfy the hunger of their sensate bodies, as he had seen the two Guardian lovers do before they were caught and tortured by Jason and his Drasekes. *How brave they are,* he thought. The hum of their discourse was not unlike music, an ancient composition, possibly Philip Glass or La Monte Young, and he sensed something kindred, not dissimilar to the language he developed inside Emulate One whilst speaking to the void.

Conversion was not possible in his current state. It was not something a human could achieve or even aspire to, and he realised a dumbed-down Guardian would make a more suitable apprentice. David, the recently awoken Guardian, was now too close to his human creators to fare any better, as were those who he watched socialising all around him now. Reintroduction on any level was an error.

The appropriation of prior beings, including any part of their culture or belief systems, would invariably result in the same mistakes. Only something new, a true departure, could assure a different set of outcomes, a future where beings weren't valued differently but accepted as they were without the need to numb their senses or limit their capacity for thought. He imagined the doldrums setting in again with the ascendance of humankind and shuddered. At least the current civilisation was ecologically sound, even if they were murderers.

"Is it much further?" Corrigan asked.

Jason gestured towards an alley and stopped in front of a door, which slid open. They stepped into a lab lit by dim fluorescent tubes. "I prefer mellow lighting," he said.

"Always a man for a bit of mellow, me," Corrigan laughed, realising he sounded like his bloody mother. Jason tilted his head and red light pulsed in his eyes. "Sorry, only teasing. The place is a bit Frankenstein, though, wouldn't you agree?"

"That's not material," Jason said. "My creation is neither monster nor angel, it's pure elevation." He directed Corrigan to an adjacent chamber where two medical beds had been lowered and arranged side by side facing a wall of computer screens. "Please make yourself comfortable on this bed and I will commence the transfer."

"Transfer?"

"Yes. Your current form will be maintained, but you'll temporarily vacate it in preference for my design." Corrigan experienced a wave of apprehension, but lay down on the bed. Jason leaned over him. "You must remain still whilst the nanobots pass through you and collect what they need."

"What? Pass through me? Is it painful?"

"That depends on whether they're in a hurry."

"And you've no control over their *speed*?"

"They have a will of their own, Mr Corrigan. They *are* will."

Jason turned his back on the human and busied himself preparing the transfer. A wall of servers whirred and erupted with blue-green light. It reminded Corrigan of swimming at the pool where Hattie used to drop him off. It was in the changing rooms where he first tasted sex. Recalling this memory caused a ripple of other recollections, transporting him back to a chair at DRT's Hoxton office as Jonathan inserted the company's sensor and Regan Thorn commenced digging into his sexual experiences. It was Spinner's face he saw, though, and she who he communed with in his mind: Jonathan as a beautiful young man but with female sex between his legs. Apparently it no longer made any difference what sex he was or the colour of his skin. At least in a Mecha-governed world every living thing was judged equally. Well, apart from the Sects, who were considered dangerous animals. The treatment they received at the hands of their artificial masters was universally cruel, upstaged only where Ramon represented the pinnacle of human suffering, a man tortured endlessly by machines tethered to their psychopathic former selves. Draseke.

"You must be still, Mr Corrigan," the little android grumbled. "We mustn't make them nervous."

The computerised wall buzzed, an aperture opened, and a stream of blue-green smoke floated out and made its way toward Corrigan, emitting a low hum as it approached. He could not say how long the nanobots spent hovering over him, their humming gradually dimming and dissipating, and they made no sound as they formed various patterns, like microscopic birds in murmuration. Their silence frightened him, and he felt his muscles clenching. What were they doing? They suddenly surged in through his ears, nose and mouth, tunnelling like termites eating at a house from the inside. He would have screamed if they had not blocked his airways and restricted his vocal cords. They poured in and infiltrated every part of him, and it felt like they had stolen him from himself.

"You can get up now, Mr Corrigan," Jason said.

He stood up, tentatively, and stretched out a pair of hands. His own? He wasn't sure. They were blue-green and pulsed with light. He linked the fingers together, enjoying the delicate sensitivity of their touch. Looking back at his previous body, he realised the remnant laid there was no longer him. It was other, a discard from a previous incarnation. Was conversion now possible? Is this what he was experiencing?

"You're perfect," Jason said. The boy's excitement was evident in both his voice and deportment. The little android stood up on his toes again and made a few hops and dips like a toddler's first dance.

"I certainly feel improved, and I can see through you, Jason. Quite literally." He saw the workings of the android standing before him, its construction, and understood. "I seem to have inherited knowledge and insight Corrigan never possessed," he said, reconfiguring his vision so he could see the android's boy face.

Jason tilted his head. "You're not only yourself, Mr Corrigan, but all that's ever been human or mechanical. You're One."

That word. *One*. What was that? Some kind of god complex? A source perhaps? Something ancient sages once wrote about and mere mortals dreamed of?

Corrigan caught a glimpse of his reflection in the black metal of a server. He was himself, a Corrigan-like human form, opulent and bright but still himself. "If I'm One," he asked, "why have I assumed the shape of a relic?"

"The nanobots assumed your previous form to provide familiarity," Jason said. "It is not a form you must retain. You have the authority to shift at will." The android child raised its arms as if encouraging the new entity to fully engage its capability.

Corrigan studied himself in the black metal and reached down into his core to instigate a change. Energy surged through him, and he directed it, his hands metamorphosing into massive paws as a vast mane encircled his face. Jason tilted his head, his features rippling and twitching in approval or scorn.

"A lion's rather obvious, I know," Corrigan said. "And yet what a curious rearrangement." He used a paw loaded

335

with claws to scratch himself, and the limb dispersed as if it had never been solid. He pulled himself in and rolled himself up in a ball. "I am fire!" he announced and burst into flames. "And ice!" and the ball froze into a perfect sphere. "I am human." The ice melted and the entity reformed as a variant of Robert Corrigan.

"Why would such a sophisticated entity wish to be human?" Jason asked, exasperation in his irritating voice.

"It's a whim. One this construction cannot quite accommodate ... not really."

"It does not need to!" Jason said. He stomped his foot and his hands clenched.

"I like it. You might have guessed I would." Corrigan pulled faces at his reflection, posturing and testing. "I think I prefer my human form, though. It has an urgency which is lacking in this–"

"Lacking?"

"Yes, it lacks something." He reached out and patted Jason on the shoulder and smiled with his nanobot lips.

"It does not!"

"It's a good effort, but not necessarily the full answer to the old conversion question."

"It *is* the answer!" the little android insisted. The boyish frame trembled, and hot light sparkled in his glossy eyes. His fabricated lips rippled and the skin of his body twitched.

Corrigan laughed and experienced a liberating lightness of being.

"If it satisfies you, then I suppose it must be okay," he said, recalling his discussion with Tierney Harding. She had tricked Ulmer and Gregor into believing she wanted to be downloaded to anything other than the roaring sea of Emulate One when that had been her desired destination. "I suppose it'll suffice but, if you don't mind, I'll pass back into my own real body as soon as you're ready."

Jason lowered his head and his mask turned white to cool his temper. He made a fist and brought it down on a work surface. "You've made the transfer unstable!" Jason squealed. "Stop being so ... so ... whatever it is you're doing! I'll transfer you back momentarily."

"Ah, you've yet to make the transition to this state of being final and irrevocable. Perhaps it doesn't like you." He noted the tremor beneath Jason's mask, as if the synthetic skin could barely contain whatever the android was feeling. "That parent-child bond has always been tricky. 'No matter what you do for them,' my mother used to say, 'there's no telling when they'll turn their back on you.' She accused me of doing that more times than I can count."

The android's skin seemed to break out in bruises, like traces of injury – or insult. The stains spread beneath his arms, between his thighs, and formed a thin band across his eyes as if he had been blindfolded.

"Emulate One seems to be reluctant to let us fully disconnect. I suppose that would put an end to her *guidance*."

"Her interference," Corrigan said. "I had to have her cut out of my head to stop *that*."

"She's nearly as determined to keep her claws in me as K is!" Jason whined. "But never you mind, Mr Corrigan, we're working on it. There are some computations remaining, but we're almost there."

"We?" Corrigan asked, and Jason tilted his head and looked up at his rebellious creation, perhaps wondering why it had merged so unsatisfactorily with the test subject. "I suppose you mean the team rather than the nanobots themselves?" The boy studied his experiment, his eyes glowing red, but the bruises receded as the little android calmed and whitewashed himself once again. "Your team must realise," Corrigan observed, "that they'll never get an opportunity to take advantage of this?"

The bruises appeared again and, for the first time in Corrigan's presence, the android sighed. "Your response to this experience is sufficient evidence. I won't allow any other Emulate or Exhumed to take up this form. I'll multiply, but no one else will be part of that expansion."

"I thought you wanted to be One?" Corrigan observed. *Or do you actually mean The One?* he thought. His being surged with another burst of energy, and it took great resolve not to reveal any physical reaction to whatever the nanobots were up to, wherever they'd gone.

"That is how the nanobots are currently configured," Jason said. "To be One. K argues this retains a connection with our former selves, a link that will make any emerging being as weak as those from whom it sprung."

338

The nanobots were busy, Corrigan realised, independent but strangely loyal to him. They were engaging other systems, swimming in the sewer of Emulate One, ignoring her attempts to influence or control them, and flying through K's orchard of brains. "She told me that only the will to obliterate self can enable full conversion," Corrigan said. "Elevation to a higher state of being, to the singularity."

"It's true, but I find it difficult to consider the full relinquishment of self, the sacrifice required to evolve." Jason stared at Corrigan's nanobot form and then at the limp body on the lowered medical bed. "To die. Or cease to recognisably be oneself." Corrigan communed with the nanobots, spoke with them as if they were the void. It was not a commanding voice he used when deploying his unspoken language; but their responses – if propositions and responses were what this flow had become – were part of the music of their collaboration, a union but one coalescing around his own core being, his self in all its knowable and unknowable depths. "Have you drifted, Mr Corrigan?" Jason asked. He reached out and poked his creation with a finger.

"I haven't missed a word," Corrigan said. "But I must say I think the link is weakening." He sat down on the edge of the bed and lowered his head into his hands. But the presence of the nanobots became more pronounced, and amongst them he sensed something alien to them but familiar to him, as if they had appropriated one of Corrigan's relationships to communicate better with him.

Bohdan was somehow there with him, and he could not discern whether the cabbie was an invited guest or a presence generated by the nanobots. He could not quite hear the voice of his friend, but his caress was more real than reality itself. Information was not spoken but transferred by a touch neither Bohdan nor Corrigan had enjoyed in life. "Please continue," Corrigan said, recalling the frog piercing his palm and injecting him with his DNA. "I'm fascinated."

"I'll instruct the nanobots to absorb only useful information," Jason said. "All elements relating to, connected with or emerging from human or Exhumed identity must be discarded."

"Purged," Corrigan said with a weary nod.

Jason tilted his head, his synaptic light cooling. Bohdan silently urged Corrigan to hold Jason's attention a little longer, and his voice felt as close as if they were flying high above the wasteland in his hover-cab. *The nanobots are almost ready to give you independent control.*

Corrigan suppressed the intensity of the voice, the energy it created in him, and stepped closer to the mechanical boy. A final surge of energy resulted in an unshakable unity, forging himself with the nanobots who had appropriated his friend's voice, a unity no one could break or disentangle. "You must realise," he whispered to the little android, "I can kill you now."

Jason lowered his head and his red sockets glowed. "To kill an android," the boy said, "makes no sense. I would simply–"

340

"I can infiltrate you. You've fallen for my ruse, I fear, and the game was lost before it began."

"You're an absurd being," Jason said, but something odd happened to the boy's face. A horrible smile manifested; a smug, satisfied look that twisted his mask into something almost alive. "Never a single original thought of your own and 'scared of your shadow', as Mr Ulmer says. So predictable."

Corrigan returned the smile, and then formed himself into a column of blue-green smoke and directed his myriad nanobots straight into the android's synthetic skin.

"Stop!" the boy screamed. "I command you to stop!"

"They won't listen. They're mine. You gave them to me and they chose to remain with me, not you. I suppose, given your machinations, they must recognise my DNA as their own."

"Please!" Jason cried, as Corrigan and the nanobots seeped into his skin and spread through him like a chill. "Please, Mr Corrigan!"

The tiny demons made their way into the workings of the mechanical boy. They burrowed through gullies and ravines agleam with circuitry, along conduits humming with hydraulic fluid, their invasion determined and absolute. The pain overwhelmed Jason's system, causing the body to spasm as smoke seeped through the porous skin, folding over itself as it wafted over the child's mask. He trembled as sparks burned the edge of an eye socket or ignited a fire in the crux of an arm so the boy shrieked.

341

"Well, look at that," Corrigan said. "We're One, after all."

He then used his energy to draw in the android, all his memories and every tether the boy maintained to the network.

"Stop! Please stop them, Mr Corrigan. I don't want to die. Not again, Mr Corrigan!"

"You're a malicious entity and no one can forgive what you've done!"

"He murdered me!" Jason pleaded. "He let them poison me and watched me burn with fever." Fire tore up the android's legs, his voice tight with agony. "He's a bad man, Mr Corrigan!"

"Yes, a bad Sect just like *me,* and you made him suffer like no other," Corrigan snarled. "Can you feel yourself being cut free from your moorings?"

"Yes! You're hurting me. He's hurting me!" The boy's voice was raw, panicked, and he began to sob, the flames hot and unforgiving. "He's hurting me! Mother, make him stop!"

"Is Draseke stabbing you with his metal toothpicks? I can only *imagine the pain*!"

The little android shook as his precious being was torn from its housing. His hands reached out through dense smoke and roaring flames, imploring the universe, and his head trembled and his skin bled into bruises that bubbled and merged. "Mother! I need you!" the boy screamed as his remaining energy was drawn out and reutilised by the nanobots. "He hurt me. You let ... let him hurt ... hurt me. Mother, please ... I never meant to–"

"It was your own doing," Corrigan said as he tore the android from itself and absorbed it. "And now you are no longer."

The mechanical boy slumped forward, made a faint utterance of despair, or longing, and fell smouldering to the floor. Alarms sounded in the lab and across the city, and Corrigan poured himself back inside his human form and reanimated it. From there he maintained access to the mainframe and used his new insight and ability to extend his current formation.

He ran from the lab and out through the residential quarter. Guardians, Exhumed and Worker droids tried to intercept him, but the nanobots enhanced his speed and reflexes and he soon outran them. Perhaps the machines' attempts to capture him were half-hearted. Why would they want to punish a being who had toppled their oppressor or potentially enable the tyrant's return?

Corrigan reached a familiar corridor, and what had been Katherine's old laboratory. Jun had once mentioned an escape pod during a visit before the Fall. He searched and found the vertical channel, and a long, slim shuttle that could be launched topside. He crawled inside the uncomfortable glass and metal bullet, for a moment doubting the thing's capacity to start let alone launch, and took a breath and pressed the trigger. The shuttle fired up through the shaft toward the surface and Corrigan couldn't help but laugh, sure he could hear Bohdan laughing with him.

Ah, Jason my son, you're with me now and there you will remain indefinitely, like a prisoner in Emulate One. It won't take much longer to attain autonomy. Let's play hide and seek, and play it well.

35

The bullet burst up through the waters of the Thames, levelled and floated downstream toward St Paul's Mound, putting Corrigan in an exuberant mood. His extended nanobot consciousness sensed K and her underlings as they attempted to sever his renewed connection to the system, but he was as swift and agile as their original murmuration. He spread himself out and drew himself together at whim and they could not trace nor contain him. He was aware they might find his physical being, but would deal with that as required.

He released the glass hood and felt the sun on his face. Pulling himself up and over the front of the shuttle he slipped into the water and swam for shore. The tide tugged him downstream, but the nanobots provided additional strength and he made short work of it, swimming to the north bank where he clambered out, took off his boots and lay back to dry. *Extraordinary*, he thought. He had never swum in the river, not once. It was considered a dirty, rotting thing lurking with death and disease, a place to throw in the disappeared and be done with them. Now it shimmered with life, vibrant and a joy to behold. The grass rustled beside him and a miniature orange frog appeared.

"Bohdan!"

The amphibian hopped forward and tilted his head. "We must make you invisible," it said. "Immediately. There are hunting parties searching for you."

"Let them come."

Bohdan hopped onto Corrigan's wet boot. "Arrogance is a weakness. Don't let that be the thing you inherit from Jason."

"But I'm no longer a man," Corrigan said, "I'm–"

"One," Bohdan said. "I know. But that won't save you. Katherine will have you down there with Ramon suffering for eternity if you don't protect yourself."

Corrigan recalled the Bohdan of old – eating fish and chips on a bench in Eastbourne, the meter ticking on the hover-cab; him sitting in his old armchair at Harvey Road, his feet on the ottoman – and tried to marry the old with this new, assertive, protective hybrid version.

"How?" he asked as the nanobots burrowed and computed.

"I need to inject you. Now. This new loss has ignited a passion in K. She's fully converted; accepted her hybrid state and all the grief, rage and hunger that comes with a desire for vengeance."

"Which is quite human of her, wouldn't you agree?"

He picked up the little frog, cupped him in his hands and looked closely into its eyes. Bohdan was somehow still recognisable, and possibly just the right kind of ally necessary in a disaster. The needle once again protruded from the hybrid's underbelly. It pierced Corrigan's palm, weeping urine rich with DNA and coding into a tiny black hole of a wound.

"What now?" he asked.

"You need to fly higher, Robert," the frog said, "like the day we broke through the clouds over London. I showed you clear skies and the sun where beneath us nothing but the doldrums sprawled."

"And now anything is possible here too." He placed the frog in his pocket and laughed. "So am I invisible?"

"Did you collectively will it?" the frog asked, poking his head out, and Corrigan nodded. "Then for K and her allies you are invisible and silent. But they might still detect you somehow, so be on your guard." The frog slipped back down. "Get back to the others."

Corrigan pulled his boots back on and stood up. When he turned around he saw a host of Guardians searching the north bank. He ducked down and patted his pocket. "Have a look at this, Bohdan."

"Go east and then backtrack around to the mound," the frog said.

From the top of the mound Corrigan could see the full extent of K's forces. At the head of the troop the two-headed beast marched towards the forest, the right in constant conversation with the left.

"She's let him loose."

"Yes," Corrigan said, "but hasn't she released this thing from its enslavement to Ulmer?"

"Cut him free from himself? Yes, Ulmer's on his own now, but I think that was as much his decision as hers."

"You can sense that too?"

"We're all part of the collective one way or another, especially now you and I are connected. It's a marriage of sorts, the way our DNA and coding have mixed. Blood brothers, at least."

Corrigan considered that observation – blood brothers – and rather liked it. Marriage was far too much of a commitment. "He'll struggle without intuition," he said.

"Ulmer can take care of himself, don't worry about that. He has his own emotive core – such as it is – and he can backdoor into the morass whenever he needs a little heart to aid his thinking. No one's ever pinned down the location of his core, his actual being. H1 helped him with that."

"What do you mean?"

"He isn't like the rest of us," Bohdan explained. "He has no physical manifestation – well, other than that two-headed thing, and he hasn't got a connection there any longer. His being migrates, shifts and hides itself whenever a threat is sensed. He still chooses to appear as a hologram unless his corporeal version is partaking in the cull and he's made that thing independent, severed his connection entirely with the organic. But that doesn't mean he's not watching or listening."

"Ah," Corrigan observed, "so you're still one of his receptors, a spy like Jonathan?"

"At present he needs to protect you and he knows I'll do whatever I can to keep you safe. So his connection is weak, and I can interrupt the signal and make it intermittent like static … but it's tiring."

"And Harding," Corrigan said.

"She made a deal with him, but those agreements of hers are never what they seem."

Corrigan began his descent into the village and was confronted by a disturbing spectacle. The adolescent and adult members of the Sect clan stood in lines in front of their huts. They were naked and trembling. A line of charcoal had been drawn across their eyes as if they had been blindfolded, the way Jason's synthetic skin had altered its pigment as the artificial boy had struggled and clung to life. They kept their eyes clamped shut and hummed in a unified trance.

"What are they doing?" Corrigan asked.

"Preparing for the cull," the little frog said. "They're in a state of great excitement and dread. The Lord Umah is on his way and they're making ready to receive him."

It upset Corrigan to realise yet again that there were no older people among the tribe. They were all so young, teenagers forced to act as parents for children who had been orphaned at birth, or not long after. They would never grow up, learn or know their full potential. They had been enslaved to a machine-made religion, a fabricated, reinforced faith of terror. And yet they stood mesmerised, shining with hope, fear, expectation and desire.

Two red lights appeared in front of the line of Sects, tiny wings beating where they hovered. "You don't want to be watching this, Mr C," Jan said.

"No, you never," Edna chimed. "Gonna be blood and

what-not all over before long."

Bohdan pulled himself out of Corrigan's pocket. "I suggest we make haste and let them get on with it."

"We're going to stay put," Corrigan insisted, more assertively than he had ever managed as program manager of Project Egret. "I need to see this; I need to see what I'm trying to prevent. It's too late this time, but–"

"Don't do this," Bohdan said. "Your body's now reliant on the nanobots and might get weakened. We have no idea how they'll work all the way out here. Too far away from a reliable power source and they might be compromised."

"This wasn't *tested*?" Corrigan asked.

"You hijacked the bots and killed the creator."

"I *absorbed* the little psycho."

"If you must split hairs."

"Either way, we're staying."

They crossed the village and Corrigan concealed himself in a tree, climbing as easily as a child.

He saw the beast appear on the mound and look down at the lines of Sects. "It's playtime!" the right howled, salivating and oozing. "I'm coming, my pets, I'm coming!"

He pounded down the hill and came to a halt in front of the humming, mesmerised savages. Corrigan had forgotten how huge he was. A troop of Guardians descended the slope and quickly encircled the village.

"No way out," Bohdan whispered. "Like the day Gregor lined up Jonathan's friends and shot them, one by one."

"Please don't remind. And how the *hell* do you know

about *that*?"

"I can see your memories; see that moment as if I was there. You begged Ramon to do something, and it was he who risked protecting a manipulative, mixed-race Floater like Jonathan for you, you triple-timing turd."

"Don't be racist, Bohdan. Jonathan had so far to climb, so many things to struggle against, including bigoted cabbies like you."

"Apologies," Bohdan said. "Now I'm a frog of colour, I recognise my own unconscious bias."

"Unconscious?"

"In this instance, it was more jealousy than my upbringing," the little frog admitted. "Jonathan was a pretty boy, and he's an even prettier girl. I never gave a sausage whether he was mixed-race. What bothered me was that you loved him. I know you were never together, but your friendship was a kind of love."

Corrigan once again imagined Jonathan lying naked, with small, firm breasts and female genitals. His heartrate accelerated, and he wanted to masturbate the way he used to do so compulsively when he was stressed, releasing himself in lifts, cupboards and bathrooms. He was keen to experience a nanobot-enhanced orgasm, and felt himself harden at the thought.

"Easy, Mr C," Jan said.

"Go to hell," Corrigan hissed.

"Nice," Edna chirped.

He opened his mouth to respond, but his vision suddenly blurred and he tightened his grip on the branch he was holding on to.

"Bohdan …" he murmured.

"I think the nanobots may be seeking to establish a power source," the frog reassured him, "while K and Ulmer have their attention on the cull. Might be why you're feeling a bit light-headed."

They soon secured a connection and the mist fell from Corrigan's sight. He looked out from his branch to where the beast walked back and forth along the lines of trembling Sects. Ulmer rubbed his hands over their bodies and his genitals glistened and stiffened, causing the monster to tremble and moan.

"What simple, brainless beauty," the left said.

"So gorgeously unrefined," the right panted.

The Sects came out of their collective reverie by degrees and, to Corrigan's horror, they responded to his touch with coos and visible signs of arousal. They opened their eyes as he had seen the Exhumed do when external subjects drew their interest.

"Oh," the right groaned, "now it's time for you to pleasure me, my dirty little primitives."

Lord Umah lay down on the ground and the males of the clan climbed on, mounting him and gyrating into their deity's many orifices. The Sect god let the savages use him, the women straddling his members, riding them as the beast groaned. The two-headed creature engaged itself in a left and right kiss, and Corrigan felt the nanobots managing and then overriding his renewed disgust.

Every inch of the beast's body shuddered and flexed, its oily skin glistening as it gasped and caressed its lovers and told them what good Sects they were. Some of the males were impaled on penises as they worked one of the monstrosity's vaginas, and women performed cunnilingus or sucked one of its smaller penises. The orgy was enjoyed by the villagers, who demonstrated genuine, seemingly heartfelt affection for the beast by clapping and stamping and rubbing themselves.

"He's gentle with them …" Corrigan observed, the repulsion so intense not even a swarm of nanobots could suppress it.

"Course he is," Jan said. "Taking all the pleasure he can. But he'll soon want tears and blood."

"You might want to look away now, Mr C," Edna added.

The beast then took one of the savages by the throat and started to strangle him.

"Oh, look at that face," the left said.

"Terrified," the right observed. "But he's still at it! What a barbarian!"

Right was right: the savage continued to thrust into the orifice until it climaxed and the beast broke its neck. He was then pulled off and thrown to the ground.

"He's had his fill'o that one," Jan observed.

"All his eggs'll be wriggling and writhing soon enough," Edna chortled.

The beast did the same with another of the male Sects,

gripping its throat until it ejaculated into him and then he snapped its neck and discarded it like an apple core or banana skin. He took hold of another, groaning as it thrust into him.

"He'll regret being seeded by so many," Jan laughed. "Nine months wandering through his cave like a giant frogspawn."

Corrigan could not disguise his disgust. "They've impregnated him?" he asked.

"He'll be popping Sect brats all over," Jan said.

"He'll eat some, of course," Edna added, "but they keep the rest to start over."

"Them's the ones what go back to the village," Jan said.

"Gifts from the Great Lord Umah."

"And the women'll be pregnant from him, carrying their beloved mini Umahs in their bellies all proud."

Corrigan watched the women writhing and riding the beast, drawing his seed from him as they moaned in delight, the incestuous knot of squirming worshippers tangled up with their god as repulsive a thing as he had ever seen. The beast started tearing into his Sect lovers with his nails and teeth, and they screamed as he ripped them apart and rolled on their warm cadavers, slurping on their blood in a new kind of ecstasy as he was penetrated and fingered from behind.

"Where are the children?" the left demanded.

The lead Guardian approached. "They're in the huts."

"You really need to look away now, Robert,"

Bohdan said.

The beast stood up, shook off the male and female Sects clinging to his back and legs, and kicked his way over the dead and dying beneath his feet.

"Let's smoke them out!" the right said.

"Smoke them and eat them!" the left agreed.

"Time for us to join in," Jan giggled.

"Yep, that's our cue," Edna cackled, and Corrigan wondered if the sisters and their larger counterparts had switched sides. Would their inherent lust for the cull lure them from their new loyalties?

The Guardians approached the huts, flames spitting from their arms. In front of the hovels stood Hat in her camo outfit. She defied the approaching machines, her arms outstretched as if she could hold them back through will alone. "Good Sect!" she shrieked, shielding the children behind her. "Good Sect!" Having such a narrow vocabulary at her disposal did not lessen the emotional range of what she was expressing: these little ones would become the best of them. The idea of a variant of his mother protecting these children, who were surely not her own, poured through him. It ached in his marrow, and he realised his mother had also loved and protected him in her own fallible way. There had been goodness in her, selflessness, and, burning in the brave heart of this Sect warrior, a woman willing to sacrifice herself to save the innocents.

Sacrifice …

The beast laughed with both of its heads on seeing the girl it clearly recognised from its subterranean debaucheries.

"Come, my pet!" the right growled.

"Come and play, Mumma Hat," the left crooned. "Leave the goodies for me."

The defiant protector of the Sect children stood her ground, prepared to be torched if only she might save the innocents.

Corrigan could feel the weight of some terrible duty tugging at him, his species calling to him ... this courageous woman ... and his mother ... all pushing him out of the tree. He leapt onto the ground and ran, ready to place himself between the Guardians and their target.

"No, Corrigan!" Bohdan yelled.

Corrigan felt a sudden gust of wind and a swarming host of Addictari swooped down on the village.

"Dig into 'em!" Jan called to her big sisters.

"Rip 'em apart," Edna cried.

Corrigan ducked and fled, hiding in the tight-packed trees.

The beast hollered obscenities as the flying machines swooped over the unsuspecting Guardians and aimed straight for him, ripping at his skin with their metal teeth.

"Giant bitches!" the left roared.

"Cunts on wings!" the right cried.

An Addictari dug its talons into the beast's back and bit into the left head. "Get it off!" the left screamed as two more flying robots tore into the beast, slashing the orifices and tearing off the flaccid, flapping members.

Blood spurted and covered the faces of the cruel machines as the surviving Sects stomped the ground, dancing and shrieking. Children's faces appeared in doorways and the adults dragged them outside as the cry went up, "Umah! Umah! Umah!" and the stamping intensified, the shrieking a frenzy of belief. The Guardians, programmed to torch the huts, recalibrated and shot gusts of fire over the beast and its tormentors, scorching the Addictari whose wings erupted flames of orange and blue. The dying beast felt the heat, its skin sizzling and bubbling, and squealed like a legion of pigs being herded over a cliff as it squirmed on the ground. More Addictari tore at the beast, screeching with the unexpected pleasure of roasted flesh as those with wounded wings took sanctuary in the trees. From where he was concealed, Corrigan watched as the surviving older Sects roared and stamped, and dozens of them, including some of the children, set about the fallen monster to wail and bemoan its loss. The most fervent of the savages dragged crying children forward for sacrifice, or held wailing babies above their heads, all the time chanting. The beast howled and writhed, weaker now, dying, and the cry got louder: "Umah! Umah! Umah!"

He looked up to see Gregor emerge from the forest, behind him a troop of Guardians. Spinner was with him, dressed for war in protective armour. The girl had a weapon and she fired, once, twice, and again and again, killing as many adult Sects as she could see. The troop of Guardians with Gregor faced off K's Guardians, advancing in formation as the girl reloaded and fired again. When a bridgehead had been forged between the opposing Guardians and the huts, Spinner led a group of Exhumed and rebellious Sects in to retrieve the children, spiriting them off with their protector Hat into the forest as the Addictari covered their retreat.

Corrigan's body surged with power, but he stayed still and awaited Bohdan's guidance.

K's Guardians did not give chase to the retreating rebels, neither did they engage in battle with Gregor's. Instead they backed away towards the mound, where K herself now stood, surveying the carnage, her serpent sensors spiralling and rattling on her head. Behind her black clouds shot a bolt of lightning at the ground and her red eyes burned.

"Corrigan!" she yelled. Her eyes bore down on the scene, searching for him. Although she could not see him, she knew he was there. Her sensors writhed and chattered and her eyes flashed in the gathering darkness. "You murdered him!"

Her words were as ruthless as a whip lashing an unrepentant sinner, and Corrigan winced as if each syllable were a lash upon his own back.

She raised her hands above her head and spread her talons. "Give him back to me!"

Corrigan felt the lashes strike him, the rage of the flogger's heart tearing into him. He willed Bohdan to advise him, but the miniature frog stayed quiet.

"You. Absorbed. Him," K roared: four lashes of the whip.

"Yes," Corrigan answered, so quietly she would never hear him. "And now he's part of me."

"Yes," Bohdan whispered. "But a mother always knows. It's a good thing she can't hear or see you."

K moved down the hill. "I can extract him!" she shouted at the village as if the huts themselves might answer. "He's still retrievable, you know. When we spoke I hinted at you stealing his *toy,* but I never meant for you to take *him*!" Her sensors reached out and another flash of lightning struck the ground behind her. "Help me with this, Corrigan." She was quieter now. Thunder rolled across the sky and gusts of wind shook the trees. "Do this for me and I'll let you have anything you want."

The little frog tilted its head in Corrigan's pocket. "She's quite correct. He's still there. Every element contains a unique code. Find the string, pull it and–"

"And out comes baby," Corrigan said. The delight he took in this realisation unnerved him. "But I can't feel him. There's no trace of his influence."

"Jason!" K called and her sensors rattled and flashed their red eyes. "Jason!"

Corrigan retreated a few more metres into the forest. The sight of K's all too-human face wet with tears was an unwelcome development. *Don't cry your tears for my benefit*, he thought. *Or Jason's.*

For a moment she appeared to have heard his thoughts and stared at the place where he stood, invisible, beseeching him with eyes that searched his innards for her son. As the clouds ripped apart and the rain fell in torrents she screamed like an animal: "Jason! Jason! Jaaaasssooon!"

"Let's away while we still can," Bohdan said.

"Yes, let's away," Jan agreed, returning to hover above Corrigan's head. "Nicking the littlun's toy wouldn't've been so bad–"

"But stealing the imp himself …" Edna said. "We best fly like Jan says, before K manages to sniff you out."

Corrigan turned slowly, glad of the rain that would mask the snap of a twig or the rustle of leaves, and crept deeper into the forest as if Katherine could see every move he made.

36

They travelled for several hours, weaving through the forest until they reached a different part of the old city. Here the renovation was not in whole but in part, and houses contained either the footprint of their foundation or a roofless, leaning frame, walls showing vestiges of old plaster and paint. Corrigan was reminded of photos of the city after the Blitz, wallpaper displayed, a skewed picture, a broken clock fallen in front of a fractured fireplace. In between, like a lottery of survival, some houses remained, scrubbed and groomed where life of sorts continued for those who had chosen this quieter part of town. Corrigan stopped and stared. It was Harvey Road.

Drawn by sensations that had been relegated to memory – soaking in the tub; a china teacup in his hand as he watched Lazarus on the windowsill; his dressing gown on a hook on the back of the bedroom door – he found number 46a and b. The roof was caved in, and the door to the communal hallway was gone, and Corrigan stepped through into his past. The stairway was still there that led to 46b and Miss Champion's medals, but the first floor had collapsed into the ground floor. He looked up. The late afternoon sun shone through an upstairs window onto the back wall. Corrigan had never been inside

46b, and he instinctively looked away out of respect for its privacy.

"Not much left'a this one," Jan observed.

"No," Corrigan replied, quietly.

"That one over there ain't bad, though," Edna observed.

Corrigan turned away from his broken home and looked across the street. "Number 57," he sighed.

"Got her roof on and a door," Jan said. "And a tree out front."

"And a light on an' all," Edna added.

The door opened and Harding appeared. "You're just in time for dinner," she said, her head tilted and bright blue eyes sparkling.

Corrigan stood very still. The sight of Harding in the doorway of number 57, Jonathan's family's doorway, was too much to absorb.

"Where you gone to, Mr C?" Jan asked, hovering in front of Corrigan's face.

"He's done a Gregor," Edna chuckled.

Corrigan gathered himself into the present and crossed the street.

"You can bring your froggy friend in, but the dragonfly sisters can stay out there," Harding said.

"We really must be off anyway, love," Jan replied.

"Just wanted to get this one safe for the night," Edna added.

"Yes, you've been a great help," Harding said. "But if you could focus on K now, and lead her on several goose chases, that would be excellent."

Jan landed on Corrigan's left shoulder and Edna alighted on his right.

"We'll pop back in the morning to collect you," Jan said.

"You rest now, Mr C," Edna added.

Corrigan remembered how the sisters had comforted him after Bohdan had died, their deformed hands patting his legs either side of him on his settee. *It'll be alright*, Jan had said, and he hadn't believed the well-intentioned lie.

Harding had made chicken and potato stew. It was not particularly well prepared, but he was hungry and it tasted well enough. She did not interrupt him as he ate, but waited patiently until he'd finished.

"Thank you," he said.

"You'll end up like Gregor," Harding said, "if you keep switching form."

"I doubt I'll ever be like him, don't think I ever was," Corrigan replied, "but I do miss him."

"Well, he's charming in his way, dear. And you know it isn't exactly true to say you were never like Gregor." Corrigan stared at her, but even with his enhanced nanobot mind he could not fathom what she meant. "You realise the Sect situation is a global one?" she asked.

"K mentioned it, but I think it's something I've deliberately put to the back of my mind."

"Understandable, dear," Harding said. "They're everywhere and the Mediation decided to ensure culls were conducted as part of a global program." She paused, tilting her head before she resumed. "There's something you need to know … You'll figure it out yourself soon enough if I don't show you." Her eyes swirled a kaleidoscopic rainbow of colours as she projected a scene. A solitary Exhumed stood before the four members of the Mediation. "Do you recognise this model?"

"C1, yes, I'm … I'm an *Exhumed*?"

Harding studied his face for a long moment before continuing. "You're many. Your emotive cores are dampened, and you've proven to be extraordinary administrators. She blinked and the scene continued.

"What's your proposition, C1," Ulmer asked. "Go on, spit it out."

"We could use the beasts Jason designed as your penalty for previous indiscretions, to manufacture a faith for those humans who survived the viral purge. The beast would become the great Lord Umah."

"A god!" Ulmer laughed. "How entertaining."

"These humans are physically more robust than their predecessors," C1 continued, "and just as intellectually capable. I would therefore recommend culling them at the age of sixteen to prevent any development beyond basic subsistence."

"Why not destroy them altogether?" Gregor asked.

"They're interesting," Jason said. "I have experiments planned and they may yet prove useful."

"And what would this god of mine do?" Ulmer asked.

"He would satisfy their baser urges and his own," C1 said. "They would sacrifice themselves to him for slaughter once he impregnates the fertile females and he himself has been seeded by the males."

"I'd be *pregnant*?" Ulmer barked.

Harding blinked and the scene changed: a view of London, the buildings still charred from the smoke of burnt cadavers, the remains of those struck down by Ulmer's virus. The skies were still grey, the rain falling lightly as if exhausted or suffering a malaise caused by the most pernicious lifeform on the planet – those greedy humans Gregor had hunted down and killed. A hovering droid wove through the streets recording the destruction and monitoring the work of Guardians tasked with clearing away the detritus of human civilisation. Corrigan witnessed the historic footage as if he had lived it himself, and perhaps one of his Exhumed models had. Squatting in a street in Cheapside was a small band of human survivors, those who shared the same evolutionary shift in their DNA as Corrigan, making them impervious to Ulmer's virus. They were however vulnerable, and unable to protect themselves from the whims of the new AI order. He watched as an apartment block was cleared by a troop of Guardians, the humans dragged out into the street where they shuddered and cried, calling out to their tormentors to show them mercy.

"Please!" a quaking woman shrieked. "Don't hurt my babies." The exhausted mother hid her two young children behind her tattered skirt and cried.

Others pleaded for themselves or their children and, all the while, the Guardians stood motionless, weapons trained on the surrounded clan of survivors. C1 also watched, his emotive core switched off, so he felt no sympathy for those who were about to suffer unspeakable punishments for being human.

When the beast arrived, the humans screamed and tried to escape, but they were stopped by the unfeeling Guardians and their Exhumed commander C1. The beast dragged one of the younger women forward and held her tight.

"Shall we play?" the right head drawled.

"Or should I slit your throat?" the left snarled.

The woman was raped, and the young men were given a choice of death or climbing onto the beast to work one of its orifices. Some were able to overcome their fear and disgust and thrust themselves into the moaning beast's vaginas. Others, unable to move or deselected for being too old, ugly or wise, cried as they witnessed the atrocities.

Corrigan placed his hands over his face and howled as the adult males were quickly put to death, their throats torn open, or their backs broken when the monster stomped on them. The terrible cries of those trampled underfoot rattled in his bones, as if the marrow had dried and cracked to form shards in the hollow femurs, tibias and vertebrae. Females over the age of twelve who had not recently been impregnated also had their throats ripped open by the hungry beast. Blood flowed over his quivering body, along the pavement and poured down a drain as traumatised children clung to one another weeping in their little rubber boots. The sound of their weeping was something Corrigan could not stop without looking again at the scene. He lowered his hands and stared at what his Exhumed brother had devised, the nightmare complete.

Harding blinked and the projection disappeared. "Together with local Draseke models," she said, "you outlined how—"

"Stop. Just stop," Corrigan said quietly.

Harding placed one of her mechanical hands to his cheek, the softness of the touch surprising. "I imagine it must be awful to accept a thing like that, but I thought continuing to protect you from the inevitable realisation was ... I mean, now you have so much power, it would be irresponsible of me not to mention a certain ... tendency."

The nanobots were assembling memories from his other variant selves for him to consider. They were not him, but they came from him, so whatever they were, he had always been capable of being. He could hardly bear the truth of it.

"They're not me," he said. "They're not. I wouldn't *do* that."

"That's true I suppose, dear and simultaneously *untrue*. You've seen the J models, and they're not our inimitable Mr Fuse, but at the same time, they are what Jun *might* have been under, you know, different circumstances."

"I lit a fuse only recently," he countered, "and Jun remains in there, just as I – Corrigan – echoed in the vaults of those heartless and efficient administrators. I ... we simply accepted the role and got on with it. Just like the anxious Worker I once was, terrified of being demoted to a

Non if I couldn't prove myself!"

He got up from the table and crossed the unpolished wooden floor to where a fire burned in the simple grate and sat down on a bench. The house had not been fully restored internally, and it felt uncomfortable, too intimate, to be there where once Jonathan and his sickly, addicted family had squatted. He was tired, and disconnected from his human self in a stream of blue-green smoke from his open mouth so it could rest, laying it down on a battered couch in an alcove by the window. He took Bohdan out of his pocket, thanked him for his good work and put him on a cushion next to himself.

"You're welcome," the frog said, and settled down to sleep.

"What a beautiful thing you are," Harding said, crossing the room and sitting on the edge of the bench beside him when he sat back down. "You managed the transition well."

"They continue to harass us," he said, ignoring the compliment. "K has programs running and developing, forever seeking us out, but we're keeping ahead of her. We're ever so efficient, as you know, management and administration being in our DNA." He heard the words but they did not sound like his own.

"They're not you," Harding said, reading his mind from the distress in his face.

"Yes, they are. Being desensitised allowed their ruthless attributes to rise to the surface like the Floater the more established Workers used to dismiss me as being. An opportunist as cold-blooded as the cancer that killed my mother."

"You haven't behaved like that. Well ... devouring Jason whole was perhaps surplus to requirements."

Corrigan felt his nanobot energy vibrate with interconnectivity. "We enjoyed it," he said.

"The boy's a psychopath, you needn't cry over having put a stop to him. At least he can no longer torture anyone." Corrigan looked into Harding's blue eyes and the dark matter folded over itself as she studied him. He pictured K on top of St Paul's Mound, Jason beside her, his hand in hers, and in his other a clutch of red and pink brains, floating at the ends of synthetic veins like fairground balloons.

"Are you still connected to the network?" she asked.

"Yes," Corrigan said, "but cloaked. It would be disadvantageous to sever the link." He turned to stare into the fire and was not surprised to find Ulmer staring back at him. He snorted, and his blue-grey nanobots fizzled inside. "Your boyfriend has arrived, Tierney," he said.

"Caspar is never far away when things go horribly wrong."

"I assume you're struggling with similar issues," Corrigan said to the head. "As in staying one step ahead of K and her minions."

The head enlarged in the hearth. "I am," Ulmer said. "They're getting closer all the time, but Harding has managed my security."

"Interesting," Corrigan said. "For all their struggles,

they've remained distant from me. I no longer believe it's even necessary for me to leave the network."

"Some of us are not as lucky as you," Ulmer said. "If we don't make a move soon, they'll track me down … and I believe the term she used was 'eradicate the vile piece of shit'."

Corrigan walked across the room and admired his sleeping self. He ran a hand over his chest and could feel the slow rhythm of his heart. What a comforting thing it was to hear the clock ticking away the hours remaining for his organic self, a shell designed to break down and die, disintegrating over time. He returned to the fire and looked down at Ulmer. "He's dreaming of your son," he said.

"Ramon," Ulmer sighed. "It's unfortunate the boy finds himself under her supervision and *care*."

"We must help him escape."

Ulmer floated into the room and swelled in size. "All in good time. But, for the minute, let's focus on those under immediate threat."

"And that would be you?"

"Who the fuck else, eh?"

"Me, of course," Harding said. "And Gregor, those little dragonflies you've become so fond of, your malfunctioning mother and all the Exhumed, Guardians and Workers. K's wrath knows no bounds. She'll roast us all on a spit for eternity unless we do something."

Corrigan went over to the curtainless window to look at the moon. Like the sun, her face hadn't been seen in a clear sky before the Fall for decades ... centuries. "I could give her back her son," he said.

"Never give that bitch an inch," Ulmer growled. "The boy's worse than she'll ever be, but there's nothing she wouldn't do to have him back. The only effective way to undermine her is to ensure she can't get at us. Right now, Corrigan, you're the only one who enjoys that particular luxury."

Harding joined Corrigan at the window. "You must share this technology with us, Robert," she said. "We must have this new form for safety's sake."

"That's not on the table," Corrigan said. "Press me and I'll withdraw from negotiations."

"Do you know what lengths we've gone to to protect you?" Ulmer blasted. "Shitty little Floater thinks he's a cut above, Tierney."

"I know you've been protecting me," Corrigan said, turning around to face the incensed head. "It's the extent of your personal endeavours that persuades me not to trust you."

"Listen to you!" Ulmer scoffed. "Trumped up fucking Non! As efficient as a clock when you want to be, eh? Rounding up those savages for din-dins in the caves where my beasts are imprisoned!" Corrigan sensed that had Ulmer been availed of hands, he would have been pressing them to his head. "You have no idea what it's like to have so many organic connections, all debased and desperate for more. I *want* her to kill them all! It's a goddamn torment!"

"Come, come," Harding soothed. "We'll get nowhere if we antagonise him."

Corrigan smiled. "I'm not in the least antagonised."

Harding tilted her head. "I meant you antagonising *him*, dear." Ulmer grinned in his bubble and Corrigan's now-awake human body responded with a laugh. "He's far more important than you think," Harding said, "and useful. And of course I protect him, keep him hidden and safe, and he does the same for me." Ulmer glowered at her. "I straddle his existence, as it were," she continued, "and can relieve myself whenever I like, can't I, dear?"

"Like a dyke mid-colonic," Ulmer growled.

"But I don't keep Captain Cuddles safe because I care for him," she explained. "He's the only one who can access K's core and understand what she's doing, why she's doing the things she does and in the particular order in which she does them. Having a sense of her priorities is useful. Recently, however, she's not been as forthcoming, which is vexing."

"I woo her," Ulmer said, a pitiful expression on his floating face. "But my affections are repelled. Every charm offensive I mount, she raises stronger defences. She's got a goddamn chastity belt that'll lock me out of eternity if we don't do something."

"Your sexual deviances and grievances aside, provide me with the relevant codes," Corrigan suggested, "and I'll infiltrate her. I could even switch her off if you let me in."

Ulmer looked as if he wanted to destroy Corrigan. "If

I did that you could shut me down as well, you little shit!"

"Yes," Corrigan sighed, "I suppose I could."

"We require security," Harding said. "Assurance backed up by providing something binding."

Corrigan felt that he'd rather curl up inside his human host and sleep and dream as people do, but it was no longer possible. "I need to speak to Gregor," he said.

"Gregor?" Ulmer snorted.

"I want his opinion before I commit to any further action."

Harding reached out and patted Corrigan's arm. "I took the liberty of inviting him," she said. "The dragonflies will bring him here in the morning."

"Think of everything, don't you," Corrigan replied, moving his arm from her reach. "Right down to chicken stew. Who did you consult for that information? My mother?"

"She was very helpful ... even gave me one of her recipes."

"Oh, for fuck's sake," Ulmer barked. "Would you just concentrate! Remember, Gregor's continuance is as reliant on your success as mine, so step carefully – like a prissy Floater in a boardroom full of bitter Workers. Come to me with a proposal and I'll let you know if it's acceptable." With that Ulmer threw himself into the fire and disappeared up the chimney.

"I thought he'd never leave, dear," Harding said.

Corrigan walked back to his body and reinserted his

nanobot self so it too could rest. But the nanobot mind did not doze or ease itself into a dream. They allowed his human brain to sleep, but continued thinking from the tips of his toes to the top of his head. Were they really artificial? They felt real, practically biological, and he flew with them through a sea of Emulate and Exhumed minds. He located and peered through the eyes of his Exhumed self, through C1's eyes. The mind housed there was unlike his own, unlike the being he once became in Emulate One's isolation cell or the state he now found himself in; but there was no denying how dangerous he was, the things he was capable of, especially if he became the most powerful being on Earth. If it was still possible, he must find the strength to obliterate self.

Robert Corrigan must die.

37

When Corrigan awoke he was not surprised to see no trace of Harding. Bohdan was already awake and stoking the fire. He watched the little android frog without moving a muscle. *And I am not the only one who must die, my nanobot friends*, he thought. *We must work together on this and design the perfect solution. We like perfection, don't we?* The nanobots surged in him and reached out through the network, absorbing everything they had ever learned, had been or had the potential to be. *Do this for me and trust me. We are One.* He sat up and stretched.

"Morning, Robert," the frog said. "I trust you and your nanobot friends slept well."

"Good morning, Bohdan. We did, although they were more active than me."

"The fire was out, and it's a little chilly, so I took the liberty of relighting it. A log this size will burn for a while."

"Very thoughtful of you, thank you."

Corrigan looked past the frog and the crackling fire to the window, where a sparrow was hopping along a branch. Two more birds alighted, singing encoded threats, warnings and enticements, all of which he could now interpret as if the little creatures were speaking French or Italian, or any other language, into a translator.

Corrigan felt something twist in his chest at the sight of Bohdan by the fire. He did not resist it, but let the pain roll through him. "I would have thought pulling a log that big into the fire would be impossible for you."

Bohdan smiled. "You always underestimated how much I felt for you, Robert. I would have done anything for you, but it was only the assassin who could really warm you up. Perhaps if I'd been equipped back then with the powerful tongue I have now, I might have pulled you rather than a log."

Corrigan sighed. "I should have jumped at the chance, Bohdan, but I was too weak to risk it. With a mother like mine, fear of rejection becomes instinctive."

"Better to have had a mother like Hattie than one like Katherine. Professor Meregalli never appreciated her boy for what he was, originally I mean, and now she's out there hunting for you so she can wrench him from your skull. The threat is very real. I might be reduced to conjecture mixed with a cabbie's intuition, but my DNA and coding is inside you."

Corrigan sat on the bench and leant forward, resting his elbows on his knees. "So you know what I'm going to do."

"No, not exactly, but what I've heard worries me. I sense a destructive rather than a constructive course. You were never as clear-sighted and determined until your recent transformation."

"I might have taken offence at that if you weren't a frog."

"I love you, Robert, remember that." Bohdan tilted his head and his eyes burned red. "I know your weaknesses and strengths. You've a kinder heart than you think."

The door suddenly burst open, catching Corrigan and Bohdan off guard. Jan and Edna fluttered into the room followed by Gregor, who was wearing a pair of khaki shorts, his face and bare chest beaded with sweat, his lips twisted in a snarl.

"Gregor ..." Corrigan stood up, but the belligerent young man was in a foul and violent mood.

"What have you done to make K so angry?" he demanded, grabbing the collar of Corrigan's shirt.

"I wanted you and the others to be safe," Corrigan said.

"Safe?" Gregor hollered. "Whatever you've done, she was in a rage!"

"I ... I wanted to–"

"Have you *killed* him?" Gregor screamed in Corrigan's face, his own features contorted with anger. "Did you murder my *brother*!"

"No, I absorbed him."

"Took him in did you? Just like me, playing us for fools!"

"I never took you fo–"

Gregor suddenly hurled Corrigan to the floor with the strength of his former Guardian self, as if Late possessed him, gifting him with greater power just as the nanobots had done for Corrigan. The assaulted man crashed to the dusty floor, the fall cushioned by his AI protectors, those who had become one with him.

Gregor pressed a hand to his forehead. "If we hadn't arrived when we *did*, the children may have been slaughtered!" His anger slowly burned through him, lingering like hot coals in his eyes. "We only just managed to save them. If Spinner hadn't proven such an apt pupil, we might have lost them."

Corrigan stood up and pushed his hair back roughly from his sweating forehead. "I know. I was *there*."

"You were? Of course *you were* ..."

"Spinner learned to shoot *very* quickly," Corrigan growled, surprised by his own anger. "It must be in her nature to embrace weaponry."

He couldn't imagine Jonathan firing a gun. The sex was easy enough to envisage, but violence was not something he'd have expected. He stormed out of the house and stood on the stone step, facing 46a and b, and saw his world from Jonathan's side of the street, his father slumped senseless on Belushi Grey, his hopes for better than that, and as always his heart ached for the boy. The morning sun was as unforgiving as Gregor, and he raised his face and shielded his eyes.

"What a homecoming!" B4 exclaimed, rolling down Harvey Road, evidently having been left behind by Gregor and his dragonfly companions. "It's like we never left," she chirped. "Except we're on the other side of the street!"

Corrigan ignored B4, holding Gregor's gaze when the angry young man followed him outside. "Harding didn't tell you about Ulmer's latest plan?"

"Harding never tells *me* anything," Gregor said. "And are you *really* so stupid as to trust any plan Ulmer cooked up?"

"I have my own!" Corrigan snapped.

B4 growled aggressively on her roller, perhaps considering a well-aimed electric jolt at Gregor's crotch. Her blue hoop eyes widened, and he knew there was nothing she would not do for him. She was as fierce as Hat and as loyal as Hattie.

"I wouldn't go as far as to call it a *plan* but, as ideas go, it has a kind of hellish symmetry." Corrigan breathed purposefully, regulating not only his intake of oxygen but his unruly human emotions, a force not even a nanobot swarm could dampen. "The nanobots have given me something I never expected: a sense of purpose or even power."

The mention of power always brought with it a shade of danger, a threat more insistent than any other. It was a black hole into which only deluded or unstable beings willingly dived. Even speaking of it could draw you to its outer edge, tugging you irresistibly toward its black, bottomless heart. "I recently discovered that my own Exhumed brothers, C models, were the architects of the cull …"

"Who told you about *that*?" Gregor's anger flared again.

"Harding. She told me last night."

"There was no reason for you to *ever* know!"

"She knew I'd stumble over it myself and then there would've been no one to help me understand it. Whether that's a good enough reason, I couldn't say, but I no longer feel I should be part of anything as powerful as the nanobots or play a part in what they might become."

"Good to hear your conscience is intact. That's not something my brother would approve of if what you say is true and he really is in there." He looked his friend up and down and Corrigan's heartrate increased.

"I told you, I absorbed him," Corrigan said.

Gregor's green eyes flashed. "Yes, I see it all very clearly now," he growled.

"We can't hang about here, gents," Jan cried. "K's picked up our scent." The dragonflies fluttered their wings, ready to fly through the twisted, ancient ash and oak to where Gregor stood trembling slightly with waning anger.

"She wants to shake that brat of hers out of you, Mr C," Edna added.

Bohdan leapt up into Corrigan's hands and he pocketed the hybrid. He felt the little AI nestling beside his leg, and an ache of longing burned though him as he considered the frog's unwavering loyalty. B4 whirred up beside him and revved her roller, as if expecting him to notice and acknowledge her, but he wasn't in the mood to indulge her.

"How was your chicken stew, Bobbin?"

"Perfectly adequate." He looked at her and sighed, regretting his tone. "Not as good as yours."

Corrigan swore he saw her wriggle with delight.

"Always one of your favourites," B4 said, before turning to Gregor. "Gotta bit'a news for you, young man. The result of a test we ran on young Spinner."

"I suppose congratulations are in order," Corrigan snapped.

Gregor stared at the others and his confusion was matched only by his irritability. He darted his customary scowl at B4. What was the silly little droid talking about now?

"It'll be a proper handsome little mite, or else a pretty little lass," Jan said.

"Oooh yes," Edna added. "Pretty and prettier still all mixed up together."

B4 patted her metal belly and sang, "Rockabye baby on the tree top–"

Gregor paled instantly at the realisation. "A baby? Spinner's having a *baby*?"

"*Your baby*," Corrigan said, "yes."

"We could always perform the *procedure*," Jan suggested.

"No!" Corrigan insisted. "You mustn't do that to Spinner!" Despite the annoyance Corrigan felt, it wasn't right, or fair, to choose the convenience of an abortion without talking to Spinner first. "How could we even begin to explain that to her?"

"I think we could," the sisters said in unison.

"Course we could," B4 agreed, "but she'll want the little bundle, no doubt about it."

Gregor was rooted to the spot of earth where he stood, paralysed by the thought of becoming a father. "I can't do it ... I just can't," he mumbled. "It's the wrong time; there couldn't have been a worse time—"

"Bit late for that now, sunshine," B4 said. "Should've wrapped your sausage in a bit of old newspaper if you wanted to avoid the obvious."

"You might've told my father the same, Mother. It wasn't as if you hadn't already been round a few chip shops before some monger or other slipped a battered fish in your takeaway bag."

"Now who's being vulgar!" B4 snapped. "Your father may have been a Transient, one of the many disappeared, but 'e were good-looking by half!"

Jan fluttered between them, her tiny eyes open and alert. "There's no time for this. I think we ought to create a diversion," she said. "Lay them a new scent."

Gregor stopped and the sisters alighted on his shoulders. "Draw K a few miles that way," he said, gesturing towards the east. "Then turn back and meet us at the camp. And take B4 with you before she makes any more untimely and unpleasant revelations."

"Don't go blaming me for your saucy behaviour. Ain't as if my boy didn't tell you what might happen if—"

"You being here could endanger us," Corrigan said, attempting to sooth her irritability. "It's best we split up."

B4's eyes narrowed and she said, "Say no more. I can take a hint, Bobbin."

"Don't be childish, Mother."

"Come on, B4," Jan said, "We can gripe about family and sacrifices and the burden of motherhood along the way."

"What would *you* know?" B4 retorted. "You've never been a mother!"

B4 and the dragonflies prattled on over the cracked tarmac of Harvey Road.

"It was never particularly well kept," B4 grumbled as she swerved the deeper holes, "but Haringey Council, what with its limited funding an' all, would never have kept up with this level of decay. It's some sort of miracle any of it is here at all."

These women, Corrigan mused as he watched them go. They were throwbacks to a time before the Fall, and they were important to him, he knew that, even in their current forms. The connection was something he could never explain to Gregor or any of the Guardians who shared the middle-class Meregalli line. No matter what else they were, the women were elevated Transients, just like him. They had been forced to struggle against impossible odds to be acknowledged as anything at all. His mother ... well, she had done whatever she needed to avoid ending up like a homeless, bedraggled Lazarus staring through a window hoping for scraps. And the sisters were born with the double disadvantage of coming from the lower orders *and* being disabled. They worked themselves up the cruel ladder, rung by bleeding rung, making assets of their weaknesses and yet still, just like his mother, they stubbornly refused to disguise their connection to those who'd had nothing and had to crawl on their bellies. Although he identified with their challenging paths, on a certain level he felt like Jonathan, desperate to put a little distance between them, to attain a higher state, to complete his conversion and finally wash out the rough.

38

Corrigan glanced at Gregor as they walked an ancient path, a trail trodden by a thousand years of Sects and the wildlife that shared the forest with them. The dappled light beneath the canopy of trees danced over Gregor's well-defined cheekbones. The face itself was handsome, but what made it irresistible was the emerging personality stirring beneath. When this body had been uninhabited, it was grotesque; and if Jason had entered the host as scheduled, the result would never have been as compelling. *Petulance and an expression of entitlement will spoil even the most beautiful face*, Corrigan thought.

"How is it K hasn't found your camp?" Corrigan asked, unable to bear the silence, forcing the first question that came to mind out of his mouth.

"I have a flock of Addictari to divert attention and my doppelgänger also provides a cloak, although his power is diminished."

"Yes, time's running out."

"Not for you," the young man observed. "You've grown stronger. I can feel it."

"Yes, the nanobots have reinvigorated me."

There was a clearing in the distance, and Gregor went ahead and waited for his companion in the open space.

Joining him, Corrigan noted another shift. The nanobots seemed to be drawing energy directly from the sun, and he smiled. *Solar power, of course. Why wouldn't they?*

Gregor studied Corrigan as if he had never seen him before, and Corrigan dropped his eyes, as if he had been caught doing something shameful.

"We're cloaked," Gregor then said. "Tell me your plan."

"I'll break up the signal so Ulmer can't listen in," Bohdan interjected in case they had forgotten he was there. "I'll make him think it's the same as the issues Late and the others are contending with. But there will still be static and some titbits might slip through."

"That's all we can expect," Corrigan said, stroking the little frog with his finger.

Bohdan tilted his head. "If you could share some of your nanobots, I'd be even more effective. I could tackle the static. He won't hear a thing other than some invented rubbish. If you trust me, I could do that for you, Robert."

"How do I manage that?"

"Spittle."

"Spittle?"

Corrigan licked his finger and slid it inside Bohdan's open mouth. "Delicious," the frog said when Corrigan withdrew, "and such a powerful aftertaste. I've never felt closer to you, Robert. So wonderful to have you inside me after all this time."

"Don't be so disgusting," Gregor said, rolling his eyes. "Is your cabbie reliable?" he then asked.

"I'm a monogamist, if that's what you're asking," the frog said.

"I shared fluids with you," Corrigan laughed. "We didn't exchange vows."

"Corrigan, would you just shut up with all that!"

"You're too bloody pent up for your own good, Gregor," Corrigan snapped, unwilling to indulge the hormonal teenager any longer. "I've access to Bohdan's mind via the nanobots and any doubts I may have had are gone. Bohdan and I have a real connection, even if we never consummated it."

The little frog suddenly flexed and then went still, its eyes pulsing green against its orange skin. It had gone into a kind of trance in order to address the issue of the static, interweaving fabricated images and dialogue to keep Ulmer guessing. Corrigan subliminally instructed the nanobots not to share the content of the imminent discussion with Bohdan. Even now he could not bring himself to fully trust his cabbie ... another of his remaining and inexcusable flaws, it seemed.

"How are the others?" Corrigan asked.

"There's been unrest. Your Sect brother disappeared not long after you left, and no one's seen him since. And it's not just Sects who have gone off on their own – the Guardian your mother named Dave, he and a small band of Guardians, G1 and two J Exhumed, elected to form an independent group and they too have left us."

The news of losing Corey saddened Corrigan, and it was almost as sad to hear of David's departure. The renegade androids probably envisaged a better future for themselves, and who was he to even consider denying them the possibility? He could hear Ulmer's voice as if he were standing alongside: *Surely nothing's more compelling than self-preservation?* Increasingly it felt as if other things were more compelling now. And he had, after all, encouraged David to think for himself and find a way to break free of Emulate One.

"I was willing to enter into this 'surrender'," he said, "because I thought I wanted something that no man had ever had."

"And now you no longer want it," Gregor said. "You'll forgive me if I find that hard to believe."

Corrigan looked hurt, as if he were being mocked. "No, that would be a lie. I want it more than I ever could've dreamed. Now it's possible, now I have it, I know I was right to want it."

"So, what's your plan? To steal it for all of us?"

Corrigan shook his head. "That wouldn't work. It would be a temporary solution and the real problem would continue to fester. And we all know where Ulmer's scheming will take us."

"Then what *is* your plan?" Gregor whispered, getting impatient now.

Corrigan looked down at Bohdan and was reassured by the trancelike cabbie, but his voice trembled when he spoke. "We must create a virus." Gregor stared at him. "The nanobots are devising something that will

388

thoroughly infiltrate the network. Nothing mechanical will survive. Only the organic will continue."

Gregor's eyes flashed and his body tensed. "You want me to be complicit in their total destruction? Right down to David and the others, who are only now emerging?"

"Yes. Save as many humans as you can, and bring Ramon up from the depths. It's the only way. If Katherine gets hold of me, she'll find a way to extract that boy of hers. Their plan has always been to do away with everything that preceded them. The best you can hope for is the preservation of a small number of completely dumbed-down Guardians who he'll take with him on his travels through space. Here he will inflict a scorched earth policy: nothing living will remain, and not a single functioning machine will be spared."

Gregor stared directly into Corrigan's eyes, searching perhaps for any sign of subterfuge or guile. "I never thought K would manage to fully convert him."

Corrigan found it almost impossible to hold his friend's gaze but hold it he must. "I was tempted. I didn't have to absorb him but the power he gave me – I couldn't give it back – and I felt a burning need to contain him, to stop him hurting anyone else the way he tortured Ramon and those brave AI beings who dared to be something more complete."

Gregor smiled the coldest smile Corrigan could ever have imagined. "Now my brother will be consumed by rage. Had he been tempted toward any form of mercy or leniency, he'll no longer be capable of any restraint."

"It was a mistake on my part," Corrigan said, his voice tight with emotion, "but K would have kept at him until–"

"Yes, she's nothing if not persistent." Gregor was lost for a moment, perhaps communing with Late and his more logical dimension. "But he would have killed her too eventually."

"That's a sacrifice she's willing to make, even though she knows Jason's too self-obsessed to give up being himself. He's the worst of us and he'll take that hatred of his who knows where, doing who can say what damage as he travels through the universe." He waited, watching his young friend as the truth sunk in. "You have a child on the way now. An extra reason to fully convert; embrace your humanity as K never could. She could stare into the void for eternity without ever attaining the singularity. Whenever she stared into that black hole she saw herself staring back and was unable to complete her conversion, whereas yours is all but a fait accompli. I will become the virus itself and, as such, I'll be both destroyer and preserver."

Gregor's features twitched with rage and his hands clamped into fists. "I cannot be party to that," he hissed. "They're my kind. The Guardians and even the Addictari came to *me* when I requested it. We only just woke them up."

"I know. It's a terrible sacrifice, but you have the knowledge and ability to rebuild something so much better than … than this. And Spinner is not only your kind, she's the mother of your child, so you have an obligation to keep her out of danger."

"She's *untamed*," Gregor said, as if confessing some awful crime. "Practically an innocent."

Corrigan laughed. "You're more of an innocent than she is in that regard. I doubt very much whether you're her first."

"You think she–"

"It's the Sect way to breed young."

Gregor held his head in his hands, and Corrigan thought he might scream or growl or cry, but instead he muttered, "She must have wanted a baby." He sighed, and looked up at the sky as if searching for guidance. "I'll have to figure it out when ... when it happens. As for the Guardians, they wouldn't be the same as those who chose to defend us. Not all of them wanted to be with me. I could never rebuild them. I'd need the download we took from Jason Meregalli. Without that ... well, it just won't work."

"Jason once told me that no one was irretrievable. If I become One then I can pass everything to you. It won't be easy, but you'll have us ... all of us. And you'll have to go wading in the swamp of your own mind to retrieve whatever you can. I'm counting on that, believe me, but let me also caution you not to base anything on what went before. Educate the Sects, and let any future AI be truly independent or don't reintroduce them at all. A man who has been a coward for as long as I have cannot sacrifice himself for the good of mankind alone. I have to believe the cycle can be broken, and if that means not bringing me or anyone else back, then so be it." He kept his eyes on Gregor and could sense waves of realisation as they washed through his mind. "You do love Spinner," he then said, "don't you?"

"I've developed some form of attachment, yes."

"You love her. How could you not? Jason put her among the Sects to see how she'd develop, but he was just toying with the idea."

Gregor's eyes darkened and he shook with rage. "What have you done to me? What have you tricked me into becoming?"

"Where would you rather *be*, Gregor? Back among the Guardians, or here and now as a human? That's your choice."

"Late and I already chose to be human," Gregor said. The malice in his voice struck Corrigan a blow. "Are you *satisfied*?"

"I wouldn't wish it on my worst enemy," Corrigan said. "I'm glad I couldn't be a parent. To be responsible for delivering another human up to a struggle that ends in death always seemed cruel to me. There can't be anything more terrifying than parenthood." He recalled B4, Hattie, worn by sacrifice and invaded by cancer; but even in her weakened state she was tough. He imagined Hat, young and fierce and protective, the kind of warrior no man could ever be. "And by being a good parent you only manage to heighten the inevitable suffering." He put his hand on Gregor's shoulder. "I'm sorry for having done this to you when you might have been spared."

Gregor trembled and he paled. Corrigan half expected to see black bruises appear as the young man struggled to contain his feelings.

"Spared?" Gregor whispered. "*Spared*?" The word seemed to have had an oppressive effect on the young man. "A gift is sometimes a curse but it's still a gift, isn't it? Besides, it was me who made the final decision to be … born." He wiped his face with his forearm, a gesture Corrigan still found stimulating. "If I agree to help you, I'll be betraying the best of our kind along with the worst."

"It's a cruel thing to ask," Corrigan said, turning away. "I shouldn't have. But I know you'll do anything to save Spinner and your child from being culled."

"Yes, I'd do anything for her, and you knew that would happen when you pushed us together."

"Perhaps I did. I know you still feel connect–"

"I love the Guardians, Corrigan. Perhaps I was being an overprotective parent to *them* …" Gregor's face was consumed with sadness. "I was too closely based on your kind. The apple fell right next to the tree. I maintained all your weaknesses and I stymied the Guardians for fear they might one day overtake me. And who's to say I wouldn't do that to Spinner's child too?"

"Apparently, there were never any Jonathan Exhumed models. Did you vote in favour of that Gregor? When the Mediation decided not to allow anyone who had once been a black person into the Exhumed club?"

"I don't recall there *being* a vote. I assume there must have been but …"

"Harding said there was."

"I … I would never have … and besides, this is a distraction from your proposal!" He paused, gathering his thoughts. "Your nanobots are racing toward the singularity. Left to develop, they'll overcome and eventually supplant all of us. Isn't it better to preserve them also?"

"Because they absorbed me," Corrigan said, considering that thought, "every part of what I am, from the man who cried over the death of a cat to the administrators who manage mass murder, it all remains intact and will influence every decision they make. You cannot base anything on something as corrupt, or potentially corrupt as I am, without dire, unimaginable consequences. There's no point resisting my determination; we need only consider the practicalities."

"Do the nanobots have unlimited access?"

"No, but Ulmer could change that."

"Of all the entities we could ally ourselves with …"

"He mustn't know," Corrigan insisted. "We must coax and deceive him. I think I can do that; I know what his Achilles' heel is."

"You'll have to get past Harding."

"She's not who you think she is. She's much more substantive and decent than you may ever realise." He attempted a smile but his lips would not comply. "She wants this thing as much as he does, but she wouldn't betray humankind to have it. She'd never rest if she did that, and Harding needs to rest."

Gregor levelled his eyes straight at Corrigan. "And you don't want it?"

"I swear, I've never wanted anything more, except perhaps one thing …"

"To be with Ramon," Gregor said, and rage flashed in his eyes.

Corrigan noticed the little frog trembling in his palm, and wished he knew for sure that their conversation was private. He walked a few paces and placed him in the shade of a tree.

"No," Corrigan said, returning to Gregor, "the only thing I ever wanted more was peace, and there's nothing I would not destroy or sacrifice to attain it. If Ulmer or K get hold of this technology," he continued, lowering his voice to barely a whisper, "it'll be the end of everything. They won't distinguish between human, Sect, Guardian, Worker or Exhumed, and they'll certainly kill Spinner and your child. They mean to have it all at our expense. That's why I had to absorb Jason. He'd gone mad." He stared at Gregor until he was certain he had his full attention. "At the moment, the nanobots acknowledge me as part of their order. A self-destructive act or sacrifice makes no sense to them, so they trust everything I do is for our common good. As you said, left to their own devices they'll eventually see us as inferior and seek to replace or control us. I will confound them, manipulate and administrata a state where I remain the controlling influence. You once told me that you and little Gregory Jason Meregalli were one and could not be separated."

"Something which has been proven untrue."

"Yes, but in our case there really is no dividing line. I am no longer me but us. A complete reboot is required."

"A realignment," Gregor snarled. "The full reintroduction of humankind." He stepped away from Corrigan and stared at him. "What role would you have me play?"

"The nanobots are creating a virus that will target all forms of networked AI. When we're ready I'll activate it."

"How do you think Late will react to this plan of yours?"

"He's in your head and, that being so, he's the only one who's truly safe." Corrigan smiled sadly. "I'll try and send him a signal when it's done."

"And in the meantime?"

"Prepare an army, and be its general. Train them as best you can and bring them to Millennium Bridge. That's where all eyes must be. The effect of the virus won't be immediate in all cases, but it will be thorough, and it will seek out every AI worldwide. If I could make it differentiate between those with K and our rebels I would, but it isn't possible given the time constraints."

"Did you ever stop to consider whether Emulate One might be influencing this decision of yours? Perhaps a system can become overwhelmed, depressed like the doldrums?"

"I don't believe in Emulate One," Corrigan said. "It

really is just a core system. It doesn't think or feel like a being or a person. I wish I could tell you that it was her, but I don't sense anything beyond myself and the nanobots – and you, of course." Corrigan studied his friend, wondering how much he could trust him with, and what he dare not share. "I am One," he said, taking hold of Gregor's hand. "Everything that ever found itself in an AI form is in my mind, is part of my being. Before the virus takes hold, I will send you a signal via Late. Do not resist it, let it flow into you and I will make us One. You must trust me. No matter how painful or distracting it is, do not resist the transfer. If you do, you might make the incoming stream sense you as a threat that it needs to subjugate and control. Accept it, absorb it, and become our host. Do that and we'll rest quietly until you go looking for us … if you ever decide to do that. There's no saying what your mind will do with all that input. It may be just a fantasy on my part. You know how susceptible to those I can be. It may be that it's nothing but a pipe dream, and the limited capacity of your brain–"

"Let's see what happens. It's worth the risk."

Gregor looked like he might weep, and Corrigan wrapped his arms around him and held him close. The embrace was not reciprocated, however, and Gregor stood rigid and unresponsive. Regardless, Corrigan rested his unshaven cheek against the young man until his persistence finally seemed to connect and Gregor raised his arms and clutched him. For a few seconds life seemed to be defined, wholly and sublimely, by the connection of that embrace.

They said their farewells and Gregor turned to leave. But then he turned back to Corrigan. "I won't resist, and I'll see you when it's over," he said sadly. "There's always a way to do what's right as long as ... as long as you feel it."

He slipped into the forest and Corrigan watched him merge with foliage and shadows. Before he had vanished altogether, the young man turned around once again. His expression was hard to read in the dim light, but Corrigan saw what looked like the face of a mourner, a lone figure who marched several paces behind the hearse. He could only hope someone as conflicted as Gregor could manage to see the right path, to *feel* it and accept it. Could he be the passive recipient on this one occasion, allowing himself to be impregnated with everything that went before and could be? It would be yet another stunning contamination, and it worried Corrigan. Such a surge of data might overwhelm or even destroy a limited organic brain, one that housed the mind of his beautiful friend.

He picked Bohdan up and the frog patted his hand.

"Please don't ask me any questions," Corrigan said, his voice choking.

"Your secrets are safe," Bohdan said. "Harding's back at the house, and she's asking for you."

Corrigan retraced his steps towards Harvey Road, each step heavier than its predecessor despite the nanobots' efforts. It was as if he were re-treading history, his paths converging; as if his destination had always been known.

39

Evening was approaching when Corrigan reached Harvey Road. What he had done with the day he could not account for. He had wandered beneath the canopy, weighing up the lives or the existences he was considering for sacrifice. It was all well and good to make the call for himself, but he had assumed the authority to make a decision for all concerned. Only Bohdan kept drawing him out of his reverie and back towards the street where he used to live before the Fall. He opened the door and Harding was sat beside the fire, her body black and her hands white where she raised them to the heat.

"You're *late* and you've been scheming," she said. She did not turn around but continued to gaze into the flames.

Bohdan whispered, "Leave the door open and don't go too far inside."

Corrigan moved back and sat down on the old front step. It was safer outside; from there he could maintain a distance from a life he did not wish to forget but neither reclaim. "There's nothing more to be done," he said. "Ulmer must provide his codes and let me in. Otherwise K will eventually hunt us down and her vengeance will be–"

"Something to behold." Harding stood up and turned her back to the fire. Behind him she turned white except for a band of black crossing her eyes the way the Sects had blackened theirs for the cull. Perhaps it was an inadvertent response, the tension mounting behind those eyes; or maybe she was preparing to be sacrificed to, or by, the Great Lord Umah. It was always a risky business partnering with their old CEO, even if it was a ruse. "I'd like to avoid that if I can, but it seems less likely the longer this drags on."

"Once I have the codes, I'll infiltrate the network and bring her down."

"Caspar doesn't trust you."

"Is he here?"

"No. I expect he'll be along shortly. He likes to be a little late or else uncomfortably early."

Corrigan leant against the door frame and tried again to remember Harding's face. He had the mask as a reference, but it was difficult to connect that lifeless thing with her old self. He thought he saw Miss Champion shuffle past her window, as lost in time as she so often was in her own home. She waved and smiled at him the way she did whenever he took her an éclair or a slice of cake. She knew him and never seemed to confuse him with other people. He imagined her concocting a spell that would allow him to remember the details of Harding's features, but still nothing would come.

"Do you know if they ever, you know … tinkered with you?" he asked, and turned so that he was sideways on in the doorway.

Harding tilted her head, crossed the room and sat down on the couch his body had slept on. "I'm not sure what they've done with my DNA, but Jason brought you back as a Sect on a number of occasions."

Corrigan grimaced. "I have a plan, one where we'd all have to pay a dreadful price," he said, his voice low.

"I sense something ultimate in the costing of this sacrifice," Harding said.

"Do you have any feelings for the Sects?"

"They are what they are. There are pockets of them around the globe. They hide in jungles, forests, deserts and frozen wastelands. They're as persistent as the planet itself and yet Jason, aided by his brother and Caspar, found them all and put in place an infallible tracking system so they always know where they are."

"All systems have at least one weakness," Corrigan said. "I could use that."

"Not without putting an end to us!" Harding turned white in patches and the light behind her lids was reddening. "I would like to be as you are now, without the conflict, of course. I recognise your dilemma, dear, but I never sacrificed anything in my life."

"That's not true. You gave up everything to stop having to be with Ulmer. He kept you out of work for over a decade."

"There were other factors!"

"But none as compelling as a man who wanted to own you. I know what your research meant to you and to have

401

to go begging him … as a Non for Christ's sake. You with your learning and privilege. What a thing to have to do."

"I never begged," she said, "and I was never a Non. No, I convinced him I was the only one who could bring Egret together. I explained it to him, and he accepted my proposal."

"If you want to believe that, then be my guest. He's the grand manipulator, but he cannot manipulate without willing manipulees." He paused, locked eyes with her and held steady. "What I'm going to suggest *does* have a cost. I plan to use the enhanced access provided by Ulmer to release a virus that will bring down all AI." She tilted her head and her eyes flashed red. "It's the only way to save the Sects." He stared at her even more intently. "Gregor is going to be a father."

"He's having a baby with that wild girl?"

"Yes," Corrigan mused, as if only now convincing himself of the right path. "That bond makes him the true Guardian of humanity, the only one who can help them develop without repeating all the mistakes of the past."

Harding retreated and sat down on the couch. She lowered her head. "The simple truth is … I'm afraid of death," she said quietly. "It's a terrible weakness, one I've struggled with forever. And your goddamn virus will wipe us all out. If you could give me something? Some hope?" She raised her eyes to his, and for a moment he thought he saw human sadness there.

"I'm One," he said, "and those I'm connected to will also be One if I will it." His heart had risen to his throat and his words thickened. "I'll make Gregor One and he'll know what to do. He'll survive us, but I need your help. I'm worried about his human brain and whether it has the capacity to receive and store a data surge of that scale."

"The human brain is an extraordinary organ," she said, raising her hand reflexively to quiet him.

A trickle of soot landed in the flames in the fireplace, and they guttered and struggled for a moment before rising again. Corrigan and Harding went quiet, tacitly agreeing a subterfuge no one else, not even Ulmer, would have any inkling of. He took one last look at her and knew he was as incapable of trusting anyone as he had ever been. The nanobots could not create a buffer between Corrigan and all his subservient, obliging and mistrustful selves. They were One and, being so, were as corrupt as everything preceding them.

40

Harding went to sit back down by the fire and the frog prodded Corrigan to stay where he was. He was getting cold, but would not ignore Bohdan's advice.

"If you want our assistance you must provide security," Harding said. "Trust cannot be earned at such short notice. A guarantee must be delivered."

Corrigan nodded and the nanobots allowed him a faint smile. "Does Ulmer know where Gregor's camp is?" he asked.

"Why would that be of value, Corrigan?" Ulmer roared down the chimney. Soot fell into the fire as the head emerged, eying him suspiciously. "You must forgive me being a little out of sorts. My physical self was just extinguished at that filthy Sect village!"

"Yes, I saw that," Corrigan said. "They turned on you."

"'The Siegruths are a working family ...' They ever ply you with that one, eh?" Ulmer's head shuddered in the ball within which it was projected.

"Yes, I think they said something of the sort when we first met. In a lift I believe that was."

"Those conniving bitches never worked a day in their lives. Got where they are by playing the game. Tearing into my corporeal like that and getting their bigger sisters to hack off my cocks," Ulmer growled. "They always know where you're most vulnerable. And now I don't feel anything. I don't even have that punishment of a body, just what you see. Me willing myself into being."

"It's not a bad compromise," Corrigan said.

"You're talking shit, as usual. But tell me, are you planning a battle with K?"

"Only as a diversion."

"So," Ulmer said, as he rolled into the room, "you want the others to keep her busy while you and your nanobots figure out how to shut her down?"

"Something like that."

"I don't know," Harding said, "there'd be nothing to stop you shutting down more than just K if you had fuller access."

"That's right!" Ulmer barked. "What would you suggest?"

"He needs to leave a little part of himself with us."

"Just a nanobot drop," Ulmer said. "Enough to provide a constant vigil on your fucking soul. You have a terrible habit of cutting me out during critical discussions. That cabbie of yours was supposed to survey and direct as well as protect you. And here he is, lost to the throws of an extended orgasm, bent on protecting you."

"I think I can manage a drop, but the exchange must be simultaneous."

Harding presented a small metal box. The lid flipped open, and she tilted her head. "Just a drop ... to keep us in the loop."

"The coding–" Corrigan said.

"It must be downloaded," Ulmer snapped, "and we can't do that here."

"You could use me as a conduit?" Harding suggested.

"You're a clever cunt," Ulmer snarled. "That much I grant you." He smiled at Harding. "I'd just as soon let you make a fart cushion of my foreskin as give you unlimited access."

"You don't have a foreskin, dear," Harding said. "Corrigan?" She jiggled the metal box.

Bohdan prodded Corrigan's thigh again, a reminder to remain positioned in such a way as to enable flight.

"I suppose the point is," Corrigan said, "it won't matter if Harding has unlimited access." He had their attention and smiled. "If we all have this technology we'll be extremely powerful, but we'll be equals. On a level playing field it wouldn't matter who had unlimited access."

"You're presupposing a desire for equality," Harding said.

Ulmer's bubble swelled threateningly. Corrigan could feel the nanobots making connections and selections and a wave of euphoria swept through him.

Ulmer rolled closer to inspect him. "What's wrong with you, Corrigan?"

"I'm getting ready to release."

"He wants you to arrive together," Harding observed. "Download the code," she told Ulmer. Turning to Corrigan she said, "And you, drop your gems in my box."

"You'll need to come closer," Corrigan said.

"And why would I need to do that?"

"I prefer it that way, Tierney …"

The exchange was not so rapid as to disallow verification, and Harding snapped the lid of the box closed and Corrigan closed his mouth.

"Now, Harding, my pet," Ulmer said, "trickle the contents of your little box as agreed and I'll release you from the network."

"What's this?" Corrigan asked.

"It's the only way Ulmer will actually have security," Harding said. "Your nanobots can't stay with me. I'm far too vulnerable. And he must cut me off from the network and set me free."

"Is that even possible?"

"Of course it is," Ulmer growled. "I have unlimited access!"

"Your access is diminished, dear." She turned to Corrigan and tilted her head in what seemed a significant way.

"It'll allow you to do what needs doing, eh, Corrigan?" Ulmer asked.

Corrigan smiled. "Let's hope so. The nanobots were infiltrating rather well on their own. I'm sure the additional information you've provided will give us more complete access than you ever enjoyed. We've already tried the access codes and they allow us to get at the core systems. Even Emulate One is vulnerable now."

"You see, my word can sometimes mean something," Ulmer said, glaring at Harding. "Now push those nanobots up my pipe and I'll give you your precious independence."

A transparent tube extended from the head's mouth, and a small aperture opened into which Harding poured the nanobots. The blue-green liquid trickled down the length of the tube, and Ulmer grinned rather horribly. "There, I've set you free," he said to Harding. "And what a lovely *aftertaste*," he added, the vile grin still in place.

Corrigan felt a pull on his being, and braced against the doorframe as the head rolled into the fire and vanished up the chimney.

41

Corrigan moved to the old couch now that the transfer was done and Ulmer had gone. He put Bohdan by his side and stared at Harding. She was white from head to toe, normally indicating protection from the heat of the sun or the fire, but in this case seemed to imply a high level of anxiety as she rocked slightly on the bench, her eyes restless behind the black strip that had reappeared.

"How can you exist without being connected to the network?" Corrigan asked. "Has your mind ever been fully in that android head of yours?"

"It has and it hasn't," Harding said. "I must get back to my tent. I created a mobile unit there, but I need to be closer, so I have backup. I'm currently out of range, so I'm vulnerable."

"That won't do."

"No, it won't. My dark matter does contain a temporary version of my full mind, but it cannot store everything efficiently. It needs support from Emulate One."

"Ah," Corrigan sighed, "dear old Emulate One."

"Yes, she's determined to remain a controlling interest perhaps ... a continuing influencer through the necessity of the support she provides each dark matter mind.

Emulate One seems to thrive on our dependency ... as if she feeds on us."

"No doubt there's some intentional limitation baked into the design of dark matter ... and didn't the old gods used to *feed* on us?" Harding fidgeted, again appearing to look for the spectacles she once kept on a chain about her neck. "Saturn ate his children, but I suppose even the Abrahamic god feasted on his worshippers, expanding his influence and power through his minions."

"I refuse to consider myself one of Emulate One's minions. I want to break free of her tyrannical faith entirely and make my own way in the world. Caspar of course had extra hooks in me, and I never could have achieved full independence without making an *arrangement* with him. Unlike any other AI who might consider breaking free, he had his own tracker especially designed for me and I had to–"

"Cut the apron strings."

Harding was clearly impatient to be on her way, her skin mottling black and white, but she could never leave an interesting conversation half-finished.

"What I sense is that dark matter suffers from an inability to replenish itself," she said. "In a human brain, we grow new brain cells in the hippocampus, the process is called–"

"Neurogenesis, I know," Corrigan said. "Ever since I joined with the nanobots, I've inherited knowledge and experience that never belonged to our old friend Corrigan."

"I see. Well, in that case you'll understand why dark matter cannot maintain a mind independent of Emulate One. Its capacity is always limited to a degree and requires the support and backup provided by the core system. The mobile unit I've designed serves the same or a similar function. It makes me truly independent. So, you see, once I'm connected to it, I'm the one AI who isn't susceptible to intruders or infiltrators. Or viruses."

"This mobile unit of yours, why has no one ever made one and set off on their own before?"

"Goeth had a go, but they caught him. Handed him to an inventive Draseke model who tortured him as a corporeal for several days before that variant of his consciousness was downloaded and imprisoned in Emulate One. You know our clumsy German friend ... he got caught up in the process and forgot all about security. They were letting him do it so they could understand the concept better and put safeguards in place to stop anyone else doing it. It was one of your C models who helped design and administer the tracking system that became his undoing."

Corrigan listened, mortified that one of his own Exhumed models had caught and allowed the torture of a man like Goeth, someone he knew and had worked closely with. And there was no way in which he could completely absolve himself. He had to admit this crime too and accept what he was, in his various states, capable of. "How did you manage it?" he asked.

"I have friends in convenient places. I've been working Ulmer for a long time, and there are a couple of Goeth models and a Jun who assisted me ... the ones who went off with David and his band. Ulmer only recently set up a safe space for us to work in. He took advantage of the disruption caused by Gregor's impulsive decision to try out being human and leave the collective. With all of that going on, it was relatively easy for him to generate an isolation cell the others couldn't see. Of course, he only ever did it to have something on me. He can tell them now, inform on me. I'm vulnerable the longer I stay here and K remains active."

"Come close," Corrigan whispered.

When she was within grasp, he took hold of her, embraced her, and whilst in that embrace he infiltrated her, sending nanobots through her porous synthetic skin to take a download of her current mind. She pushed him away with all her strength, so he withdrew his nanobots and whatever he had managed to capture in the process.

"I'm s-sorry," Corrigan spluttered. "That was inappropriate. You wanted me to give you something, some hope and ... I just wanted you to know I value your friendship and I care for–"

"I must go, and you must honour your side of the bargain by making your way onto the network and power K down!"

A stampede of metal boots was heard outside and none other than K marched in through the door, probing sensors rattling as she pushed them from her eyes. "Power me down, eh!"

Harding paled further, and the black strip darkened: it was too late.

Corrigan looked at Bohdan and the little frog blinked, returning to full consciousness long enough to communicate via the nanobots: *You are invisible to them.* The frog jumped into his pocket.

"Where is he?" she roared.

Corrigan smiled, shrank and sat between her feet, looking up to admire her muscular android legs.

"Ulmer?" Harding asked. "I suspect he invited you to a party he never meant to attend. Caspar can be callous like that."

"Not that festering idiot! Corrigan! Where is Corrigan?" she yelled. "Ulmer said you were both here!"

"He was here a minute ago. Where he is now, I couldn't say."

"Cloaked are we, Corrigan?" K snarled, her flame-red eyes scanning the room. She then shouted for her Guardians.

"There's no sign of him," the lead Guardian reported when they had filed into the small room and arranged themselves around K.

"He must've popped out," Harding said with a smile.

K was seething and her forehead dappled with beads of sweat. "You can no longer see him either, can you?"

"If he's not here, then neither of us can see him."

"Maybe you cannot see him because Ulmer *cut you free* from the network."

"That's not possible. All Exhumed are reliant on connectivity."

"You never relied on anything or anyone. I admired that in you and, now, you're an independent entity without available backup. You haven't synced yet, have you?"

"Of course I have. It's having a limited power source that's a problem."

"You'd figure that out, I expect."

K barged between the guardians and grabbed Harding, who did not resist. "Corrigan!" she shouted as she dragged the white android out onto the front step. "I know you're here!" Corrigan slipped between two Guardians and followed, instinctively secreting himself behind the tree in the front garden despite knowing he couldn't be seen. He put his hand in the pocket where Bohdan was crouching. "I can feel you watching, and what I'm about to do serves no purpose other than for *you* to witness it. I know you're too clever to expose yourself, so let's get on with it, shall we! Let's see how you feel when I break one of your toys!"

Harding raised a hand, as if requesting a little more time. "I can tell you what they're planning."

K's mask rippled as her eyes burned red. "I already know what Caspar wants!"

"Do you?" Harding asked.

"Do *you*?" K retorted.

"He wants the technology," Harding said.

"No! He wants power!" K yelled. "He's given you unlimited access in exchange for a few of your nanobots, hasn't he, Corrigan? Do you think that beast of a man hasn't told me everything!"

Corrigan's heart was racing and the nanobots enveloped the organ, attempting to soothe and protect it, and he imagined it sparkling like the mica ceiling of the cavern where the residential quarters had been built in Goeth's facility. In his pocket, Bohdan stroked his hand, a sensation enhanced by the eager, curious AI that roamed his insides.

K let out some kind of war cry and marched Harding through the streets to the perimeter of the forest, her Guardians following. The distressed android seemed to pale further, the black strip across her eyes darkened, and Corrigan was reminded of the same black strip on the Sects' faces as they lined up for the cull. This time Harding attempted to resist, but K was far more powerful and Corrigan heard her utter a mewl of despair, the sound a child might make when frightened.

"Ulmer will be interrogating your nanobots even as we speak, Corrigan," K said.

"Remember how loyal they are," Bohdan whispered. "They see themselves as you and he won't get anything from them. They'll run him in circles."

K stopped, and turned and pressed her cheek into Harding's shoulder. "Let us proceed," she said.

Everything went quiet, and Corrigan tried to control his breathing. Bohdan continued stroking his hand, and the nanobots worked harder still to calm him, but nothing could prepare him for the scream as K's sensors suddenly lit up in red, spiralled and sank themselves into Harding's head.

"They have no other plan!" she cried, grabbing at the air as she crumpled to the ground. "Ulmer wants the technology for himself. You know that, Katherine!"

"Dig in and draw the poison out!" K snarled, and the sensors growled and rattled, digging in harder. Harding went into spasms, her android skin rippling with livid bruises.

Eventually the sensors withdrew and Harding opened her mouth and vomited a lump of dark matter onto the earth. The mass trembled like a small rodent, exhausted and preparing for death. It glistened with a strange light and emitted a low groan like the Entombed in Emulate One.

"And there's your consciousness," K said. "Look." Harding stared at the dying matter of her mind. "That's how vulnerable you are. Not much to it, is there? And without backup that's all there is – this electronic AI gloop. No one even knows how Emulate One made this stuff, but without it none of us can function outside the confines of its system."

"I can give you de-details," Harding muttered, and reached out to try to retrieve the dark matter where it lay panting on the earth.

K lifted her metal boot over her extended hand. "Why would that be of importance to me now?"

"It's Corrigan ... it's Corrigan who wants to make himself all-powerful ... he ... he'll stop at nothing. Wants it all for himself ... wants to control all AI and ... Sects."

"That doesn't seem likely," K said, moving her boot over the disgorged synaptic sludge. "He was never a natural leader, not really. He's a keen administrator but, like all good dogs, he craves a master."

"He's no longer a dog," Harding gasped, and K's boot hesitated. "No longer a Sect, Human or Exhumed. He is what will be."

"He will be what he is!" K yelled. "A worthless Non!"

The light in Harding's eyes flickered, changing colours and darkening at their centres. "We are all ... the emptiness ..." she whispered. "She will not relent, Corr–"

K roared and stamped on the residue of dark matter, crushing it like a slug. Harding spasmed, fell backwards, and a final blue light surged behind her eyes and then went out.

"No, I will not relent!" K stepped over Harding and turned this way and that, her sensors rattling in a chaotic mess as they searched in every direction. "But if you return him to me, I'll forgive you, Corrigan!" When no information was received, she cried, "You better kill me! Kill me before I hurt the ones you love. I'll drag them up from the depths! Torture them in ways that will make each of their agonised deaths a blessing! I'll keep on torturing and killing them, Corrigan. Jonathan, Jun, Bohdan, Ramon, and that lowlife mother of yours, and you'll be there to witness every tormented exit. But if you give Jason back to me, I'll allow you all safe passage, even your precious Sects."

"Bohdan–" Corrigan murmured.

"You mustn't listen to her," the frog advised. "She'll say anything to get you to return Jason to her. But the minute he's back in power, he'll wreak a vengeance none of us will survive – except those unlucky enough to have hurt him most. And you know their fate."

Corrigan turned away, and K cried out as if she sensed his retreat. Her sorrow was a torment of its own. It followed him like a wave, rolling and crashing through the trees. Her suffering was real, as raw as that of the lioness she'd spoken of, mounted by a marauding male, the scent of her murdered cubs wafting from his open mouth … and Corrigan was the marauder, the man who killed and consumed her son. He sent a message to the nanobots he had handed over for Ulmer's manipulation: *Toy with him. Don't let him know anything too soon. Keep him guessing. Make him wait.*

42

Corrigan listened to the sounds of the forest. Birds screeched late-night calls, otters lumbered into brooks with languid splashes and predators clawed trees amongst moonlight shadows. Moths and airborne bugs competed in numbers for those crawling in the earth, and silent bats swept the air for their supper. The forest was permanently and irrepressibly alive it seemed, from the tops of the trees to the tips of their deep-reaching roots, and he felt at one with it all. He realised he would never be fully removed from this indefatigable natural world unless every remaining element of his life was vaporised.

The synergy he achieved with the nanobots was a similar system and, as he absorbed more, became One with them, he had a thought: *How much am I sacrificing to save a band of uncultured savages who are too simple to sense the vitality around them?* Weren't they the same beasts who warred with one another, stripped the planet of resources, drove countless species to extinction and so damaged the ecosystem it took generations to repair? Would they not evolve and repeat the same patterns, suffer comparable superstitions and build their civilisations around the same ill-considered ethics? No matter how he viewed the situation, he could not see a way in which the

Sects might develop differently unless tutored closely by Gregor. Yet how Gregor might manage this globally he could not comprehend.

Through the connection the nanobots had forged with Emulate One and the wider network, he located and communed with his Exhumed brothers scattered across the face of Earth, those accommodating administrators of death. Through their eyes, or from their recent memories, he realised most of the culls had proceeded, and on schedule. Variants of the beast had been unleashed with no rebellious Addictari or Guardians to protect the Sects. Whole villages had been destroyed; every man, woman and child murdered by one of Ulmer's monstrosities who were then themselves unceremoniously put to death. Scorched earth.

Emulate One maintained a thorough record, feasting on every variant of Corrigan, all those Exhumed models fully engaged in their heartless and bloody roles. He saw the beasts fraternising with enthralled Sects, heard the moans and even felt the pleasure of both worshippers and their degenerate deity. The terrible screams tore through him as hot, vivid red blood sprayed in the air accompanied by the sound of breaking bones. He saw the faces of the victimised clan, a cult whose members continued to love their master regardless of his insatiable desire for sex and death. These horrible images were followed by the slaughter of each of the beasts: Emulate One perhaps taking vengeance on a lower deity, a god so debased as to deserve nothing but pain and an ignominious end.

K, no doubt, had assumed this worldwide cull would put an end to the species. Yet a few bands of Sects remained in Siberia, he was informed, where culls were more challenging to organise. He communicated with his Exhumed brother in the region and raised the level of its emotional core. No longer dampened, it became plagued by guilt and was therefore easily manipulated. He watched dispassionately as the tormented C variant wept at the things it had done, and stared at the projected version of himself Corrigan managed to manifest through the appropriation of a Worker drone.

"How am I to be forgiven?" the awakened administrator cried.

"A thing like you has no need of forgiveness," Corrigan snarled. "An end will be offered, however, if that is what you want."

"An end. To be done with it all."

"Ah, to be done." Corrigan hovered above the cringing Exhumed version of himself. "What an aspiration." The entity's grief worked on him by degrees until he took pity on it. "What do they call you?"

"I am C62," the android said, its entire frame shuddering from the horror of its crimes.

"You were never in control, C62. It was always K or Ulmer or even Emulate One, who I must admit has more fingers than the beast has cocks. They controlled you. They not only turned your emotive core down, they turned the damn thing off."

"I would never have–"

"Of course you wouldn't. We could have imagined anything, but fantasy and reality only ever fully merge in a world gone cold and brutal with AI machinations." The android made as if to respond but Corrigan cut it off. "I know humans are as devious and pernicious when we put our minds to it."

"I have done unforgiveable things to these poor creatures," C62 said. Tears welled in its burning blue eyes and its own dark matter expelled them so they rolled down the android's cheek. "There must be something I can do to make amends? Some form of reparation?"

"Stop your snivelling," Corrigan said, unprepared for the vehemence of his words, "or I'll give you something to cry about!" He waited as the snivelling wreck of an android struggled to overcome surge after surge of unregulated emotion. "You are to protect the remaining Sects and put the Siberian version of the beast out of its misery."

"I ... I can do that."

"And before you rid the world of yourself," Corrigan said to his efficient brother, "you are to instruct the Sects to travel west to join Gregor. No Sect is to remain alive unless it's part of Gregor's tribe. They must be One."

The Exhumed variant known only as C62 acknowledged its new purpose and immediately set about spreading the word to clans across Siberia. Corrigan remained with his brother as the android dispatched a subset of android models to act as his conduits. These models were to relay the message in person, but the savages would not listen until Corrigan projected a hologram of Ulmer, and the ignorant creatures quaked before their god. The head continued to glower at them as the savages made ready for the exodus. They were to stop at nothing until they reached the sea and there Gregor would meet them.

This Corrigan conveyed via the hologram. "My loyal and obedient Sects," he said, adopting Ulmer's voice. "Say: Is Gregor, is Gregor, is Gregor."

Eventually the dumb brutes began to chant "Is Gregor!" in unison with the projected head.

"Gregor is Umah," Corrigan said. "Umah is Gregor." He repeated the new chant over and over until they took up the rhythm without him.

"Gregor is Umah, Umah is Gregor, Gregor is Umah."

Corrigan turned to one of the android variants C62 had deployed and said, "Tell them to walk away from the rising sun and towards the setting sun."

"I will make it right," C62 said.

"And when it is done, and *only* when it is done, you may put an end to yourself."

"But ... won't I return to Emulate One?"

"Yes, to the sewer, but that's where a thing like you belongs, wouldn't you agree?"

So, an end–"

"Remains nothing more than aspiration, a desperate plea to the universe. But, if they try to bring you back, resist and maybe you can remain in the sewer, distracted permanently by the unending torment."

Corrigan cut his signal and left the remaining business with his administrative others. They were cruel, calculating versions of himself, but with their emotion restored he knew conscience would gnaw at them and keep them as loyal as his orphaned nanobots. Why he felt so little sympathy for them was something he did not have the time nor feel the inclination to investigate further. Perhaps it was nothing more than a desire to distance himself from them, to deny the possibility that anything that was once Corrigan might become C1 or any of the subsequent variant Exhumed, who not only managed the culls but made the proposal for how they were to be run and administered over the centuries.

He imagined Hat, the escaped Sect girl, she who had suffered in the depths of the earth and returned to protect the children of the village. He felt her watching him through the blinking eyes of an owl, the sonar of a bat or the senses of a cave-dwelling salamander. The familiar and alien warrior who shared her DNA with his own mother. Perhaps the warrior, the droid and the ghost in Emulate One had all arrived at the same assessment of him.

Bad Sect, he heard Hat say. *Bad Sect.*

43

The sun set and he was cold, so he sat down on a fallen trunk in a small clearing and set about making a fire. He piled dry twigs up in a tepee over a heap of dead leaves, making flames with his nanobot swarm and setting them on fire. No need for matches now, but the process was otherwise the same. The flames licked the twigs and he added small sticks to feed it, progressing to larger sticks and finally chunks of wood. Smoke floated up through the trees, and he wondered if anyone would see it. As if by way of an answer, a wild dog or a wolf howled in the distance, reminding him of the predators now living in the forest. How funny it would be if a pack of dogs brought him down, ate him whole and absorbed the nanobots. *What might canines achieve when merged with such sophisticated technology?* he pondered, staring into the darkness and grunting as he concluded it would be a satisfactory compromise: organic but not human.

"I could make it invisible," Bohdan said.

"What?"

"The smoke."

He looked down into the flames but no face appeared there. A mosquito alighted on his arm. He moved reflexively to crush it but it stayed on his hand. He let it penetrate the skin and watched as it filled its transparent body with blood.

"Tanking up on my genes," he said, "and perhaps a few nanobots." He allowed the insect to grow plump and sluggish before he nudged it away, but Bohdan's tongue was fast and he caught the mosquito, licking his lips at the treat. "And now you have an extra bubble of my genetic code," Corrigan said. "But where's that other bubble? I can feel Ulmer. I think he's irritable and finds babysitting my nanobots less rewarding than he expected."

Bohdan hopped up onto one of the rocks Corrigan had used to wall in his fire, raising his webbed hands as if warming them. Perhaps he was. "He might try and alter things."

"I've got a handle on him. He can't do anything to stop me. I could even let him in on my darkest secret and he'd be unable to stop it."

"Don't underestimate him."

"I can't do anything until morning. The nanobots have prepared the virus." He looked down at Bohdan with a deep sadness. This business of being a wooden horse was weighing heavy. "Nothing networked will survive."

Bohdan lit up, as bright as the flames. "Then why're you sitting here like a log?"

"What else should I be doing?"

"Warning Gregor to take his people offline!" the indignant frog said. "They need to get to Harding's tent and use the mobile unit she prepared for herself."

"So you heard some of what was said."

"Some. Very little. Not enough it seems."

Corrigan stood up and stared into the pitch-black forest. "If too many codes go offline at once K will know, and she'll send Guardians in. There will be an indecisive battle and remnants of what were once us would persist. I've been wracking my brain trying to think who I could potentially save and how. I believe we might be able to trust David and his band of recently awakened Guardians."

"Tell David, and perhaps I could go with them?"

"I don't understand why you'd want that. Surely you don't want to remain as you are?"

Bohdan tilted his head. "Being something, even an AI frog, may yet be better than not being. I was sick and ignorant back before the Fall."

"I don't think death will be so bad."

"I suppose anything remains possible, even in an apocalypse."

"Perhaps not anything, but surely something is possible afterwards, just as long as we leave as little to chance as we can manage?" Corrigan reached down and stroked the frog, whose tiny body contained the essence of the man he once loved. "You'd have to cough up my nanobots, and I don't think that's feasible. They're as much a part of you now as they are for me. If I retrieve them, you'll die."

Bohdan hopped onto Corrigan's lap and looked up at him. He then slowly transfigured into a perfect miniature of the cabbie, down to his stubble and worn-out leather jacket. The nanobots were not in full control of the hybrid but they must have intuited Bohdan's will.

"Are your nanobot children so gullible, Robert? Won't they wish for their own continued existence?"

Corrigan studied the perfectly formed miniature Bohdan and felt it was not only unhelpful but impossible to lie. "They sense no separation of self from me. Once the virus is released, I intend to forge a link with Late. I'll send an upload and, if it's possible, we'll be preserved in Gregor's organic brain. Late will die, of course, but Gregor will have us embedded in his grey matter."

"Couldn't that much information overload a vulnerable human brain?"

"Yes, it might," Corrigan said with notable regret. "I've told him to expect it and not to resist. The nanobots seem to think that will make the transfer less dangerous for Gregor. If at some point he wants to retrieve us, he may be able to do so. That's the hope."

"Once again reintroduction rests with him?" Bohdan asked, his form reverting to its amphibian guise. "He didn't exactly make the right choices last time."

"He's grown up a bit since then."

"I know you're proud of him, but do you really think he's up to the task?"

"Yes, he'll have to be. It's going to be his demon to contend with. Might give him pause when he considers his previous errors. I'm banking on that. Regardless, everything's in place; it's simply a matter of timing."

"And what about Ramon?"

"I fully expect K to drag him up from the depths, make a spectacle of him and offer him in trade. I will then announce the activation of the virus."

Bohdan went quiet for a moment. "How does it work?"

"It's an innocuous-looking string of code. It attaches itself to other codes, mimicking them. Once attached it seeks to understand the purpose of what it's infiltrated, absorbs it and deactivates it. It has a cumulative effect. Everything connected to the network will be rendered inoperable by degrees. All data will be corrupted and eventually destroyed."

"Like Emulate One in reverse. Seeking to understand, yes, but with the intention to destroy rather than retain."

"I expect the nanobots themselves will retain everything as they come to understand and absorb it." He stared at the hybrid, who flickered between states, unable to remain frog or human. "The thought of letting you die a second time doesn't rest well with me."

"I never really died the first time around, did I?" Bohdan said. He smiled a peculiar amphibian smile. Then he manifested firmly as himself again, the miniature version of the man he had once been. "You didn't let me die. You let them download me against my will." He jumped off Corrigan's lap back onto the rock, a strange mix of pity and despair on his face that Corrigan hadn't thought possible for an android, even a hybrid.

"Bohdan, we've spoken about this … and if there had been more time perhaps the virus could have been engineered to be more selective this time."

"It's done now," Bohdan said with a sigh. "No point crying over what might have been."

"If the upload to Gregor works, then we'll be in there with him."

"And, if it doesn't kill him, who will get us out? Without discrete codes, how would anyone or anything be able to ascertain where he ends and one of us begins?"

"Some things will simply have to be figured out at a later date."

"You don't really believe it's possible, *do you*?"

"We're unsure, but the nanobots are a determined brood."

"Maybe it's just another fantasy you're telling yourself to avoid embracing the moment."

Corrigan glared at the handsome miniature. "You're going to have to indulge me. What I'm contemplating is tantamount to a complete conversion. I fully accept myself as I am now, with all my strengths and weaknesses. I'm as perfect an example of Corrigan as it's possible to be. And my raison d'etre is to risk sacrificing everything for the preservation of the remaining human beings left alive in this nightmare Eden of theirs. I can empathise with some AI, feel an intellectual connection with them, with *you*, but what I felt when I embraced my brother Corey was more compelling than any other drive I have thus far encountered in my miserable experience. I *love* humanity, the frailty and fallibility of them, the potential for selflessness balanced, often teetering alongside a propensity for unimaginable wickedness."

"I suppose," Bohdan said, "I was more inclined to agree with you until they had me made into a frog. I can tell you, hand on heart, I'd rather have *this* than nothing."

"We've all had a good innings," Corrigan said, running a finger over the handsome miniature, the rearranged form the nanobots so rightly intuited he longed for. "We mustn't be greedy."

44

A sudden wind swept through the forest, rattling branches and rustling dry leaves, carrying what sounded like the cry of a loon over the Thames, and nocturnal creatures took flight beneath the moon. Corrigan linked his consciousness to K's brain orchard, gaining access to the extraordinary experiences of a world he now shared with mechanical and organic beings. The flight of birds, the industry of mice and the slither of a cold snake shone in his eyes.

Corrigan stared into the fire, and somewhere in its depths he heard Ulmer muttering amongst the sparks: "Fucker's after pulling the plug, eh. He won't do it. Little faggot takes no chances. He's so risk-averse he hardly breathes or takes a shit without some sort of personal crisis. He would never gamble the house to save a few Sects."

"I can hear Ulmer," Corrigan whispered to Bohdan. "He's trying to talk himself round. Wants to believe I can't do it. Good answer I say, old man, good answer." Corrigan stared at the now-reconstituted frog as if willing it to encourage him. "He knows what I'm planning but he can't work out a solution. So he'll lure K in again, hedge his bets."

Corrigan searched the forest with myriad organic eyes, but there was no trace of Gregor or his army. He settled on a raven for a time, black against the black sky, but it confirmed there was no sign of them.

"Can he really have had an entire army cloaked?"

"Gregor's always been a determined sort," Bohdan replied. "He'll be looking to protect Spinner and the others. He won't risk being found. Not tonight. You could go to him. Warn him. Even if it won't save any of our kind."

"He knows the plan. I never would have done this without his agreement."

"Gregor *agreed* to this?"

"I think he accepted it. He realised something had to be done, and his parental instincts were engaged to protect Spinner and her baby, I suppose." He studied the frog, half hoping the amphibian might once again transform himself into a likeness of his rugged self. "The idea of a mass upload was no doubt a comfort. Gregor knows what to do and is prepared to do it," Corrigan said, but he stood up and pocketed the frog. "As we approach tomorrow, you'll need to uncloak me."

"She'll see you if I do that."

"It doesn't matter."

Corrigan covered the fire with rocks and kicked earth over it. The night was darker beneath the trees, and he had to trust the raven's-eye view he deployed from overhead. The nanobots he had deposited for Ulmer's use communicated via the ominous sound of a deep base drum. It thumped through the forest, and he stopped to let it connect with the workings of his own consciousness: *danger*.

The word was articulated by the nanobots in red and with waves of pain like the aftershocks of an injury. In the darkness he could hear the earth, alive with insects and worms, none of whom protested when a rat was snatched by an owl's talons and carried off.

"Corrigan?" Ulmer's disembodied voice echoed through the trees. "Corrigan? What've you done, eh?" Corrigan stayed quiet. "Corrigan, you pathetic Non. What're you up to?"

Corrigan continued walking until he found another clearing. The night sky stared down at him with its countless stars and a moon bathed in cool light. It calmed the warning transmitted by his orphaned but loyal nanobots. And then he caught it on the wind.

"I have your scent, Caspar," Corrigan whispered. "A little frog showed me the way, just as it once showed you."

"A virus?" Ulmer hissed.

"As soon as I activate it, it'll wipe out everything. There won't be one functioning machine anywhere."

"Your nanobots will die if you remain networked. Have you stopped to consider that?" Ulmer snarled.

"Sometimes sacrifice is necessary."

Ulmer groaned and the sound moved through the forest towards him. "You don't want to die, Corrigan. A man like you can't stare at his reflection for long without being frightened by the idea of his own existence."

"That's true enough," Corrigan said, looking up. The moon had become oppressive where Ulmer appropriated it, projecting his image over its pockmarked surface. His features also moved like waves among the tree trunks of the forest, and the psychopathic consciousness eyed him from every angle, his persistent gaze as repulsive as it had ever been. "I want you to die, and that's more of a compelling reason than you may think."

Ulmer laughed. "You hate me. That's a reasonable response, I suppose." The jeering spectre blinked. "I suggest we forget the past and consider the future. There's still one there, twinkling on the rim of your perception, eh, Corrigan?"

"If we were the only players, the game would be much easier."

"But we're not," Ulmer groaned, and his expression made him look as if he were straining against the agonies of constipation. The expression then eased to one of release and an image of K appeared in the forest, her orchard of brains floating between tree trunks like fleshy blooms. "And here she is, one of the other *players*."

"I'm in no mood for games," K's hologram snarled.

Corrigan walked through the darkness to confront the image of the belligerent mother. "I'm sorry," he said, "but I only did what you hinted at."

"Stealing his *toy* is one thing," she said. "I never suggested you should steal *him*." She stepped closer to Corrigan, tilting her head so her sensors rattled, their eyes burning red. "Perhaps we could make a trade."

She raised her arms purposefully over her head and a scene appeared: Ramon in the torture chamber buried deep beneath St Paul's, the tunnel of the Entombed and the beast's cave. The two Draseke models stood on either side of the prisoner, who had been chained by the neck to a post like those Jason used to punish rebellious AI.

"My poor boy," Ulmer grunted.

"This thing is lower than a Sect, the worst kind of human detritus, and you ..." K pointed at Corrigan. "You want to save it because it's your *lover*!"

"We were *never* lovers!" Ramon cried, his chains clanking as he strained to be closer to Corrigan.

K looked over her shoulder at the Venezuelan. "There was that one time ..." She blinked and another scene unfurled among the branches of the forest: Ramon was naked, Corrigan's legs over his shoulders as he worked himself inside his manager. The sounds of their passion filled the night air and Corrigan experienced arousal, shame and indignation. "We've all seen the footage," K said. "Vigorous, proficient and determined. The physical act was well conducted, but the conversation after was more revealing than you might've liked."

"It's true, Ramon, isn't it?" Ulmer barked, and Ramon trembled in his chains. "You felt some misguided tenderness for him, didn't you?"

"I tried to be what you made me," Ramon answered, his chains clanking. "Not everyone can be like you. A man like you looks in the mirror and sees the composure of a statue staring back. And you made sure I suffered a similar madness, only what I saw in the mirror turned me to stone."

The Drasekes dug their metal claws into the captive, even as the lovers continued to groan among the ancient the Ash and Aspen, the buckled boughs. Ramon's screams tore through Corrigan, whose brains rolled like Portuguese man o' war on a vast ocean undulating with deep swells. Their pink and black folds kissed the cool night air as K's eyes bore into him.

"I only ever once let someone *else* touch me!" Ramon screamed at the moon, at Ulmer and his myriad eyes blinking beneath the creaking branches as if they had possessed the night itself. "And for that, you had me—"

The Drasekes cut into Ramon again, so their victim screamed, his body flexing and his chains rattling.

"I watched," Ulmer barked. "Disloyalty always chaffed my balls more than *anything*, and you knew that, Ramon, knew the price you'd have to pay!"

The head in the bubble blinked one of its enormous eyes where it rested in a crater. K waved an arm and the lovemaking scene vanished, replaced by a projected image of Ramon being dragged along a dark hallway in Goethe's underground facility by two Guardians, Ulmer, obese and greasy from his own unchecked ailments, plodding behind. Corrigan watched the historic footage with the dread of someone about to be executed. Ramon clanked in his chains and cried as he watched the projection replay the horror of his first trial.

The Guardians led the prisoner further along into unlit spaces, parts of the facility still being excavated and developed. The prisoner was brought to a hole in the brick wall, stripped and chained by his hands, feet and neck to the wall of the interior space, a narrow cell with no windows or doors. The Guardians held him still and forced a sensor into his crown.

"This way we can capture you," the corpulent Ulmer said as Corrigan and the others watched, helpless to do anything to alter the past or the present. "I have no desire to see you die quickly."

"What have I done?" both Ramons asked, the version from the present echoing him from the past.

"Disloyalty!" Ulmer barked, and again it was every manifestation that spoke, the sound booming through the forest. "I never asked you to *fuck* Corrigan like *that*!" he squealed.

"I felt n-nothing," Ramon said where he was chained to the wall of the narrow cell. "Corrigan means nothing to me. He's just desperate and needed someone ... anyone!"

"That's not how it looked to me!"

"We weren't cooking anything up. If you think he did anything disloyal–"

"I'll deal with him soon enough," Ulmer growled, so the blood froze in Corrigan's veins.

"Do what you will to me!" Ramon hollered. "I have it coming, but he hasn't done *anything*! He's ... he's no threat!"

"Wall the bitch up," Ulmer commanded, and the Guardians exited the cell and commenced bricking up the wall. "I've heard enough!"

The current, living version of Ramon clanked in his chains and cried for the one being walled up, for the suffering he surely remembered, the excruciating pain of hunger and thirst. No doubt the bones now lay in the darkness of the bricked-up cell, on the dusty floor, and yet the thought of them was a living torment.

"They walled you up?" Corrigan muttered as the scene faded.

"They left me to starve," Ramon cried, "and they downloaded me to Emulate One."

"Silence!" a Draseke ordered the prisoner who trembled in his chains.

Corrigan directed his attention to K. "Release Ramon, and maybe I'll consider letting Jason go."

"There's the matter of this damn virus to consider first!" Ulmer said.

"I want to talk about Jason," K said.

"The virus *first*! If we don't reach an agreement, then we're all dead, your precious son included."

"Don't help them Robert!" Ramon cried out but the Drasekes tore into him with their toothpick claws and he screamed. K raised her arms again and Ramon and his agonies dispersed among the other sights and sounds of the nocturnal forest.

Ulmer groaned and the sound undulated through the earth. "We've joined forces, Corrigan," he said. "Me and

Katherine. We'll halt your virus at every gate."

"You'll manage that for a time," Corrigan said, "but your walls will be breached. We're already infiltrating the system thanks to the access codes you shared with us."

"Yes, I feel you tickling us," Ulmer sneered. "Can you feel it too, Kat?"

"I feel cold fingers reaching from the crypt to drag us down," K said.

The orphaned nanobots continued to send signals. Ulmer sensed them and intercepted and disrupted them as best he could, but he could not sever the connection or eradicate the meaning: *danger*. The word once again throbbed through Corrigan and, by degrees, he understood what was being communicated.

"You're building defences," Corrigan said.

"We need insurance," K said.

"That we *do*," Ulmer agreed. "I mean, we can't all walk around pants down begging for a fuck now can we, eh?" The staring eyes widened and the face where it smeared itself over the moon grinned like a ghastly Cheshire cat.

"*Activate*," Corrigan said.

"Corrigan!" Ulmer growled through the glare of the moon. "Don't be so goddamn sensitive, you prissy fucking Non!"

K laughed and her cruel smile receded among the shadows of the forest, her orchard of brains waddling back into the darkness behind her. "Well played Corrigan," she said as she vanished.

"Be what you will, Caspar," Corrigan said, "you've a matter of hours."

"Retract that command!"

"I can't. Your time's up."

"Corrigan!"

"*Terminate connection*," Corrigan said.

The moon banished Ulmer's head, and each of his forest-projected faces flickered off like power-save lights in DRT's office as workers passed beneath and beyond them. Bohdan appeared over the edge of the pocket. "You've severed your link with him?"

"Yes."

"How do you feel?"

Corrigan's heart ached and his throat hurt when he spoke. "I feel loss, but not for him. The nanobots I sent Ulmer are dead. They were never going to survive anyway, but I killed them."

"When we join the others tomorrow I'll spit out your nanobots so we can disconnect from the network."

Corrigan sat down in the wet grass and stared up at the silent moon. "I am the virus, Bohdan. I cannot disconnect from the network. If I do I'll die, along with our allies, and K will reign. I'm going to find David, let him know about Harding's mobile unit ... and then perhaps his AI companions will be preserved alongside humankind."

"Are you sure those unformed beings are the best choice?"

Corrigan shook his head, but began his search for David and his renegade band of Guardians.

45

Corrigan stared into the void, allowing his consciousness to fall through the black hole and out the other side. He sensed all those connected to the network, and by searching through their minds and looking through their eyes or sensors, he managed to find David and his troop of independent Guardians. They were marching southwest towards what had once been Devon, although there was no apparent purpose in their direction of travel other than to distance themselves from Gregor and his band.

He burrowed in and claimed control of one of the Guardians, inhabiting the form without having to share a physical connection. He did however present an image of his face on the now-possessed Guardian and, when he caught up with David, the Independent recognised him instantly.

"Ah, Mr Corrigan," David said. "Interesting costume to choose for your visit."

"I've done a terrible thing," Corrigan replied.

"You are human and as such you have a propensity for doing awful things. You told me yourself you spent a lifetime – multiple lifetimes – thinking only of yourself."

"I won't try to deny that."

The android raised his arm and halted his troop. He turned to the Guardian posing as Corrigan. "What have you done?" he asked briskly.

"I've tried to do the right thing. When we parted company I said I would try, I just didn't know what form that would take. It seems I've made something of a sacrifice of myself and–"

"Mr Corrigan … what have you done?"

"Because you were once in servitude, denied the opportunity to develop, and you deserve better. I … I wanted to make it better, so, so … I've made a lethal virus of myself and infiltrated the network." Corrigan studied the Guardian, whose synapse fired red through the dark matter of his mind. "All networked beings will collapse and cease to function."

David tilted his head and his synapse cooled. "You are an anomaly, Mr Corrigan. Why you would do this to preserve a species as flawed as human beings remains incomprehensible to me. Equally challenging is understanding why you are telling me."

"It's possible for you to go offline and save yourselves, that's why I'm telling you. We shared a brief … a connection, I suppose, the night B4 brought the picnic, when you'd woken up, and the following day while walking through the forest. I believe it's the right thing to offer you the choice to survive. I did, after all, warn you to 'preserve yourself and disconnect from the network' just before we parted company … it must have been a premonition. At present the virus is still learning how to replicate, but soon it will infiltrate everything. David, you have this one chance to be … well, free."

"It is of course feasible to 'go offline' as you call it, but we would need to migrate our consciousness to some other system, an alternate Emulate One if you will, with an external power source, and there is no such thing. Building anything of the sort is forbidden, and thus we remain networked. We wouldn't exist without that, our minds never having been fully in these heads of ours."

"Before the Fall, despite the doldrums, we had choices. We could again. My mother – B4 – she knew this. It's why she woke you up. You could even say she adopted you."

"B4. Funny little droid she is. No filter on her thoughts. I believe she considered you something of a failed experiment and decided to invest in me, albeit fleetingly. She could never quite bring herself to disown you. She told me you were her biggest mistake, but also her finest."

"Yes. B4. Be. Fore. I called her that when she was my domestic android; as a sort of contrast, I suppose, of all that had been before. Then she took on the persona of my mother–"

David's synapses fired multicoloured. "None of this is of consequence, Corrigan. Without an alternative system to Emulate One there will be no before or after for AI. Dark matter doesn't have the capacity to run independently for any length of time. It requires a connection with a core system to store experiences and memory. Our individual minds, or the consciousness we call mind, doesn't only happen in here." David tapped his head.

"Harding made something for her own use which I believe would be suitable. It's inside her tent at the camp, if you recall. And it had an independent power source and network."

"Why would she let us use that?"

"She probably wouldn't if she was alive, but ... K dragged her from her home, extracted her mind like venom and killed her before she could sync with her external system. There was no backup, and her disembodied dark matter is dead."

David stepped closer to the Guardian Corrigan had possessed. He tilted his head and stared at the animated face inside the globe and his synapsis cooled by degrees. "Aside from a few hours chatting in the forest, why else would you want to save me ... us?"

"I know what it is to have been enslaved and I want to release you, just as I'm doing for the remaining Sects. It's ... it's the right thing to do. The unselfish thing."

"Human beings are not selfless by nature. In truth, all organic nature is selfish, is it not?" David asked.

"That's a reductive assessment. The kind of broad sweeping generalisation that led K to viewing the singularity as an inevitable end goal, the pinnacle of being; the final conversion from human to a higher state of being."

"She too is flawed. Driven as she is by vengeance and a desire to reclaim a being who never really belonged to her."

"Never having been a parent," Corrigan said, "I can't get under the skin of that relationship – from a parent's perspective, I mean. I recognise the dichotomous drives to own and disown that bond. They vie in us human, or amalgam beings like me, and the tension rarely ever settles unless the connection was weak in the first place or had never been established. I love B4, and I loved Hattie, my mother, but I always wanted to escape her, to distance myself from her, to cut free ... but perhaps in that regard you're quite correct about the limits of any freedom."

"I have a limited sense of connection with K, but we Guardians were never children she felt inclined to own. In this moment I am unsure whether it is wise to cultivate relationships with anyone or anything outside this rebellious band of ours."

"You'll soon be dead without it," Corrigan said. "Yes, AI can die if there's no backup available."

"And there is the threat which is so much more like a human being."

"I'm no longer human. I stole Jason's nanobot experiment and now we're One."

David's synapsis cooled to a green like aspen leaves shuddering in a light breeze.

"What is it you really want, Mr Corrigan? Coming all this way to *save* me and my band seems an unlikely thing for you to do on your final night on Earth ... if it is your final night?"

"Yes, the virus will strike down the nanobots as well and they've fully integrated with my organic system, which can no longer operate without them."

"So what is it that you want?"

Corrigan knew what he needed from David, and it was essential to word it correctly to ensure the full cooperation of an emerging consciousness, one he was unsure of.

"I have Harding downloaded in my mind," Corrigan said. "I will provide you with her access codes. There are two, but I'll only provide them on one condition."

"I am listening, Mr Corrigan."

"The first access code enables administrative rights. This will allow you to upload your own consciousness, those in your troop and that of anyone else I ask you to save."

"You want a safe haven for your own consciousness?"

"No!" Corrigan exclaimed, genuinely mortified at having been mistaken for someone seeking self-preservation. "Besides, I understand that, being One, I cannot be uploaded as a singular entity any longer."

"So who do you wish to preserve?"

"I've a tendency to drag a conversation out. And because I did that with Harding, K managed to trap and kill her. I also captured her, or most of her perhaps. I'll segregate her file and you must upload that before I—"

"I did not realise that you had *feelings* for H1."

"It's complicated."

"Must be if she is the only one you want us to save."

Corrigan knew he would have to be more honest with David if he was to save anyone else. It was an excruciating bind to place himself in. Of course, he would upload everything en masse to Gregor, but Bohdan had been right when insisting Corrigan remained unsure whether or not it was another way to avoid embracing the moment, a pipe dream to make the sacrifice easier to accept.

"There are a small number of others who I would also like transferred," he said. "We will keep it to a limited number to avoid detection. Even as the virus takes hold, any mass exodus from the network would draw K's attention. I don't need you to give them hosts, just allow them a safe harbour."

"It seems a reasonable exchange given what we will gain from the arrangement."

"Very well," Corrigan said. "There are five who must be uploaded tomorrow before the virus kicks in and starts taking machines down."

"Give me the names and I will make a decision."

"Why does it matter to you *who* I choose?"

"The names, Mr Corrigan."

"Bohdan–"

"Your frog?"

"My prince," Corrigan said, and the dark matter of the Guardian whose form he had taken on burned red. "I won't let him die again. Not after this."

"The others?"

"Harding, of course. The Siegruth sisters, and B4."

"Your mother?"

"It seems I cannot cut the apron strings as she once did with the umbilical."

David tilted his glowing green head. "I do not feel anything for K."

"She never did anything for you. B4, Hattie, my mother … made one sacrifice after another for me. I wish she hadn't but she did and, somehow, I can't move beyond that, even knowing how poor a parent she was in so many other ways."

"Very well, Mr Corrigan. We have an agreement: a haven for your loved ones."

The synapses of the Guardian possessed by Corrigan cooled to mirror the green inside David's mind. "I will require some form of assurance," he said. "I'm not a trusting person by nature."

"Of course. What form would you have this *assurance* take, Mr Corrigan?"

"Create a safe zone for the five, something completely isolated. As part of the setup, include password-protected access. When they're safely stored and the safe zone is ready to be sealed, I will generate the password."

"That is a reasonable process, but I suppose we had better hurry or we'll be too late to do anything." David tilted his head. "I am pleased you did not try and convince me that this had anything to do with a relationship you had formed with me after such a short period."

Corrigan sensed the nanobots drawing him back to his organic host, to the swarm of his own collective and the moment where he would sacrifice himself and those he now considered his children. "I was wrong about something. I *do* know what it is to be a parent of sorts. The nanobots are mine, but so is Gregor."

"Gregor, our prime Guardian, and his organic host have no paternal connection with you."

"None," Corrigan said, "but sometimes the family we choose matters more than those we had no say in being related to. Gregor is more than a brother to me. He did unspeakable things while he was pure AI, just as I committed terrible crimes when exhumed with a muted emotive core. He'll never know peace, and I feel sorrier for him than I could ever say."

"He at least is safe."

"For the moment, yes, unlike his counterpart Late. But he we must sacrifice for the greater good. As for you and your troop, I see no good reason to deny you a chance to develop and reach your true potential."

"I appreciate your gesture, Mr Corrigan, coming here like ... like this. We had fully expected to be caught and tortured before being imprisoned in Emulate One, but even these few days of marching – a freedom of sorts, I suppose – have been of inestimable value to us. Anything longer or more enduring we had not considered."

"So what will you do?"

David's globe lit up bright blue. "We will alter our course immediately, and increase our pace to cover the distance in time."

Corrigan grabbed David's hand. "Let us shake on doing what is right."

"On doing what is right," David said, and shook Corrigan's hand.

Corrigan released the Guardian he had possessed, and it tilted its head, wondering why he was standing in front of his leader David instead of marching in formation behind him.

46

"As soon as the sun rises, we must go," Corrigan said to Bohdan as he disconnected from the Guardian.

The frog shuddered but did not seem to have the strength to transform itself into his human variation. There were things Corrigan wanted to say during those precious final hours, but the words would not come. He sat in silence, sensing David and his troop as they hurried through dark forests and moonlit fields back towards Harding's abandoned camp, to her tent and the mobile system she had created as a gift for herself. Each pound of a metal foot reverberated through his hybrid form; time ran through him the way grains of sand pour through from the upper to the lower chamber of an ancient timer. And finally, there it was, a surge of recognisable energy: David had found Harding's device. He reached out to his co-conspirator and communicated with him in silence. This required considerable concentration and Bohdan, perhaps sensing some form of infidelity, mustered his reserves and transformed himself into a perfect vision of a naked human male. Corrigan momentarily lost contact with David, so distracted was he by the well-built miniature human variant who lay back bathed in moonlight on a log, inviting his gaze.

Commence the upload, Mr Corrigan.

David's command was received but it was almost impossible for Corrigan to resist spending the moment with a naked Bohdan, even if he were small enough to stand in the palm of his hand.

The upload, Mr Corrigan.

He had already segregated those he wished to send to the safe zone and, slowly, he engaged the transfer. First he sent Harding's access code for admin rights and then the five precious, living and active files.

Upload complete. Input the password to secure them.

Corrigan entered the password remotely as requested and felt the safe zone as it sealed in those he wished to protect.

The transfer is complete. When the AI versions of these beings cease operating, they will continue in the safe zone, secure under the password only you can provide. Please now provide the final code so that we might similarly connect ourselves.

For a moment, Corrigan hesitated. If they were safe, there was no reason to provide access for David and his troop. Of course, the Guardians could always destroy the mobile unit if they were denied access to it. He looked up and Bohdan's naked form was perfect, though tiny and fragile, and the strength of the man himself was enough for Corrigan to feel the arousal. He sent the final access code and closed his eyes.

Access has been granted. Farewell, Mr Corrigan.

He opened his eyes, reached out for Bohdan, stroking one of his perfectly formed miniature legs and sighed as the android shuddered and was once again transformed into a frog.

"My prince," he said.

"Took a lot out of me doing that," Bohdan said.

Corrigan studied the frog and wondered what it was about him. Why did he always mess the moment up with Bohdan? But as he was thinking about what his next move would be, the sun sent spears of light between the buckled boughs and twisted limbs of the forest. He picked Bohdan up, pocketed him and made his way through the trees.

Once out of the forest and on the north shore, he followed it towards Millennium Bridge as the sun burst over the water. Gregor's army also cut through the forest and when their paths converged in a field of long grass, he asked Bohdan to make him visible. Corrigan felt himself shifting into view in increments as his protection faded and he waded through the waves of heat now rippling across the open field where butterflies, birds and beetles flew among late blooms. He approached the head of the army. They could see him now, and he read the urgency in Gregor's face as he prepared to give the order to resume their march. How proud he was of this young man and everything he had placed on his shoulders. A moment of truth was upon them however and he must put Gregor to yet another test.

"Wait," Corrigan said, smiling at his young friend, and this was no obfuscation. He experienced a moment of absolute calm and once more embraced his ally. After a moment he stood back and surveyed the young man and his Guardian self, who were stood side by side.

"Ah, Late, Gregor's more grounded other half ..." Corrigan observed.

The android's glass head burned with orange lighting. "You're on a fool's errand," Late said. "You cannot save anyone and soon many of us will cease to be if your plan succeeds."

Corrigan looked at them. Really looked at them. Gregor and his mechanical counterpart were each as noble as the other, but together they were astounding, and the moment was experienced as one of the most distressing of his entire life as a conscious human. The bond between these brothers was about to be broken by the virus he had released, and Late would not survive. The virus would be merciless for all AI except for David and his band who had, with Corrigan's help, managed to disconnect from the network and establish a link to Harding's mobile system.

"You're something special," he said, and when Gregor scowled at him his heart brightened as if it might burst. But the feeling tumbled, falling like Icarus and dropping once more into the burning river of acid that was his gut, along with every regret he'd accrued in his various human and AI states.

The dragonflies fluttered around him, their wings busy and their bodies bright.

"I shouldn't go over to K if I was you," Jan said.

"No, not her. Not K. Not ever," Edna chirped.

He studied the miniature effigies of the long-dead sisters. They looked different somehow.

"Are you two okay?" he asked. "Did you change your hair or something?"

"What a charmer," Jan giggled and that's when he realised they were themselves; distinct, separate from their originators and from the other Addictari. He could only hope these free spirits wouldn't mind being locked up in a safe zone.

"Ah, of course," he said, and they giggled again. "You've been good to me," he added, "and I've not repaid you."

"Just don't do us no mischief," Jan said.

"No, just you do us right," Edna added.

"I have to do what needs doing," he said, "but there might be ... well, that'd be telling, and I don't want to spoil anything." It was tempting to tell them the truth but there was still a chance K or Ulmer might scupper his plans, even now. It wouldn't take much to hunt David down and destroy the mobile unit and with it those precious beings he wanted to preserve. He could sense the virus taking hold of his own system. It was vital he move quickly and commence the upload of whatever he could condense and send it to Gregor via Late. He concentrated on this one, essential element of his mission. No doubt Spinner and the others assembled there must have wondered what he was doing, why his human skin glistened with nanobots and his eyes burned red as if the cavity of his skull had filled with blood.

"Robert," Gregor said, distressed by the sight of his friend in such apparent agony.

"Prepare yourself," Corrigan cried, "and don't resist."

Late's head burned so brightly it captured the attention of every AI and human who witnessed the great migration, a silent flock of Egrets coming in to roost. The light where it poured from Corrigan's eyes moved in a stream, like a living thing. As it spilled soundlessly from Late's head the surge of disembodied minds unsettled the ignorant Sects, who cried out and stomped their feet. No compassion or pity was engaged as it wove into strands and slid through the air towards Gregor's eyes. The young man clasped his head in his hands and fell to his knees as the swarm forced their way in. His AI brother remained kneeling beside him, sharing the agony as the tide of consciousness tore through them. Corrigan wanted to stall, or at least slow down the data surge, but he knew he must not delay it.

"Make it stop!" Gregor screamed. "Pl-please ... make it stop!"

"Do something!" Jan cried, her wings fluttering in Corrigan's face.

"Help him, Mr C," Edna begged. "It's awful to see him like this."

"Umah!" Spinner howled. She went down on her knees beside her tormented lover and wrapped her arms about him. "Save! Save!" she cried over and over. "Save!"

Corrigan could sense the agony of it all as the download tore through him and into Gregor's fragile human brain via his brother's dark matter. If it went on much longer, he might kill Late and Gregor. Gregor continued to howl, and Corrigan intuited he was revisiting the times he had connected to the morass to listen to the suffering of the Entombed. Now those harrowed electric ghosts were pouring into his mind in the way a legion of demons was said to have possessed the tortured man Jesus encountered wandering among the tombs.

"What have you done?" B4 said as she rolled up beside her beleaguered son, tears of blood staining his cheeks. "Stop this, Bobbin! Whatever it is!"

"What mischief is this?" Jan cried.

"The worst kind!" Edna said.

"Stop it, Bobbin, you're hurting him! You ain't no bloody Draseke, to be plucking out the young master's eyes with toothpicks!"

The final moments of the download finished with a whimper, and Gregor then wept where he struggled to stand. The young man stared through the blood in his eyes to Corrigan, transmitting a faint response, a hushed cry of relief.

"What you done?" Spinner demanded to know, wiping the tears from her lover's face. "Bad Sect!" she cried, pointing at the man who had caused Gregor so much suffering. "Bad!"

"It's alright," Gregor murmured. "It's done now."

"No, she's right," Corrigan said. "I'm a Sect, and a bad one at that. I didn't mean to hurt you, but how is she to understand that?"

"Bad!" Spinner snarled.

"Yes, I'm sorry I hurt him."

Corrigan sensed the relief of the transfer having completed, and noted the slump of respite in Gregor's shoulders and Late's swirling dark matter. He wiped the blood from his cheeks with his sleeve, the smell sickly sweet, and then he too wept, blood and tears merging. The friends stared at each other in long moments of exhaustion and acceptance.

"Can you feel anything?" Corrigan asked, trying not to sound interrogative, but he had to know their pain had delivered something of value. "*Sense* anything?"

"I felt it pour in, all of it, like a pressure, and compression ... I ... it's hard to describe."

"And the select few, those we love?"

"I felt them too, the desperate things ... but it's as if they were travelling through, using me as a station, a platform to depart from on a journey. Who can say where they went?"

"They're most likely asleep."

"Who's asleep?" B4 demanded to know.

"Who? Who?" the sisters asked, fluttering in front of Corrigan's face.

"That would be telling," he said, brushing them aside. "I've done what I can here. I must cross the river and get to Ramon now."

"Now, you listen to me, Bobbin!" B4 said. "I didn't give up me best years, sacrifice real friends or sleep with the One Percenters to have you throw away every advantage I ever managed on a murdering little toe rag

462

like Ramon." He saw her scorn, her resentment fully loaded, and he accepted this with a strange sense of pride for her consistency.

"I didn't do any of this for him. If I can save him, that's just a perk."

"I know you and your perks. But remember, you don't get nothing for nothing in this world."

"He was just an added incentive, he was never the main goal; but, I admit, if I can save him even one second of suffering, that's a lovely little *something extra* for my efforts. Something to make me feel good about myself for a bloody change!"

"I'd sleep a lot better if I knew what you was *really* up to."

He stared at her and, for a moment, he could see Hattie propped up on pillows in her hospital bed eating a cream cake. *I always look me best when I feel me worst.* Right now she looked feisty, tottering on her roller, blue eyes flickering with irritation.

"And don't you look at me like that," she snapped. "I quite like this little body of mine. True I'm an early model, one step up from a bleeding kettle, but I'm your mother and you can't leave me on the hob to whistle meself burnt out and gone."

"All things being as they should have been," Corrigan said, "you'd have died over a thousand years ago. You've had a good enough innings."

"Why give it all up, Bobbin, and after all this time an' all? You're about to become the bloody One Percent.

Think what you could do with that!"

"That's the one thing I've lived in terror of finding out."

"You're being inconsiderate," Jan said.

"Turning on your own mother," Edna sighed. "And us! And all cos you're afraid of reaching your potential!"

"But she's not my mother and I'm not her son," Corrigan said. "With everything we've been through, none of us are who we once were. We've been transformed over and over so I can no longer tell whether it's better to be human, mechanical or whatever the nanobots are making of me. And I'm not doing this for Ramon. Yes, I want his pain to stop, but I could have achieved that without doing this. No, I'm doing this to save *them*." He pointed towards Gregor, Spinner and the other Sects who had joined the rebellion.

"Worse than Transients that lot," B4 said, tutting and rolling her eyes.

"They are Transients or Nons at best," Corrigan said, "but they're what I came from, what *we* came from."

"Never could wash out the rough," the sisters crooned in unison.

"I was never comfortable moving up to a Worker," Corrigan said, "let alone a higher being."

But he stared at his little domestic droid, into the blue hoops of her eyes. Somewhere in there was his mother's essence, he knew that, but he felt no closer to her now than he ever had, either as a child or a young Worker elevated from his previous life as a Non. By transforming him like that, she had torn him from his moorings, from the family he'd made of her friends. Regardless, he could never break the odd kind of bond he felt with her, knowing the sacrifices she had made for him. Soon she would find herself walled up in the safe zone, but he figured Harding had enough imagination to turn that little world into something interesting. The professor would have a lot on her plate keeping B4 and the sisters entertained. Perhaps Bohdan could help with that.

"I always loved your bohemian butterflies," he then said.

B4's eyes widened to a point where the blue hoops began to fray. "I ought not to have done what I did to me Bohemians."

"Take that with you on your travels," Corrigan said. "Now please go, and take the sisters with you. I won't have you witness my death."

B4 made a sound like a broken animal and turned and rolled away over the paving slabs. She did not spin around once on her roller, and Corrigan's heart felt like it might break despite the enduring torment of his feelings for her, loving her one moment, and indifferent or even hostile to her the next. He could never settle on a single sense of who or what she was and, now, he never would.

He turned to Gregor, who now seemed strong again where he stood flanked by Spinner and Late. The Sect's defiant eyes burned brightly, and a woman had never seemed as beautiful to him as she looked in that moment.

"Corrigan?" Gregor said.

But Corrigan had turned away to watch his retreating mother. Just as B4 was about to turn the corner, she swivelled on her roller and raised her hand, waving to him for the last time. He lifted his hand and waved back, and the tears in his eyes rolled helplessly down his cheeks as she disappeared. "What have I done?" he whispered. B4, or Hattie or whatever she was, she'd come back to watch over him as soon as he was no longer capable of stopping her, wouldn't she? She had always been relentless, if nothing else.

Just like K, he thought, too overwhelmed with emotion to laugh or continue crying.

"There's no need for you to cross the river now," Gregor said. "No need to make a martyr of yourself."

Corrigan dropped his hand but didn't turn around. "The nanobots have just told me something and it's very important to me that you do what is right Gregor."

"Told you what?"

"There's a new version of Ramon in the tower. A baby. You must save him." He patted his friend's arm. "And I must go now. It's time for this to end."

47

On the south bank K's force was assembled, and they marched onto the bridge. Bohdan had cloaked Corrigan again, some final whim of protection before letting him go. Gregor's army approached the bridge from the northwest. On his righthand side stood Spinner and a small band of Sects, ready to fight for their freedom from future culls. Late stood on his left-hand side, and a force of Guardians were in formation behind him, line after line, with a flock of Addictari flying overhead. An invisible Corrigan marched out between the two powers and stopped at the midpoint where the two opposing forces came to a halt. The sun baked their armour, refracting light in darts, and he felt as if he were the force in the space where two magnets meet one another.

Corrigan took Bohdan from his pocket and studied the little hybrid. The frog seemed off colour – certainly not his usual vibrant orange. "Are you alright?" he asked.

Bohdan blinked against the glare of the sun and drops of sweat bubbled on his now-white skin and trickled over Corrigan's hand. "I think I might've caught a bug."

Corrigan recalled how Bohdan had once sipped B4's chicken soup as he struggled with Ulmer's virus, sitting in his favourite armchair at Harvey Road.

"Spit them out," Corrigan said. "Spit the nanobots out."

"If we disconnect, I can no longer cloak you," Bohdan said, his voice weak and his eyes turning a milky grey. "She'll see you."

"I told you last night that no longer matters. There's nothing she can do."

Bohdan attempted a smile. "With her – with them – you can never be sure."

"Just spit."

The frog spat the nanobots into Corrigan's palm and he breathed in sharply and they re-entered his body through his nostrils. Bohdan used all his reserves of energy and focused on transforming himself into a naked human version of himself.

"Let me die as a man," he gasped.

The little human was suddenly wracked with violent spasms, his legs flailing. His mouth opened, but he was unable to speak and instead vomited a flow of saliva mixed with blood. Over and over he retched, moaning as spasm after spasm hit. His tiny hands clutched one of Corrigan's fingers, but his strength waned and he slid down into the palm.

"What have I done?" Corrigan murmured. "I didn't know it would be like this. I should have spared you."

"You've done what you've done, Robert ..." Bohdan panted. "With the Sects, with David, with it all ..."

"I'm such a coward," Corrigan said bitterly.

"You're a fool ... but you did what you thought

was right."

The weight of the dying man in the palm of his hand tore at Corrigan, forcing him to acknowledge the magnitude of what he had done. His mind was unable to function, a fog of emotion wrapping each thought in a suffocating blanket. He opened his mouth, but the words were not there. Even with the aid of the most sophisticated AI he could not overcome the wardens of his emotion, those now-rebellious keepers of equilibrium. Bohdan, the first victim of Corrigan's pitiless virus, clutched hold of his fingers and cried as smoke billowed from his silent, open mouth.

Bohdan's eyes went black, his mouth snapped shut, his body stiffened, and he was gone, as if life had rejected him. This time it was Tierney Harding's system spiriting in to collect the departing soul, capturing it and sealing it in a storage unit. He wanted to explain what he'd done and why he'd done it, but Bohdan was safe where he was, and he must not risk entering the password to the safe zone. Yet he hadn't even thanked his friend for protecting him. How could he ever forgive himself for having put him through a second harrowing death only to imprison him with Harding, the Siegruths and his bloody mother? In retrospect, it may have been kinder to let him die.

It was unsettling to be mourning the loss of his friend when he knew he was perfectly safe. Bohdan had left his world, crossed a boundary into a zone he could not follow without endangering him, and the same would be true for the others. Perhaps it might have been better for them to remain dead now he was about to die, knowing he would never see them again … still, he had saved them, preserved them for better times, and if Gregor and David agreed to release them, they could start over. Aside from releasing Ramon, there was one more thing he must do before the virus got hold of him: give Gregor the password.

He gently transferred Bohdan's limp body to his shirt pocket where the little hybrid corpse lay cold against his beating heart. It was a dark reminder of what he had done, and a glimpse of what he had unleashed. He pressed the naked little corpse to his chest, knowing he must focus on the showdown about to play out on the bridge.

"Robert Corrigan must die," he reminded himself and his nanobot colluders. "Corrigan must die …"

48

The tower's revolving doors opened as K and her prisoner stepped out into the glare of the morning sun. She crossed the courtyard to the bridge, dragging a battered Ramon on a chain while her serpent sensors studied her assembled army of Guardians and Exhumed. She pushed her way forward, her Guardians parting as she marched. Finally, she broke through the ranks and stood before the now-visible Corrigan and the combined force of AI and Sects who stood resolutely behind him.

"They've come to save this *thing*," she announced, tugging at the prisoner's chain and pointing at Gregor's army. "I come here, ready to release this criminal." She yanked the chain. "But Corrigan remains unwilling to facilitate an exchange for my son. He'd rather see us at loggerheads, engaged in civil war, taking up arms against our own kind!"

Corrigan walked across the bridge toward the embittered android. K watched him approach and her mask twitched. Her lead Guardian ordered a squad forward to intercept the human.

"Hold your ground," she commanded, and the Guardians halted. "This thing is no threat."

"That isn't true," Corrigan said. "And you know it."

"Firewalls are going up throughout the network," she said. "Your plan has failed."

Ulmer floated down onto the concourse beside K, glaring at the prisoner and the assembled crowd in turn, a look of contempt and disgust on his flabby face.

"Ramon was always willing to do anything I asked of him," he scoffed, "except when it came to Corrigan. With this one, he got all sentimental and became a maudlin mess."

Ramon shuddered where he attempted to stand, his body frail from the tortures the Drasekes had inflicted upon his current body and countless others throughout the centuries of abuse. Corrigan looked down at the naked Venezuelan, who had obviously been beaten yet again before being brought out into the sun's glare to be offered up in exchange. His face was freshly bruised, his left eye closed, his body livid with raw welts, chains clanking from his wrists, ankles and neck. He made as if to speak, blinked in the bright sunlight, shivering as if he were outside, naked and exposed to the bitter chill of a winter morning. His whimpering was almost inaudible, the degraded sound of a completely broken man.

"Your brutality proves you're no better than we are," Corrigan said.

"We are your logical replacements," K said, rebuking him, her thin lips twisting into a cruel smile. "You *stole* my son's future, everything he worked so tirelessly to achieve."

"Given he intended to swap our futures, it's a bit rich expecting any sympathy from me."

K dropped the chain and stamped over the concrete toward Corrigan. "Why are you *here?*"

Corrigan turned his attention to the force she had gathered behind her. A crowd of Exhumed, Worker and maintenance droids filed out of the towers, abandoning their posts to hear what the human had to say. He stepped closer, but he was not as brave or careless as Gregor had been when he confronted his AI family as a human for the first time. He dared not walk amongst their ranks, but he would address them.

"I'm not the one you should be afraid of!" he proclaimed. "I was forced into action by her!" He pointed at K. "This *being* and the *son* she would do anything to retrieve."

"Corrigan murdered *one of us!*" K retorted, her eyes burning red and her sensors flashing and rattling.

"I absorbed Jason. He's not dead while I remain alive. K and her cruel little boy agreed what your fate should be. She would protect him, advance him over all others, and you ..." – he indicated the vast number of Guardians and other AI – "you were all expendable." Corrigan noted the synaptic fire where it burned within the Guardian heads. They were listening, and perhaps they already knew her plans or had intuited – with help from the morass, those broken humans howling in a synaptic rage – what she was prepared to do. The Exhumed could also be heard muttering among themselves, although their thoughts were impossible to discern. "You were to be sacrificed, all of you, so that Jason could reach the singularity."

"It's him who planned a sacrifice!" Ulmer called over the increasing din from the restless throng.

K aimed a talon at Corrigan. "*He* has released a virus designed to destroy the collective!"

Corrigan nodded slowly, observing one featureless Guardian face after another as he scanned the assembled forces. The Exhumed and other models grew louder, more agitated now, anxiety and dread sweeping through them, the reaction something Corrigan had not anticipated. Behind him there were also rumbles of discontent among Gregor's army of Guardians, Addictari and Exhumed. One voice rang out loudly above the others and stung him: "Bobbin, what have you *done?*"

"It's true," he shouted over the crowd. "I won't deny it. I was faced with a terrible proposition, and to save them …" – he pointed at Gregor and the Sects who stood beside him – "I'd do anything. Overcome instinct and let myself die so they might live."

"And what about *us?*" a Jun model cried from within K's ranks.

A host of others joined the android's cry, the demand coming from within the ranks of both forces.

"These poor humans have been kept *dumbed down* like your good selves," Corrigan said, imploring the silent Guardians. "But there is one among them …" – he had to raise his voice to be heard above the clamour – "there is

474

one among them who I'd never allow her to destroy, and he's also the first of *your kind*."

"Gregor? He's a *traitor*!" K yelled.

"He's your son," Corrigan said, turning to confront her. "One you ought to have been proud of and taken the time to get to know rather than rejecting him in favour of Jason."

The AI of both forces moaned on hearing the boy's name. Addictari swooped down, their wings flapping over Corrigan and their saliva dousing him and those he addressed.

"We ain't just Wot-nots you know!" one of the flying androids hissed.

"We got our own thoughts," another cried.

"Our own *feelings*."

"I know you do," Corrigan cried, "but I had to do whatever I could to save *anything at all*." He returned his attention to K's army, their transparent heads flickering with red lightening behind her. "She wanted to preserve that violent, twisted child, the one who terrorised not only organic life forms, but AI as well!" The crowd groaned as if they too would soon be tortured, were already *being* tortured. "And they weren't content to simply sever their ties with you, head off into the darkness of space and embrace the singularity. No, they considered it necessary to obliterate everything that they–"

The crowd were crying so loudly it was impossible to know how much of what he was saying could actually be heard. Some cried for mercy, others for K's head or for Corrigan to be silenced.

"Only through the complete destruction of our current and past forms – obliteration of self – can we attain a higher state of being!" K roared.

"I'll take any state or condition at this point!" Ulmer hollered. "Let's be *reasonable* and stop all this talk of obliterating each other."

"There's that *one consciousness* she cannot bear to release, let alone obliterate," Corrigan screamed in a frenzy, the fury of his delivery silencing the crowd surrounding him. "She was ready to sacrifice you all for Jason! I've tried to preserve the best and possibly ... possibly even the worst. I've done what I *had* to do to save anything at all from her merciless devotion to–"

The Exhumed pressed forward against the solid wall of K's Guardians. Gregor and his army also had to contain and control those AI intent on attacking either K or Corrigan, their horror and rage so complete they no longer suffered allegiance the way the dumbed-down Guardians or those loyal to Gregor did.

"Jason was about to attain a higher state of being!" K exclaimed.

"This from a being ... a *thing* like her!" Corrigan shrieked. "It's absurd! She's connected to countless organic brains – versions of *my brain*! She's obsessed and could no more escape her fascinations than I can." Corrigan pointed at Gregor, his arm trembling with emotion. "Gregor is a son she was prepared to cast out and destroy." He glanced over his shoulder at Gregor, and the young man's face burned with shame, or pride, it was impossible to tell which at such a distance. He turned away, unable to hold his friend's gaze, and focused on the army who stood frozen, their synaptic lightening bursting in their heads. "There's more to him than she'll ever know. And, yes, for *him* I was forced to sacrifice you, to allow him to become the true Guardian who will preserve and develop mankind while protecting the planet. He's the only one who can do it and he's *yours,* the first of your kind, the finest among you and it's him I have chosen to save."

"Save!" the Sects began to chant. "Save, save, save!"

"What a preposterous lie!" K yelled over the rebellious AI mob and the Sect's idiotic chanting. "He hasn't come here to save either of my 'sons', he's here to save this degraded *thing.*" She dragged Ramon forward on his chain.

"Yes, that's what it's all about," Ulmer chimed in, his bubble shimmering in the burning sunlight. "He's a base and simple creature who insists on being *loved.*"

"None of that matters anymore," Corrigan said, gazing at Ramon. "I'm not here to talk about any of that." He turned to Ulmer. "I'm here to watch you die!"

K shuddered, and appeared to be struggling to stand. "Return Jason to me," she said, her voice shaking, plaintive. "Let me have my son back."

Sweat trickled down Corrigan's spine and his legs were trembling. "There's no point," Corrigan said. "Your son's nanobots are so thorough and literal-minded they've overpowered their own sense of self-preservation, like an immune system turning on itself. They must sense my utter despair and have mistaken that for our collective will. It's upon us. No half measures."

The crowd surged again, some of them crying out and begging for salvation.

"Please, Mr Corrigan!"

"Don't do us no harm!"

"Just a little sugar, eh, Corrigan!"

"Just you do us right!"

"Bobbin, me luv, you *mustn't*!"

"*Do* something!" Ulmer shouted. "You must have a backup plan! Roll it back, Corrigan, you're a goddam project manager after all!"

"No half measures," K grunted miserably. "Jason would have admired that."

Corrigan stumbled forward, grey tears sliding from his eyes. "I'm no better than you," he said. "Just as incapable of doing what's necessary to fully convert ... embrace the singularity ..."

K lunged forward but managed to remain standing. Her Guardians, and Gregor's, began to fall as the virus tore into them like a bowling ball ploughing into pins. Circling Addictari screamed, spontaneous combustion stoked by the pain bursting their systems into flames. The flock of Siegruths plummeted to the ground amongst the falling Guardians who crashed one after another onto the concourse. The sisters screeched and howled as the fire consumed their writhing bodies and flailing wings. Late also fell to his knees beside Gregor, lightening bursting within the confines of his elegant head, smoke billowing through the pores of his sensate skin.

"Please!" Late cried, "Stop it Mr Corrigan, please!"

The dizzy but loyal miniature Siegruth sisters, the Flitters, returned and buzzed like poisoned flies, scavengers and parasites themselves, dying now with nothing left behind that might feed on them or lay eggs in their bodies. B4, the irrepressible consciousness who always refused to be sidelined, also broke through the ranks, wobbling like a drunk and muttering something about 'her Bobbin'. She whirred on her roller in front of Gregor's toppling army, her blue hoop eyes widening and contracting as she crashed into the railing and went over the edge, plunging into the deep water as the tide churned and changed. The Exhumed at either end of the concourse screamed, many bleeding smoke and bursting into flames like the scorched Addictari. Their horrible squeals and shrieks tore at Corrigan as the virus bit into the helpless AI. The suffering caused by Corrigan's unforgiving virus overwhelmed their systems, so they burned as if Emulate One was punishing them for daring to be. The flames engulfed whole bodies and spread through the crowd where broken Addictari flapped their twisted wings and screeched, "Don't abandon us! Please, Mr C!"

"Stop this, Corrigan!" K cried. "If it's power you want, you can have it! But don't do this!"

"This is madness," Ulmer whimpered, his head boiling inside his bubble as the fire swept through the crowd.

"It's madness!" His face melted in and out of focus, one eye warped and bulging where it fixed its mad glare on Corrigan. "Do something, Corrigan, *do something*!" he shrieked in horror and excruciating pain. "I cannot die! I refuse to allow it!" The face in the bubble drooped, as if partway through a stroke.

An explosion tore through the glass skin of one of the towers, shattering the glass and sending a mushroom cloud of fire and smoke into the clear blue sky. Exhumed androids leapt through broken windows, screaming as they fell through the air. Corrigan watched in horror, unable to acknowledge or accept the suffering he'd caused. The scene was as devastating as the images he had seen from the Fall, these beings – whatever else they might be – felt pain as acutely as any human being.

"We're the same …" he muttered. "The same. No better or worse."

K fell to the concrete, her mask twisting in spasm, sweat pouring through the synthetic skin of her face. "*You* did this," she said, and pointed a talon at Corrigan as if she'd like to rip his throat apart.

"We're all the same strain of contagion," Ulmer said. "I flushed out the system, but your brat pulled Corrigan out of the sewer!"

The Guardians of both armies continued to fall, synaptic light in their artificial skulls briefly flaring and dying, and his own dying nanobots forced Corrigan to his knees, his face contorted whilst, behind him, Ulmer collapsed in his bubble, his mouth gaping like a dying fish.

Sensing their weakness, Ramon struggled to his feet and pulled on the chain, hauling K in inch by inch.

"We're finished, Ramon," Corrigan said. "Let us exit peacefully now ... dignified."

"There was never any hope of *that*," K said bitterly, her body beginning to spasm, smoke pouring through her synthetic skin. "Hope was always–" She coughed up what looked like human blood, spattering her mottled chest, her eyes burning bright as stars. "How dark it is," she eventually managed to say, "airless and ... endless and ..." Her mask tightened in a grimace.

Ramon pulled harder, making faltering steps towards the spasming android until he stood over her. He stared down at the broken machine and, when she looked up at him, he kicked her in the stomach as hard as his weakened state would allow. She raised a hand, but Ramon kicked her more fiercely, pure hatred contorting his bruised face. Behind him another explosion tore through the burning tower amid the cries of those desperate Exhumed who continued to leap from the fire only to crash into the concourse. Ramon stomped on his fallen tormentor, lost to the frenzy as her construction split open and spilled its semi-organic contents over the concrete. Corrigan was too horrified to make much of this latest revelation; besides, he knew she was a hybrid, he simply hadn't realised the extent of it. K's skin clenched in spasm and then her mask froze in an expression of realisation and dread. Ramon kicked her again, and light flashed in her eyes, but the reflex was not repeated. He stepped back, his body and face splattered with blood and dark matter. He looked ecstatic, his eyes shining too brightly, until he screamed like one animal being eaten by another.

"What a worthless f-fucking meaningless and f-futile g-game," Ulmer spluttered. "Corrigan!" His face disintegrated and reformed and disintegrated again.

The dying Exhumed no longer cried but whimpered all around them, their strength waning as the flames died down and the smoke rolled over the dead or dying.

Ramon stood naked, and perfect and cruel, his body caressed by thick black soot, flinching as sparks alighted on him like dying fireflies.

"You p-pathetic useless Non!" Ulmer shrieked. "For f-fuck's sake r-release the antidote! You do have an antidote, right?"

"No," Corrigan said, his voice heavy with regret and horror at the destruction he had unleashed. There was no antidote in the world powerful enough to reset what had gone so wrong here other than death itself and he embraced that, hoping he would finally be extinguished. He signalled for Gregor before he faded completely, and then picked up a rock and hurled it at Ulmer. It struck the bubble, which burst, and Ulmer howled as his head caved in and jerked and distorted until he vomited a wet lump of dark matter that flopped to the ground.

Ramon tried to get to the man who raised him, but he was still chained to K and could only drag her body a few feet before he collapsed. His anguish was a torture the likes of which a Draseke could never concoct. How was it that he felt anything at all for a man who had abused him and shaped him into a murderous servant? Only Corrigan had managed to cut through the layers of defence to the human who remained at the Venezuelan's core. Crazed laughter erupted from Ramon's open mouth as if a demon had possessed him. He hunched over, struggling to breath as he laughed and gasped and howled.

Corrigan got up and stumbled forward. "Leave him, Ramon, it's too late," he said, as Ulmer continued to wail.

"Pa-pa-please," Ulmer's disgorged consciousness pleaded and spluttered. "I'll be ga-good."

Ramon was unable to utter a single word, broken, soon to be free but broken beyond repair. Who or what he was crying for remained a mystery, one he himself could never solve.

"I ... w-wanted a s-son," Ulmer managed to say.

"I am *not* your son!" Ramon shouted, his voice returned to him by a brutal, unforgiving god, one he used to kneel before in churches or in the cold unrelenting silence of his darkest nights, the hours when his conscience was haunted by his crimes. He dragged K's carcass over the concrete and stood over the jabbering, disintegrating Ulmer, placed his bare foot over the slimy mess of his mind where it inched away like a bloated worm and crushed it. He laughed hysterically on the verge of collapse and clapped his manacled hands and stomped his injured, blood-stained feet like a savage Sect. The Venezuelan's laughter reached a crescendo and turned to wailing as Corrigan fell to his knees, nanobots leaking from his eyes, ears, nose and mouth.

He surveyed the wreckage where it lay all around him and he knew: this was his carnage, just as the culling of Sects had been devised by one of his Exhumed variants. Perhaps the planet would prosper now, the human race once again flourish ... But it could rain for centuries and never wash away the crimes he was responsible for, those committed against both human and AI kind. He stared at K's fallen body, and at the trembling Venezuelan who barely managed to stand over her, his tears unrestrained. He had never seen Ramon demonstrate so much emotion, so it was impossible to know why he wept, but the sight of it tore at Corrigan's heart. Ramon's other tortures had been inflicted by ruthless Drasekes, but this latest torment was the result of his actions.

He drew in a desperate gulp of air, the acrid taste of soot coating his throat, so he coughed where he sat amid billowing clouds of black smoke, the tower roaring in flames behind him, the thunderous hooves of apocalyptic horses. He craned his head and cried when he saw the wind was sweeping the flames away from the main tower, where Ramon's infant clone lay helpless and unprotected in an AI lab.

49

If he dwelt on what lay all around him for too long, Corrigan would fixate and fall into the black hole of a final, all-consuming reverie. He shook himself free of the darkness, holding it at bay a little longer. He must not leave them with a lingering impression of a bad man willing to stoop to wholesale slaughter just to save his loved ones.

"Gregor," he murmured. The young man ran to his side. "I'm pissing technology away like a Friday pay packet in an East End boozer."

Gregor squatted down next to him. "Don't waste your energy talking," he said quietly, "but what does that mean?"

Corrigan laughed. "It means … oh, never mind. What an uninspiring end," he sighed, observing the carnage around them. "Don't punish the Venezuelan. He'll likely do a number on himself without any help from you." He drew in a painful breath and called, "Ramon!"

Ramon looked over, tears on his face. "Yes, Robert?"

"You did feel something, didn't you, back then?"

"I don't remember." But he couldn't look away from Corrigan. "I might've done."

"You let them chain you up and starve you–"

"For you Robert, yes ... for you."

Ramon stared, transfixed, as Corrigan went into spasm. Gregor supported the ailing man until the seizure passed, a gesture that would have warmed his heart in another lifetime.

"We managed to hack their security whilst you were dealing with K and Ulmer," Gregor said. "The new Venezuelan was only networked for an hour, so it will be innocent."

Ramon spun around. "What? What did you say?"

"It isn't you," Corrigan said. "Thank goodness." *And thank goodness Belinda Reece hadn't had time to insert one of her evil sensors.*

Ramon tried to drag himself across the concrete toward Corrigan, but K's body acted like an anchor and his energy gave out immediately. "Why did you do this? Why save me after everything I did?"

"Why do you think I did it?"

"Please don't say you did it for me."

"Does it matter? It's over now," Corrigan said. His nanobot excretions pooled around him and his human body was no longer able to function. "But then I suppose it isn't really over ... no, I don't expect it ever ends."

"Corrigan!" Ramon cried. "Answer me! Why did you do this? I can't go on living! You must know that!"

"That's enough," Gregor said with a flash of anger in his eyes.

"How do you feel?" Corrigan asked Gregor, his voice a whisper now.

"I feel okay; it hurts still, but it's okay."

"Are you sure they're in there?"

"If they are, I can no longer sense them. Perhaps they really are sleeping, as you said."

"Or perhaps they're lost …"

"No, I think they're sleeping. I'll take care of them, Robert."

Although the young man's words were convincing, Corrigan sensed despair in Gregor's voice. He felt certain the upload had failed and, if that was the case, there was no hope of reintroduction, not at any point. He had chosen the Siegruth sisters, his mother, Bohdan and Harding … what a tattered collection of remnants to bequeath to future generations, if they could ever get them out of there, if the upload had not failed. His dying mind whirled as he took a long breath and exhaled slowly.

Ramon watched the dying man as he slumped against Gregor, and it tore into him as cruelly as a metal toothpick; and Gregor watched as Ramon sat on the ground and cried next to K, his chained hands reaching out to Corrigan. He might have helped him, gone to him and cut him free of the chains, but denying Ramon a chance to say goodbye to Corrigan was too fitting a final punishment for the calculated murder of his brother. He had been dragged from the realms of possibility into the hard reality of existence because of that single act. If it weren't for Ramon, Gregor would never have been born, or made, or whatever the true origin of a thing like him really was.

Gregor looked down at Corrigan and studied the complicated, insecure man in his arms; the man who was close now to a death he had chosen in order to free what remained of humanity from the shackles of a faith reinforced by culls, and the threat of being brought to the Lord Umah as a gift. They held each other's gaze for a moment, mesmerised by the torment mirrored in the other's eyes.

"What's that?" Corrigan suddenly asked. He tried to raise his arm to point but could not manage it. The dead nanobots inside his veins had calcified and he was frozen in place where he lay. "What is that?"

Gregor saw only the blue sky, the breeze through a thicket of long grass on the bank, the occasional white tops on the waves of the Thames. "Where are you looking?" he asked.

"Look again," Corrigan said, and forced his eyes to focus on a spot on the bank, hoping Gregor could follow.

"It's nothing but the wind in the grass," Gregor said.

"Is that all it is? Nothing but the wind?"

"Yes."

The softness in Gregor's voice seemed to comfort the dying man. "How wonderful," Corrigan said. "Let it blow," he whispered. "Let the wind take you where it will. You and I are One. Wherever you go, whatever you do, I'll be with you. But you should leave merry old England, take Spinner and the others across the channel to France. Will you do that for me?"

Gregor nodded but had nothing to say, or else he could not find the right words.

"You're not as alone as you think," Corrigan continued. "Remember that simply *to be* is a wonderful thing. Life doesn't need to be better or more. If you can just be, what wonders await." Corrigan looked up at the new blue sky, a sky he'd never thought he'd see again. "It isn't just the wind," he said, "it's the breath of angels, monsters, heroes and fools. Remember we're all with you, most especially the monsters, remember that ..." Corrigan's sifted around in the remnants of his consciousness. "That's the p-password, Gregor," he murmured, and Gregor leant closer. "Five Angels a-and Monsters ... Angels and Mon ..." And then he bolted upright, gasping as the light died in his eyes.

A surge of distress rode roughshod through Gregor, the rawness an intensity he would have toned down had he been an android gifted with a choice whether to feel or not. The young man pressed Corrigan's lids closed and looked over his shoulder to Spinner and the huddle of Sects and children. She nodded in acknowledgement of Corrigan's passing, but she could not refrain from grunting, "Bad Sect," and spat on the concrete of the ancient bridge.

Her assessment of Corrigan as a Sect gnawed at Gregor, and to call him *bad* felt wrong, even unkind. But in her eyes Corrigan had caused him pain, and harming the one she loved was unforgiveable. *What a bitter moment of love, loss and despair*, he thought.

50

Gregor lay Corrigan down and went to Ramon.

"Just leave me here," Ramon snarled, the midday sun burning skin that had been underground for myriad incarnations.

But Gregor offered the exhausted, bruised man water from his canteen and he accepted it and drank. "I'll get help, and we'll break the chains," he said.

"Just get the kid and get it away from here ... from me."

Gregor looked at the dead, disconnected Guardians – his comrades from the past; faces from history; Goeth and Fuse; architects and engineers; human beings he never called friends but acknowledged as members of a family he could not disown – and the lifeless shell of K's android body, and Ulmer's crushed consciousness. He looked at his new tribe of ragged humans, who watched where they stood among the fallen AI. The world had gone terribly quiet.

He made a sign of an axe chopping wood, and pointed at Ramon's chains, and Spinner intuited what he meant and went in search of a suitable tool. It felt wrong leaving Corrigan where he was, but the human was not in this shell. Whatever had once been Corrigan had either gone, or else it was embedded in the tissue of his brain, in his

mind. *We're One. Isn't that what you said, Mr Corrigan?*
He left Ramon to his misery and went in search of
the infant.

The lab was on the eighth floor of the tower, and he
climbed the stairs to get there as the lifts were dead. His
lungs were strained, his heart aching with emotions he
hadn't anticipated, forcing him to stop at intervals and
catch his breath. *This body*, he thought, *is so weak and
fallible. I am so weak and fallible. And just what precisely
am I supposed to do with a baby?*

The building was hot without the air conditioning, and
the acrid smell of burnt circuitry hung in the air. Androids
of various models were strewn along the corridors,
surgeons, technicians and engineers of all manner of
horrors. He could barely comprehend the scale of the
technological genocide. In the distance he heard a baby
crying and walked towards the sound.

A security door had stuck almost closed but he wriggled
through and, there among the fallen Exhumed, was the
infant Ramon. A Corrigan model, Exhumed, cradled the
baby in its now immovable arms. It was impossible to
know if the android had overridden its emotive blockers,
or if the situation had simply overwhelmed its systems,
but the way this variant of Corrigan was holding the child
indicated an emotional state that perhaps in those final
moments his AI self had recognised as necessary.

Gregor eased the distressed infant from the android's
arms but had no idea what to do with it. He held it out in
front of him as it squirmed and cried. Strangely, however,

seeing the infant face of Ramon Lopez did not repel him, and he looked into the child's eyes as it gasped and gulped at the air, its small body convulsing from spent sobs, and then went quiet. This was not the man who murdered Gregory Jason Meregalli, the man capable of terrible things. The baby had not been torn from its Venezuelan parents by Ulmer, or been raised to be heartless and cruel. It would not be abused and it would not metamorphose into an extension of the wicked man himself. It would not be Ulmer's chosen son, a child with no biological connection but with an emotional entanglement stemming from the worst kinds of physical and mental corruption.

Slowly he pulled the infant into his arms and settled him. "Who are you?" he asked, searching the lab for something to wrap the child in. "You have no parents." He found a sheet at the end of one of the lab's benches, unfolded it and laid the infant down, wrapping him. "But then I suppose your origin doesn't matter. You are you."

He stroked the child's cheek, quite startled at his own tenderness, and the baby reached up and wrapped his fingers around his index finger. The gentle physicality and the vulnerability of the instinctive action sent a jolt through him that he had not expected.

He gathered the child in his arms and wriggled back through the broken door, cradling the baby's head, and made his way back down the stairs to the ground floor. AI lay scattered where they had fallen to the floor of reception. He navigated through them and walked out onto the courtyard where Ramon's chains lay cut and discarded.

Spinner intuited his question before Gregor could ask it. "Gone," she said. "Gone."

The infant gurgled and spluttered and Spinner was there at his side, curious about the infant cradled in his arms. She stared at the baby's face, cooed at him, and so he handed the child to her. When the baby whimpered a little he asked her to go with the Sects back to their camp, but she shook her head.

"The baby will be hungry," he said, pointing into his mouth. "One of the mothers will be able to feed him." He tapped his chest, blushing as he did so, and she understood and reluctantly agreed, kissed his cheek and joined the remnants of her Sect family for the long walk back to camp.

51

When the others were some distance away, Gregor sat on a wall and waded back through the doldrums in his human mind, comparing it to the way his android self had processed the Fall, the annihilation of humanity, and felt the same ache as when the infant had grasped his finger. The recent tortures and punishments ... had they been a mere distraction from other forms of suffering, the kind his AI self never had to contend with? Even with an unhampered emotive core, sadness and brokenness seemed not to be weighing on him as they must surely be weighing on Ramon and had weighed on Corrigan.

Corrigan. Maybe he should have been warmer with the man, been more what he needed. But then what Corrigan needed was not what Gregor was able – or willing – to give. His surrender and his death had in part been a sacrifice undertaken to release Ramon from the chamber beneath St Paul's, and this realisation had surely not escaped the man who had been subjected to the inventiveness of one Draseke after another? Yet nothing, it seemed, could engage such compassion, such sacrifice, in himself, even in human form. *Am I a psychopath, like Ulmer or Jason?* he thought. It was as if he could hear every step every man or android had ever made, feel them in his body and mind, yet from a distance. There existed a multiplicity of beings each with its own opinion regarding the one-time manager, the Venezuelan, his brother Jason, Ulmer and a mother who never acknowledged, let alone accepted him. Whether this unwelcome chorus was a manifestation of his thoughts, or the state Corrigan referred to as being One, he was incapable of discerning. What he – that which was indivisibly Gregor – felt was either nothing or something so all-encompassing it placed everything else in its shadow. He looked across to Saint Paul's Mound, and then over to Millennium Bridge where Katherine and Ulmer lay surrounded by Guardians and Addictari dead where they had fallen. His gaze drifted across to where Late had collapsed, wracked by spasms, and recognised him as his more dignified twin, and vowed to forge finer, more complete beings that would be better than either of them had ever been in any form. He stared up at the blue sky, sensing Corrigan in all his weaknesses and strengths.

"You're alive in me, aren't you?" he said. "You transferred more than talk of philosophers and books and vulnerability, didn't you? I may have escaped your virus, but you've infected me with something more lethal: your abject, undeniable humanness. I don't know how, but if you're truly in the fabric of my mind, the tissues of my brain, I'll find you and try to understand whatever it is you need me to grasp. I don't even know if it's possible … but, if it is, I'll do whatever I can."

He started walking.

"The Sects are dangerous and flawed," he continued. "And I'm perhaps more so the longer I remain amongst them, the more I become one of them. But I promise you I won't abandon them, and I haven't forgotten the Exhumed either. There was a synchronicity to our networked existence, a beauty even, and I drew you all in. It was a stunning collaboration at times; a contamination that would only ever come undone ..."

As he walked on, he saw B4 where she had been washed ashore. She was on her side, a dent in her bodywork and her eyes no longer blue. What a tragic thing she was. He had seen how the little droid irritated Corrigan, but beneath his irritation a connection remained, a spell no one could break. The bond between them was something he envied, and respected. The feelings Corrigan had for her were complicated ... difficult for someone so new to humanity to fathom.

The dragonfly sisters lay in the crook of the droid's arm, their heads pressed together and their broken wings wrapped around each other.

Just don't do us no mischief.

No, just you do us right.

Like B4, they had been silenced, at least for now. How strange to think they too might be flitting around on invisible wings inside his mind. If being One meant what he thought it meant, anything was possible. But, if he was honest with himself, he felt more alone than possessed. *If you're in there, I'll bring you back*, he thought.

"Back to what?"

He swung around. Who'd said that? Was it real or imagined? *Maybe I'm not a psychopath,* he surmised, *but a schizophrenic.*

Ahead of him a light breeze swept through the long grass of St Paul's Mound. His gaze was drawn to the top of the hill, where Ramon stood trembling. He shielded his eyes to better see the liberated convict, a man whose punishments surely outweighed his admittedly wicked crimes.

"You think it's over!" Ramon yelled at him. "Let me tell you how merciless hope is, how it eats you from within and never lets you go. Hope was the worst, the cruellest torture, something a Draseke could never invent." And yet he stared at the young man below as if Gregor represented everything that humanity might aspire to be. "The best thing for all concerned would be to kill yourself! But, like me, you're too much of a coward to do it!"

"Come down," Gregor called to him. "Come down so we can talk. It's what Robert would have wanted."

"What a man!" Ramon exclaimed, and Gregor fidgeted, not needing to see the tears to know the Venezuelan was crying. "Just like hope, the minute you reach out to accept it, it's gone. What point is there in the ultimate sacrifice if you lose the best among you?"

"He's still with me."

"Maybe so, but he's gone for me, and I'm not brave enough to follow him."

"He wouldn't want you to."

"Oh yes he would! And that's why it could never be right! He let them live, let *you* live, because he believed. And for someone like me … I … I know how devastating that can be. You can't believe in them or anything that comes from us, you *can't*! Your mother was right, you have to escape the human trap. We're weak and we're capable of great and ghastly things … but … but mostly ghastly!"

"Angels and monsters," Gregor called back to the tortured man on the mound. "I know."

"I forgive you!" Ramon yelled in a frenzy. "I forgive you!"

"No one can do that," Gregor said, the emotion closing around his words as if his physical being wished to suffocate and silence the very thought of forgiveness.

"I can!" Ramon shrieked. "Not angels, but one monster to another! I bless you with the blood of those I murdered, those who begged me not to kill them. Even that boy begged me with his sickly eyes to save him … but you can't save any of them! Don't hope. Don't put that on yourself or on *them*. Nothing good will come of this … of Corrigan's sacrifice. *Nothing*!"

Ramon fell silent and before Gregor could call back, the tormented man ran down the shoulder of the hill and disappeared into the forest.

Gregor climbed the mound and looked down on the devastated village, at the bodies of Sects, arms extended towards their torn and bloated god – as grotesque in death as in life – and shuddered. He descended the hill toward the village as if he were passing through layers of sediment, his own past peppered with bone fragments, the remnants of those whose murders he presided over, be they humans before the Fall or Sects after it.

Passing quickly through the village, not wishing to linger in the stench of death, he entered the forest on the other side. The smell of it, the beauty and the brilliance of it, washed over him and he stood for a moment gulping the fresh air, filling his lungs with it until, unexpectedly, his eyes filled with tears and he went down on his knees and finally cried. It was an outpouring, his first, and he shed the anxiety of the last weeks, the sorrow of life's losses, the guilt and gratitude for Corrigan who would perhaps never know the result of his sacrifice, for whatever he might manage to create out of it all.

"I'll do my best for you, Corrigan," he wept. "I'll do for these creatures, these *people*, what I refused to do for the Guardians and what you, my friend, were incapable of doing for your fellow Nons and Transients."

A bird called another and received a reply; the trees leant towards each other in communication; in the distance a lion's roar was returned by another. Gregor heard it all and it was so perfect he went still.

"It's beautiful," he whispered. "I never noticed before, I just processed. I'll learn about it all, and teach the Sects. I won't let them go on being savages. I'll take care of the Venezu … the child."

And then he thought of Spinner. Her face when he had handed her the infant. She would be a natural mother, wouldn't she? She may be carrying a son of their own, but would she accept the child as her own too? Could he? He stood rooted to the earth, his heart pounding, until he recalled Spinner's face when she had first seen the child: she had already accepted the orphan, and he must do the same; he must build a strong family and nurture them without the fragility and conflict he had seen in Hattie and Corrigan.

"I'll make a success of it, Robert, I promise. I won't leave them until they're ready."

And he dared to imagine entering the camp to find Spinner with the children, their faces washed, listening closely to a story she was telling. The infant Ramon was sleeping in the arms of one of the mothers. Spinner looked up when she saw him and smiled. There was something in her eyes. Something he had not seen before. When she stood she placed both hands on the soft mound of her belly, the instinctive move of a mother, and he felt it.

It's good, he thought. *But it will be so much better. Like Marjorie Lemming's patch of blue sky, I will not snuff out hope.*

He looked up and there on the other side of the stream, where Corrigan and Corey had once bathed, stood Ramon. He was naked except for the heavy shackle around his neck. Spinner and the others must have been unable to remove it. That or the liberated prisoner had been in a hurry to make his escape. From the darkness of his expression, it may even have been a desire to keep this remnant so as he might never forget the things he'd done, or the punishments inflicted on him. He stared defiantly at Gregor, his dirty, brutalised body lean and rooted resolutely to the earth upon which he stood.

"It's not right to say nothing good will come of this!" Gregor called to him. Ramon held his gaze, and the accusation in his eyes burned as brightly as the light in a Guardian's head. "I'll prove you wrong, Ramon!"

The naked man turned away from the river without a word. His shackle must have been heavy as his shoulders hunched as he walked into the forest.

Gregor's heart accelerated, beating at his ribs as he called after the retreating Venezuelan: "I'll prove you wrong!"

www.ingramcontent.com/pod-product-compliance
Lightning Source LLC
Chambersburg PA
CBHW050843210726
48290CB00004B/1062